T0182725

"Jess Lourey is a master of the coming-of-age thriller, and *The Quarry Girls* may be her best yet—as dark, twisty, and full of secrets as the tunnels that lurk beneath Pantown's deceptively idyllic streets."
—Chris Holm, Anthony Award–winning author of *The Killing Kind*

PRAISE FOR *BLOODLINE*

Winner of the 2022 Anthony Award for Best Paperback Original

Winner of the 2022 ITW Thriller Award for Best Paperback Original

Short-listed for the 2021 Goodreads Choice Awards

"Fans of *Rosemary's Baby* will relish this."
—*Publishers Weekly*

"Based on a true story, this is a sinister, suspenseful thriller full of creeping horror."
—*Kirkus Reviews*

"Lourey ratchets up the fear in a novel that verges on horror."
—*Library Journal*

"In *Bloodline*, Jess Lourey blends elements of mystery, suspense, and horror to stunning effect."
—*BOLO Books*

"Inspired by a true story, it's a creepy page-turner that has me eager to read more of Ms. Lourey's works, especially if they're all as incisive as this thought-provoking novel."

—Criminal Element

"*Bloodline* by Jess Lourey is a psychological thriller that grabbed me from the beginning and didn't let go."

—*Mystery & Suspense Magazine*

"*Bloodline* blends page-turning storytelling with clever homages to such horror classics as *Rosemary's Baby*, *The Stepford Wives*, and *Harvest Home*."

—*Toronto Star*

"*Bloodline* is a terrific, creepy thriller, and Jess Lourey clearly knows how to get under your skin."

—Bookreporter

"[A] tightly coiled domestic thriller that slowly but persuasively builds the suspense."

—*South Florida Sun Sentinel*

"I should know better than to pick up a new Jess Lourey book thinking I'll just peek at the first few pages and then get back to the book I was reading. Six hours later, it's three in the morning and I'm racing through the last few chapters, unable to sleep until I know how it all ends. Set in an idyllic small town rooted in family history and horrific secrets, *Bloodline* is *Pleasantville* meets *Rosemary's Baby*. A deeply unsettling, darkly unnerving, and utterly compelling novel, this book chilled me to the core, and I loved every bit of it."

—Jennifer Hillier, author of *Little Secrets* and the award-winning *Jar of Hearts*

"Jess Lourey writes small-town Minnesota like Stephen King writes small-town Maine. *Bloodline* is a tremendous book with a heart and a hacksaw . . . and I loved every second of it."

—Rachel Howzell Hall, author of the critically acclaimed novels *And Now She's Gone* and *They All Fall Down*

PRAISE FOR *UNSPEAKABLE THINGS*

Winner of the 2021 Anthony Award for Best Paperback Original

Short-listed for the 2021 Edgar Awards and 2020 Goodreads Choice Awards

"The suspense never wavers in this page-turner."

—*Publishers Weekly*

"The atmospheric suspense novel is haunting because it's narrated from the point of view of a thirteen-year-old, an age that should be more innocent but often isn't. Even more chilling, it's based on real-life incidents. Lourey may be known for comic capers (*March of Crimes*), but this tense novel combines the best of a coming-of-age story with suspense and an unforgettable young narrator."

—*Library Journal* (starred review)

"Part suspense, part coming-of-age, Jess Lourey's *Unspeakable Things* is a story of creeping dread, about childhood when you know the monster under your bed is real. A novel that clings to you long after the last page."

—Lori Rader-Day, Edgar Award–nominated author of *Under a Dark Sky*

"A noose of a novel that tightens by inches. The squirming tension comes from every direction—including the ones that are supposed to be safe. I felt complicit as I read, as if at any moment I stopped I would be abandoning Cassie, alone, in the dark, straining to listen and fearing to hear."

—Marcus Sakey, bestselling author of *Brilliance*

"*Unspeakable Things* is an absolutely riveting novel about the poisonous secrets buried deep in towns and families. Jess Lourey has created a story that will chill you to the bone and a main character who will break your heart wide open."

—Lou Berney, Edgar Award–winning author of *November Road*

"Inspired by a true story, *Unspeakable Things* crackles with authenticity, humanity, and humor. The novel reminded me of *To Kill a Mockingbird* and *The Marsh King's Daughter*. Highly recommended."

—Mark Sullivan, bestselling author of *Beneath a Scarlet Sky*

"Jess Lourey does a masterful job building tension and dread, but her greatest asset in *Unspeakable Things* is Cassie—an arresting narrator you identify with, root for, and desperately want to protect. This is a book that will stick with you long after you've torn through it."

—Rob Hart, author of *The Warehouse*

"With *Unspeakable Things*, Jess Lourey has managed the near-impossible, crafting a mystery as harrowing as it is tender, as gut-wrenching as it is lyrical. There is real darkness here, a creeping, inescapable dread that more than once had me looking over my own shoulder. But at its heart beats the irrepressible—and irresistible—spirit of its . . . heroine, a young woman so bright and vital and brave she kept even the fiercest monsters at bay. This is a book that will stay with me for a long time."

—Elizabeth Little, *Los Angeles Times* bestselling author of *Dear Daughter* and *Pretty as a Picture*

Praise for *The Catalain Book of Secrets*

"Life-affirming, thought-provoking, heartwarming, it's one of those books which—if you happen to read it exactly when you need to—will heal your wounds as you turn the pages."
—Catriona McPherson, Agatha, Anthony, Macavity, and Bruce Alexander Award–winning author

"Prolific mystery writer Lourey tells of a matriarchal clan of witches joining forces against age-old evil . . . The novel is tightly plotted, and Lourey shines when depicting relationships—romantic ones as well as tangled links between Catalains . . . Lourey emphasizes the ties that bind in spite of secrets and resentment."
—*Kirkus Reviews*

"Lourey expertly concocts a Gothic fusion of long-held secrets, melancholy, and resolve . . . Exquisitely written in naturally flowing, expressive language, the book delves into the special relationships between sisters, and mothers and daughters."
—*Publishers Weekly*

Praise for *Salem's Cipher*

"A fast-paced, sometimes brutal thriller reminiscent of Dan Brown's *The Da Vinci Code*."
—*Booklist* (starred review)

"A hair-raising thrill ride."
—*Library Journal* (starred review)

"The fascinating historical information combined with a story line ripped from the headlines will hook conspiracy theorists and action addicts alike."

—*Kirkus Reviews*

"Fans of *The Da Vinci Code* are going to love this book . . . One of my favorite reads of 2016."

—*Crimespree Magazine*

"This suspenseful tale has something for absolutely everyone to enjoy."
—*Suspense Magazine*

PRAISE FOR *MERCY'S CHASE*

"An immersive voice, an intriguing story, a wonderful character—highly recommended!"

—Lee Child, #1 *New York Times* bestselling author

"Both a sweeping adventure and race-against-time thriller, *Mercy's Chase* is fascinating, fierce, and brimming with heart—just like its heroine, Salem Wiley."

—Meg Gardiner, author of *Into the Black Nowhere*

"Action-packed, great writing taut with suspense, an appealing main character to root for—who could ask for anything more?"

—Buried Under Books

PRAISE FOR *MAY DAY*

"Jess Lourey writes about a small-town assistant librarian, but this is no genteel traditional mystery. Mira James . . . flees a dead-end job and a dead-end boyfriend in Minneapolis and ends up in Battle Lake, a little town with plenty of dirty secrets. The first-person narrative in *May Day* is fresh, the characters quirky. Minnesota has many fine crime writers, and Jess Lourey has just entered their ranks!"
—Ellen Hart, award-winning author of the Jane Lawless and Sophie Greenway series

"This trade paperback packed a punch . . . I loved it from the get-go!"
—*Tulsa World*

"What a romp this is! I found myself laughing out loud."
—*Crimespree Magazine*

"Mira digs up a closetful of dirty secrets, including sex parties, cross-dressing, and blackmail, on her way to exposing the killer. Lourey's debut has a likable heroine and surfeit of sass."
—*Kirkus Reviews*

PRAISE FOR *REWRITE YOUR LIFE: DISCOVER YOUR TRUTH THROUGH THE*

HEALING POWER OF FICTION

"Interweaving practical advice with stories and insights garnered in her own writing journey, Jessica Lourey offers a step-by-step guide for writers struggling to create fiction from their life experiences. But this book isn't just about writing. It's also about the power of stories to transform those who write them. I know of no other guide that delivers on its promise with such honesty, simplicity, and beauty."

—William Kent Krueger, *New York Times* bestselling author of the Cork O'Connor series and *Ordinary Grace*

THE
REAPING

THRILLERS

The Quarry Girls

Litani

Bloodline

Unspeakable Things

SALEM'S CIPHER THRILLERS

Salem's Cipher

Mercy's Chase

BOOK CLUB FICTION

The Catalain Book of Secrets

Seven Daughters

CHILDREN'S BOOKS

Leave My Book Alone! Starring Claudette, a Dragon with Control Issues

YOUNG ADULT

A Whisper of Poison

NONFICTION

Rewrite Your Life: Discover Your Truth Through the Healing Power of Fiction

THE REAPING

A STEINBECK AND REED THRILLER

JESS LOUREY

THOMAS & MERCER

Text copyright © 2024 by Jess Lourey

Published by Thomas & Mercer, Seattle

www.apub.com

Amazon, the Amazon logo, and Thomas & Mercer are trademarks of Amazon.com, Inc., or its affiliates.

ISBN-13: 9781662513985 (paperback)
ISBN-13: 9781662513992 (digital)

Cover design by Caroline Teagle Johnson
Cover image: © Joanna Jankowska / ArcAngel; © Cosma Andrei / Stocksy

Printed in the United States of America

To Shannon, an excellent writer, retreater, sprinter, and friend

The nice thing about living in a small town is that when you don't know what you're doing, someone else does.

—Frequently attributed to Immanuel Kant

CHAPTER 1

Rannie
1984

Rannie slipped into the forest for a peek at the forbidden.

His heart thumped with excitement . . . and a slice of guilt.

He took a deep sniff. He liked the way the forest smelled in autumn, like God had scrubbed it with maple syrup. And it wasn't just its smell. The crisp fall air felt *closer* somehow. All up inside his clothes and hugging him. It got him so buzzed that he was about to kick a rock—he was eight, his happy had to escape somewhere—when he realized it wasn't a rock at all.

It was a turtle.

Not a dime-a-dozen snapper, either. This one had a domed back, dark green and speckled, the shell plates laid out in a pretty honeycomb pattern.

"You shouldn't be out here, girlie," he said in his high-pitched boy voice, squatting. Oaks and elms towered over him, their red, brown, and gold leaves muted by the fading light. "Not out in the woods, not when it's going on dark o'clock. That's no place for a turtle."

Rannie glanced to the west, the direction the turtle had been traveling from. He was proud he knew his directions. People said that about Randolph Tervo—"Rannie" to everyone he met—that he couldn't get lost in the woods no matter if you blindfolded him. That's how he knew the turtle'd been coming from the swampboggins.

He tapped her shell lightly with his fingernail. *Click click.* "I can carry you closer to the river," he said, "which is the direction you were headed, in case you don't know. But I'm not allowed to get too near the water. Not the river you're going to, not the swampboggins you came from. I made a promise. That okay?"

The turtle craned her head toward him. He was delighted to see she had a yellow chin. "Well, aren't you as pretty as a picture." He picked her up to check her underbelly. It was chocolate brown with brushstrokes of black. He stole only a quick peek before he set her back down. He wouldn't like being plucked from the ground so someone could stare at *his* belly.

Don't do anything to others you wouldn't want done to you.

His big brother, Veli-Pekka—Pekka to friends and family, and in Alku, they were one and the same—had taught him that. Not much stuck in Rannie's head, but that saying did, that and north-south-east-west.

He gazed down the path in the direction he'd been headed. Toward Sandwich Rock. That's where Pekka was right now, and maybe another twenty minutes of walking would bring Rannie to him. Well, not *to* him. Pekka had been clear that he and his friend were camping alone in the woods tonight, that they'd be knee-deep in Man Business, the kind of stuff a boy shouldn't be exposed to. Rannie had been forbidden to join.

Pekka hadn't said it mean, so Rannie figured he'd see for himself.

Though he'd struggled with whether he'd want someone spying on *him.*

That was why he was feeling the pinch of guilt, why he hadn't reached the forest until just now, the sky shading to the color of plums. It'd taken him that long to decide he wouldn't mind at all if someone wanted to watch him do stuff. Heck, he *loved* company. Ask anyone in the whole town of Alku and they'd tell you: Rannie Tervo was good at directions, and he enjoyed people.

Still squatting, he peered through the shadowy woods. An owl hooted overhead. He ignored it. The river was a thirty-minute walk to the east, and if he was carrying a turtle, he'd definitely have to walk. No animal wanted to go from walking to hurtling (*a hurtling turtle starts to curdle*), Rannie knew that right now.

He groaned. There really was no choice. He couldn't leave the turtle to the elements, not at near dark, not in these woods full of hungry animals. He picked her up and marched straight into the hardwood and pine, trying not to think about all the bumpy crawlies he was probably strolling right over, or the Man Business he was missing, and especially not how terrifying it was to be in the woods alone, at night.

He kept going until he heard the river song.

"This is as far as I can go, girlie," he said, placing her gently on the ground. She immediately began shoving leaves away in a turtle version of speeding. He smiled. Once he saw she was gonna be safe, he tore back to the path as fast as his thick legs would carry him. He tripped a few times. Leaped to his feet. Ran again, not bothering to wipe off his knees or his hands.

He'd almost made it back to the main path when a heavy branch cracked behind him. He stopped cold, his heartbeat galloping through his ears. It was the one thing he'd feared. He'd heard stories of the monster, of course. The veri noita. His mom wouldn't let him attend the academy on the hill no matter how much he begged (*you're too cool for school, Randolph*), but every Alku kid knew about the Finnish blood witch, how she'd chitter through the woods and down the alleys during reaping season, searching for a naughty child whose toes she'd eat like grapes. None of the kids believed in her, at least that's what they told Rannie when they dropped by to play, but courage came at garage-sale prices when there was a mom and a light switch nearby.

"Hello?" he whispered.

Nothing.

He shivered, swallowing a hot pebble of fear, and rushed out of the devil-belly woods. The sun was fully set, the air cooling fast. Good thing he'd dressed warm, in a thick flannel shirt and a wool cap. He tugged the cap low and glanced back at the forest he'd just stepped out of. No movement, just shadowy layers of darkness. Surely there was no blood witch hiding in there, haunting the woods in search of children to reap (*your imagination will make you pay one day, Randolph*), but what about a bear? Or a wolf? He slid his hand into his pocket, searching for his great-grandpa's Victorinox pocketknife. He found it, smooth and heavy. Touching it immediately calmed his wild horses. He drew a deep breath. Glanced at the pale half wheel of moon cheese rising in the east.

It was enough to light his path.

He squared his shoulders and took off toward Sandwich Rock, making quick progress now that he was back on the trail.

Sandwich Rock was actually a whole hill of gray boulders on the far side of an open field, but two specific rocks gave it the name. The bottom one was big as a car, as round and smooth as a giant's skipping stone. On top of it rested a nearly identical boulder that leaned slightly forward. The whole thing looked like a great big stone sandwich with the top slice a little off kilter, almost like you could shove that slice off if you leaned into it. That was a trick on your eyes. That rock was going nowhere fast. Rannie and Pekka had climbed every inch of it, and the top boulder didn't so much as *think* about moving.

Rannie and his brother used to be as close as a container to its lid, but now that Pekka'd started college up the road, he had his own life. At least that's what he told Rannie, though he'd sounded sad when he said it. And sure enough, since then, Rannie didn't get to see Pekka nearly enough. That was all he planned to do, really. Watch Pekka and his college friend, Hector, camping.

See Pekka without *bugging* Pekka.

They wouldn't even know Rannie was there. Unless they wanted to, of course. Unless Pekka said something like, *I really wish my brother was here.* You better believe Rannie would charge out of the forest then, grinning and ready to hug.

Rannie smelled the campfire before he saw it, the rich scent reminding him of safety and home. He hurried to the edge of the clearing, across which his brother had set up a tent smack against Sandwich Rock's face. It was a good location. Not only were the rocks sturdy, but the top boulder's slight overhang offered protection from the elements. The fire crackled a few feet away from the tent, its orange tongue licking the air, mesmerizing Rannie.

One man sat by the fire, one man stood.

"Your turn," said the seated one. Not Pekka. Hector. Rannie'd met him earlier. Pekka had brought him to the house, introduced him as his "good buddy," asked to borrow the tent and some sleeping bags. Hector had dark eyes and a nice smile. He'd made a point of talking to Rannie, of asking him if he was having a good day.

Rannie was thinking how nice it would be to have a friend like Hector when he realized he was standing out in the open like a silly duck waiting to get shot. He was a good forty yards from their camp, but still. He darted behind a pine tree, its sharp scent like furniture polish, and peeked out with only his eyes.

"S'nough," Pekka said. He was swaying, hands held out toward the fire.

Rannie squinted. It looked like his brother talking, but it didn't *sound* like him. The words were rumbly and heavy, like they wanted to stand up but couldn't. The Pekka Rannie knew was always confident, his speaking voice crisp and clear. Was that really him? The firelight cast his face into shadow.

Across the field, Hector laughed. "The game was your idea," he said. His words were heavy, too, but they didn't run together like Pekka's. "And *because* it was your idea, you can't quit." He held up a bottle. It held liquid the color of honey in the firelight.

Whiskey.

Rannie's shoulders sagged. If drinking was what twenty-year-old men did in secret, that was about as exciting as watching bread rise.

He'd hoped for something better. Secret missions, or epic battles, or three-legged sack races. Rannie'd seen those at school, when he spied on the kids playing, and they looked like a pure good time.

"Sssshhhhhut it," Pekka said, "or the Finnish witch'll get you. She doesn't like pushers."

Rannie's attention sat right back up. He'd never heard Pekka talk about the veri noita, not outside of the fairy-tale books he'd read to Rannie when he was little, when their mom and dad were attending the meetings.

Say your prayers and get to bed on time when there's a reaping, or the veri noita will swallow your toes!

"Ha," Hector said, chuckling. "I'll take your Finnish witch and raise you La Llorona."

Rannie liked how Hector's voice went warm, like a purr, when he said *yarona.*

"You dare to challenge veri noita on her home turf?" Pekka exclaimed, using the same pretend-angry voice he did when reading Rannie stories. "Beware!"

Hector was really laughing now. "Man, so you *can* joke. I wondered."

Pekka started to giggle. He waved a dismissive hand at the whiskey bottle Hector was still offering him. "B'right back."

Pekka disappeared behind Sandwich Rock, out of Rannie's sight.

"Pekka take-a leak-a, Pekka take-a leak-a," Hector started singing softly, poking at the fire with a stick. The sparks danced. "Hey, man," he called over his shoulder, "did you bring the chips?"

Chips! Rannie loved chips. His mom didn't allow store-bought food at home, but sometimes Pekka sneaked him some. Rannie watched with great interest as Hector rustled around inside the lump next to him—a knapsack?—then stood, wobbling, and turned toward the tent.

"Pekka take-a leak-a," Hector mumbled, shambling forward. The scream of the tent zipper split the air. Hector vanished inside.

"Found 'em!" he called out. "Found the chips!"

Just then, a high-pitched laugh pierced Rannie's eardrums like the sharp end of a screwdriver.

Not a laugh, he realized, his blood icing.

A cackle.

He blinked at the kaleidoscope fire, shaking his head like a dog. He caught a flash of something black and quick behind the flames and felt a burst of terror. It was followed immediately by numbness. Was the air getting hazy? Warm, too. His chest squeezed, and he reached out to the pine tree to steady himself. He wanted to lie down, but an enormous, ancient scraping sound from Sandwich Rock got his pulse racing. Turning to look took so much effort that sweat broke out along his forehead. He wanted to sleep so bad, but he knew he couldn't, not now.

Because the top boulder was wobbling.

Impossible. Was it an earthquake? Rannie'd never personally felt one, but everyone knew Alku had quaked on the day of its founding, way back in 1881. It was the land welcoming the Finns to their new home, that's what their history said.

But the earth wasn't moving now.

Only the top boulder of Sandwich Rock was. Wasn't it? Or was the enormous stone the only thing that was still, and everything else in the world was tipping?

Rannie dropped to his knees, suddenly too weary to stand. He wanted to throw up.

"The rock," he called out. Or at least he wanted to, but the veri noita had stolen his voice. That was what this was, wasn't it? The monster coming to reap Hector for challenging her. She'd cast a spell on Rannie, too, making him feel like he was dying. He curled his toes inside his boots. He wanted to tell her that he was an Alku kid, his blood pure, that he was a Finn through and through and a good boy, but he was so jelly-bone tired that all he could do was lie down on the pine needles and close his eyes.

"No. No. No."

The word knocked at Rannie's skull, starting quiet and growing steadily louder. He sat up slowly and leaned around the tree, rubbing at his face. Pine needles dropped off, leaving itchy dents. Pekka was kneeling on the far side of the clearing, swaying back and forth.

Something was wrong with the picture.

It took Rannie an upside-down moment to figure out what it was. The top boulder of Sandwich Rock had slid all the way off. It'd landed smack-dab on the tent and the fire, destroying both.

Hector was nowhere to be seen.

"No. No. No."

"Pekka?" Rannie stood, stumbling toward his brother. "You okay?"

"No no no no noooo," Pekka was wailing. He was facing Rannie, the cheese moon outlining the shape of his skull. Rannie thought how much Pekka looked like their father in that moment. Old. Sad.

"What is it, Pekka?" Rannie was close enough now that he could touch his brother's shoulder. "Where's Hector?"

Pekka's eyes widened. "You," he said, jerking back. It sounded like an accusation, but then his voice softened, resigned, understanding. "*You.* How long have you been here?"

Rannie shrugged. Pointed at the top rock, which was now upside down alongside the bottom rock. "Is your friend under there?"

Pekka shuddered, stood. When he spoke, his voice was sobered by fear. "We should go back to town. We should get help."

Rannie's eyebrows pushed together. "If Hector's under there, he's squashed like a caterpillar. Flat. Flatter than flat. There's no rush."

Pekka suddenly looked scared.

Rannie didn't like that. "Did the monster come out?" he asked.

A noise in the woods startled them both. Something large, lumbering in the other direction.

"Yeah, buddy," Pekka whispered. "Yeah, it did."

CHAPTER 2

BCA agent Harry Steinbeck lived his life by three principles:

1. Insight adheres to structure.
2. Structure provides safety.
3. Safety requires you let no one in.

If he kept his two worlds separate—his current ascetic life as a Bureau of Criminal Apprehension forensic scientist, and his past as a teenager whose sister was abducted—and hung on to those three tenets, he survived. But now, as he blinked at the banner hung above the hospital door, pastel Easter eggs and pink-nosed lambs adorning its edges, an oily chill spread through his gut.

'TIS THE SEASON OF FORGIVENESS

The words offered a cruel irony to Harry, a man returning to his past for the first time in years, reminding him that the wall he'd built between his worlds was made of tissue paper. He'd thought he could keep neat TV-tray compartments for the Before and the After, that by making the obligatory calls to his mother—Christmas, Mother's Day, Thanksgiving, birthdays—and meeting her for dinner once a year at a restaurant of her choosing in Saint Paul, he could keep his meat separate from his potatoes.

But now, here he was, back in Duluth, the tray smashed.

His partner, Agent Evangeline Reed, aimed her chin at the banner as she patted her jacket pockets. "Catholic hospital. I guess they're allowed to run ads for Jesus."

The distant sound of a car revving drew Harry's attention. The early-afternoon sky was muddy, the ground snow-covered. A freak blizzard had pounded the northern Minnesota port city of Duluth the previous night. The snowbanks lining the sidewalks were thigh-high, and wicked-looking icicles glittered on the roof's edge like deadly twinkle lights. The hospital itself was a large, modern building with multiple floors and wide windows lit up from within.

"Got any gum?" Evangeline asked.

"I do not." Harry grimaced. "And I never will."

The hospital entrance was automatic, so he couldn't open it for her, but he hung back so she could enter first. He loosened his deep-blue cashmere scarf and unbuttoned his merino-wool peacoat in anticipation of the heat. He was rewarded when the whoosh of the sliding door released a wave of warmth, the sharp scent of disinfectants mixing with the cold, crisp outdoor air. The chatter and beeps of a packed emergency room washed over them. He studied Evangeline's straight back and squared shoulders, her white-blonde hair in a crisp ponytail at the crown of her head. They'd taken baby steps toward developing a friendship at the end of the last case they'd worked together, a double abduction from the '80s that the media had dubbed the Taken Ones. This trip north, if they didn't get out within a day or two, would put their nascent relationship at risk.

Evangeline didn't know what he'd done when he lived here.

Her shoulders tensed as if she could read his thoughts. "Do you smell that?" she asked as they both scanned the ER.

A person increased their risk of getting the flu by 3 percent in a hospital waiting room, measles by 13 percent. Harry reached into his pocket for hand sanitizer. He knew better than to offer Evangeline any. "What?"

"Fear," she said. "Blood. Rubbing alcohol." She shuddered. "I'd rather be naked onstage than in a hospital."

"Yet you chose to become a homicide detective." Harry said it mildly, returning the nod of an officer on the far side of the emergency room. From here, he couldn't tell if the man's uniform was midnight blue or black. He rubbed the antiseptic into his hands, slid the bottle back into his coat, removed a crisp mask from his pocket, and snapped it over his mouth before following Evangeline across the busy floor. A few heads turned as they waded through.

They ignored them.

"Homicide detectives don't spend nearly as much time in the morgue as TV would have you believe," Evangeline said over her shoulder, pitching her voice to be heard. Her tone was sharp, but she was teasing.

At least Harry hoped she was. His chest hitched. She couldn't possibly believe he got his information from a *television*, could she? He sighed as he realized he had to be sure. He raised his own voice to carry over the ER's thrumming chaos. "You realize that I know, more or less, how a homicide detective spends their days, right?"

It wasn't that his ego needed her to acknowledge his intelligence. Far from it. Rather, this was the first investigative case they'd work as co-leads. It was crucial they understood what the other knew. Evangeline had been a homicide detective with the Minneapolis Police Department for ten years before becoming a crack agent at the BCA. Harry was a forensic scientist with nearly twenty years' experience in collecting and processing evidence. He'd worked closely with police departments all over the state and was the scientist requested by name when the crime scene was particularly complex.

And so he knew, on average, how much time homicide spent in the morgue.

He needed Evangeline to know he knew.

The case demanded it, and Harry Steinbeck gave everything to his cases.

"Evangeline?" he asked when she didn't respond.

She groaned dramatically. "Christ on a cracker, Steinbeck. For this partnership to work without me strangling you in your sleep, I'm going to need you to develop a *fleck* of humor." She held up a hand, her thumb and pointer finger nearly touching. "Not a whole sense. Just a *fleck. Obviously* you know a detective's duties. It was a joke. You know, the thing normal humans say to one another to lighten the mood? Or didn't your hard drive come with that chip?"

Harry suppressed a grin. They'd nearly reached the far side of the ER. Most of the people waiting appeared to be suffering from a mix of shoveling- and snowblower-related injuries, their backs bent or their hands wrapped in blood-soaked towels, with a sprinkling of what sounded like stomach viruses thrown in for good measure.

"You must be Agent Steinbeck and Agent Reed," the uniform said when they reached him, leaving his station in front of a door marked AUTHORIZED ADMITTANCE ONLY. He shook Evangeline's hand and then Harry's. Harry was pleased the officer had started with Evangeline. It was a low bar, acknowledging a female agent, but it wasn't one every cop cleared.

"Nice to meet you," Harry said.

"I'm Greg Davidson." He was in his late twenties with a broad, honest face, his grip firm. "If you follow me, I can take you to the morgue. The medical examiner just started the autopsy, but Detective Emery can catch you up if necessary."

He held the door open.

Over a dozen bacterial colonies live on the average doorknob. The thought came unbidden. Harry tamped it down.

"When was our victim brought in?" Evangeline asked as she passed him, removing a mitten with her mouth and then yanking a notebook out of her pocket.

Davidson waited to answer until the security door closed, dropping the noise level at least seventy decibels. "Around midnight last night."

He indicated they should follow him down the white hall lit with buzzing fluorescent bulbs.

"And who found him?" Evangeline asked, falling in behind.

Harry had received that information earlier this morning when Deputy Superintendent Ed Chandler asked if he'd be willing to drive to Duluth at the request of one Detective Dale Emery. Harry had almost said no. Every return trip to the northland was one more chance for him to be found out, to be connected to the truth of his past.

But when he'd skimmed the file, he'd realized he couldn't turn this one down.

Unsolved. Juvenile victims.

Detective Emery had requested a cold case agent in addition to someone from forensics. When Chandler asked Harry what he thought of working with Evangeline on this one, Harry said he'd be happy to. And he would. She was a good agent. Harry had filled her in on the case on the drive up.

What she was doing now, seeing if the details Officer Davidson shared corroborated what they'd already been told, was good basic investigative work.

"Pizza delivery person was the one who discovered the body," Davidson said, one hand resting on his belt. "At 11:54 last night."

"That's a dick move," Evangeline said, tugging off her other mitten and shoving it into her pocket.

"Excuse me?"

She quirked an eyebrow. "Ordering pizza during a snowstorm."

The officer's lip twitched, but he didn't respond. "We believe the pizza gal missed walking in on an active murder by minutes. She thought she maybe saw someone leaving, but she couldn't be sure. The snow was coming down as thick as stew. Door was cracked open when she reached it, no lights on. She knocked. No answer. Peeked in, didn't see anyone. Not at first." He made a noise like a cough. "Then she saw it on the floor."

"It?" Harry's tone made clear he didn't approve of the word choice. Victims never relinquished their humanity, dead or alive.

"Sure, I suppose, *him*." Officer Davidson's tone was grim. "But once you see what's left, you'll understand why 'it' makes more sense."

"Lead the way," Harry said.

CHAPTER 3

Detective Dale Emery swiveled from the autopsy suite's viewing window. He was in his midthirties, a hair taller than Harry—maybe six two—and rangy. He had a strong nose, an easy smile, and thick sideburns that would not have looked out of place on a 1970s Elvis Presley.

He offered a handshake to them both, just like Davidson had. "Thanks for coming." He nodded at the window. "You'll see it's not your standard PM."

Harry stepped up to Emery's left side, Evangeline to his right. The PM—the postmortem—was being conducted on a white male laid out on the autopsy table. The pathologist had her back to them and was leaning over the victim's head, obscuring it. The body was covered in what looked at first glance like speckles of dirt, with a cluster of entrance wounds on the belly and chest. The Y incision had not yet been made, which meant that the pathologist was still completing the external exam.

The speaker relayed her observations as she made them, her voice crackling. "Tasmanian Devil tattoo, upper left shoulder. A three-inch keloid just below."

Harry had his scarf loose around his neck, his winter coat draped over his arm. Beneath, he wore a cream-colored oxford and a blue tie decorated with gold chess pieces. The ties were one of the few displays of whimsy he allowed himself.

"Not standard how?" he asked.

At that moment, the pathologist moved, revealing the victim's head. Or what was left of it.

"Holy hell," Evangeline muttered. They'd been told there was a traumatic cranial injury in addition to the bullet wounds, but not the extent of it.

"Yeah." Detective Emery scratched a sideburn. "Looks like someone stuck it in a meat grinder."

There was that word again. *It.* "Victim's name?" Harry asked, though he knew.

"One Peter Gordon Weiss of 1472 Superior Way."

Harry wished he were inside the exam room for a closer visual, but the Bureau of Criminal Apprehension had no jurisdiction of its own. The organization was unique to Minnesota, started in response to the Chicagoland gangsters terrorizing the area in the 1920s. It began small, basically a traveling backup team designed to assist law enforcement across the state at their request. A statistics division was added in the '30s, and in 1947, the BCA built the first forensic science laboratory in the region. It soon became one of the finest in the nation, renowned for its crime scene processing and evidence analysis. Since then, the BCA had not only added more agents and field offices but also founded one of the first dedicated cold case departments in the country.

Their agents did important work, but their lack of jurisdiction meant they needed to tread lightly. It was human nature to be territorial, and police officers were no exception.

"Do you have more information on the weapons used?" Harry asked.

Emery pulled at his nose. "To smash the head? No clue. Best guess on the holes in the body is they were made by double-aught buckshot from a 12-gauge at intermediate range." His elbow twitched toward the exam room. "We'll know for sure at the end of this."

"A shotgun, for chrissakes." Evangeline leaned so close to the glass that her forehead touched it. She still wore her winter coat, though it was now unzipped. Most Minnesotans knew not to pack away their winter gear before May because of stealth snowstorms like the previous night's, but Evangeline hadn't even taken hers out of her car. Harry had witnessed her grab it from her back seat when he'd rolled up to her apartment this morning to drive them the two and a half hours north. A McDonald's bag plus two empty water bottles had tumbled out of her Toyota along with the black parka whose pockets she was currently searching.

Harry wasn't sure she'd have retrieved the trash if he hadn't been watching.

Then again, in his limited experience, cold case agent Evangeline Reed didn't do much of anything unless she wanted to. She appeared immune to social pressure, especially when it came to tidiness. Though her messy habits made Harry twitchy, he'd never seen them interfere with her job. He suspected they were a nesting protection she'd adopted either to keep people at arm's length or as a rebellion against the repressive environment she'd been raised in.

Until age seventeen, Evangeline had lived in a commune run by a cruel but charismatic man by the name of Frank Roth. She'd escaped when the feds apprehended Roth for tax evasion. The arrest had been a media circus. The women and girls of "Frank's Farm" were led out, paraded in front of the cameras, each of them displaying signs of active shock, all of them wearing sack dresses in plain gray cloth with their long hair twisted into a bun. A photo of a plate-eyed Evangeline had made the cover of *Time*, the headline Communes in Your Backyard.

Looking at the image had pinched Harry's heart, though he hadn't known her then.

Evangeline pulled back from the viewing window, unaware of Harry's mental wandering. "Did the pathologist cover that speckle bruising before we got here?"

Emery shot her a glance. Evangeline's petite size and milky-blonde hair gave the impression she was younger and less capable than she was. Harry wondered if Detective Emery would make the mistake of underestimating her.

It would be at his peril.

"She noted it," Emery said, "but wouldn't speculate as to what had made it."

Harry approved. The job of a scientist was to observe and record, not guess, at least not so early in the autopsy. Case in point was the speckle pattern. It looked like dirt or blood spatter at first glance, but a trained eye could see what appeared to be swelling below each patch of discoloration. He was impressed but not surprised that Evangeline had caught it.

"I'd like to take the clothes and fluid samples back to Saint Paul with us at the end of the autopsy," he said. "Is that possible?"

"No problem on the fluids," Emery replied. "You'd be saving us a trip. Can't help you on the clothes, though." He tipped his head toward the victim. "He was naked as a jaybird when we found him, just like you see now. Wiped clean, too. Same with the scene. No blood, no sign of struggle, just the corpse and the powerful stink of chlorine bleach." Emery scratched his left cheek, the sideburn making a sandpaper sound beneath his fingers. "Which made the luminol as effective as a black light at a Grateful Dead after-party, by the way. Whole place lit up like a glowstick."

Harry winced. Luminol might be helpful in revealing blood patterns, but its chemical reaction often destroyed other evidence. He preferred to work a scene first, reserving luminol as a last resort. If Weiss's murder location had been bleached, however, there'd be little for it to damage.

Though in Harry's experience, nothing disappeared without a trace.

"There wasn't blood beneath the victim's head?" he asked.

Emery studied what was left of Weiss—the pink-purple meat, the shock of white skull fragments. "Yeah, there was blood, but not a whole man's worth. Just a trickle. He was either killed off-site, or whoever killed him cleaned up and then skedaddled before the pizza arrived."

"What time was it ordered and then delivered?" Evangeline asked.

"Ordered around ten, call came in from his landline." Emery rubbed the back of his neck. "But the storm backed up everything. Pizza wasn't delivered until right before midnight."

Harry studied Peter Weiss's remains. Long toenails, short fingernails. Graying pubic, arm, and leg hair. A swollen belly suggesting he'd been a regular drinker, though the rest of his body was long and lean. One visible tattoo, the Tasmanian Devil on his shoulder. The ear nearest the viewing window was intact and the only part of Mr. Weiss's head in approximately the spot it should be.

Emery continued. "Whoever did this to him had over two hours to mash him good, if they dove in right after he ordered."

Except that wasn't quite right. "Mashed" would've laid Weiss's head flat, destroying the ear or at least moving it to a new location.

"Can you send all photos to the Saint Paul lab?" Harry asked.

Emery grunted in the affirmative and offered the file he'd been holding. "You can have a look at these for now."

Harry flipped open the folder. The first photo was a driver's license shot, Weiss staring unsmiling at the camera, gray hair trimmed short, a thick horseshoe mustache framing his mouth.

Evangeline nodded at it. "The men like their facial hair up here."

Emery was poised to scratch his magnificent sideburn again. He dropped his hand.

Harry swallowed an involuntary smile and flipped to the next photo. It featured Weiss on his back, head obliterated, leg folded beneath him in a gruesome imitation of a runner's stretch. The linoleum floor below was clean other than a small pool of blood gathering beneath the damaged skull. But there was something off with the cranial injury, something Harry couldn't put his finger on. He'd ask Deepty Singh, one of two scientists he trusted implicitly back at the Saint Paul BCA lab, to enlarge the photos for a better look.

"No question why I called you guys, right?" Emery's tone was light but his jaw stiff. "It's got Matty the Mallet hammered all over it, pun intended. Same as the 1998 cold case."

19

Evangeline tossed Harry a tight glance.

The unsolved murder of the Korhonen family in the town of Alku, a village sixteen miles southwest of Duluth, haunted the northland. Husband, wife, and three children under the age of ten murdered as they slept, all five of their bodies riddled with double-aught buckshot, their skulls destroyed by blunt-force trauma. They were the reason Harry had accepted the case. He knew nothing about the parents, but those children had been innocents. He couldn't have handed the file back to Superintendent Chandler this morning for love or money, though he knew what he was risking by returning to Duluth.

Everything.

So instead, he'd checked the contents of the go bag he kept in his office to make sure they'd meet Duluth's climate, and then he'd pulled up the old files. The Alku cold case, like this one, had mirrored the MO of Minnesota's most notorious serial killer: Mathias Millard, a.k.a. Matty the Mallet, so called because he bludgeoned five women and two men before his 1990 capture. Millard had worked as a traveling salesman for GrainLed, a Midwest-based multilevel marketing company known for its breakfast bars and horse-pill-size vitamins. After he was caught, he famously claimed he'd never killed a customer. All his victims had been hitchhikers he'd picked up, driven to a remote location in his wood-paneled station wagon, tortured, blasted with a shotgun, and then pulverized with a rubber mallet until their heads were more liquid than solid.

Exactly as had been done to the Korhonen family.

The only hitch in tying Mathias Millard to the Korhonen killings? He was behind bars at the time, imprisoned at the Carlton County Treatment Center's medium-security nursing home just north of Alku, rendered mute and immobile by a stroke he'd experienced two years earlier.

No other viable suspect had been found.

The mass murder was relegated to Minnesota's cold case files.

Where it had moldered, until today.

CHAPTER 4

At the end of the autopsy, Emery had requested Evangeline and Harry meet him and his deputy at the Carlton County Treatment Center, or CCTC, a mile north of Alku. He wanted them present as he performed his due diligence in "interviewing" Matty the Mallet. Emery had argued that tagging along now would save them time later if the BCA elected to reactivate the Korhonen cold case, a decision that only Superintendent Chandler could make.

Harry had agreed.

After the site visit, he and Evangeline could head home with a clear conscience, back to the safety of skyscrapers and the certainty of science. Harry knew he'd been foolish to come up here. The past was too near. When you went home, you came back to the person you used to be, for better or worse.

In his case, much, much worse.

"So tell me," Evangeline said as she drove. "What's it like to return to your old stomping grounds?"

As if she'd read his mind, *again.* He was just able to stop himself from glancing sideways at her. When they'd first been thrown together in Costa Rica to follow up on a suspected homicide—a case that still wasn't solved, as far as Harry was concerned—they'd been babysitting more than investigating. The Taken Ones abduction that they'd worked a few months back? He'd been her forensics contact, but that investigation had been all hers. Weiss's homicide was the first time they would be acting as true partners, though their time on this case would be short-lived. They'd only been called north to consult on the murder and determine whether there was merit in reviving a potentially connected cold case. Harry hoped they'd be driving home tonight.

He'd researched her tenure at the Minneapolis PD before they'd gone to Costa Rica, of course. He had no intention of traveling out of the country with a complete unknown. He found she had an exceptional clearance rate. No write-ups, no dings on her record. Yet more than one officer he asked about working with her had wanted to tell him she wasn't right. "Witchy" was the word they'd used. He'd shut them down. Harry Steinbeck didn't truck in gossip, and he certainly didn't truck in magic. Still, the way she'd seemed to know facts she had no right to during the Taken Ones case, how she sometimes appeared to pluck thoughts from his head, like just now? It rippled the skin at the back of his neck. He held himself rigid. "Being back at my old stomping grounds is fine."

She snorted but didn't push it. "'Fine' it is." They drove in silence for a few more minutes. Harry found himself ridiculously worried to think anything. Evangeline wasn't a mind reader. She was a good agent, that was all.

"Lucky you requisitioned a big ol' four-wheel drive," she finally said.

Harry hadn't objected when she'd demanded the keys before they took off for Alku. He was surprised she'd let him behind the wheel as far as Duluth, actually. He didn't take it personally. Evangeline preferred to control all aspects of her life, including where she drove. If Harry had been raised by a man who hadn't allowed his children to choose so much as the clothes they wore, he imagined he'd react similarly.

"It wasn't *luck*," he said, his eyebrows meeting over his nose. "I checked the weather before I picked it."

The steering wheel gave a jerk. Harry's hands flew to the dashboard. When he glanced over at Evangeline, she was smiling innocently.

"Slippery roads," she said.

The highway *was* shiny with ice, two feet of snow blanketing the ditches on each side. If the temperature remained above freezing through the week as predicted, the roads would soon be released, the snow withering like a scene in a stop-action film.

Harry planned to not be here to see it.

"You know anything about Alku other than what he told us?" Evangeline asked, tipping her head toward Emery's car just ahead of them.

During the autopsy, the detective had offered an overview of the village where the Korhonens had been murdered, starting with the fact that its actual name was Uusialku.

"Leave it to the Finns to throw every vowel they can at a word," he'd said.

When Harry raised an eyebrow, Emery qualified his comment. "My grandpa's Finnish. I'm allowed to make jokes. Anyhow, everyone, including the folks who live there, calls it Alku. The CCTC, where Matty the Mallet is serving his time, is their only industry. It started out as a hospital, then was converted into a psychiatric institution, and now it's a nursing home for convicted killers. They're physically incapacitated but still dangerous. Most of the Alku citizens work at the CCTC, including the Korhonen adults back in the day."

"And including Peter Weiss before he was murdered," Evangeline murmured, watching as the pathologist removed Weiss's heart and dropped it onto the scale.

"It was verified in 1998 that Mr. Millard couldn't walk?" Harry asked.

Emery nodded. "It wasn't for lack of trying that they couldn't pin the murders on Matty, but his legs were two noodles back when the Korhonen family said their final goodbye. I can't imagine they're any better now, and it's a shame. Folks in my line of work've been chafing to solve this one. It's the kind of case that's measured in careers, not years."

Harry knew the gnawing pain of an unsolved homicide. Every law enforcement officer who'd served more than a few years had at least one. The pain of it was magnified when the victims were children.

"Is it possible Mr. Millard is communicating with someone outside the prison?" Harry asked. "I know he's unable to speak, but does he have access to a computer?"

"The CCTC doesn't allow prisoners computer time," Emery had said, scratching his sideburns. Harry thought what a relief it would be to shave those off. "The inmates have a library. They have a monitored pay phone. They have movie night, they have an exercise room, and they have an outdoor field. No internet."

Evangeline cleared her throat, bringing Harry back into the present, to the SUV and the heat blowing from its vents distributing the sweet, sticky smell of the vanilla air freshener she'd bought at a gas station on their drive up. "Harry?" she said. "I asked you what you knew about Alku."

"Sorry." He released his grip on the dash. It'd been a few minutes since Evangeline had swerved, but his body had yet to relax. "My mind wandered. I don't have much more to offer than what Emery gave us. Small town. Unincorporated, so no record of the exact population, but I can't imagine it's higher than four hundred. I'd like to do more research once we return to Saint Paul."

"When do you think that will be?"

A speck of green in the distance announced that they'd soon reach Alku's perimeter. "If the meeting with Mr. Millard doesn't provide any surprises, we'll be home before midnight." The thought was balm to his soul. He *would* survive this visit. He'd return to the Cities still himself.

The current version.

He would follow his first principle, adhere to structure, and go by the book, but he'd do it quickly because everything was screaming at him that he needed to escape this area as soon as possible. The scent of Lake Superior crack-thawing in the spring, the awesome sight of the Aerial Lift Bridge as they'd driven into Duluth, the blaring horns of barges entering one of the largest inland harbors in the world.

It all reminded Harry that he was the reason his sister had never been found.

CHAPTER 5

Harry's mother, Myrna, had never been particularly warm, but she seemed to try her best to parent. That changed when Caroline was born ten years after Harry.

Myrna couldn't seem to lay eyes on her daughter without criticizing her. It started with telling her she cried too much, or wet too many diapers. And then when she became old enough to walk, it became, "Caroline, stop that incessant humming! Can't you see I'm trying to have some peace? Caroline, did you eat a cookie? You know it'll make you fat. Caroline, you smell like a wet dog. You must have forgotten to take your bath."

One sunny summer afternoon, when Harry was sixteen and Caroline six, the harsh words reached a fever pitch. When Harry found his baby sister hiding in her bedroom after a particularly harsh tongue-lashing, he decided on the spot to whisk her away for the day. It didn't matter that he barely had his driver's license or that Myrna would most certainly not let him take the car if he asked.

"Caro," he asked, kneeling by her. "Do you want to visit the traveling carnival that's in town?"

She and Harry shared the same arctic-blue eyes, but where Harry's hair was dark brown, Caroline's was so blonde it was almost white. With her button nose and cherry lips, she looked like a doll, and when she heard the offer of escape, it was like the sun had risen on her face. She nodded and jumped to her feet, dropping the crayon she'd been clutching. That's when Harry noticed she'd been drawing clouds on her wall. Myrna was going to *flip*. He grabbed Caroline's pudgy hand, her fingers wrapped tightly around his, and they made their escape.

Caroline had been so excited on the drive that she was trembling in her seat. "Can we ride the Ferris wheel?" she begged. "And consume cotton candy and mini doughnuts?"

That's how she talked. It was like she'd been born an old soul. "You got it," Harry said indulgently.

And he was true to his word. They rode the Ferris wheel, the carousel, the giant slide, Caroline giggling the entire time. He bought her a corn dog and mini doughnuts and bright-pink cotton candy. He even won her a stuffed teddy bear. The day seemed to stretch on forever.

He knew there'd be hell to pay when they returned, sure. He'd left a note that Myrna would see when she woke up from her afternoon nap, but she'd be fuming, and it would only get worse when she smelled the fried food on Caroline. But when he looked over at her buckled into the passenger seat on the drive home, clutching that teddy bear, her cheeks sticky with sugar, he knew it was worth it.

The recollection of that magical day brought a smile to his face. It was rare to have a purely happy memory of Caroline. His mind, likely balking at the unfamiliar sensation, yanked him from the warmth to the icy reality of that morning at the BCA, just before he'd learned he'd end up in Duluth today. He'd gone to work early to put the finishing touches on a case that had kept him late in the lab for more than a week: a teenage girl had been killed while working the graveyard shift at a gas station in the western suburbs. Harry's lab had been sent the evidence to process, but there was a long line ahead of it. He'd checked it in, assigned it a number, and then gone to the cantina for a coffee before starting in on the day's scheduled processing.

It was chance that the television in the cafeteria had been playing the interview with the murdered girl's mother. She was understandably distraught, her face swollen with tears. A single mom, she'd raised her daughter without any help, financial or otherwise. She'd received news of her only child's murder while in the middle of a double shift at a local diner.

"Please," she'd sobbed at the camera. "I don't have my girl. I need justice."

Those words had cleaved Harry in two.

I don't have my girl. I need justice.

It wasn't unusual in the BCA to work long hours, so when he stayed at the lab well past his required shift to make time for the murdered girl's case, no one asked questions. He was able to pull a DNA profile from the evidence they'd received. When he obtained no matches in CODIS, he forwarded a portion of the DNA to a private lab and called in every favor to have them do a rush job: developing the BCA's sample into a single nucleotide polymorphism profile, the DNA type used by genealogical databases. Once that was done, he reached out to a San Francisco acquaintance, a woman in the private sector creating a meta-crawler that culled profiles from across all commercial ancestry sites. With the information she provided, and after several late nights that turned into early mornings, Harry narrowed the DNA association to two men.

One had died three years earlier.

The other was an accountant and married father of two who lived within walking distance of the suburban gas station where the girl had been working the night she was murdered.

Gotcha.

He'd brought Superintendent Chandler the information at 7:00 a.m. Neither of them should have been in so early; neither was surprised to see the other. Chandler had grunted a "good work" and told Harry about the Korhonen family and Peter Weiss cases. Was that what this trip was? What his entire career was? Penance for what he'd done to Caroline?

"A nursing home for serial killers." Evangeline drummed her fingers on the steering wheel, jerking Harry back into the present yet again. "That's about as creepy as it gets. And it's Alku's main industry." She pointed out the window. "What do you think the word means?"

It took Harry a moment to realize she was referring to the name of the town, spelled out on the sign they'd zipped past: Uusialku.

"I don't know," he said, rubbing his hands over his face. There was no percentage in living in the past. "I don't speak Finnish. It might not even be a word. It could be someone's name."

He felt her studying him. What was she thinking about as they cruised through the landscape of the worst moments of his life? He started to itch just under the skin. The discomfort had begun on the drive to Duluth, building until he wanted to take steel wool to it, but talking about the case, watching the autopsy, the activity had silenced it. Out here, though, there was too much space to think. The snow-crusted fields spread out as far north and west as the eye could see, an eerie moonscape. His shoulders didn't unknit until they crested a hill and Alku's rows of wooden houses replaced the numbingly white-gray terrain. Many of them were deep red, a startling contrast to the snow. The rest were white and brown, their lines simple.

Evangeline and Harry were quiet until they reached the town's central square.

Harry sat at attention, pulse hammering in his neck.

"Ho-lee Hannah," Evangeline said, her free hand dropping to her waist, hovering near her firearm. "Have we driven onto the set of *The Twilight Zone*?"

Ahead, a body dressed in black was tied to a stake in front of a small church, a burlap sack covering its head. Children in costumes choked the streets alongside it, their merry faces jarring alongside the staked figure. They wore brightly colored, shapeless clothes, their cheeks painted red and dotted with freckles, towering witch hats perched on their heads. Each child carried a sack, and most of the children were sucking on old-fashioned candy sticks and staring at the SUV as it rumbled past, ignoring the macabre corpse strung up behind them.

Harry got the unsettling feeling he and Evangeline had driven back in time. It wasn't until they were parallel to the black-clad figure that he realized the "corpse" was a mannequin, VERI NOITA painted on a wooden sign hung around its neck.

"Must be some sort of cultural celebration," he said, still tense.

"Old-school Easter." Evangeline's hand had moved away from her firearm, but she didn't sound like she'd relaxed much, either.

"What's that?" Harry asked.

She jabbed her thumb back toward the church. "If I'm not mistaken, these *folks* have a little pagan mixed in with their Christianity."

Harry's forehead furrowed. "Why'd you say 'folks' like that?"

"What do you mean?"

He turned to her, mystified. "You said 'folks' like you were giving it air quotes, like you weren't so sure they were even people."

She shook her head. "It's not that. You don't see it?" She made a frustrated noise and pointed at a cluster of children, two women standing behind them, their flat eyes locked on the SUV as it passed. "And there." She nodded toward a huddle of men leaning against pitchforks in front of what looked like it used to be a diner, the word CLOSED etched in soap on its window. "And there," she said, indicating a group of teenagers.

"I don't—" Harry had been about to say he didn't see it, but then he couldn't look away.

It was subtle, something a click off. The townspeople seemed ordinary at first glance, but on closer inspection, it became clear that their foreheads were a little too large, their necks a bit too long, their movements languorous. Any one of them standing alone, Harry wouldn't have noticed it. When gathered together, the echoed effect sawed at his nerves.

"You see it now," Evangeline said, her voice grim. "It's not just the kids dressed like witches. They're *all* pretending to be someone else."

CHAPTER 6

"Take a right here." Harry's voice came out harsher than he would like. The brief and unnerving glimpse into Alku had unsettled him, but that wasn't Evangeline's fault.

She shot him an annoyed look. "At the 'Sanitorium for Consumptives'?" she asked, exasperated.

Seemed the town had agitated them both.

They'd circled back to complete an extra circuit through Alku—more children dressed as witches, more lingering, disconcerting stares, more craniofacial abnormalities—and had managed to lose Emery in the process. They now found themselves a mile north of town on County Road 98, the area heavily wooded, velvet-green pine trees choking off what little light trickled down from the gloomy sky. None of the side roads they'd passed indicated that the Carlton County Treatment Center was nearby. Not advertising a prison was standard practice, but they'd been unable to find any signage at all other than the decaying ten-foot stone pillar with the words SANITORIUM FOR CONSUMPTIVES inlaid in white pebbles down its front.

"Detective Emery mentioned the treatment center had been repurposed," Harry said. "It might be this."

Evangeline exhaled heavily, but she took the road straight into the guts of the forest. It rambled through the thick hardwoods before forking. The left road continued as gravel, disappearing into the forest's dark mouth. To the right, it became pavement leading directly to a wall of ominous razor-wire-topped chain-link perimeter fencing. A guard hut was stationed nearby, a man inside.

Harry fought the uncharacteristic urge to gloat.

"Don't say it," Evangeline told him before rolling the SUV to a stop near the gate and opening her window. She held out their badges. "Agents Van Reed and Harry Steinbeck of the BCA. Detective Emery should have arrived just ahead of us."

The guard lacked the wide forehead and long neck they'd witnessed on the Alku people. Harry was caught off guard by the relief he felt. The guard's face was lined, white hair tufting out from beneath his winter cap. He examined their IDs over the rim of his bifocals before returning them and offering them a clipboard to sign in on.

"What's the dirt road back there lead to?" Evangeline asked while she wrote down their names, jabbing her pen at the gravel they'd just turned off.

The guard studied her curiously. "You serious?"

"As a throat punch." She handed him back his clipboard.

"Good news, then." The guard winked. "That's the road you're taking to meet Emery."

Evangeline glared at the gate in front of them. "But we're here to visit the prison."

"Understood. But Emery said to meet him at the school. It's adjacent to the prison."

"There's a *school* next to the *prison?*" Evangeline asked.

The guard's eyebrows crinkled. "Lady," he said, "you don't know the half of it."

He returned to his guardhouse, as if that were a normal way to end a conversation. Evangeline waited a moment before she jammed the vehicle into reverse and squealed backward, a scowl pulling her mouth.

"He could have just told us," she said. "Same with Emery, for that matter. He *very specifically* told us to meet him at the CCTC."

Harry didn't think she expected a response, so he kept quiet. It brought him some warmth that she seemed to dislike being in the area as much as he did, though certainly for different reasons. He thought again how nice it would be to return to Saint Paul tonight, to his orderly life, his bed, his lab.

His mother wouldn't even know he'd been this close.

They backtracked to the fork, this time choosing the left. It soon became clear the road hadn't always been dirt. It'd been paved once upon a time before falling into disrepair, leaving chunks of asphalt poking like black warts through the iced gravel. The thick pine and hardwood forest crowding the road brought to mind Harry's mother's favorite poem, one she read to him when he was little.

He was surprised to find the memory wasn't entirely unwelcome.

"The woods are lovely, dark and deep," he said quietly.

"But I have promises to keep," she responded in the same low voice.

A burst of pleasure surprised Harry. "You know the poem."

"I wasn't raised by wolves." Evangeline tossed her head. "Though it would have been an improvement." She flashed Harry a welcome grin before glancing at her phone. "Dead zone," she said. "No reception since Alku. Did you check if we had any going in?"

"No," Harry said, just managing to bite his tongue before he asked her not to look at her phone while driving. "But it's not unusual to dip in and out of pockets up here. As you've seen, it's sparsely populated."

They took another corner, finally leaving the tree cover. Harry felt a moment of disorientation, a clenching low in his stomach, as he studied the unexpected view suddenly laid out before them.

They'd gone from the thickest forest he'd ever driven through to a scene straight out of a gothic novel.

"And is it unusual for there to be castles?" Evangeline asked in wonder.

CHAPTER 7

"Castle" wasn't entirely accurate.

The yellow brick structure leaned more toward manor, the main building made of three sprawling levels before turning into turrets, one on each side of a soaring tower capped with a witch's hat of a roof. A pair of three-story wings jutted off the main building, unturreted but still impressive. The Romanesque windows were topped with intricate sculptural elements, maroon accents contrasting richly with the yellow brick.

Two men—one wearing a white lab coat, the other in tan scrubs—stood at the top of the marble stairs that poured out of the center of the main building. Detective Emery and Officer Davidson had driven separately and parked side by side beneath an open-air carriage house. They were in a heated conversation near their vehicles, barely sparing a glance as Evangeline and Harry pulled into the circle drive.

Evangeline shifted into park and turned off the SUV, craning her neck to stare at the massive building. "It's like something out of *Downton Abbey*."

Harry's eyebrow shot up. "You watched the show?"

"No." She zipped her coat. "But I saw a commercial for it once."

They exited the vehicle and made their way toward the arched front door, walking through crisp, pine-scented air. The manor's grounds were framed by the same dense woods they'd just driven through, unbroken except for the razor-wire-topped perimeter fencing dividing the trees to the east. The prison? If so, it was invisible other than the fence, the thick forest muffling the outside world.

Emery and Davidson broke off their discussion and strode over, Davidson's movements stiff. Harry wondered what they'd been arguing about. Could be unrelated to the case. Davidson had seemed subservient to the detective back in the autopsy viewing room, barely uttering a word.

"You get lost?" Emery asked when they met up at the base of the stairs, an easy smile sliding onto his face and lifting his sideburns.

"You said we were meeting at the Carlton County Treatment Center," Evangeline said. "This is not that."

Her face was placid. Harry was impressed. If he'd never met her, he'd have no idea how near to spitting nails she was.

"Thank you for coming," the man in the white lab coat said from the top stair, cracking the tension gathering below. He held out his arms, his voice deep and rich with a faint accent. "This is the CCTC. I'm Pekka Tervo, head psychiatrist."

Tervo had what Harry was already thinking of as the Alku neck and forehead, though the smile lines etching his cheeks softened the dominant features. He also had round glasses and eyes of the palest blue, so light they seemed to glow. The man standing next to Tervo, on the other hand, had a face like a garter snake. Eyes close and flat, thin mouth, pointed nose.

"Sign out front says 'Sanitorium for Consumptives,'" Evangeline responded evenly, though Harry suspected she'd start swinging if she didn't get a straight answer soon.

"I can see your confusion," Tervo said, descending a step. "That's what we were originally called. We've undergone a number of changes in the 140 or so years since."

Evangeline cut her eyes to Harry. She'd caught the peculiarity of the "we," too. Tervo was a man who deeply identified with his place of employment.

"Now we're an administrative building as well as a school for the children of Alku." He indicated the tower and turrets behind him before dropping his arms and nodding vaguely toward the perimeter fencing, his expression growing sober. "With our former employee housing now a medium-security treatment center on the other side of those trees." His smile returned. "Why don't we go inside and I can give you a tour?"

"After you," Emery said, gesturing for Evangeline and Harry to lead the way.

The itching was back. Harry didn't want a tour. He wanted to interview Mathias Millard, and then he wanted to leave.

But once inside, he was impressed despite himself.

The foyer held the bones of a majestic entrance, looming over them like a shabby queen who still knew her worth. The ceilings were thirty feet high, two grand staircases curving elegantly upward at each end of the vast space. The floor was a white tile inlaid with a pattern of blue squares with loops for corners. There was even a dusty chandelier strung high in the middle, glass teardrops catching the murky light streaming through the large windows and transforming it into a thousand tiny rainbows.

But the walls needed fresh paint, the floor tiles were chipped and yellowed with age, and the foyer had been retrofitted with flimsy room dividers and a ridiculously small desk that gave the space the feeling of a temporary encampment.

Tervo led them across the expanse, his shiny black shoes clicking on the tile. He nodded at the woman behind the front desk, her face expressionless beneath her high Alku forehead, her lips so thin as to almost disappear. She held that blank gaze until her eyes landed on Harry. They widened and then dropped. Harry wasn't comfortable with the reaction, but he was accustomed to it. He understood his symmetrical features and his clothes—according to Van, they were more *Mad Men* than mad scientist—set him apart. His grandfather had been a debonair dresser, always wearing his signature suits and fedoras. He'd taught Harry the joys of dressing sharp. Fortunately, after the initial surprise, most people accepted his appearance without comment, though Evangeline had once asked him, after a pair of new BCA interns had literally tripped over each other when he and Evangeline walked past, how it felt to be "a hot piece."

He'd been horrified by the question, but she'd seemed genuinely curious, so he answered honestly. "It's a distraction."

She'd laughed out loud. "Only you would say that, Harry Steinbeck."

Her response had warmed him, as did the memory of it. He held on to that comfort as Tervo led them behind the dividers and to a door, one of several. Harry guessed they'd been the administrative offices when this was a functioning hospital, but they appeared empty now.

"Please," Tervo said, waving at the open door, "go inside and have a seat. Silas, will you bring warm drinks for our guests?"

The snake-faced man had yet to speak. When he did, his tone was sullen. "Like what?"

Tervo opened his hands, palms up. "We'll offer them coffee, tea, and history."

Emery cleared his throat. "Thanks, but we don't want to put you out. I'd like for you to tell Agents Reed and Steinbeck what you can about the Korhonen case, and then we'll pay a visit to Mr. Millard. After that, we'll be on our way. Shouldn't take too much of your time, Dr. Tervo."

"As I tell everyone, call me Pekka. Please." He smiled gently. "And I'm happy to give you the CliffsNotes version of the Korhonen tragedy, though I'm not sure how any of it's connected to Mr. Weiss's death. I don't believe they could have known each other. Mr. Weiss would have been barely a teenager when the Korhonens were killed."

"As I mentioned on the phone," Emery said, "I'm not at liberty to share any details at the moment. You were living in Alku back in 1998?"

Pekka appeared momentarily unsettled. Harry couldn't blame him. Emery had obviously told the man one of his employees had been killed, nothing more. It made sense he'd want more information, particularly about how the Korhonen family and Mathias Millard were coming into play.

But Pekka seemed to quickly make peace with the situation. He clasped his hands, almost like he was praying. "That's correct. Living in Alku, working here alongside Jarmo and Janice."

"That's Mr. and Mrs. Korhonen?" Evangeline asked, tugging out her notepad.

Pekka nodded. "Jarmo and I were in the same year at school. We both grew up in Alku, both went off to college at the University of Minnesota in Duluth. Jarmo studied to be a nurse, and he became a mighty fine one. He met his wife, Janice, at college. She fit right in here. Worked the front desk, that spot where we just passed Hannele. Their two oldest children attended school in the west wing here, like most Alku kids. Their youngest . . ." His voice cracked. He cleared his throat, then continued. "Their youngest was only one when they were all taken from us."

"I'm sorry," Harry said. He considered himself good at reading people, and Pekka was genuinely grieving their deaths, or at least the memory of them.

"Thank you." Pekka inhaled deeply through his nose. "We'll never recover from the loss, but we've learned to abide. We continue to hold out hope the case will be solved."

His voice was mild, but Harry detected a sliver of resentment, maybe chiding. If Emery also heard it, he made no indication.

"We'd like to solve it, too, Pekka," he said brightly. His face curved into slyness for only a moment, the expression gone so fast that Harry wondered if he'd imagined it. "You said you were going to give the agents a quick-and-dirty dip into the CCTC history?"

"Certainly." Pekka's face relaxed, pride visible on it. "Our Finnish ancestors settled this region in 1881. Specifically, seven families from northern Lapland, some of them doctors, all of them landowners. America, like the country they were leaving, was caught in the grip of a tuberculosis epidemic, and so once they arrived, the families elected to pool their resources and open the Uusialku Sanitorium for Consumptives."

"What does it mean?" Evangeline asked. "'Uusialku'?"

Pekka's smile lines deepened. Harry put the man in his late fifties. "It means 'fresh start,' and that's exactly what this was for those seven families and the people they treated. The sanitorium consisted of the original buildings you saw when you drove up. The tower building that we're in now has always housed the administrative center. Patients stayed in the west and east wings. People traveled from all over Minnesota for treatment. After the epidemic waned, we transitioned to a center for what would now be referred to as high-needs residents. We cared for them using the Kirkbride model of fresh air, healthy food, and honest work."

That "we" again. If Harry were a gambling man, he'd place money that Pekka's family had been one of the original seven.

"We were a successful institution in that we were able to get many folks well enough that they could return home. The ones who lived here became like family to us. That all changed in the late '80s." His mouth tightened. "State-level funding changes forced institutions such as ours to release our clients into the community. Without patients, we couldn't pay our bills. We were at risk of closing our doors permanently when the state announced they were accepting bids for a privately run medium-security facility for prisoners who required care more suited to a nursing home environment. We threw our hat in the ring." His cheek twitched. "When we were chosen, we had two years to retrofit our facility to meet the security requirements. Only the Willow Building, originally a dormitory for our workers, had the necessary infrastructure. That was back in 1989. A few of us thought adding the prison would be a temporary shift in our mission. We changed our name to the Carlton County Treatment Center because our ultimate goal was and continues to be to turn the east wing here into an inpatient drug and rehabilitation center, and then expand that to the west wing, and finally, potentially, to reclaim all of our buildings. Get back to our roots of helping folks in need."

It was clear Pekka's first choice would *not* have been to establish a prison on the grounds. Harry wondered how that affected his ability to provide therapy to the prisoners, or if he had an entirely different role here.

"Thanks for that overview," Harry said. "It was compelling."

Emery tossed Harry an appraising look before returning his attention to Pekka. "Yeah, thank you. That was a good orientation. I'm embarrassed to say I only knew a part of it, and I've spent my whole life in the region. Bet you're glad you heard it too, eh, Greg?" he asked, pretend-punching the officer's arm.

Evangeline briefly studied Emery and Davidson before turning her attention to Tervo. "Would it be all right if we visited the prison facility now?"

Pekka nodded and stood.

Harry felt the squeeze of anticipation, one that shamed him given the circumstances. His purview was facts, evidence, the lab. As a result of his job, he'd seen hundreds of criminals up close, many as a result of testifying against them in their trials.

Still, he'd never visited a nursing home for serial killers.

CHAPTER 8

Rannie
October 1987

"Alku on perhe, perhe on tärkeintä."
   Alku is family, family is everything.
   It was Rannie's favorite part of church. Everyone murmuring the same words. It sounded like wind through golden grass, scratching an itch right behind his heart.
   It also marked the end of the service.
   They'd be released to the basement, where there'd be a potluck and laughter and backslapping, in just a few moments. The smell of blood dumpling soup floated through the floorboards, and Jarmo Korhonen's new wife, Janice, had promised Rannie before the service that she'd brought karjalanpiirakka, the rye-crust potato pies slathered with boiled eggs and butter that Rannie couldn't stuff into his mouth fast enough.
   Rannie liked Janice.
   She was an outsider—Rannie's mom, Ansa, made sure everyone knew—but she worked hard to fit in. She was funny, too. She'd made the goofiest face when she first tried salted black licorice, like her mouth wanted to pack up and leave but the rest of her had to stay out of politeness. It was like the face she made when she first heard a veri noita story. The pastor included one in every sermon. It was as expected as an "amen," but Rannie happened to be peeking at Janice the first time

she heard about the blood witch. When the pastor started that Sunday's veri noita tale, Janice double-taked at her husband like he'd tell her it was a joke, a pull-my-finger dropped right into the middle of church. When he didn't, Janice's face crumpled, and it wasn't even one of the worst veri noitas Rannie had ever heard.

"In a quiet Finnish village nestled between rolling hills and lush forests," the pastor had begun, "there lived a powerful sorceress known as the Blood Witch. She used her magic to protect those true of heart. But one fateful day, a handful of disloyal villagers decided they knew better than the veri noita and were tired of living by her rules. They banded together, bringing their sharpest knives, and stabbed her a hundred times."

Janice's bottom lip was trembling. Rannie wanted Jarmo to put his arm around her and comfort her, but his attention was trained fully on the pastor. It seemed to Rannie like maybe Jarmo'd requested the veri noita's origin story today for Janice to hear, and that's why he was hanging on every word of a tale he'd heard countless times.

The pastor continued. "Because the veri noita was so powerful, they had to bind her hands and feet in her grave and balance a scythe over her neck so she'd be killed all over again if she came back to life." His voice dropped. "With the veri noita defeated, the disloyal villagers next turned to the original seven families, the veri noita's truest followers." He began breathing heavily. "They murdered all their children, every last one of them, in an event that came to be known as the reaping."

The pastor paused here, his watery brown eyes connecting with his parishioners. "With their children gone and the veri noita believed defeated, those poor folk, those seven families true of heart, had no choice but to flee the village they'd called home. They made new lives, created new families, in this land." He held up his arms. "And do you know what they discovered?"

He patted his chest, pausing dramatically. Rannie was leaning forward in his pew. He knew this part from memory. "They discovered that the Blood Witch had escaped her grave by tunneling down, through the earth. She popped up right here in Minnesota."

Rannie glanced down at the floor like he always did, waiting for her bloody, bent claws to tear through the floor and clutch his ankle. When the pastor struck his pulpit, Rannie wasn't the only one who jumped.

"She wanted to make sure we never repeat the mistakes of our past. But also"—Rannie was mouthing the words right along with the pastor—"to protect us. If anyone threatens Alku, the veri noita *will kill them.*"

Janice gasped.

The pastor nodded at her, like he'd expected that reaction. "Because of what happened in Finland, the veri noita knows the threat can come from within as well as without. That's why none of us can ever give in to darkness and cruelty. Especially the children."

Rannie squirmed in his seat. This was his least favorite part.

"You must always be respectful, children of Alku. If you ever stray from the path of obedience, the veri noita will know. She will demand another reaping. She'll rise from the cave in which she lives, her eyes gleaming and her teeth gnashing, and search for misbehaving children, those who have been cruel or selfish and did not put Alku first." His voice was growing louder, higher, and he was making a point of tipping his head at each child in the church. "The last thing you will smell is the rich, black dirt of the motherland, before—with a slash of her gnarled hand—she will slice open your throat."

Rannie realized he'd fisted his hands at his sides. He forced them to relax. That was the end of this particular story. He wished he could tell Janice it was over. She was crying, quietly. But then the pastor moved on to one of Rannie's least favorite sermons, the parable of the sower, and his mind wandered.

That day had been rough for Janice, but over time, she seemed to not mind the veri noita stories so much. Like everyone else, she just sorta let them flow over her, probably so she could get at the good food in the church basement, too.

Mr. Esko bumbled into Rannie, bringing him back to the present. Everyone was supposed to shuffle out of their pews, but Rannie had been so busy daydreaming about food and friends and veri noita stories that he'd lost track of where he was. Rannie was a good daydreamer, that's what Pekka said. His wandering mind made their mom unhappy, though.

"You don't want to be rotten at the top of the tree, Randolph," she'd say, tapping her noggin. "It's nothing but bad from there." But she'd say it with love, promise he could be her little peräkammarin poika—a man who never moved out of his parents' house—forever.

Rannie hurried to catch up to Ansa, who'd already reached the aisle. She wore his favorite dress, the blue one with yellow flowers. He became so busy counting the buds (*one flower, two, three flowers for you*) that he didn't realize his mother was heading behind the altar rather than toward the basement stairs until she disappeared into the vestry. His father, Pekka, and Jarmo were already inside, plus the heads of the other original families except for Mr. Esko, who was right behind.

It was crowded.

Rannie wanted to leave, but he didn't want his mother to notice he hadn't been paying attention, *again*. He settled for making himself small, tucking into the coats before she noticed he'd been on her heels.

"This isn't necessary," Jarmo was saying to Nils, Rannie and Pekka's father.

Rannie's father was a man who always looked unhappy, but now he seemed ready to punch the walls, his face as dark as a storm cloud. Rannie's hands automatically moved to cover his behind.

"Not necessary?" Nils was saying. "Is it *necessary* to feed our families?"

The other six patriarchs were nodding. An Esko, a Wenner, a Harju, a Virtanen, a Laine, a Korhonen, as it had been written. Jarmo Korhonen was young for a patriarch, only Pekka's age, but the men in his family didn't live long, that's what Ansa said. Rannie and Pekka's mom was the only woman allowed in these meetings. She didn't let anyone, including and especially tradition, tell her what she could take part in.

"Of course feeding our families is important," Jarmo said. He had a great wave of thick dark hair that he kept pushing back from his face. "But we must find another way. We can't invite monsters into our community, no matter how dire our circumstances. How can we have evil so close and not become evil ourselves?"

"I side with Jarmo," Pekka said, drawing all eyes.

Pekka was allowed at the meetings because a Tervo man had always led them, and Nils wanted to prepare his son to take the mantle. That's what he told anyone who asked. But Pekka wasn't supposed to speak—even Rannie knew that.

Jarmo seemed so grateful for Pekka's voice, though. "Yes," he said. "We can find another way."

"The past is gone," Mr. Esko said. He was Rannie's dad's best friend. "The buildings are all but empty, and there's no patients to fill them up. Opening the prison is our only option."

"I don't know," Ansa said, her tone nasty. "Maybe Jarmo is right. Maybe the veri noita will protect us from the bill collectors."

Everyone except Jarmo and Pekka laughed. Rannie shivered. His movement drew Pekka's attention.

"Little pitchers have big ears, Mother," Pekka said.

Ansa whirled to see Rannie cowering near the wall. She loved him, he knew that, but she might be mad he was here. Mad like she always seemed to be at Pekka. The two of them fought a lot, almost as much as Ansa fought with Nils.

He wished they didn't.

"The veri noita hasn't been back since Sandwich Rock," Rannie said, his hands going to his ears. They didn't feel bigger, but he was sure he was the pitcher Pekka had been referring to. "I think we're safe."

The way Pekka's face fell, Rannie knew he'd said the wrong thing.

"Enough of this," Ansa said sharply. She turned her attention to her husband. "This isn't a discussion. We must put Alku first. *Always.* There's no other option. It's time for an offering."

Rannie's father nodded and reached into the large built-in cabinet alongside the wall and began pulling out the straw and willow-branch masks. The patriarchs, Pekka, and his mother were already donning their white robes. When they pulled on their masks—haunty animal faces with skull-socket eyes and no mouth—they hardly even looked human anymore. A few willow twigs fell to the floor. Mom said the only thing she didn't like about the masks was how messy they were, but they had to be constructed in the Old Way, using only their hands and items from the forest.

Don't ask about the mask, just say yes to the mess.

Jarmo was the last to reach for his. He looked at it like he'd rather cut off his own arm than wear it. But when the goat appeared in front of him, he pulled it on.

Rannie exhaled, his stomach relaxing.

Everything was going to be all right in Alku.

CHAPTER 9

Both Harry and Evangeline remained silent as the man named Silas led the two of them plus Emery and Davidson down chipped concrete stairs and into a vast basement that smelled of mold. They threaded the sanitorium's furniture graveyard, including stacked hospital bed frames, dusty file cabinets, desks, even some exam tables, their rotted tie-down straps and rusting footrests taking the shape of torture devices in the weak light filtering in from high, dirty windows. The air felt close and heavy. Harry was about to don his mask when they broke free of the spooky piles and into a blessedly uncluttered hallway with the same inlaid tile floor as the main level.

Where they came upon a high-tech security door with an electronic card reader near its handle, as out of place in this dim and dusty basement as an iPhone on a stagecoach.

Evangeline glanced from it to Silas, her face washed in disbelief. "The prison is underground?" she asked.

"No," Silas said, his affect flat. "The prison isn't underground. But the staff entrance to reach it is."

"A nice trick in the winter," Emery said. His tone was light.

Evangeline hugged her arms. "Missing a real opportunity to host a seasonal haunted house here," she said. "The hall of horrors back there was something else."

Harry wanted to empathize with her discomfort, but he knew she hated to be thought of as weak, so he said the only thing he could think of. "This basement would be too dangerous for children."

She scowled at him, unease taking a back seat to her annoyance.

Harry felt a warmth in his chest. He was glad he'd been able to distract her.

Silas tugged at the badge clipped to his waistband and presented it to the card reader. A double beep was followed by a click, and the door opened. "The tunnel runs under the fence," he said. "There's another security door at the far side. That one also needs a card, plus there's always a guard stationed at it. Back in the day, the asylum workers needed to be able to travel between their job and where they slept. That's why it's connected by this tunnel."

"Asylum?" Harry asked, following Silas through the door. He'd smelled a faint sour odor, like clothes left wet for too long, since they'd left the main floor. He'd thought it was the basement, but he now suspected it was the man leading them.

Silas shrugged. "I like to be honest." He held the security door until they were all inside the curved tunnel. The section they stepped into was washed in acid-yellow light, but the tunnel beyond was as dark as ink. "That's what this place used to be. An asylum. Tervo doesn't like us calling it that, believes it was some high-and-mighty place before the prison came in, but the truth is the truth." He coughed and released the door. "Those 'high-needs residents' had a different perspective on their time here, that's all I'm saying. You get out back, you'll see what I mean."

Harry wouldn't be surprised if that were true. Care for the mentally and physically disabled had been far different in the early part of the previous century. It wasn't unheard of for patients to be tied to beds for days or kept in a large room like animals, where they were tossed food and hosed off but otherwise ignored.

"What's out back?" Harry asked.

Another shrug from Silas.

"Did you know Peter Weiss?" Emery asked.

Silas didn't even bother lifting a shoulder this time. He started marching forward, activating the motion sensors. When the group crossed an invisible line, a new ten-foot bank in front of them was drowned in cold light, turning the infinite black ahead and behind so dark that it looked like it was moving. The effect was eerie.

"Yeah, I knew him," Silas finally said, still walking.

Click. Lights turned on in front.

Click. They turned off in back.

"But we weren't friends or anything."

Another long pause. Silas was an unhurried man. "I'm only an aide," he said. *Click.* "I do the grunt work." *Click.* "Weiss was a nurse with seniority." *Click.* "Top of the heap over at the prison, and he let you know it. Bragged about every damn thing." *Click.* "I usually avoided him, for that reason alone. Last I saw him, he was all puffed up with something new. That's just how he was."

"You get along, at least?" The strain in Evangeline's voice was palpable. Harry, who'd never felt claustrophobic in his life, was becoming convinced spiders were dropping down from the ceiling and slipping inside his collar. He brushed at his shoulder. How long was the tunnel?

"Sure," Silas said, continuing to pause between each piece of information, a perfect counterpoint to the lights' ominous heartbeat. "I suppose we did." *Click.* "We were both outsiders." *Click.* "Most everyone who works here is related to those original seven Dr. Tervo was talking about." *Click.* "They have to bring us in to fill staff holes, but they don't like it." *Click.* "They don't like it one bit."

Harry found his mouth opening, found himself about to say he'd prefer they walk back—or better yet, run; were the spiders now in his hair?—and simply drive to the prison, when a final bank of lights came to life, revealing a door in front of them like a magic trick.

Harry exhaled loudly.

"Here we are." Silas slid his serpent eyes toward Harry and locked them in place while he leaned forward with his badge. "Made it to the prison."

CHAPTER 10

The guard standing outside Mathias Millard's cell, his signature Alku craniofacial features on full display, was firm. "No visitors."

Though they'd only seen the portion of the prison visible from the basement entrance to the western end of the first floor, the interior reminded Harry of a 1960s bomb shelter. Brutal, with poured cement floors and walls. Thick windows that didn't open. At least two levels, judging by the stairwell they'd passed.

Unlike the manor, however, this building was bustling.

Uniformed guards policed the hall. Orderlies in scrubs wheeled prisoners. Most doors they passed were secured, a card reader out front, a thin, reinforced rectangle of window in each revealing a person inside.

Only one door had a guard stationed outside it, though.

The cell of Mathias Millard, a.k.a. Matty the Mallet.

"We got the visit okayed in advance," Emery said, his voice rising. "In fact, we just left Dr. Tervo. He sent us over here." Emery placed his hands at his waist, revealing his badge. He, Davidson, and Evangeline had left their sidearms at the basement guard station.

The guard's eyes flicked to the badge. He was older, possibly in his seventies, his forehead so high it was beginning to curve back on itself. His hair was buzzed short, which served to accent his long neck. His Adam's apple bobbed in response to Emery's words, but he didn't move from his position blocking the door. "No visitors."

"I'm going to need to talk to your immediate supervisor, Mr.—"

"Esko," the man said. He glanced to his right as if for support, but the hallway was suddenly empty. "I was told to direct you back to Dr. Tervo if you had any questions."

"There must be some mistake," Evangeline said. "As Detective Emery just told you, Dr. Tervo is the one who sent us here. We won't take much time."

Esko stood his ground, blocking the narrow cell window. "I'm sorry."

"C'mon," Emery said, drawing himself to his full height. "I didn't drive all this way—"

"I'm afraid it's my fault."

The voice belonged to a woman hurrying down the hallway toward them. Harry had watched *One Flew Over the Cuckoo's Nest* a dozen times before he turned ten—his father had been a quiet, kind man with one peccadillo: he loved Jack Nicholson movies with a blazing passion—and if this woman wasn't a dead ringer for Louise Fletcher's Nurse Ratched, Harry didn't know who was. She wore a white lab coat open over a gray sweater and skirt. Her legs were covered in thick gray tights, her feet in crepe-cushioned white shoes.

"Pihla Tervo." She approached Harry with her hand out, startling him. "Head nurse here."

He shook it. Her gaze lingered on his face for a moment.

"Pleased to meet you," he said. "I'll defer to Detective Emery."

She nodded and turned to the detective, who'd puffed himself up when she went to Harry first. "I'd hoped to catch you before you made the trek over. Mr. Millard had a seizure about twenty minutes ago. He's not in any shape to receive visitors."

"We only need to verify his condition," Emery said.

"Still." She smiled, but Harry recognized the steel beneath it. "I am sorry. I can notify your department once he's feeling better."

Pihla stationed herself next to the guard who'd identified himself as Esko. She held herself as stiffly as a soldier. There would be no broaching the threshold.

Emery must have read the same message. He nodded crisply. "I'll await your call."

Harry was disappointed, but there was little choice. It would be an ordeal to get clearance to override the medical staff even with a time-sensitive reason, which they didn't have. By all accounts, Mr. Millard had been confined to both a wheelchair and this facility for twenty-seven years.

They were turning to leave when Evangeline stopped. "Agent Van Reed," she said, facing Pihla as if something had just occurred to her. "I'm Harry's partner. Just one quick question."

Pihla's mouth tipped downward.

"Does he have shoes?" Evangeline asked.

"Excuse me?" Pihla said.

"Does Millard own a pair of shoes?"

Pihla's head jerked, like she was fighting the urge to glance behind her at Millard's door. "No," she said. "He wears a special kind of sock designed to improve circulation in paraplegics."

"That's it?"

She nodded stiffly. "That's it."

"Thanks," Evangeline said.

The five of them returned the way they came, Silas in the lead. Emery kept sighing and glancing at his phone in a way that suggested he was waiting to get reception. Davidson tipped his head at a guard they passed, the gesture one of familiarity. Evangeline and Harry walked side by side.

At the anteroom leading back down into the tunnel, Silas led Emery and Davidson through the security door. Harry was holding it open for Evangeline when his attention was jerked to the bank of windows lining the eastern wall, facing across the exercise yard. He'd caught movement at the edge of the yard. Evangeline stiffened. Had she seen it, too? Harry released the door, separating the two of them from Emery and Davidson, and strode to the window. The sun had broken out of the clouds and was glittering off the sharp snow, turning it into a field of diamonds. Two hundred yards beyond was the perimeter fencing.

Evangeline was joining Harry at the window when a bellow of fear ricocheted off the cold concrete walls.

CHAPTER 11

Evangeline and Harry charged down the hallway. By the time they located the source of the commotion, two guards and a nurse were already there, trying to calm an agitated man in a wheelchair sitting in the center of a large room. He was young, no more than thirty, with floppy brown hair and wild eyes.

Harry and Evangeline stepped toward him.

"Get me out of here!" the man screamed, straining against the men holding him down. "They're gonna come for me. They're gonna get me, too!"

The room appeared to be a common area, a large and dismal white-walled space dominated by an old but functioning floor-model television, the stack of board games on top of it gathering dust. A bank of windows looked out at the snowy rear yard Harry had just been staring at. Two other prisoners were in the room, also seated in wheelchairs, pointed in the general direction of the television.

"The witch is gonna suck my blood, too, just like she does to Matty!" He managed to break an arm free from Esko, the same guard who'd prevented them from entering Millard's cell. "You wait and see. You just wait."

He stopped struggling and slumped in his chair. "Please get me out of here," he said, his tone beseeching. "Please."

His gaze traveled over Harry's shoulder. Whatever he saw made his eyes bulge.

Harry followed the man's stare to Pihla. "You're all right, Amon," she said, stepping into the room. "Did seeing the officers pass by upset you?"

But they hadn't passed this room or this patient. Harry was certain of it.

"It's okay," the man named Amon whispered, all the fight drained out of him. His eyes dropped to his hands, which were twisted in his lap. "I really didn't see much. Didn't see nothing at all, in fact."

"Please bring him back to his room," Pekka said, appearing in the doorway. His hand hovered over his forehead and then suddenly moved to smooth his hair. He exuded almost a preternatural calmness. "His recreational period is over."

Pekka swiveled to address Harry and Evangeline, a serene expression on his face. "I'm so sorry about the situation with Mr. Millard. My wife"—here he tipped his head at Pihla—"informed me about his seizure after you'd left for the tunnel. Let me walk you back so I can answer any questions you may have."

On the return trip to the main building, Pekka shared that the young prisoner, Amon Dooley, had a history of hallucinations. He'd also murdered three women over the course of a year, all of them truck stop waitresses. He'd been working the Tilt-A-Whirl at a carnival just outside Boston when he was caught.

"After he was brought back for his trial and sentencing, he started out in Stillwater maximum security," Pekka said. "When he was diagnosed with a degenerative neurological disorder, he was transferred here. He doesn't cause trouble, usually, but he's been here a few years. He knows it's Easter, and he knows how we celebrate."

"How *do* you celebrate?" Evangeline asked.

Pekka smiled disarmingly. "You saw the little witches when you drove through town." It was a statement, not a question. "The children dress up and travel door-to-door, wishing everyone a healthy year in exchange for a bit of candy or a colored egg. It's a Finnish tradition, with our own special twist. Our ancestors believed the veri noita—the blood witch effigy in front of the church—protected them. It's a fairy tale, really, but one we keep alive for the kids." He coughed. "We also have a more traditional Easter service. After, we gather as one large family for a meal of roasted lamb with mämmi for dessert."

"You should try mämmi if you get a chance," Emery said, his first words since they'd started the journey back down the creepy tunnel. He, Davidson, and Silas had been waiting for them at the station where their weapons had been held. His stiff posture suggested he'd been annoyed Harry and Evangeline had run off without him, but he'd accepted their explanation without comment.

"I do recommend it," Pekka said, grinning at Harry and Evangeline. "It's not much to look at, but it is delicious. A rye pudding swimming in fresh cream, and we swirl in red currant preserves." His grin faded. "Please don't judge us for our traditions. They keep us connected. Even something as foolish sounding as the veri noita is vital to our sense of community."

CHAPTER 12

"What the hell was all that?" Evangeline asked from the driver's seat.

Harry sat next to her, studying the front of the manor. "It was a lot."

Pekka had reconfirmed Mathias Millard's paralysis on the journey back to the basement below the admin offices, told them they were welcome to return tomorrow when he was recovered from his seizure, and walked them to the front door. Emery and Davidson had climbed into their cars, Evangeline and Harry into the SUV.

"You think? The whole place feels like a madhouse." Evangeline rubbed her face. "And did you see how Amon Dooley looked at Pihla, like he was afraid she'd cut out his tongue if he kept talking? And let's not forget how Silas smells like old yogurt and, oh yeah, remember how the whole town of Alku felt like driving through a horror movie?" She was quiet for a moment. "So, are we coming back here tomorrow?"

A cold trickle worried its way through Harry's core. Their attempt at the one task they'd agreed to complete before returning to the Cities—verify Mathias Millard's incapacitation—had been a bust. Still, it was dangerous for Harry to stay so close to Duluth. He was startled by the urge to punch something.

"We have to, don't we? We can't leave until we confirm Mr. Millard's state." He held his phone toward the SUV's ceiling, as high as he could. "Still no reception."

"You sure?" Evangeline asked.

"I am."

She started up the SUV. "Put it on airplane mode when we get back on the county road," she said. "Then flip it back to regular. It'll search for the network again."

They drove in silence through the fairy-tale woods, following Emery and Davidson.

"I'd be okay not spending the night in Alku," Evangeline said. "I'd have to sleep with one eye open."

They broke out of the woods and onto the pavement. "It worked," Harry said, staring at his phone in disbelief. He began typing and then exhaled. "And that problem may solve itself. No hotel in Alku." He typed some more. "Also, no Airbnb." He made a frustrated sound in the back of his throat. "Aaannnd I just lost the connection."

He kept flipping from airplane mode to cellular again, airplane mode to cellular, desperate to connect with the current century, but there was no cell tower to be found. By the time he admitted defeat, they were already in Alku. His scalp tightened. The streets were empty, but the simple white wooden church was lit up from within and vibrating with sounds of worship.

The veri noita with a burlap sack over its head was still strung up in front of it, except a new sign had been hung around its neck.

It read BEWARE THE REAPING, painted in blood red against a white background, but it looked scrawled on tagboard rather than etched in wood, like someone had hurried to make it while they were at the CCTC.

Evangeline was gripping the steering wheel with both hands. "We'll stay in Duluth. There's gotta be a ton of hotels there."

"No." For the second time that day, Harry's voice was sharper than he intended. He tried turning inward, calling on his qigong breathing to calm himself. He didn't speak again until they left the village limits. The sun hung low on the horizon, casting a dull, muted light over the barren landscape. "I'm sorry."

"Harry . . ." She trailed off.

Evangeline didn't open up to many people. In fact, Harry wondered if he was her closest friend, and he barely knew her. He knew she thought he was a good man. That would change if she discovered the truth about his past, and the longer they stayed in Duluth, the more inevitable that outcome seemed. But he'd made a deal with himself long ago that he wouldn't risk his career to hide his shame. He wouldn't gamble with the lives of victims who depended on him for justice.

He and Evangeline were needed up here.

"Please," Harry said. He meant *please don't ask me why I'm not myself,* but he wouldn't say it. "I'm tired. That's all. We can drive toward Duluth, find a place on this side of the city so we don't have so far to return tomorrow."

Evangeline was quiet for a few beats. He thought she was about to agree when: "Wait! Didn't we pass a little motel on the way here? About ten miles this side of Duluth?"

Harry closed his eyes. It was a relief to have a break from the grim white snowscape, interrupted only by the occasional bare tree, its skeletal branches grasping toward the eerie sky. Within seconds, he was able to call up the image of the motel. "That's right. The Pine Lodge? That'll work." He paused. Tried to gauge her mood. "As long as they have two rooms."

Evangeline snorted with laughter.

Harry felt his own smile.

When they'd landed in Costa Rica on their first case together, he'd almost offered to sleep in the car when they were told the hotel only had one room for the two of them, but somehow, they'd made it work. That's where he'd learned she suffered regular nightmares, the intensity of which he'd never seen. The deeper they spiraled into the case, the more vivid her night terrors became.

He'd *also* witnessed up close her brilliance as a detective.

It almost overshadowed her irritating messiness.

"We've got a few minutes until we get there," she said. "Let's run over what we know."

Harry was happy to focus on facts. "Peter Gordon Weiss, thirty-nine, white male, was murdered last night. He suffered a severe cranial injury and was shot with what appears to be a 12-gauge shotgun, both events happening back-to-back regardless of which came first. He was either killed at his apartment and then the apartment was scrubbed, or he was murdered elsewhere and his body relocated to his home."

"Though the pizza was ordered from his landline," Evangeline said, repeating a detail Emery had offered as they watched the autopsy. "Suggesting it's the former."

Harry nodded. "He worked as a nurse at the Carlton County Treatment Center, tasked with caring for disabled violent offenders. The CCTC is the same place Jarmo and Janice Korhonen were employed in 1998, when they and their three children suffered severe cranial injuries and were shot with a 12-gauge shotgun, though again, we don't know which injury came first."

"Much blood on that scene?" Evangeline asked.

Harry grabbed the file from his briefcase and paged through it.

"Yes," he said. "All five killed on-site, and in quick succession." The sun was dropping like a weight, so he turned on his phone's flashlight and aimed it at the file. "The techs on scene at the Korhonen home took exhaustive photos, thankfully. I'm going to ask Deepty to comb through them and see what story the blood tells us, but my first impression is that they were shot—and likely dead—before they were . . ."

"Brutalized."

Harry nodded, more to himself than Evangeline. He flipped through the images. Husband and wife, in bed, their pajamas and the mattress beneath them nearly black with gore. Their eyes, noses, and mouths had been forcefully rearranged, a deformed Picasso painting of people at rest. Both their ears appeared intact and—more or less—located where they should be, just like Weiss's. Depending on the tool used, blunt force should have destroyed the facial features as well as relocated the ears. What sort of instrument had done this precise and grotesque damage?

"Meanwhile," Evangeline continued, "one Matty the Mallet, famous for taking a hammer to his victim's faces, is living at the same treatment center where our adult victims worked."

"Rendered incapacitated by a stroke two years before the Korhonen family murder."

"As far as we've been told, anyhow." Evangeline cleared her throat, finally dropping one hand from the steering wheel. "That town and that treatment center give me the willies."

"Facts," Harry murmured, doing his best to keep his own jitters at bay. One of them had to remain on solid ground. "Science. That's how we'll solve this. Not willies."

"Here's a fact for you," Evangeline said, jabbing her thumb backward in the general direction of Alku. "More than a few of those folks looked like they were related."

"Not unusual, given what Pekka told us," Harry said, snapping the file closed and returning it to his briefcase. "A small group immigrated here, and they've remained tight-knit."

"Hmm." Evangeline rubbed the back of her neck. "Do you remember hearing about that town in west-central Minnesota? Lilydale? Founded by Germans who were selectively inbreeding off one bloodline."

Harry's eyes squinted as he looked back through time. "Vaguely. It made the news back in the '60s, didn't it?"

"Something like that."

He turned off his phone's flashlight. "I believe there was visible evidence of inbreeding in that case. The Alku people we've seen so far seem entirely healthy."

They stayed quiet for a few moments, lost in their thoughts.

"I don't like private prisons," Evangeline said, breaking the silence.

Harry was surprised by the subject shift. "Why?"

She shook her head, the movements sharp. "For the obvious reasons. Capitalism and justice don't mix. If prisoners are a product, and more product equals more money, you're going to look for ways to make—and keep—more prisoners."

"The CCTC is a safety net more than a prison," Harry pointed out, though he shared her opinion on privatization. "Men already incarcerated who need more care than a regular facility can provide them."

Evangeline's jaw muscle jumped. She wanted to argue with him, but she was holding her tongue. It was so unlike her. She'd been treading lightly all day. Why?

"What did you see at the fence line?" he asked. "Back at the prison."

"Before Dooley screamed?" Evangeline put her elbow on her window ledge and leaned into her hand while she drove. "I dunno. An animal? Nothing? Except we both saw it, didn't we."

"We did," Harry agreed. "It was brown. Brown against the white snow, just outside the perimeter."

"I'd like to walk that fence after we visit with Millard tomorrow," Evangeline said. "Check for any breaches." She slid him a glance. "If we decide to take the cold case, that is."

When he didn't respond, she caught him off guard with her sudden warmth. "Harry, I'm gonna say this once. You've been wound tight as a clock since we arrived. I can't imagine how hard it is to come back here, to be reminded of your sister. We *don't* have to stay. There's a whole stack of cold cases waiting for me back at headquarters, and I'm sure you have plenty of blood and guts to analyze. We'll do important work no matter where we are. We don't have to do it here."

He considered her words, his duty, the risks. He was surprised—and more than a little unsettled—to realize that her unexpected kindness had bought him some small grace. He made up his mind on the spot. "We're going to stay at least through tomorrow." He drew a deep breath. "If it takes longer, I ask only one thing."

"Anything."

"We spend as little time in Duluth as possible without sacrificing the case." He was embarrassed to say the rest, but it was necessary. "I don't want my mother to know I'm here."

"Understood," Evangeline said.

Harry had been ready for questions. She asked none. He felt his shoulders unknit.

A glow ahead indicated the motel and, across from it, a small restaurant. The trapezoidal neon sign in the lodging parking lot read PINE VIEW LODGE in green and yellow. Below was a smaller, square, changeable letter-board sign that promised DIAL-UP INTERNET! and MAGIC FINGERS BEDS! in every room. The motel had eleven green doors set in a single-story, dirt-colored building, with a room marked OFFICE on the far end, its whole face glass. An elderly man watched TV behind the counter, crawling light reflecting on his face.

Only four of the doors had cars parked in front of them.

"Jesus," Evangeline said. "I guess we know where the serial killers take their prom dates." She parked near the office and grabbed her duffel bag from the back seat before hopping out. "I hope you have quarters."

CHAPTER 13

"How is your room already like this?" Harry asked, his throat growing tight.

Evangeline glanced up from the scuffed desk she'd set her laptop on. They had adjoining rooms with connected doors. Hers had the same layout as his: a damp-looking bed covered with what Harry assumed was a spectacularly flammable flowered bedspread. A CRT television, as deep as it was wide. A pockmarked desk and chair. Two bedside tables with mismatched lamps. A matchbox-size bathroom, its dim lighting a blessing.

The difference between their rooms? Evangeline had eaten four small bags of potato chips, drunk a bottle of soda, and apparently gotten disoriented on the way to her trash basket. On top of that, her duffel bag had exploded.

She squinted as she studied him. "I've legit never seen someone look *aghast* before. Well done." Her gaze traveled around her room, pausing on the garbage strewn on the floor. "We can work over on your side if you prefer."

Harry nodded briskly and stepped back into his room, breathing quickly and shallowly. His mother had destroyed the house—ravaged it—after Caroline's disappearance, not allowing the staff to clean for weeks. *This is not that. This is Evangeline, being her messy self. It has nothing to do with my sister.*

Evangeline gathered her laptop and followed, oblivious to his distress. "I figure we get up early tomorrow and do some old-fashioned door-to-door before we head to the CCTC," she said as she strode into his bedroom. The three suits Harry had packed—one navy, one black, one chocolate brown—hung on the metal rod that passed for a closet. His suitcase rested on the foldable holder but was closed. If he couldn't keep bedbugs out, he could at least slow them down. Evangeline took it all in with a flick of her eyes. "We'll check out the house the Korhonens were living in, talk to neighbors, get the lay of the land before we head over to meet with Millard," she finished.

Harry winced when she flopped on his bed still wearing her boots. He decided not to say anything. He was going to remove the bedspread before sleeping anyway. He paused to get his breathing under control. "Good idea."

She flipped open her laptop. "Kyle said he'd scan the Korhonen phone records for anything suspicious, plus go through Weiss's phone and internet records, if Emery okays it."

Agent Kyle Kaminski was Evangeline's number two. He was ambitious on top of being an excellent researcher. Harry respected him. He wished he were here now so Harry wasn't alone with Evangeline in this cramped space. He wasn't sure where the proper spot was to stand. It was important Evangeline feel safe and respected, but they were in what was essentially a bedroom. His options were limited to sitting on the desk chair that had one sticky wheel and a stain on the seat or leaning near the bathroom door.

He chose the latter.

"I just got off the phone with Deepty," he said, reclining awkwardly against the doorframe. "She's going to carve out time tomorrow to process the evidence Duluth agreed to drive down for us today. A shell was found at the scene of the Korhonen murder, and she believes it's still in evidence storage at the BCA, so she's going to look for that, too. Plus, she and Johnna confirmed they'll go over the Korhonen and

Weiss crime scene photos checking for anything that may have been overlooked."

"Great." Evangeline peered at her laptop screen. "We're getting the help we need. I—"

A pounding at the door brought her to her feet, laptop slapped shut. Harry pushed off the wall, images of his sister suddenly consuming any other thought. Trauma did that to a person, no matter how long ago it had happened. Centered the eight ball of their ugliest fear and turned every sight, sound, and smell into a potential cue. But Harry had long practice in silencing his. He and Evangeline exchanged a glance. She strode to the window. Peeked out through the curtain.

"It's two kids and a grown-up." She sounded surprised.

Harry joined her at the window, his heart still tharumping. *It's not the day Caroline went missing. I am not that person. I am near Duluth, but it's twenty-five years later. I am now a man who helps people. I have resources. I can manage this.*

He looked outside.

Directly at his missing sister.

"Harry!" Myrna Steinbeck stood at the bottom of the main staircase. Every hair on her head was perfectly curled, her peach pantsuit was immaculate, and she was beside herself. "Will you call the head of catering? Because they're telling me down here that I didn't order sun-dried tomato crostini, and I *know* I ordered sun-dried tomato crostini. Three dozen."

Harry put down the gel he'd been trying to apply. Back when they'd been dating, Jennyfer Baldwin's favorite song had been the Goo Goo Dolls' "Name," and if he styled his hair just right, he could pass for John Rzeznik minus the cleft chin. That's what he'd been aiming for in his en suite bathroom, until his mother had yelled for him. He suspected his father had scheduled an overseas trip specifically to avoid this Easter garden party. Myrna was high-strung in the best of times, but she became a tornado when she hosted "events." With her husband gone, she was recruiting her son to do what she believed every man was born to do: defend her honor. Harry was accustomed to helping her, but today he had other things on his mind.

Important things.

Well, really only *one*: seeing Jennyfer.

They'd headed to different colleges in August, Jennyfer to Sarah Lawrence, Harry to Brown. They'd declared their love their senior year of high school—on the Ferris wheel at the same traveling carnival he'd sneaked Caroline to a couple years earlier—but Jennyfer had decided she wanted to go to college as a single woman. He'd respected her decision, but that hadn't stopped him from daydreaming about her while he listened to lectures on biology, anatomy, chemistry, knowing she was only three hours away. He enjoyed college but couldn't seem to stop imagining his first girlfriend's laugh, her quick mind, her midnight-black hair, and the way she always smelled like cinnamon apples.

His feelings had started tipping toward desperation.

It was chance they were both scheduled to be in Duluth this weekend. A coinciding spring break. A mutual friend having a party. For the first time since she'd broken up with him, Harry was going to see Jennyfer.

Heat bubbled low in his stomach at the thought of it. He believed that somehow, if he could get his hair just right . . .

"Harry, are you listening to me?"

Myrna wasn't going to give up. He'd forgotten how intense she could be. Well, not forgotten so much as locked it away.

"Coming!" He gave himself one last glance in the mirror. Good enough.

Caroline was standing outside the bathroom door when he opened it.

"Harold," she said in a high, singsong voice, holding both hands with her pinkies raised, "will you please tell the gardener that the leaves are falling off the oak tree in direct opposition to my request that they stay put? And while you're at it, could you please inform the sun that I'd like it to stay in the sky for an extra hour?" Her voice tilted British. "But only for today."

Harry chuckled. Given their age gap, there was no conceivable reason they should be such good friends. Yet she was his favorite person, had been since the day she was born. "If Mom overhears you mimicking her, she's going to make you stay home so all her friends can fawn over you. You know that, right?"

A crease of worry marred Caroline's perfect forehead. She was still preternaturally beautiful, but she'd lost her baby fat and now looked far older than her age. "I'll tie sheets together and climb out my bedroom window to escape if I have to," she said, the crease deepening.

She'd been sliding in and out of moodiness since he'd come home. He should talk to her about it, find out what was wrong, but not today. She was probably just bothered by Myrna being Myrna, and that was a dragon best left unpoked. He hooked his arm around her shoulder and guided her toward the stairs. "That shouldn't be necessary. As long as we both do our time now, she'll let us go." He tried to steer his brain away from images of Jennyfer. Black hair. Dancing eyes. "Remind me again where you're headed this afternoon."

She clasped her hands beneath her chin. "Why, I'm going to the land of fairies, where the sky is lemon colored and the clouds taste like cotton candy."

"Hmmm," Harry responded. "Beats Duluth in April. I think the clouds taste like road salt here."

Caroline's vivid imagination could be off-putting for some people—particularly Myrna—but it was one of the qualities Harry appreciated most about her. Their father was a bottom-line businessman, their mother a social climber who'd been a promising scientist before she became pregnant with Harry. He'd grown up in a stilted *Grey Gardens* atmosphere until Caroline's birth. She'd turned their household into something warm and alive, sometimes silly, never dull.

Maybe that's why Myrna had always seemed to hate her.

"You shouldn't lick the clouds in Duluth," Caroline informed him seriously, tossing her hair. "They're made of fiberglass." She wriggled out from beneath his arm and leaped onto the top stair, turning to give him a mischievous smile. "You're going to see Jennyfer tonight, aren't you?"

Was he that transparent? "Among other friends," he said defensively.

"Well, if you get bored, me and my homies will be bedazzling purses, and that's only the start of our wild activities." She waggled her eyebrows. "You're welcome to join us."

Harry grinned. "I'll keep that in mind."

"You should." She started to match his smile when a shadow crept across her face. "There's something stupid I want to tell you, but I don't know if I should."

He nodded indulgently, but his mind had already wandered back to Jennyfer. Was she single? If not, he'd play it off like he just wanted to be friends. He might even lie and say he had a girlfriend of his own.

"Harry, Caroline," Myrna called from the bottom of the stairs, "how many times must I yell for you two?"

She stood below them with her hands on her hips. Physically, Harry was her son through and through. Fine-boned and striking in a way that stopped people on the street. Personality-wise, he hoped he had more in common with his sister, who, for the record, his mother had *not* yelled for. Myrna never passed up a chance to be angry at Caroline, though. Harry sometimes wondered if she was jealous of Caroline, of her opportunities, of the easy way she walked through the world.

He descended the stairs, putting himself between his mother and his sister. "I'm sure I can handle this alone, Mom," he said. "Caroline is busy at the moment. She's doing me a favor."

He turned to wink at his sister. She'd always appreciated it when he shielded her from Myrna. He thought he caught the shadow back on her face, but her smile erased it.

"I sure am," she said, skipping down the hall toward her bedroom.

CHAPTER 14

Harry pulled his mind back from that day, the last he had seen his sister.
There's something stupid I want to tell you.

That's what Caroline had said to him.

His sister would be in her thirties now. This girl outside his motel room looked barely old enough for kindergarten. Her pale hair, the ghosts of his past so close. It'd all conspired to throw him off his game.

Evangeline opened the door. The ice of April poured in. "Can we help you?"

"Yes." The man speaking was huge. Not overweight or even particularly tall so much as solid, with fists as big as softballs hanging at his sides. His apparent strength was offset by a cherub's face. "We biked here from Alku. I could keep biking all the way to Duluth." He smiled. "That's how strong I am."

"Hush, Rannie," the boy at his side said shyly. "These two don't want to know about any of that." He offered his hand to Evangeline, who shook it. "I'm Max, and this is my little sister, Honeybee. She doesn't talk at all. The big guy is Rannie, and he does nothing *but* talk." Max smiled, revealing a mouth crowded with teeth too big for his narrow face.

Harry put the boy at nine or ten. Rannie must be in his forties, though it was difficult to be certain.

"Are you here to help?" Rannie asked. "Is that why you came?" He peeked into Harry's room, his thoughts seeming to escape his lips the moment they entered his head. "Is that a teee-veee?" He said the word oddly, each syllable drawn out.

Evangeline tossed Harry a look. It said *take over*. He realized he'd never seen her interact with children outside of a single fraught encounter on the Taken Ones case. Did kids make her uneasy?

Rannie was squinting at him. "What's your name?"

"Harry Steinbeck. This is my partner, Evangeline Reed."

Rannie's expression grew doubtful. "Hairy?" He pointed at Harry, though they were standing only feet apart. "Pinky makes more sense. Cuz there's no hair on your face and only a regular amount on your head. Somebody should have told you that a while ago but they were maybe too scared, or they forgot."

Evangeline cough-laughed.

Harry ignored her as well as Rannie's comment. "We were thinking of walking across the street for dinner," he said, telling a white lie. *He'd* been thinking of it. He didn't know if Evangeline had, but he certainly couldn't invite children and what appeared to be a vulnerable adult into a motel room. He would find out why they were here somewhere well lit and public, where they'd feel safe. "Care to join us?"

Max, Honeybee, and Rannie looked at each other, their expressions pained. Finally, Max said, "Sorry, but we can't stay long." He threw his arm protectively around Honeybee.

"They have a teee-veee in the restaurant, Max," Rannie said in a stage whisper. "I can see it from here."

"Yeah, they sure do, Rannie." Max patted his tree trunk of an arm. "But I don't think we should go in there. We have to be getting back for church."

"You said you're all from Alku?" Evangeline asked.

They nodded solemnly.

"That's got to be over half an hour on bike," Harry said. "What did you come here for?"

Rannie opened his mouth, but Max—who was clearly in charge despite his age—nudged him hard. "We're just passing through," Max said.

Harry's radar went off. It was full dark out. "We'll give you a ride home," he said firmly.

Max kept pushing back, but when Harry made it clear that either they rode in the SUV or the SUV would follow them all the way home, he relented. It took five minutes and some maneuvering to fit both bikes—Honeybee had ridden on Rannie's handlebars—into the back of the vehicle with enough remaining room to buckle Rannie and the two children into the rear seat.

"I still can't believe you all biked here," Evangeline said as she pulled out. "Wasn't it cold?"

"We're used to the weather," Max said.

When Harry swiveled to look back at the boy, he saw worry on his face. It seemed unlikely they'd biked all this way to only peek at the agents. Did they have some information about the recent murder? He knew that the straightest route wasn't always the quickest, though, especially when dealing with children.

"In answer to your earlier question," Harry said, keeping his voice light, "we're here to help the Duluth Police Department solve a crime."

"You *are* police officers!" Max said triumphantly. Rannie high-fived him over Honeybee, who was buckled in the middle.

Harry had a hard time not smiling. "We're actually agents with the Bureau of Criminal Apprehension. We're based out of Saint Paul. How'd you know we'd be staying at the motel tonight?"

"Lucky guess," Max said, but Rannie wouldn't leave it at that.

"It's the only motel around," he said. "We came because we need you to know."

Max made a hissing noise. Harry's pulse picked up.

"Know what?" Evangeline asked, glancing in the rearview mirror.

Rannie started talking fast. "There's bad luck in Alku. Good people but bad luck. I don't sleep, you know. I never sleep. But if you follow the rules, you're safe."

"Rannie!" Max closed his eyes for a moment. "We don't talk about Alku outside of Alku."

"There's a blood witch there," Rannie continued, like he couldn't stop once he'd started. "You can't go to the river. You can't go to the swampboggins. If you do, she'll get you. She's a monster." His whole body began trembling. "She'll getcha if you go where you shouldn't go! It's about time for another reaping, don't you know!"

"Rannie!" Max patted his arm, then pulled his little sister closer to him. "You got to calm down and be quiet. It's okay. We're okay. We're in a car. We're safe."

Rannie nodded, but his eyes were glazed. It was only when Honeybee touched Rannie's cheek with her tiny hand that he began to relax.

"So that's all you came to tell us?" Evangeline asked as they pulled into Alku. "To watch out in Alku because there's a witch?"

"Something like that." Max sounded frustrated. He stared out the window. The streets of Alku were still empty, the small white church lit up like a torch, mournful singing emanating from it. "Will you drop us off there?" he asked.

Evangeline grunted and pulled to a stop.

"You don't like kids, do you," Max observed.

Evangeline blinked at the rearview mirror, then laughed. "Not automatically."

Max's face was serious. "It's okay. I don't like all grown-ups, either."

He helped his sister out of the SUV, closed the door behind her, and then guided her to the sidewalk before returning to help unload the bicycles. Once the bikes were leaned against a tree, Max took his little sister's hand and Rannie's and led them into the church.

Harry and Evangeline watched them go.

Evangeline was the first to speak. "What the hell's in the water here?"

CHAPTER 15

"Don't even ask," Evangeline said as she slid into the diner booth across from Harry the next morning. Her hair was bound in its standard smooth ponytail, but she had greenish-gray circles under her eyes.

He'd watched her step out of the motel, clutching the note he'd taped on her side of his interior door. She'd glared at the world as she stomped across the road toward the diner, her hands shoved into the pockets of her black, puffy jacket and her shoulders bunched up around her ears.

His glance dropped to the plastic-coated menu. "The oatmeal is good."

She groaned. "Of course you ordered oatmeal. Did you ask them to hold the brown sugar and raisins so they didn't corrupt you?"

He saw no reason to tell her that he had, in fact, requested that the oatmeal be served plain. "How'd you sleep?"

She picked up the menu. "What did I say? 'Don't even ask,' that's what I said, and here you are *asking*."

She began scanning the breakfast offerings. He figured their morning pleasantries were over, so he was caught off guard when she spoke.

"I had weird dreams," she said, her face still on the menu. "I think they took place at the CCTC, inside a cell. There was a square-shouldered man sitting on a bed, his back to me. I couldn't get him to turn around." Her face tightened. "The cell was *liquid* with evil." She blinked rapidly, and then her eyes lasered on Harry. "The dude looked a little like you from behind."

The Lipton tea he'd been served suddenly went down sideways, and Harry began coughing. Evangeline pulled some napkins from the silver dispenser and handed them to him. He wiped at his eyes as he weighed his response.

Did she know about him?

He balled up the napkin and cleared his throat. That was ludicrous. Evangeline couldn't dream about things that she hadn't witnessed, couldn't possibly watch bygone crimes unfold as she slept. No one had that ability. She was simply having nightmares. *Not* ones about him. *Not* about the horror in his past. "Nightmares make sense, given that we visited a nursing home for serial killers yesterday. The latest science suggests that dream sleep resets our brain chemicals by washing them in cerebrospinal fluid and tidies up the thoughts and emotions of the day by consolidating them. It could be your brain was processing feelings about Mathias Millard."

Evangeline was sticking out her tongue when the server, a woman in her fifties with the posture of a career waitress, appeared. She sported what Harry's mom had called "hot roller hair," blue liner circling her eyes. Her name tag read LYDIA.

"What can I get you, love?" she asked Evangeline.

"Full stack of pancakes, side of bacon, and coffee with cream." Evangeline handed her the menu. "Thank you."

The waitress headed back to the kitchen. The diner seating area was a single room, the walls hung with enlarged, faded photos of lakes and ducks. The far corner held a jukebox, but no music played. Only one other booth was occupied, filled with a young couple taking selfies as they held up cinnamon rolls nearly as large as their heads. Two stools at the counter were taken by hunched men wearing ball caps, matching up to the two long-haul trucks parked in the motel lot.

"I did some research on Alku last night," Harry said. It'd taken him more than an hour and a borrowed cord from the office to get the dial-up to work. "Care to hear it?"

"Hit me." Evangeline gratefully accepted the steaming white mug Lydia brought over. She inhaled deeply. "Nothing better than fresh diner coffee after a crap night's sleep."

"What Pekka told us about the founding of Alku lines up."

"You like him, don't you." Evangeline tipped a tiny pot of cream into her mug.

He drew his chin back. "You don't?"

"Jury's out. Those little round glasses he wears remind me of the Nazi gear in *Indiana Jones* movies." She shrugged and brought the conversation back to his research. "So, seven families came over from Finland?"

"Yes, in 1881." Harry leaned forward. "It was suggested they were fleeing persecution, though from who or what, I couldn't find. They opened a tuberculosis sanitorium, which eventually transformed into an institution for people who were unable to live on their own." He frowned. "The CCTC has had awful names throughout the years. Historically appropriate, but awful."

"Such as?"

Harry was surprised by how difficult they were to say out loud. He paged through his notes, though the names were burned in his brain. "The Carlton County Sanitorium for Defectives. It was changed to the Institute for the Feeble-Minded in 1895, then updated to the Colony for the Feeble-Minded, Dumb, and Epileptic."

She whistled. "That branding does *not* stand the test of time."

Harry had to agree. "Those were accepted medical terms in the late 1800s and early 1900s, but I'm glad the language has evolved."

She tried to peek at what he'd written down. "Where'd you find that info?"

"Wikipedia," Harry said reluctantly. "Though I first searched for primary sources."

Evangeline smirked, but before she could make fun, a stack of six fluffy pancakes appeared in front of her, three glistening strips of bacon alongside.

"Syrup?" the waitress asked.

"Yes, please," Evangeline said, accepting the dispenser. "Do you have whipped cream?"

The waitress winked. "Be right back."

Evangeline smeared the melting butter pat across the top pancake, then bit into a crisp bacon strip. Harry's arteries hardened just watching her.

"It's strange," she said, "that they were driven out of Finland."

"According to Wikipedia," Harry amended. It had pained him that the only information he'd found had been crowdsourced.

"Sure, according to Wikipedia," she said, talking with her mouth full. "But didn't Pekka say the original founders were mostly in the medical field? You'd think they'd be in high demand during a pandemic." She grabbed a napkin from the stainless-steel dispenser and wiped her mouth. "I suppose Finland's bad luck was Alku's good."

Lydia set a bright red-and-white canister of "whipped topping" in front of Evangeline. "If there's one thing Alku doesn't have, it's good luck," the waitress said, wiping her hands on her apron. She glanced from Evangeline to Harry. "Can I get you two anything else?"

Evangeline paused, hand halfway to the whipped topping. "You could tell us more about Alku's luck."

The waitress glanced toward the door and held her elbows. "Don't get me wrong, it's full of good people. Good people and bad luck. There was a bear attack in the woods over by the treatment center, back in . . ." She turned toward the kitchen. "Mel! When was that black bear attack in Alku?"

A man whose face was more hair than skin appeared in the serving window. Harry noted he wasn't wearing a beard or mustache net. He pushed what was left of his oatmeal away.

"Eighties, maybe?" the cook said.

Lydia turned back. "That sounds right. Two out-of-towners mauled to death by a wild animal, and do you know what the folks of Alku did? They started a fund for the family left behind. Raised tens of thousands of dollars."

"That was very kind," Harry murmured.

"You don't know the half of it," Lydia said, putting her hands on their table. "They're going to open a new—"

The bell above the diner door tinkled. Lydia glanced over, as did Harry. Two men strode in. The first was Silas, the garter-snake-faced nursing assistant who'd escorted them through the tunnels yesterday. The second wore a feed cap and a Carhartt winter jacket. His hat was tipped back, revealing a high forehead. When he swiveled to lock eyes with Harry, he moved slowly, languorously, his neck overlong.

An Alku man.

"I'm so sorry," the waitress said, her expression growing pained. "I should leave you in peace so you can eat."

She scurried back to the kitchen, her quick departure leaving a cold squeeze in Harry's chest. Evangeline glanced over her shoulder at the men as they turned to walk out as abruptly as they'd arrived. Then she dug into her pancakes.

"We've got our work cut out for us here," she said around a mouthful of food.

Harry could only nod.

CHAPTER 16

Pekka appeared mildly startled by what Harry was telling him, his eyes magnified behind his round glasses. "You say Rannie stopped by your motel?"

"Yes." Harry crossed one knee over the other, straightening the pleat on his top leg. He'd chosen the dark-chocolate suit this morning.

He and Evangeline had driven directly to the prison after breakfast, the building far less dramatic on the approach than the school. From the outside, it resembled a midcentury high school or clinic with a large employee parking lot crammed full of cars. Pekka, who said he had offices in both locations, had been waiting for them after they cleared security. Once they'd been informed that Detective Emery was running late and wanted them to go ahead without him, they'd requested a private moment of Pekka's time before interviewing Mathias Millard.

"As I said," Harry finished, "he and the children seemed more curious than anything."

Pekka leaned back in his chair and steepled his fingers. His office was small and windowless, the paneled walls reminiscent of a 1970s rumpus room. And if Pihla shared features with Nurse Ratched, Harry realized Pekka bore more than a passing resemblance to William Redfield's Dale Harding in the same film—slightly weak-chinned, self-contained, gentle. "Rannie is my brother," he said. "Younger, obviously."

"And the children he was with?" Evangeline asked.

"Max and Honeybee are good kids." Pekka's eyebrows nearly met above his nose. "You may be wondering what a forty-seven-year-old man was doing with two children he's not related to. Rannie has fragile X syndrome with a moderate intellectual disability. He's in many ways an eternal child." His smile grew wistful. "My mom used to call him her peräkammarin poika. A man who never leaves home."

"He lives with your parents?" Harry asked.

Pekka shook his head. "Rannie lives with Pihla and me. Both my parents have passed."

"I'm sorry," Harry said.

"It was a while ago."

Evangeline tugged out her notebook. "Do you and Pihla have children?"

Harry swallowed a grimace. He didn't think it was a relevant question, but Evangeline had more field experience than he did. He would trust her interview methods.

"Unfortunately, no." Pekka stood abruptly.

"Just a couple more questions if you don't mind," Evangeline said, still sitting, her expression guileless. It made Harry uncomfortable to disregard social mores. He had to fight to stay in his own seat with Pekka standing. Evangeline continued, seemingly oblivious to both men's discomfort. "You mentioned earlier that the town had seven founding families. Could we get a list of their names and some further information on them?"

"Of course. All the town records are contained in the church. They're accessible to the public by appointment."

"Not in the city hall?" Evangeline asked.

"We're unincorporated. No city hall."

Evangeline studied what she'd just written in her notebook. "Were the Korhonens one of the original families?"

Pekka glanced back at his chair like he wished he hadn't left it so quickly. "They were."

Evangeline nodded. "There's a diner across from our motel. The Viking Corner Café, which isn't on a corner."

Pekka smiled faintly and reclaimed his seat.

"Our waitress there mentioned a bear attack a while back. Do you remember it?"

Pekka's smile disappeared, his face growing pale. He rubbed his eyelids behind his glasses. "It happened near the school, actually," he said. "Not one hundred yards from where you parked yesterday. The police said the victims were two young hikers who'd gotten lost. They must have spotted the building through the trees. They'd almost made it when some sort of animal attacked them."

"The town put together a donation for their families?"

"The board, yes," Pekka said.

Harry was taken by the misery Pekka suddenly exhibited, just like when he was talking about the Korhonens yesterday. "That was generous."

Pekka waved his hand, trying to minimize Alku's response. "It was a tragedy. Communities look out for one another in tragedies." His attention moved to a spot between Evangeline and Harry. "Silas. Mr. Millard is ready?"

Harry turned. The nursing assistant was again wearing tan scrubs. He was staring at his own feet, but it wasn't a submissive gesture. If Harry were to name it, he'd call it *calculating*. His sour odor was still evident.

"As ready as he can get," Silas said.

"Very good. Please take the agents to meet him, and then be at their disposal for as long as they need. And when Detective Emery arrives, do the same for him."

"Which is it?" Silas asked his feet.

"Excuse me?" Pekka said.

"Am I to help these two, or am I to help the cop?"

"These two now, Detective Emery when he arrives, *Mr. Smith*," Pekka said evenly. His line of work must give him practice in dealing with personalities.

"All right, then." Smith spun on his heel and began walking away, not waiting for Evangeline and Harry.

Evangeline hurried to catch up. "Why'd you leave the diner when you saw us this morning?" she asked him.

He didn't turn or slow. "Had nothing to do with you," he muttered. "Decided I didn't want a greasy breakfast."

"They have oatmeal," Evangeline said, winking at Harry. When Smith didn't respond, she pivoted. "Who was your friend? The guy you came in with?"

"I've got no friends." Smith picked up his pace. "That fellow and I just happened to walk in at the same time."

And walk out together.

But Smith wasn't interested in talking.

They found the prison quieter than the day before, the faint egg-and-sausage smell of a cafeteria breakfast lingering on the air. Guards were stationed at the entrance points, but otherwise, the halls were empty. Harry and Evangeline passed the recreation room where Dooley'd had his outburst. He wasn't among the prisoners who were either watching television or staring out the windows. Harry found himself curious about their daily routine. All the inmates were incapacitated, either due to age or illness. Were they given enrichment activities? Regular physical therapy? Or was the CCTC simply the waiting room between prison and death?

"Is there a meaning to the decoration on the floor?" Harry asked, watching the blue squares with their looping corners pass underfoot. He'd admired it yesterday in the Gothic school, but he was realizing it was the only beauty in this otherwise squat and ugly institution.

"You got me," Smith said.

Evangeline glanced down. "Reminds me of the Command key on a Mac." She addressed Smith. "Did you know Jarmo or Janice Korhonen?"

He snorted. "I'm not that old. It was the '90s, right? They only let townies work here back then, townies plus a handful of nurses and guards with special training. I bet they wish they could still run the place that way, but they're not reproducing fast enough. They have to bring in us outsiders." He scratched his shoulder beneath his scrubs. "To work, anyhow. I hear they only let the descendants of the original settlers live in the Alku city limits. Their blood must be pretty watered down these days, but there you go."

"How long have you worked here?" Harry asked.

"Three years." Smith took a left. The halls weren't marked, no colored arrows on the floor. It would be easy to get lost.

"Any problems with inmates in that time?" Harry continued.

"Naw," Smith said. "They come here because they used to be dangerous, but they're toothless now. All bark, those who can talk, but no bite."

"What about Amon Dooley?" Evangeline asked. "The one who was so upset about the veri noita yesterday?"

"Veri noita?" Smith wrinkled his nose. "Try very *nothing*. That's all superstition. A Finnish bogeyman."

"Did Peter Weiss believe in her?" Evangeline asked.

Smith tossed her a cold look. "Guess he's the only one who can answer that. Too bad he ate his own mouth, thanks to the business end of a hammer."

"How do you know that?" Evangeline's tone was sharp.

Smith's cheek twitched and his eyes shuttered. "I got friends in the hospital."

Before Harry could ask a follow-up question, Evangeline stopped abruptly in front of a metal door that looked like the rest, except the strip of security window on the cell was blacked out. There was also a heavy-duty bolt latch in addition to the electronic security lock. "What's in this room?" Her voice was urgent.

"Evangeline?" Harry asked.

"Do you smell that?" Her eyes were wide, her mouth rigid.

Harry thought she was referring to Smith's odor, but when he stepped closer, he caught a whiff of something like fresh-dug black dirt. "What is it?"

"The smell? I'm not sure." Evangeline lowered her voice. "But this is the cell I had a nightmare about last night."

Harry felt a wave of unease. She said she'd seen an evil man inside, his back to her, a man who resembled Harry from behind. He rubbed his face, bringing his mind back to logic. The cell was either empty or there was a prisoner inside. Either way, it wouldn't be him, chained to the wall in some creep-show twist.

Evangeline leaned around Harry to look at Smith. "What's in here?" she asked again.

"It's empty," he said, his eyes back on his feet.

"I'd like to look inside."

Smith shrugged. "Don't have a key."

Evangeline grabbed the bolt and slid it back with a thunk. She reached for the handle.

"Evangeline," Harry cautioned. Forget his burst of paranoia—they didn't have permission to look inside. He understood that she was troubled from her nightmare, but it was impossible she'd had a dream about this specific cell. It wasn't worth risking their goodwill over.

She grabbed the handle and twisted. It didn't budge.

"Told you," Smith said. "I don't have a key. Also told you that it's empty."

"It's got two locks?"

Smith dragged his eyes to hers. "Guess so, if you can't open it. You want to see Matty the Mallet or not?"

CHAPTER 17

It didn't matter how many killers Harry had seen, he was always surprised by how unremarkable they were. They were simply men, often smaller than average, frequently with a low IQ, and with either extremely poor or alarmingly effective social skills.

Records indicated Mathias Millard fell on the distressingly effective end of the scale. He'd been an award-winning salesman in his prime, with glossy brown hair and a build like a bantamweight fighter, his eyes glittering with a cunning intelligence. The man slumped in front of Harry was a shell of that. This era's Matty the Mallet spent his days in a wheelchair, visibly wasted legs perched on the footrest, hands twisted in his lap, head listing to one side. His eyes were open and rheumy looking, his remaining hair a frothy patch of white above each ear.

"Mr. Millard," Harry said, crouching in front of him. "I'm Agent Steinbeck of the BCA, and this is my partner, Agent Reed. We were hoping to ask you some questions."

Smith snorted. Harry ignored him.

"Are you willing to talk to us?" Harry said.

"Check it." Smith knelt next to Harry, a penlight in his hand. He flashed it into the prisoner's eyes. Millard's pupils constricted, but he didn't blink. "See? You can knock, but ain't no one home."

Harry glanced back at Evangeline, who pursed her lips. *Dead end*, her expression said. Harry stood, knees creaking. "Thank you for your time, Mr. Millard."

"You're welcome," Smith said in a falsetto voice. Then he laughed.

"We'd like to walk the fence line now," Evangeline said, glaring at him. "Just to make sure there's no breach."

"That won't be necessary," Pihla said from the doorway.

The woman had a disturbing habit of appearing out of thin air. Her brown hair was gathered in a crisp bun at the nape of her neck. She wore a white coat, her eyeglasses hung around her neck by a black cord. "We assigned two guards to check the fencing just yesterday, after we received word of Mr. Weiss's murder."

Smith seemed to shrink into himself, reacting to Pihla far differently than he did to Pekka.

"Still," Evangeline said brightly, "we'd like to look while we're here. I'm sure you understand."

Harry marveled at how Evangeline was consistently able to match the energy of whoever she spoke with. It disarmed them. This case was no exception.

"I'll inform the guards," Pihla said reluctantly, glancing at the silicone overshoes protecting Harry's custom-made brogans and Evangeline's ankle-height boots. Then she smiled without showing her teeth, like a crease in leather. "Are you sure you're dressed for it?"

"We'll manage," Evangeline said. "Smith, will you show us the way?"

The first thing Harry noticed in the courtyard was the uncanny hush. The prison at their back and the woods circling them muffled the world beyond while amplifying every sound they made: the sharp crunch of their shoes through the snow crust, their labored breathing as they navigated knee-deep drifts to reach the fence line, the startling scream of a hawk taking wing from a nearby pine.

The second thing Harry observed was the single track of footprints on the inside perimeter. He walked toward it.

Evangeline stopped and turned, her breath escaping in white puffs. The weather tomorrow was forecast to return to the midforties, where it had hovered before the freak snowstorm, but it was well below freezing at the moment. "What is it?" she asked.

"Look," he said, bending and placing his hand as close to the nearest footprint as the fence allowed. It was only a few inches longer. "Did you see any female guards inside?"

"Or men with dainty feet?" She took out her phone and snapped a photo of the footprints with Harry's hand by them for scale. "I did not. In fact, the only female I've seen inside is Pihla. Remind me to ask her who checked the fence line." She glanced back at the prison, a two-story concrete eyesore, then off toward the thick evergreen forest, its rich green needles scenting the air. "The woods are beautiful."

Harry agreed.

"And the people inside that building are keeping something from us."

Harry agreed with that, too. "It could be unrelated to either case."

"It could," she said, sliding her phone back into her pocket. "But tell me, fact man, how statistically likely that is."

Harry stared off into the woods. Everything had been all wrong since the moment they'd crossed into Duluth. Something was slippery about the photos of the Korhonen and Weiss crime scenes, the town of Alku made him uneasy on a primal level, the CCTC seemed to be hoarding secrets, and Caroline felt both closer and farther away than she had in over two decades. But he couldn't follow the fear, the doubt down, down, down, or he'd never get back up. "I'd rather keep looking for information." He indicated the path in front of her.

She rolled her eyes but started walking again. The narrow trail inside the prison yard continued. Evangeline paused when a flurry of tracks appeared directly on the other side of the fence, so much activity that most of the individual footprints were obliterated. They made a trail back into the forest.

"This is a popular viewing spot. Lookie-loos coming to check out the serial killers?" Evangeline took another photo, and then glanced back toward the prison. Her voice dropped. "Speaking of, does it look like someone is watching us? Third window from the bottom right."

Harry shaded his eyes from the cold spring sunshine. "Impossible to tell."

Evangeline sniffled, changing the subject. "You get the impression Pihla is in charge back there?"

Harry considered it, the wind nipping at his cheeks. "Pekka seems to defer to her, and both Dooley and Smith appeared to be intimidated by her."

"Mmmm. Something like that. But not exactly that."

They both started walking again, sinking back into their thoughts. They'd made nearly a full circuit of the exercise yard when Evangeline made the call. "If any of the prisoners are sneaking out to hunt at night, they're not escaping through here." She made a surprised noise. "Hey, is that an actual flower blooming? Over there, just on the other side of the fence."

Harry followed the invisible line from her pointer finger to the tender yellow daffodil poking through a shallow patch of snow, the murky sunlight bathing its cheery face. Looking at it made his heart ache.

Daffodils had been Caroline's favorite flower.

And there it was, the past cracking open and flooding the present just as it had when Rannie and the children showed up at their motel room the night before.

He tried to hold it at bay.

He'd have had better luck plucking a bird from the sky.

"Thanks for getting me out from under the Wicked Witch's thumb," Caroline said.

She'd disappeared while Harry called nearly a dozen catering companies until he found one that had sun-dried crostini available and could deliver them on Easter weekend. He'd agreed to pay an exorbitant amount to have them hustled over in time for the party.

"Where did you get those?" he asked, pointing at the buttery daffodils she held. "Please don't tell me it was Mom's garden."

Myrna Steinbeck's flowers were for show, never picked. They were allowed remain in their landscaped backyard until their bloom passed, and then they were disposed of by gardeners. April had so far been uncharacteristically warm—1998 was predicted to have the hottest summer in years—creating a furious explosion of multicolored tulips, saffron daffodils, purple-and-white crocuses, and sherbet-colored ranunculus. The profusion didn't mean Myrna wouldn't miss a bouquet of daffodils.

"You know I love them." Caroline dipped her nose toward the delicate petals. "They're so hopeful and silly. I'll bring them to Olive's as an Easter present. Mom can't criticize that, can she? A hostess gift."

Caroline knew better than Harry that Myrna could criticize *any-thing* she did. Her best bet was to become invisible. Harry considered asking her if Myrna was treating her better, worse, or the same since he'd moved out, but that was a conversation that could wait. "That's where you're going? Over to Olive's?" She was a new friend of Caroline's, one Harry hadn't had a chance to meet yet. From what he gathered, girls changed friend groups a lot at Caroline's age.

"Yep." She still had her face tucked in the flowers, but her voice sounded off.

"Caroline?"

She looked at him. The tip of her nose was dusted with pollen. With her ice-blonde pigtails high atop her head, she looked her age. It was a relief. The way she was developing, how she carried herself. She'd seemed to age years rather than months since Harry had gone off to college, and he didn't like it.

"I'm fine, big brother," she said, laughing at his expression. "You go back to worrying about whether or not you can get your hair just right for Ms. Jennyfer."

He watched her skip up the stairs.

Staring at the daffodil outside the prison, almost twenty-five years to the day since he'd last seen his sister, he had the same thought that he'd had every day since: he'd give his life to return to that moment, to make a different choice, to derail the horror just around the corner.

CHAPTER 18

Evangeline and Harry stood in front of 2840 Willow Street, Alku, Minnesota, the site of the 1998 Korhonen family slaying. The two-story farmhouse-style home—like all the houses on this street—was a deep red with white trim, a steeply pitched roof, and tall, narrow windows.

Its interior was dark.

They studied the house, the slate sky hanging low overhead. A sharp wind was sneaking down Alku's streets, biting and snapping at exposed flesh, leaving it red-slapped.

"The sidewalk is shoveled," Evangeline observed.

"I see that."

"I wonder who lives there now."

Harry glanced up the street at four children who had turned the corner and were walking toward them. He recognized Max and Honeybee. They were joined by another boy and girl, their winter caps pulled so low he couldn't see their hair color. "Maybe they can tell us."

Evangeline's mouth tightened as they neared. "Don't you all have school today?" she asked.

Max grinned. "Nope. We get a long weekend for Easter."

"I'm Arlie," the new girl said. Her red cap had a rainbow-colored pom-pom. Her nose was sprinkled with freckles. "I'm ten. This is my friend Fred. He's twelve, a year older than Max."

Harry smiled. Their jobs would be a breeze if everyone were as open as children. "Nice to meet you both."

Evangeline jabbed her thumb at the house. "Any idea who lives here?"

Max's eyebrows disappeared into his hat. "No one. That's the Korhonen place."

Harry took a moment to process. "It's been empty since 1998?"

"It's the Korhonen place," Max repeated slowly, his tone suggesting he wanted to be kind but that Harry and Evangeline were maybe not so smart. "There's no Korhonens left, so it's empty."

Harry and Evangeline exchanged a look. "Who shovels the sidewalk?" Evangeline asked.

Fred smiled shyly, revealing a gap between his top two teeth. "Everyone."

"That's right," Max said. "After a snow, we all get out and shovel for one another. We don't stop until the whole town's done."

"Must be nice." Evangeline was already turning away from the kids. She held her phone up to Harry. "I'm going to call Kyle, see who the house is registered to. If I can get reception, that is."

She ambled up the street, out of earshot. The children were staring at Harry like they expected him to say something.

"Where's Rannie today?" he asked.

The kids all looked away. Max finally spoke, grudgingly. "At home, I think. Our parents got a call we shouldn't play with him for the next couple days."

While we're here, Harry thought. "Who made the call?"

Their faces cinched up tight. Harry didn't want to push it. They were children, after all.

"Looks like a nice day to sled," he said, straightening the cuffs of his deep-blue peacoat.

"Naw," Arlie said, kicking at the ground. "Snow's too icy now that it's half melting."

Harry nodded. Honeybee drew his gaze, a sweet little smile on her face. She had two flaxen braids peeking out from beneath her lemon-colored hat. Braids just like his sister used to wear when she had outdoor chores to do.

"She likes you," Max said, studying Harry. "And she doesn't hardly trust anyone."

It was a curious phrasing, using "like" and "trust" interchangeably. Harry was about to ask about it when a door opened up in a red house at the end of the street. A woman stepped onto her porch and began shaking a rug loudly, staring pointedly in their direction while the runner made cracking sounds in the cold air.

All four children jumped like they'd been shocked.

"We need to go," Max told Harry. He hurried his sister and friends away.

"Maybe you could bring us some candy, though," Fred called over his shoulder, a slight whistle escaping between the gap in his teeth. "Or a magazine. We like rock and roll."

Arlie punched him in the arm, and he ducked his head. They crossed the street so they didn't have to pass in front of the woman glaring at them. Then they disappeared down an alley.

"What'd you do to them?" Evangeline asked, rejoining Harry. "Offer multivitamins and help with their homework?"

An uneasy feeling had settled on Harry's skin like glass dust, and it was beginning to worm its way into his bloodstream. The children of Alku knew something the adults didn't want them to share. Add that to the pile of mysteries they were already dealing with. "Did you get a hold of Kyle?"

She held up her phone. "Not enough reception for a call, but we could text. Kyle said the house is owned by a corporation, same one that owned it in 1998. Same corporation that's owned it since the house was built, as a matter of fact. Over a hundred years ago."

A salty knot was forming in Harry's stomach.

"There's more," Evangeline continued. "That same corporation owns every building in this town."

"And who owns the corporation?" But he already knew the answer.

"Seven families," she said. "The Tervos, Korhonens, Eskos, Wenners, Laines, Virtanens, and Harjus."

Harry exhaled. He stared to the north, toward the CCTC. He felt like he could see it looming, though it was impossible from this distance. He tried to skirt the truth, but there was no use. "This is bigger than we thought." He rubbed his face. "We have to stay longer."

Evangeline sighed. "Yeah, we do."

He kept his gaze to the north. "You see them staring at us?"

Evangeline turned a full circle. "Holy shit."

He'd first noticed it when the children walked away: faces peering from the houses, some shadowed by curtains, others brazenly scowling.

He bit down hard on his teeth.

Something was rotten in the town of Alku.

CHAPTER 19

Evangeline and Harry crunched down the street, electing to walk the three blocks from the former Korhonen house to the church where Pekka said they could access the town records. Curtains lifted and dropped, lifted and dropped as they passed. An icy sheet of unease slid down Harry's back.

"Gives me the creeps," Evangeline said, following Harry's cue and acknowledging the movement without looking directly at it. "Do you think Silas Smith was telling the truth about only direct descendants being allowed to live in town?"

"I'd say it's a distinct possibility."

They reached the end of Willow Street and stood at Alku's main intersection. There was no post office, no restaurant, not even a hardware store. Not open, in any case. All the storefronts were shuttered, some covered with actual blinds, others white soaped. The only visibly functioning business was a grocery store. A man on the other side of the window clutched a broom and stared blankly at Harry and Evangeline.

"This town is dying," Harry said matter-of-factly, taking a sharp right toward the Uusialku Lutheran Church.

"I'd say it's dead." Evangeline glanced ahead and exhaled loudly. "Oh goody, we have greeters," she said under her breath.

Pihla Tervo was perched on the church's top step, a familiar-looking woman standing next to her. It took Harry a few beats to recognize the thin-lipped employee who'd been at the CCTC front desk when they'd first visited yesterday. Neither woman wore winter gear, only their regular clothes, as if they'd known exactly when Evangeline and Harry would arrive.

Harry suppressed a shudder.

"Hello!" Evangeline called out. "Pekka must have told you we were coming."

Harry detected the tension in her otherwise cheerful voice but didn't think they could.

Pihla's mouth curved in an imitation of a smile. "He mentioned you'd like to have a look at the church records. Somebody needs to show you where they are."

Evangeline mounted the stairs and offered her hand to the woman next to Pihla. "I'm Agent Reed. I believe I saw you at the school yesterday, but we didn't have a chance to meet."

The woman's eyes drifted toward Pihla, as if seeking permission to speak, but she caught herself and clasped Evangeline's hand. "Hannele Virtanen. Wife of Torben."

Wife of Torben? Harry hoped his face didn't betray his shock. He stepped forward. "I'm Harry Steinbeck. It was kind of you both to come down to help us. Shall we go inside? You must be chilly."

The two women stood in front of the door for an extra beat, like sentries, before Pihla moved to open it. The smell of incense wafted out, but it wasn't the frankincense and myrrh Harry was accustomed to from the Catholic church of his youth. This smell was spicier, more herbal.

The church interior had been stripped clean of all evidence of Easter. Come to think of it, the veri noita was no longer out front, either. Harry wasn't sure if the townsfolk customarily cleaned up that quickly or if the presence of law enforcement had hurried them along. In any case, the nave and sanctuary were austere, free of any decoration save crosses. Harry counted thirty rows of pews split down the middle and leading to the altar, on which hung a simple white cloth.

"You'll see that our house of worship is humble," Hannele said.

"But it serves its purpose," Pihla responded, like a litany. "This way, please."

The women led Harry and Evangeline down into the basement. The majority of the space was used as a dining hall and kitchen, but there was a small room just off the stairs. Pihla opened its unlocked door and held it ajar, the basement's harsh overhead light glinting off her high forehead.

Evangeline entered. Harry found he was reluctant to follow. There wasn't a clear threat, but he suddenly didn't want to give the women a chance to close them inside.

"Probably too tight for both of us," he said from just outside the threshold.

Evangeline clicked on a light and shot him a questioning glance. He shook his head once, the movement contained. She glanced around the room. "Not much to see in here except filing cabinets. Lots of them. And regular wood cupboards. What do you keep in them?" she asked Pihla. "Birth records, death records, marriage records?"

"That," Pihla said, slowly extending her long neck to study Harry curiously even as she answered Evangeline. "Plus land sales."

It took all Harry's willpower not to step away from Pihla. The slow movements, the dispassionate gaze. She reminded him of a hungry insect.

"And divorce records?" Evangeline asked.

This got Pihla's full attention. She regarded Evangeline frostily. "This is where we *would* keep those."

The unspoken *if we had divorces* hung in the air. Pihla and Hannele were still poised on each side of the door's exterior, obviously waiting for Harry to enter. Yet he couldn't do it. Was there a logical reason? No. Did it make any difference? Also no. He was at a loss for how to proceed when Evangeline flicked off the light and stepped out of the room, closing the door behind her. Harry was washed in inexplicable relief.

"It's good to see where you store those," Evangeline said. Her smile was gentle, but her eyes were hard as glass. "Thank you. And that room is the only place you record births and deaths?"

"Again, yes," Pihla said.

"Who else would want to know?" Hannele asked, her head swiveling on her neck in a way that chilled Harry.

"Who indeed," Evangeline responded. "And your corporation owns all the buildings in town?"

A look flashed between the women. "Yes," Pihla said.

"Who runs the corporation?"

"The board," Hannele offered. "It's loose, though. We're all family in Alku."

Harry finally found his tongue. "And both of you can trace your lineage back to the original founding seven?"

Pihla laughed, and suddenly, the spell was broken. They weren't two praying mantises plotting to lock Harry and Evangeline in a cupboard under the stairs. They were professional women, almost motherly in their demeanor.

"It's a pretty tenuous connection," Pihla said. "Watered down. I'm an Esko by blood, a few generations removed. If you'd told me back in elementary school that I was going to marry a Tervo—Alku royalty—I'd have called you a liar."

"Come now," Hannele said, her tone teasing. "I remember you writing Pekka's name in your notebook."

"A girl can dream." Her laughter melted, but the warmth remained. "I was so intimidated by Ansa, Pekka's mother. She had the presence of a cat, a woman who could take or leave you. *She* was a straight descendant from the original settlers. That's why she kept her last name."

"I forgot that!" Hannele said.

Pihla nodded. "Mother Ansa met her husband, Nils—Pekka and Rannie's father—in nursing school. He was a doctor. They treated me like a daughter as soon as Pekka and I were engaged, of course. It was from her that I learned the importance of kaupunki on perhe—the community as family. My own parents were lax on that front, despite having spent their lives in Alku. But Ansa led the charge when it came to keeping the traditions alive, right up until the day she died. Pekka took over after that." Her smile faltered.

"When did she pass?" Evangeline asked.

Pihla's expression wandered. "I believe it was 1997, though I'd have to check the records to be sure. I remember it was a year with a big snowstorm. So much shoveling!" She blinked as if clearing her thoughts. "I walked right into the past, didn't I? We really do need to get back to work, Hannele and me. You're sure there's nothing else we can do for you?"

It was a clear dismissal, a common Midwestern tactic of nudging people to leave by offering something you hoped they would decline.

Evangeline had no qualms about accepting. "We'd like to go inside the Korhonen house," she said.

Pihla's and Hannele's faces iced right back up. "It's unlocked," Pihla said, "though I can't imagine what you expect to find."

"Likely nothing," Harry said, silently thanking Evangeline for her forthrightness. "But it's important that we're thorough."

The women were obviously waiting for them to leave, so he waved Evangeline forward so he could protect her back as she went up the stairs. He noticed a few straw-like twigs—willow?—tucked in the shadows of a stair. They were so out of place that he picked them up, planning to throw them outside.

"I'll take that." Hannele dashed forward to grab the sticks.

The force of it scratched his hand. He turned, startled.

She was smiling as she held them up. "Just something left over from Easter." The smile dropped off her face, leaving an eerie vacancy. "Now go check out that house, you two."

CHAPTER 20

Rannie
May 1, 1990

Rannie shot upright, leaves and dirt falling off him.

He'd done it again. He'd fallen asleep outside.

He'd meant only to visit Sandwich Rock, to search for mushrooms in the narrow shelter created when the top rock tipped over six years earlier (*always room in the gloom for a mushroom*). But the day had been so hot—out of character for May, his mother said—that once he'd crawled into that dark space between the massive stones, he hadn't wanted to leave. So he'd taken a long nap, everything in his brain so nice and black and soft.

When he hurried outside the makeshift cave, though, he realized that most of the afternoon had crawled away. Had he missed Hela? *Oh no! Oh no oh no oh no.* He crashed through the woods toward the Sacred Spot. The special clearing behind the school and what was now a prison used to feel connected to both buildings, but not anymore, not with the high, sharp fence separating everything.

But it was still sacred, his mom said. It was still where they held their ceremonies.

He sniffed the air but couldn't smell the helavalkeat, the bonfire they burned on this holy day. There was supposed to be singing and dancing and a feast, too, everyone wearing their masks, but when he tipped his ear, all he heard was forest sounds.

Had he missed it all?

His heart thunked down to his belly. This was no good. No good at all.

Mom would be furious.

He spun when he heard a *ssshhiiing* sound behind him. The veri noita? His blood electric-thudded out of his heart. Not the veri noita. Those were stories. Stories! It was his mom he needed to worry about. She'd been gone so much lately. Gone from her body, that was, lights on, no one inside. He hated the way she smelled, too, the sweet-sour liquor seeping out of her pores. It scared him. Ansa had always been so strong, never drank, ran the whole town. But for the last couple weeks, she hardly left the house. Rannie wished he knew what had upset her so he could fix it. It was like she didn't care about anything all of a sudden.

She'd care about Hela, though.

And she'd as *sure as sugar* care if Rannie had slept through it.

Hela represented the Old Ways, the Finnish May Day celebration of fertility. That's why it was still held in the woods. The Alku Originals all donned their branch masks—some owls, some rabbits, some mice, some goats, all with scabby black eyes and no mouths—and they sang behind those masks, and they danced with bells on their feet, all of it to keep the evil spirits away and bring in a good crop, even though they didn't farm anymore, not really. His mom said the patients on the hill were their crop, and here, in the US, it was more important than it had ever been in Finland that they ensure a successful reaping.

Rannie groaned when he thought of the yummy sima, fermented honey water with raisins and lemons floating in it, that he'd probably missed, and the fresh fried doughnuts that Jarmo Korhonen always made with the big fryer he'd haul to the clearing for the party. He'd fry up munkki and tippaleipä, its bird's-nest shape extra good for holding on to the powdered sugar he'd dust it with.

Rannie's mouth filled with liquid thinking about it. He gave his body an extra burst of speed, and just as he was about to give up hope, he heard it. The music! They were still celebrating! He smiled all the way down to his toes. He kept running, tree branches slapping and dragging at him, until he glimpsed the orange light of the bonfire peeking at him through the trees, smelled the sweet, greasy odor of the munkki. Yes! Jarmo was still at the fryer, pouring dough in.

Rannie ran straight to him, ignoring the dozens of masked towns-people dancing around the fire. "Two, please," he told Jarmo.

He knew that's who was behind the fox mask because the fox was the Korhonen haltija—protector. He grabbed a paper plate and held it out expectantly.

"Rannie." Jarmo's voice behind the keen fox face was chiding. "You can't enter the clearing without a mask." He searched the crowd, prob-ably looking for Ansa. The whole village was scared of her. Rannie wanted to tell him he shouldn't be, not these days, not the way his mom was now.

"Two, please," Rannie repeated.

"I can't." Jarmo shook his head. "You know the rules."

Something dark slithered inside Rannie, like an ol' snake that was waking up. He was about to tell Jarmo a third time that he better see some doughnuts on that plate *real quick or someone is gonna feel sick* when a siren screamed up the access road to the prison. The musicians stopped playing. Everyone froze.

"Jarmo," a woman in a goat mask called out. "Come with me. Now."

Rannie would have recognized his mother even if she hadn't spo-ken, even if she were wearing a different mask. She was the strongest of them all, even stronger than the men, Rannie thought. Made of concrete, inside and out.

Used to be, anyhow. At least she hadn't slurred her words just now.

Jarmo shut off his gas burner without question and took off behind Ansa.

Rannie wasn't sure what made him follow.

Maybe he thought he could remind Jarmo about the munkki when he finished whatever business he was headed toward. Maybe it was because before Rannie had gone mushroom hunting, he'd overheard his mom say a skeleton crew would be working at the prison tonight. He wasn't sure exactly what that was, but he wanted to see it for himself, maybe help his mom if she needed it.

No one should be alone in the bone zone.

Ansa and Jarmo made good time through the forest, taking a well-worn path. When they hit the perimeter, they dropped their masks and raced around until they reached a prison door set in the fencing, one that led directly inside the building. Ansa pulled a key from her pocket and let herself in. Jarmo followed, allowing the door to close behind him on its own. Rannie managed to dart forward and sneak a twig in before it sealed shut. Jarmo and his mother were too worried to notice. Bright red lights bounced off the low clouds, but Rannie couldn't tell if it was an ambulance or a police car.

He counted to three, opened the prison door, tossed the twig, and crept down the hallway.

He didn't have far to go.

Pekka stood outside a cell just around the corner. His face was white.

"What is it?" Ansa demanded.

"A prisoner. He's dead." Pekka sounded far away even though he was standing right there.

"Heart attack?" Ansa craned her neck to peer into the cell. Rannie could only see the edge of that doorway, but whatever his mother laid eyes on made her reach out to the wall for support. "Holy ghost. What did that?"

"What do you think?" Pekka said wearily.

"The men in here are poison!" Ansa yelled. "Poison. You never should have let them come into our hospital."

Pekka shrank. Rannie wished he could protect his brother from their mother's wrath, but he'd never figured out how. She loved Rannie all the time, but she only loved Pekka when he did his job right. But she had it wrong this time. It wasn't Pekka who'd wanted the murder men to move in here. In fact, both Pekka and Jarmo had been dead set against it, and they were both standing right here. Why wasn't either one reminding Ansa that *she* had been the one who insisted they become a prison so they could pay their bills?

"The man who killed with the hammer was this one's cellmate, wasn't he?" Ansa asked sharply.

Pekka nodded, his expression miserable. "Weiss was in there with them over an hour ago, doing physical therapy. When he came back, Millard was covered in blood, his cellmate dead. Weiss called the police."

"Where's Millard now?"

Pekka pointed at the next cell over. "In there."

Ansa flashed her key at the door. The cell was directly across from Rannie's hiding spot. When the door opened, he could see inside the room plain as day: a man sat in a wheelchair, staring blankly ahead, speckled with dark-red drops as if he'd just butchered chickens. Behind him stood a tall, thin man with a mustache like a horseshoe around his mouth. Was that Weiss? Was he the skeleton crew? He looked bony enough.

Ansa crouched in front of the wheelchair man. "I know who you are," she hissed. "I know what you did."

His eyes flashed and his head bobbed, but he didn't seem deadly. In fact, he looked to Rannie like he was scared.

A commotion from the front of the prison made Ansa stand and hurry out of the room. "Don't touch anything," she told Pekka. "We'll let the police deal with . . . that. Jarmo, follow me to the tunnel. I want to make sure nothing in the school was disturbed." She shook her head. "I swear, I'm going to have to live forever to protect you all."

She and Jarmo disappeared from Rannie's view. Pekka followed slowly.

Rannie was dying to peek inside the cell that everyone was so worried about. He knew he'd get caught if he did it, but he couldn't help himself. He darted forward out of the shadows. Stood in the doorway.

Tried to make sense of the mess in front of him.

There was a body lying on a prison cot, but it looked like someone had poured tomato soup and raw hamburger onto the pillow where the head should have been.

Rannie didn't realize he was crying until he tasted salt.

He stumbled backward. He heard a sound like corn husks rubbing together. He thought it was the man in the wheelchair, laughing, the bony Weiss man still standing behind him.

CHAPTER 21

"Unlocked," Evangeline confirmed, turning the brass knob of 2840 Willow Street's front door. "Why do I think that's true of every house in this town?"

"Because we've stepped back in time, partner of Harry?" he asked. He was massaging the flesh around the scratch left by the twig. He'd rubbed antiseptic gel into the wound, but he'd like to put salve and a bandage on it as well. Too bad his first-aid kit was back in the motel room. He wouldn't make that mistake again. It would travel with them in the SUV moving forward. He was unprepared for Evangeline's whoop.

"You *can* crack a joke, partner of Evangeline. Good. I was beginning to feel like I was the only normal one out here." She punched his arm lightly. "Why didn't you go into that storage room with me, by the way?"

Harry tried to sit on his smile and failed. "It gave me the willies."

"That's two, Harry Steinbeck," she said, smiling back. "You might want to slow down so you don't break anything."

The warmth between them felt good after the ominous opening and closing of curtains as Alku kept an eye on them on their return walk to the Korhonens'. It was uncomfortable to be watched so closely in a town that seemed more like a single monolith than hundreds of individual, independent beings, like Alku itself was an immense, torpid beast, the long-necked citizens its eyes and hands.

Evangeline entered the Korhonen house and flicked on the light. The foyer flooded with brightness. "Someone's paying the electric bill."

"Or they're on a hive system."

Evangeline flashed him a look. "How so?"

"They work together," he clarified. "They worship together. A single corporation owns all the property. I wouldn't be surprised to learn there was a communal wiring system connecting the houses, too."

"That's creepy." Evangeline surveyed the entryway. There was a living room to the right, furnished with a plain but sturdy couch and chair plus a bookshelf. Opposite the bookshelf was a standing radio, the design popular in the 1940s. The dining room was straight ahead.

At its center was a table set for five.

"But not as creepy as *that*," Evangeline said, pointing. "A table waiting for the Korhonens? It's straight out of a horror movie. One town, one hive."

Harry shook his head in wonder. The radio looked like it could be flicked on and swing music would stream out. The couch had dimpled spots as if the owners had just stood up to grab a drink and would be right back. "It's a museum."

"Do you think it's stayed like this for twenty-five years?" Evangeline ran her mittened finger along the top of a shelf. "If so, someone's dusting."

"Let's check the refrigerator," Harry said.

"Good idea." Evangeline followed him into the shadowy kitchen, their footsteps echoing across the wood floor. The counters were clear, and the glass-fronted cupboards were empty except for dishes. The refrigerator was turned on but contained only a single orange box of baking soda.

If someone was staying here, they weren't eating here.

Harry pointed toward the doorway they'd just walked through. To its right was another door, presumably leading to the basement. The wall between the two was the perfect location for a telephone, but it was bare. "No phone, no phone jack."

Evangeline nodded. "I didn't spot any cable jacks in the living room, either. No magazines, no TV, just books and that big radio."

Harry felt worry like a cold breath on his neck. They were missing something very big, but for the life of him, he couldn't figure out what it was. "Let's check the second level."

When Harry and Evangeline took the stairs, he couldn't stop himself from glancing behind, his chest tight. It felt like there were still eyes on them, even indoors, but he saw no evidence of a camera.

The main bedroom was to the left of the upstairs landing, the second, smaller bedroom to the right. The gray light of a setting sun turned the shadows liquid. Harry wasn't surprised to find the bed and crib in the primary bedroom were made; same with the two children's beds in the other room. Everything in the Korhonen house was set up as if the family could walk back through the front door at any moment and resume their lives. Evangeline, still wearing her gloves, gently pulled back the patchwork quilt on one of the kids' beds.

"White sheets," Evangeline said. "I almost expected to see twenty-five-year-old blood."

The play of light across the area above the bed caught Harry's eye. The odds of uncollected evidence remaining were so low as to be negligible, but Harry still pulled a latex glove on over his uninjured hand and stroked the wall.

"Check out this stippling," he said.

Evangeline eyeballed it, then walked to the other bed. "It's on this wall, too."

Harry crossed the hall into the main bedroom, Evangeline at his heels, and discovered the stippling surrounded the queen bed as well as the crib. "Birdshot?" he asked.

Evangeline shook her head. "The shooter would have had to be in the room to make some of these angles. Even birdshot would have penetrated the wallpaper at that close range. Besides, buckshot, not birdshot, was used in all five killings. If it had missed a victim and hit the wall, it would have blasted straight through the top layer of plaster, at least."

Harry agreed. "Design element, then?"

Evangeline glanced around. "It's on most of the bedroom walls, but it's concentrated around the beds." She stepped back into the hall. "There's some around the doorways, too. Remind me what the prevailing wisdom is on whether it was their head injuries or the buckshot that killed them."

Harry closed his eyes, visualizing the report as well as the crime scene photos. "Like with Weiss, the head trauma and the gunshots happened so close together as to be impossible to differentiate which was the fatal injury, but with the Korhonens at least, logic suggests they were shot first. It would be difficult to bludgeon five people without waking at least one of them up, and blood evidence points to all five of them dying in their beds. It makes more sense the victims were shot quickly, and then the killer bludgeoned them."

"Why?"

Harry opened his eyes and turned. Evangeline was staring out the second-story window toward a house across the street. "Why what?" he asked.

"Why shoot them and then take something to their heads, or vice versa? That sort of violence suggests it was personal, which might make sense for the parents, but the children? No one hates kids that much."

Harry felt a pressure at the base of his throat as something occurred to him. "We agree Mathias Millard is largely incapacitated?"

"As sure as we can be without a medical exam. His legs were emaciated."

Harry rubbed his knuckles. "What about his arms?"

Evangeline's eyes widened as she realized what he was suggesting. "Someone shot the family so that they couldn't move or fight back while Matty did his thing?"

Harry nodded. "We have to consider all possibilities."

Evangeline screwed up her face. "That would mean that at least one person at the prison is in on it. Someone with a key, someone who can come and go without arousing suspicion. Seems like a long shot. What would be their endgame?"

"I don't know," Harry said.

Evangeline planted her fists on her hips and shook her head so vigorously that her ponytail hit her cheeks. "This town reminds me of my childhood. Not the face of it. The belly."

Harry considered what he'd heard of Frank Roth, the commune leader and Evangeline's assumed father. Before his arrest, Roth was known as "the friendly farmer." His organic jams, jellies, pickles, and homemade bread were sold at farmers' markets and even some Minnesota grocery stores. His smiling face was plastered on every label, his eyes deceptively kind beneath the straw hat. Roth had been good at many things, but he'd *excelled* at marketing. Once he was arrested and the media started digging, they found a different story, one riddled with cruelty and abuse.

Harry was about to ask her if that disconnect between the surface and the reality was what she meant when his phone buzzed.

Evangeline raised her eyebrows. "You have reception?"

"Apparently." He scanned the message, his pulse drumming nicely. "It's Detective Emery. He's back at the Duluth police station. He says they've got something new on the Weiss murder."

"Call him," Evangeline said.

Harry pressed the call option. No reception. He tried a text response. It bounced back immediately. "Whatever connection I had is gone."

"It might be time to head to Duluth," Evangeline said.

Harry wished that weren't true, but he had to face facts: they were guaranteed to be up here for at least three more days. There were too many leads, too many loose ends. Good thing he'd packed enough clothes. They'd get in and out of the Duluth police station and head back to the motel so he could do some more research. The faster they figured out what was up with Alku, the sooner they could leave.

He might get out of here unscathed. Stranger things had happened.

He was still thinking that as they pulled up to the station.

He even hung on to it as they exited the SUV.

That's when he saw his mother.

CHAPTER 22

Myrna Steinbeck was a striking woman. Silver hair cut close, ice-blue eyes, a sharp nose. He could smell her signature perfume—Fracas, the scent of sweet white tuberose and power—from a distance. She held herself straight and still in front of the station doors, waiting for her son to come to her.

Harry had the oddest feeling of being pulled forward and punched back at the same time.

He loved his mother.

He loved her the most when she wasn't around.

After a few moments of hesitation, he approached, unsure as always whether to hug her or shake her hand. He chose the embrace. "Mother."

"Harry." She held herself rigid in his arms.

He was reminded of a disturbing experiment he'd read in a freshman-year psych course. In it, rhesus monkeys were separated from their mothers, isolated with two surrogate contraptions, one made of chicken wire and holding food, the other made of cloth and offering only comfort. The baby monkeys invariably chose the soft "mother." He'd had only the chicken wire option growing up, but he'd gotten lucky, compared to Caroline.

"Why didn't you tell me you were in town?" she asked.

He released her and stepped back. "I'm working." He didn't want to offer details—that should be enough—but he struggled not to fill the silence between them. Thankfully, Evangeline appeared at his side, holding out a mittened hand.

"Hello. I'm Van, Harry's partner at the moment."

Myrna stared down her nose at Evangeline's mitten, then scanned her face. The women were about the same height, both of them strong and poised in their own ways.

"Pleased to meet you," Myrna said, turning back to Harry without offering Evangeline her name or hand. "You'll come over for dinner." It was a command.

He didn't bother asking how she'd heard he was in town. She was well connected and she loved gossip, though she'd deny the latter. She'd probably received a phone call shortly after he'd entered the hospital to witness Weiss's autopsy. It could have been a nurse, a doctor, a janitor. Someone would have let Myrna Steinbeck know that her son was in the area.

And she would have been *enraged* to hear it secondhand.

"They're waiting for us inside the station," Harry said.

Myrna arched one eyebrow. "You have to eat. I'll hold the meal until you arrive."

Apathy settled over him like an iron blanket. This was how it was with Myrna.

"Evangeline," Harry said formally. "Would you like to join me at my mother's house for dinner after we finish up here?"

She was watching him and his mom, her eyes sparkling. "Wouldn't miss it for the world."

Harry nodded. He didn't know what Evangeline was expecting, but he could guarantee she was going to be disappointed. "I'm not sure how long this will take," he told his mother, "but we'll try to be at your house within the hour."

"I'll tell the cook." She seemed ready to say more, but instead, turned on her heel and strode to her car.

"The *cook*?" Evangeline stood at his elbow.

"Her name is Miriam," Harry said. "She's worked for my mother for so long that they're more friends than employer, employee." But that wasn't exactly true. Myrna didn't have friends. She had acquaintances, and she had acolytes. "Shall we talk to Emery?"

CHAPTER 23

The receptionist directed them to Davidson, the square-jawed officer who'd first met them in the emergency room.

"Emery's out on a call," he said from his desk. "Said he'll be back in a couple hours but that I should show you what we found."

Harry was trying to stay focused. Would his mother be rude to Evangeline? She already had been, honestly. But of course that wasn't his real worry. His real worry was that his mother would talk about that day. Haul the ugliness of it into the room but put her own spin on it, a spin made of lies.

"Let's see it, then," he said, his voice short.

Evangeline flashed him a look.

"Not a problem," Davidson replied, nodding genially.

Harry's mind had already wandered. Dinner would be quick. He'd make sure of it. And then he'd ask to be taken off the case. He'd been lying to himself—Myrna's appearance had confirmed that much. He couldn't remain in Duluth, and he was fairly certain that leaving wouldn't hurt the case. He'd visited the CCTC and the Korhonen house. They'd gotten a feel for Alku. Any physical evidence had been gathered and shipped to Saint Paul. The rest of his work he could do in his lab.

Harry wished he were there right now.

Davidson opened a folder on his desk, plucked the eight-by-ten-inch photograph on top, and flipped it so they could examine it. Dead center, enlarged to the length of Harry's hand, was a spent shell casing, a lurid red plastic against the white background.

"Twelve-gauge?" Evangeline asked.

"Yup." Davidson tapped the photo. "The company hired to clean Weiss's apartment found it."

Harry felt his chest tighten. They'd been told there was no physical evidence left at the scene. "How was it overlooked earlier?"

Davidson raised his hands. "Not our fault. It'd been tucked between Weiss's mattress and box spring. Tucked deep. No way it went in there accidentally. It might not even be related to the case, but Emery thought you should know about it."

"Thanks," Harry said. "Can it also be sent to the BCA lab in Saint Paul?"

"Already on its way." Davidson dropped his hands and leaned forward. "But you can't run ballistics on a shotgun shell, can you?"

"We can look for distinctive toolmarks on the casing," Harry said, his brain working as he considered all the angles. "See if it bears resemblance to the shell recovered at the Korhonen murder scene. But without a weapon to compare it against, we aren't likely to find anything conclusive." He thought of the clean metal, the modern machinery, the sharp angles of his lab. "Whoever hid it under the mattress may have left some DNA, though."

"Was this it?" Evangeline asked. "The shell casing is the only new lead?"

Davidson nodded.

As he did, Harry sighed. There was no putting it off any longer. It was time to head to his childhood home.

Harry wanted to give Evangeline an abbreviated version of what to expect on the drive over, but how to prepare someone for the Steinbeck mansion? He'd grown up on the estate, so he hardly noticed the size of it, or the way the forbidding gray of the bricks mirrored the steel of the great lake behind it. The same was true of his mother's larger-than-life personality; he was so familiar with it that he was unsure how it would be perceived by someone from the outside.

He decided to start with Myrna.

"She inherited the estate," he told Evangeline. "Her grandfather—my great-grandfather—was a lawyer who invested in North Shore banks and mines. Both made him very rich. My mother is quite brilliant in her own right. She earned a biology degree. She was considering medical school when she met my father and became pregnant with me. She pivoted to full-time mom. She had my sister, Caroline, when I was just about to turn ten." He rubbed his forehead. "We all loved Caroline."

Evangeline had let Harry drive since he knew where they were going. He realized she was watching him, rapt, as he pulled back the curtain on his childhood.

"Your father?" she asked.

"Was a CFO for a successful aircraft manufacturing company in Duluth. He was a bit old-school in his view of gender roles in a family, but he was a good man and a supportive father. He died a few years past. Heart attack."

"I'm sorry," Evangeline murmured.

Harry followed the curving road along Lake Superior, the ice across the endless body of water reflecting back the moon in a way that felt primitive and ancient. "My mom can be . . . overbearing. She's always been that way. Don't take it personally. Oh, and the estate she lives in is huge."

He stayed quiet until they pulled past the gates.

The ten-bedroom, eight-bathroom mansion stood stoically against the frigid air, its vintage-style lighting casting an eerie shimmer across the massive house and transforming the dark expanse of the lake behind it into a bottomless pit. When Harry turned off the SUV, the crunching of their tires on the driveway gave way to the gentle creaking of branches burdened by heavy snow.

They sat in that soft noise for a few beats.

"Holy shit," Evangeline finally said. "You could give the CCTC a run for its money."

"Hardly," Harry said. "And not me. My mother."

Evangeline slid him a look but said no more. They stepped out of the car, into air scented with pine and woodsmoke. Myrna waited for them at the front door, guided them to the dining room table, and sipped her cordial while Miriam, with her thick glasses and hip-swinging walk, served them a traditional dinner. Harry felt largely numb through the entire meal, was left to wonder if his mother had sensed it the moment he'd crossed the Carlton County line, felt his presence even before he entered the hospital, heard it like a whisper on the wind, and had stocked up on groceries.

Or, rather, had Miriam stock up.

The ham was succulent, the scalloped potatoes creamy, the green bean casserole like a hug from his past, yet it tasted like ash in his mouth. The conversation had been superficial, with Myrna asking both Harry and Evangeline vague questions. It was like being forced to perform in a play about politeness. Harry couldn't wait until it was over.

"Seconds?" Miriam asked as soon as his plate was clean.

"No, thank you," Harry said. She'd been hovering since they'd sat down, her hair now full silver but her eyes as kind as ever. He didn't like that at her age she was still serving, but he also knew from experience it'd do no good to protest. "It was well prepared, but I'm full."

Once the plates were cleared, Myrna shot an arrow into the heart of their trip. "I hear you're out at Alku, digging at the story of that poor family that was murdered the same year Caroline went missing."

If the synchronicity of the dates surprised Evangeline, she gave no sign, just continued to stir her tea.

"That's right." Harry pivoted from the topic of his sister automatically, relieved to discover his mother had invited them over to gather gossip. "What do you remember about the murders?"

Myrna toyed with her napkin. She'd hardly touched her food before Miriam had removed her plate. She'd refilled her cordial glass four times, however. "It was an odd little town well before that. Your father thought he might have relatives there."

Both Harry and Evangeline stiffened. "Excuse me?" Harry said.

She nodded. "He brought you there once when you were a child. On a drive out to Colorado." Her eyes got a faraway look. "His company was thinking of expanding, and your father thought it would be a fun idea to drive out to look at the new site." She adjusted the pearl bracelet at her wrist. "Do I look like someone who enjoys *road trips?*"

"Dad was related to someone at Alku?" Harry asked. His heart was still beating sideways.

Myrna lifted one shoulder, let it drop. "I don't think anything came of it. He said they sent you both on your way, that it was a short visit, a whim, really. He might have a little Finnish in him, and you might, too. So might most of Minnesota, though not like they do in Alku." Her voice suddenly grew melancholy. "You grow old. Your losses accumulate. It happens everywhere, but there's fewer distractions in a small town."

Harry was about to ask her whether she was all right when she held up a hand, as if anticipating his question. "I know Alku is a dying town, that's all I'm saying. Not many children want to live out on the Range anymore, not once they get a taste of the real world. It's happening here in Duluth, too. We're too stodgy for the next generation." Here she shot Harry a glare. "But in Duluth we have the port, at least. Fresh blood every week, for all the trouble it brings. Now tell me how this Weiss killing is connected to that poor murdered family."

She was as sharp as ever. "I didn't say they were linked," Harry said.

"No, you didn't." She smiled. "And there was nothing in today's paper. It was a lucky guess."

"We can't discuss an active investigation," Evangeline said, the comment earning her a side-eye from Myrna. "And in fact, we should be going. We still have work to do tonight. Research, communication."

Harry felt a surge of gratitude. "Thanks for dinner," he told his mother. "You sure we can't help clean up?"

Myrna's eyes grew misty, the sadness back. "Easter was Caroline's favorite holiday. She would have loved this food."

"Mother . . ." Of all Myrna's reactions to Caroline's disappearance, her playing the role of a bereaved mother disturbed Harry the most.

"I know, I know. You don't want to talk about your sister."

Harry's chest twisted. It wasn't that. It truly wasn't.

"Do you think you'll be back to visit before you return to Saint Paul?" she asked.

"No," Harry said truthfully, though it shamed him. "I think we'll be too busy."

Myrna's eyes cleared. "Well, since you can't say no twice, there's this: I've set up a date for you. Just friends, if you like, but she's a lovely woman."

Myrna threw Evangeline a look that suggested Evangeline was the opposite. Harry would apologize for his mother later. At the moment, he was overcome with a coughing fit after he'd swallowed too hard. A *date*? Set up by his *mother*?

"Excuse me," he managed. He got to his feet and made his way to the nearest bathroom, a powder room for guests still decorated in the soft pinks, frilly towels, and seashell soaps his mother had favored in the '80s. Inside, he drank water from the sink to soothe his throat and then washed his face. When he reached for a towel, his arm was exposed, revealing a corner of a puckered scar. He yanked his sleeve down quickly, catching his reflection in the mirror. He had his mother's face.

Funny how he forgot.

When he stepped out, he could hear Myrna and Evangeline talking down the hall. He couldn't imagine what they could be conversing about. He meant to go straight back to rescue Evangeline, but he found his feet taking him in the opposite direction, up the stairs, and suddenly, he was standing outside Caroline's room.

He hadn't been inside it since the day she disappeared.

He was reaching for the knob when the memory cut through his skull.

Harry had gotten so busy helping his mother track down the crostini that he was running late for the party. But that was a nerd thought. College freshmen shouldn't care what time a party started. Besides, Harry had absolutely no claim on Jennyfer's time or attention. But he didn't want to think about that. He just wanted to see her. Would her hair be the same? Would she be dressing edgier now that she'd escaped Duluth? Did she still smell like cinnamon apples?

These were the thoughts in his head as he raced out the front door, car keys in hand. That's when he realized he hadn't said goodbye to Caroline. He'd see her in the morning before he returned to college to finish up the quarter, but Caroline missed him—he knew it from the letters she wrote. Their mother was a handful in the best of times, but her personality had apparently ramped up since Harry left.

On an impulse, he hurried to Caroline's room.

Stood outside her door, hand on the knob.

Had the wild, ridiculous thought that he wanted to put her in the car and drive her away, like the day he'd ferried her to the carnival to escape Myrna's constant criticism, but this time, they'd drive and drive and never come back . . .

"Harry?" his mother called out.

He ran his hands over his face, the past crashing into the present. He wasn't nineteen, his hair slicked back with gel, neck sprayed with Armani's Acqua Di Gio Pour Homme, his body hot for Jennyfer

Baldwin. Caroline wasn't behind the door listening to TLC and layering on lip liner and glitter eye shadow.

It was the house, the time of year, the smells of Easter cooking.

The absence of his sister echoed all around him.

"Be right there," he called back. He felt feverish.

He returned to Evangeline and his mother without ever opening his sister's bedroom door.

CHAPTER 24

That night, in the bathroom of his smoke-scented Pine View Lodge room, Harry washed his hands and face, keeping his toiletries stored inside his leather travel kit so they didn't touch the shelf. He'd brushed his teeth and donned his Ralph Lauren silk pajama set. He was tired, exhausted really, yet rather than go to sleep, he sat on the corner of his bed.

Studied the lighter on the scarred bedside table.

Evangeline had called Superintendent Chandler on the drive back from Myrna's. Given what they'd so far discovered, Chandler officially reopened the Korhonen cold case and told Evangeline it was theirs if they wanted it. Duluth PD would take lead on Weiss's murder, and there'd be transparent communication between the two agencies.

Myrna would be thrilled to have him so close. No, that wasn't exactly right. She'd feel *smug* having him so close. Purposeful. All the while, the memory of Caroline would haunt him, begging for justice.

Evangeline would find out. She would discover who he really was.

He stared at the lighter. He could release the pain. Add another scar to his body.

The sudden blare of a true crime podcast in the next room startled him.

"Sorry!" Evangeline called through the wafer-thin walls.

It was enough, barely. A reminder that he wasn't alone, not tonight, not really. Harry felt a pain in his chest as he slipped the lighter in the drawer, disappointed he'd come so close. He needed to take better care of himself. He stood, grabbing a towel from the bathroom. He laid it on the crusty carpeting and sat cross-legged on it, beginning with a meditation. Tuning out the heater's phlegmy cough, the occasional hum of traffic, he imagined the sweet thump of his pulse. He breathed in through his nose, paused for three, out through his mouth. In through his nose, paused for three, out through his mouth.

Once he was completely present, he stood and practiced *dan tian* breathing, which began with a traditional smile from the heart. It had taken him four years to master this simple and transformative state of mind. He felt himself immediately shedding tension. He then moved to Lifting the Sky, gliding through the motions until he was able to stop counting. At some point, he locked into himself.

He remembered that he didn't need to find the answers, he only had to find his way back to *here*.

To himself.

And he was saved, for one more day.

CHAPTER 25

"Your mom's intense," Evangeline said over breakfast. She was tucking into the Hungry Trucker—three eggs, four slices of bacon, two pieces of toast dripping with butter-colored oil, and hash browns that glistened. She didn't eat frequently, but when she did, she—as she said—"cameled it."

"You don't say," Harry said, spreading the cashew butter he'd brought on dry wheat toast.

"I *do* say." Evangeline dipped a corner of her bread into a bright-orange yolk. "I didn't bring it up last night because you seemed shook, but I figured I'd open the door if you wanted to talk about it."

"I don't." Harry bit into his cold toast.

She shrugged. "Suit yourself. If my mom was a controlling tyrant who wandered around a big ol' mansion with only occasional help and with *toys* in the corner, though, I'd want to talk it through with someone."

"Toys?" Harry set down his toast. It was all he could do not to drop it.

"You didn't see 'em? I only did because I got lost on my way back from the bathroom. There's a whole second living room full of jump ropes and board games and even those little bouncy chairs you hook to the ceiling. Your mom running a day care?"

"Not sure." *Myrna shouldn't be around children.* "We don't talk much."

She snorted. "You don't say."

Harry didn't take the bait. He was too busy trying to make sense of this new information. "She's probably gathering items for a charity drive. She enjoys things like that."

Evangeline began scrolling through her phone, apparently already bored with the conversation. "No reception, obvs. We're still on for talking to Emery before deciding next steps?"

"We are."

After eating and paying for the surprisingly cheap breakfast, they took off, Evangeline behind the wheel. The view coming into Duluth had always captivated Harry. You'd come over a hill, and suddenly it was there, the port city laid out below like a tiny harbor painting done in black and white. As you dropped down, Duluth proper emerged to the left, looking like a city built with a child's wooden blocks, cylinders and triangles and squares stacked high. To the right, the silver and steel of industry sprouted like metal monsters on Lake Superior's vast shores. He couldn't look at the beautiful, treacherous lake and not think about the hundreds of shipwrecks that lay at her bottom.

"Looks like the sun is coming out," Evangeline said.

Harry was surprised by a surge of warmth toward her. Their personalities were orange juice and toothpaste, yet there was something *true* about her. Something *pure*. It was her intelligence, her commitment to a case, certainly, but there was something else. She'd had a hard life, a childhood steeped in trauma, but rather than come out the other side bitter and wanting to punch down, she'd committed to protecting others.

As much as she regularly annoyed him, Harry was lucky to know her.

He glanced up at the slate-colored sky, noting the lighter patch where the sun should be. He didn't want to tell her about lake-effect weather, how Lake Superior made Duluth its own unpredictable ecosystem, how there would be no pure sunshine today.

Instead, he said, "Sun would be nice."

When they parked in the PD lot and approached the building, she held the door open for him. "After you, partner of Evangeline." She made a sweeping arm gesture and a slight bow, an impish grin curving her mouth.

He walked through, not minding the role reversal. It was not respecting a woman that made him uncomfortable. If she wanted to hold the door for him, more power to her.

They located Emery in his office, his sideburns freshly trimmed. The pallor and sag of his face suggested he'd pulled an all-nighter, but his expression brightened marginally when he spotted Evangeline. "Don't you look like a breath of fresh air."

Harry was surprised by a fire in his belly. Evangeline was an attractive woman. He shouldn't be caught off guard when other people noticed. Yet his voice sounded sharp when he said, "We stopped by last night."

"Davidson told me." Emery pulled at his nose. "He also said he passed on all the new info."

Evangeline dropped into one of the two chairs across from the detective. "What's your best guess on how that casing got between the mattresses?"

Harry considered correcting her—it was a mattress and a box spring, not two mattresses—and then realized it was an example of what Evangeline would call "fussy," something he was trying to move away from. If nothing else, this trip to Duluth was making him consider he might be a hair over-reliant on his need for precision. He held his tongue and took the other seat.

"No clue." Emery squeaked his chair back and laced his fingers behind his head, grinning at Evangeline. "Thought you big-city detectives might have some insights."

Evangeline glanced to Harry, offering him lead.

"We visited the CCTC yesterday, met Mr. Millard, and walked the fence line," Harry said. "We concur with your assessment that Millard is unlikely to be involved in Weiss's murder."

"You *concur* with my *assessment*?" Emery shot Evangeline a look, inviting her to join in on the ribbing. Her expression remained stony. Emery frowned and returned his attention to Harry. "Well, thanks for *concurring*. That means we've dead-ended."

"There's something off with the town," Evangeline said firmly.

"Off how?" Emery asked.

Evangeline and Harry had talked about this at great length. They had no facts, only gut feelings. Harry believed the latter without the former was not worth mentioning. Evangeline disagreed.

"The people there behave like they're hiding something," she said.

Emery shook his head dismissively. "Finns, I tell you. They're a secretive people. Alku is wholesome, trust me. Just a little more insulated than most." He paused, measuring his next words. "What do you know about violence tourists?"

Harry had to stop himself from making a scoffing noise.

"Excuse me?" Evangeline asked.

"People paying to be involved in violence. With both the Korhonen and Weiss murders, the victims were shot and then bludgeoned. What if they were shot to immobilize them, and then the tourists come in and do the smashing? Use their big money to fulfill some effed-up fantasy."

Evangeline snorted. "I think that's gold-plated bullshit and that you should get off the dark web."

Harry agreed wholeheartedly with the message if not the delivery. Violence tourism was not a reality in the United States, despite what some conspiracy theorists believed. He was disappointed in Emery for suggesting it. A detective should know better.

"We also haven't confirmed the sequence of the violence in the Korhonen case or the Weiss case," Harry said. "If my lab discovers anything definitive, we'll pass it on, but until then, it seems more likely both cases are connected by something more mundane."

Emery shrugged. "No bad ideas in brainstorming."

"There really are," Evangeline said dryly.

Harry tensed, but Emery just laughed. "I like your energy, Van. No punches pulled. So, I have no new info for you, and you have none for me. Makes me wonder what exactly I can do for the two of you today."

"The BCA has decided to take the cold case," Evangeline said.

Emery brought his hands flat onto his desk. "Glad to hear it."

"While we're here, we'd like to look at the original Korhonen case files, anything that hasn't been digitized," Harry said. "Plus, anything you have on the hikers killed in the '80s."

Emery's forehead creased. "What's that now?"

"We heard two people were mauled by an animal near the CCTC back in the '80s," Evangeline said. "Pekka Tervo confirmed."

"Before my time." Emery appeared genuinely troubled. "It was an animal attack, you say?"

"That's what we were told," Harry said.

"If it was an accident, and if it was that long ago, we likely won't have any information on it. The records get purged of nonessential information every couple decades. But I'll see what I can dig up. In the meanwhile, let me get you what we have in-house on the Korhonens." He punched a button on his phone, requesting an assistant to walk them to the records room.

It took until they were led out for Harry to name Emery's expression when he'd heard about the hikers being mauled.

He'd been worried.

CHAPTER 26

"One box?" Evangeline asked when Emery's assistant brought it to them in the shabby interrogation room they'd been assigned.

"Yep." The assistant was in her twenties, long earrings in the shape of cherries swinging as she nodded. "One box."

"Thanks." Evangeline waited until the woman left. She turned to Harry. "How about you look through it while I do some research on my phone."

Harry removed the box's top. He was relieved to see only paper and photographs inside, no physical evidence that would have rapidly deteriorated in an uncontrolled climate. Since Emery's comment about violence tourism, he'd been worried about the department's standards.

"What kind of research?"

"I want to check out the conspiracy sites," she said, already staring at her screen. "Emery's comment earlier gave me an idea."

Harry blinked. "You *can't* be serious."

"Oh, but I can be," she said, scrolling. "But I'm not looking for anything banana pants, like rich folks paying to hammer people's heads in. I want to dig deeper into the original founding of this town, find stuff outside the mainstream. Reddit might offer me some insight."

Harry truly couldn't tell whether she was pulling his leg, but he trusted her to manage her own time. He dug into the box, skimming each document before placing it into one of three piles: notes, photographs, and miscellaneous. He hoped it had all been digitized, but he'd need to check against the BCA system files.

"Hold up, now," Evangeline said, skimming her phone. "There's a professor of folklore studies at the University of Helsinki who's written a whole article about the Alkuans, as he calls them."

"It's like Christmas in April," Harry said dryly. He'd only half heard her. He was texting Deepty to find out if she'd tracked down the Korhonen scene shell casing. He hadn't come across even a single photo of it in the box. He also let her know he wanted her to prioritize running the shell cap that was being delivered by the Duluth PD.

"Not Christmas," Evangeline said. "The article is behind a paywall. I'm going to email the guy directly."

"Good plan," Harry said.

Deepty responded immediately. She'd discovered the Korhonen casing exactly where it was supposed to be, and she'd jump on the Weiss casing as soon as it arrived.

He missed professional procedures, crisp communication, and good Wi-Fi. He returned reluctantly to the Bankers Box. He was squinting at a handwritten note on the side of the initial ballistics report when the door to the interrogation room opened and a woman peeked in.

He recognized her immediately.

"Harry?" she said, smiling. "Myrna told me I'd find you here. Time for our date!"

CHAPTER 27

"I couldn't believe when Myrna called to say you're back."

He hadn't seen Louise—or Lou, as she now liked to be called—in more than twenty years. Her unruly strawberry-blonde curls had been tamed in a neat, professional bob, her smile lines were permanent creases in her face, and the oversize heavy-metal T-shirts and black leggings she'd worn all through the '90s had been replaced by a checkered pantsuit, but her dimples and dancing eyes were the same. Their parents had been friendly back in the day, playing cards together in the winter. The adults would drink and deal, and Lou and Harry would hang out.

They now sat in Pickwick Pub, the hundred-plus-year-old restaurant with a million-dollar view of Lake Superior. The interior was dark wood and leather. Harry hadn't stepped foot inside since high school. Back then, it'd been his parents' favorite restaurant. It felt oddly welcoming to return.

"I'm not in town for long," Harry said. The lunch menu was as he remembered. Dinner club fare—Cobb and spinach salads, burgers and sandwiches. "Do you know if the Manhattan clam chowder is still the best?"

"To die for," Lou confirmed. "Same with the onion rings. Want to split an order?"

"I don't eat fried food."

Lou smiled. "No, you wouldn't, would you? You were so . . . *healthy*, even in high school."

That startled him. He'd always thought of his need for structure as a response to what happened to Caroline. Had it started before then?

She put her menu down. "It's good to see you, Harry."

"You too." He meant it. They used to be close. "You made it to law school?"

"I did. Brought that law degree back here. I work for the city, in fact. The plan was to stay as long as my parents needed me. They passed a few years ago." She shrugged. "I found I didn't want to leave."

"I'm sorry. I should have checked in with you."

"And I'm sorry I missed your dad's funeral. I was in Europe." She grabbed his hand. "But can we skip the rest of the apologies? How are you doing?"

He considered sidestepping the question. "Been better."

"Figured." She glanced out at the lake, the wind creating dramatic frost heaves, glorious blue ice shards poised seven feet high. "Especially this month."

"You remember?"

She sighed. Released his hand. "Of course I do. It's the only time of year your mom shows up to church, but that's not why. None of us will ever forget." She looked back at him. "There's been no news? No sightings? No breaks in the case?"

Harry shook his head once, sharply. "You know Myrna thinks we're on a date."

She chuckled. "I do. She's met my wife several times. Refers to her as 'my friend.'"

Harry grimaced. "I'm not surprised. And I'm sorry."

"Not your fault. I know how Myrna's always been. Frankly, I was surprised when she started fostering."

Harry had been about to take a sip of water. The glass dropped with a thunk, water sloshing over the edges. "What?"

Lou nodded, handing him her cloth napkin. "She became a licensed foster parent last year, maybe the year before? She's got enough room in that place. I figured maybe she was just lonely. In any case, it's a great service. The county is overloaded."

He dabbed at the spilled water. "I had no idea." That explained the toys Evangeline had seen. Should he call social services? Report the way that his mother used to be?

Lou studied him with compassion, misreading his silence. "No one blames you for leaving, Harry. If it were me, I might never come back. Speaking of, tell me about the case that brought you up here. Fill me in on Evangeline, too. She really would have been welcome to join us."

Evangeline had insisted Harry go out for lunch without her, promising she'd finish cataloging the file box and then catch a ride to the motel from one of the officers. He'd been grateful. It had been strange enough, her meeting his mother. Worlds colliding and all that.

He filled Lou in on their partnership, such as it was. As he talked, he tried to imagine his mother fostering other people's children. It simply did not fit in his brain.

"And the case?" Lou asked.

He shared only as much information about the Weiss murder as had appeared in the papers.

"I read that he worked at the Alku prison." Lou's eyes narrowed. "Lots of bad luck coming out of that town."

Lydia, the waitress at the diner, as well as Rannie had said something similar. "You're familiar with Alku?"

"Our school went on a field trip there, to the town plus their school in the woods. Remember?"

Harry startled. He did not remember, just like he hadn't recalled his father taking him there. "When was it?"

She chuckled. "Don't look so worried. We were kids. Late '80s, I think."

It would explain why the CCTC had appeared familiar to him when he and Evangeline had first pulled up. He was unsettled by his lack of specifics, though. The town felt like such a presence. How could he have erased two childhood memories of having visited?

"They handed out salted black licorice," Lou continued, gently nudging his memory. "You loved it. Everyone else thought it tasted like feet."

Harry closed his eyes. Something was emerging from the fog. "I think I do recall that. Everyone gave me theirs on the bus ride back." Was there more detail he could tease out?

"That's right," Lou said, beaming. "The nuns had it drilled into our heads that we had to be polite, so we all pretended to like it so much we wanted to save it for later. You were the only one telling the truth." She chuckled. "That whole town was an experience. There's Finnish, and then there's *Finnish*. It's like they were lost in time. Their governance has an interesting structure, too, if I remember correctly. Unincorporated, run by a board made up of the descendants of the original settlers."

"That's right," Harry said, glad to be back on solid footing. His mother may have done him a favor by connecting him with Lou, and not only because he was glad to see an old friend. "Any idea how that works in terms of the day-to-day town functions?"

She tapped her chin. "I'd have to look into it, but my best guess is that they have bylaws, maybe the original ones from when the town was founded, organizing things like what can be built and where."

"Would that information be on the public record?"

"Not necessarily. It's not a requirement in Minnesota. A bank would have the bylaws on file if the folks of Alku ever borrowed money as a corporation, but I don't think they've used a bank. They have a reputation of being really tight with their secrets *and* their money. I can ask around if you'd like, see what other info is available."

"I'd appreciate that." Harry smiled for the first time since he'd seen Lou.

"There it is," she says.

"What?"

"The famous Harry Steinbeck grin, breaking hearts for four decades. I thought it might be gone for good." Her mouth quirked. "It's nice you're home, Harry. I hope you stay for a while. Put some ghosts to rest."

CHAPTER 28

Put some ghosts to rest.

Harry didn't think that was possible. Besides, it wasn't a ghost.

It was his sister.

Which explained why he found himself in front of the Elizabeth Ann Seton Academy, the private Catholic school that he and Lou had graduated from.

The school Caroline *should* have graduated from.

The building was foreboding. He hadn't noticed the Gothic heaviness of the North Shore when he'd lived here, but now that Evangeline had pointed it out, he saw it everywhere: his childhood home and the mansions flanking it, his school, buildings like the CCTC dropped onto the prairie, their heavy stone shoulders leaning into the wind and the ice.

It felt like sleepwalking to open the academy's front door and stroll down the empty hallways. The high school scents of acrylic paints, cafeteria lunches, and cheap cologne carried him back. He thought of gray matter and stored memories, portals to his past flying open as the familiar odors pressed on his amygdala like a doorbell. He imagined he heard whispers, giggles hidden behind hands, but when he looked, no one was there, only the sound of his shoes tapping against the laminate flooring.

It had been foolish to come here, foolish bordering on inappropriate. He was turning to leave when the office door opened.

"I'm afraid we're closed for the holiday break," a nun said.

She was twenty-five years older than the last time he'd seen her, but the wimple encased a face he knew well. "Sister Catherine."

She stepped into the hallway, her gentle face folded with confusion. Suddenly, it cleared. "Harold Steinbeck!"

She held out her arms, and he went to her. Ivory soap and frankincense, the scent every Elizabeth Ann Seton kid smelled firsthand at the most difficult moments of their teen years. If there was a better smell, Harry didn't know it. He held himself still while she patted his back. He tried not to think how much she'd shrunk or how brittle she felt. Sister Catherine had been his guidance counselor. She loved all the kids, but she told him she loved him the best. That's what she told every student at Elizabeth Ann; her magic was that they all believed it.

She leaned back, her hands remaining on his arms. "What are you doing here?"

"I was in town."

She smiled and nodded, waiting patiently for the rest.

"I had lunch with Louise Devon, and we started talking about school, and about Caroline, and . . ." He shrugged, his eyes growing hot. "I came here."

Her forehead furrowed. "Come into my office, won't you, Harold? I have a kettle on."

As a child and then a teen, Harry had thought Sister Catherine's Earl Grey tea tasted like perfume. He hadn't developed a taste for it in the intervening years, but he was glad for its warmth as he contentedly listened to her talk about her students and the school over the years and then caught her up on his life of the last two and a half decades.

"And right now?" Sister Catherine smiled. "What are you doing in Duluth this very moment?"

He didn't want to bring the violence of his work into the peace of the school. "I'm here with my partner investigating a crime possibly connected to Alku."

Her mouth tightened. She rested her mug on her desk so she could clasp her cross. "The Korhonen family."

"You remember them?"

She nodded. "I didn't know them personally, but a crime of that nature sticks with a community, particularly when it involves children."

"Lou mentioned over lunch that we used to take field trips out to Alku."

Sister Catherine's smile returned, though it was tinged with melancholy. "We did. They were so kind to let us in. We learned about their religion, a delightful mix of old-country beliefs and Lutheranism. They allowed us into their school and their kitchens as well, to see how they made their traditional foods. It was like a village frozen in time." She reached for her tea and took a sip. "They requested we stop visiting after the Korhonen tragedy, and could you blame them? They were such a tight-knit community. It must have shattered them."

He wouldn't have brought it up, but since they were on the subject: "I also heard two hikers were killed in or near Alku in the '80s. It would have been around the same time my class visited the town. Do you remember that?"

"You *heard*?" she asked in a chiding tone he recognized. "I've *heard* no such thing."

Her favorite saying had been *gossip dies when it hits a wise person's ear*. She was the one who'd instilled in him the importance of never listening to hearsay. He thought of Evangeline once telling him she got her best information from gossip. What would she and Sister Catherine make of each other?

"You're smiling," Sister Catherine said.

"Just thinking of a friend of mine. My partner, actually."

She nodded, waited, and when he didn't offer any more, returned the conversation to its path. "I know nothing of two hikers being killed." Her cheeks sagged. "I'm sorry to hear you've never married, Harold, or had children. I always thought you'd make an excellent father."

"Well." He felt a corner of his heart break off. He'd had the same thought, but it landed differently coming from Sister Catherine. He began to put on the coat he'd set across his lap. "I appreciate your time. It's been wonderful to see you."

Her chuckle was warm. "Hint taken." She stood and walked around the desk and took his hands. Hers were dry, bird-light. "May I say a prayer for you?"

"I'd be honored." Harry hadn't attended church since Caroline disappeared, but he recognized Sister Catherine's offer for the love that it was.

They bowed their heads. After a few moments, she squeezed his hands. He looked into her eyes, brown and beautifully wrinkled at the corners. He was surprised to see unfathomable sorrow.

"The dead don't want us to mourn, Harry." She squeezed his hands again. "They don't want for anything; they're with God."

His heart bucked as he imagined the relief of confession. He could tell her about his sister right now, reveal the awful truth of that last day. Maybe even confess what he'd done to his body since to blot out the self-loathing. But her eyes were so trusting, so loving. He couldn't bring himself to say the words.

"Don't you see?" she continued. "We shouldn't do *anything* for the dead. We have only one job on this earth, and it has to do with the living: we must love those put in our path as hard as we can, every day."

Harry didn't want her to say more. He didn't know if he could bear the guilt of hearing it. "I should go."

She nodded, but she wouldn't release his hands. Instead, she tried to pull him closer. "I worry about the children of Alku. Don't you?"

The subject change caught him off guard. "What makes you worry, Sister?"

She stared at a faraway spot. "They looked so scared when we visited that last year. The same year Caroline disappeared, the same year the Korhonens were murdered." She frowned, shook her head. "Such a terrible time. I remember thinking that I wished I could take all those

Alku children with me." She patted her own cheek as if to wake herself up. "But that was twenty-five years ago. They'd be all grown up now. No longer afraid."

Harry thought of the Alku adults he'd met so far.

Pekka, Pihla, Rannie, and Hannele, wife of Torben.

Not unafraid. Rather, bent to the shape of their fear.

He stood and kissed the top of her wimple. "Thank you, Sister," he said firmly. "I need to get back to work."

She finally released his hands and grabbed her opposite elbows. "Say hello to your mother for me."

He wouldn't tell her a lie, and it would disappoint her to hear he'd never share with Myrna that he'd visited the school, so he just smiled.

The sun was shining when he exited the academy, causing rivulets of melting snow to pour across the sidewalks. Evangeline had been right about the weather, damn the lake effect. He inhaled deeply. There was no air so fresh in all the world as the wind straight off Lake Superior. He hopped into the SUV and cracked the window.

He thought about Alku's children as he drove back to the motel. Had Max and Honeybee, Fred and Arlie, seemed afraid? He was digging through his memory for the details and realized they absolutely had been. It was in their furtive glances, their bowed shoulders, an air of desperation that no child should carry.

The realization caused a heat to build in his chest. It took him a moment to recognize the feeling.

Conviction.

He could run back to Saint Paul. He wanted to, desperately. But he would not.

He'd stay and help Evangeline investigate as best he could.

For the children.

He had no illusion that remaining in Duluth and solving the case—if such a thing were possible—would erase the pain of his sister's disappearance, or his terrible guilt.

It was his job. That was all. No more, no less.

Weiss's murder suggested they were dealing with an active threat, and his brief time with Sister Catherine had reminded him who he was. He wouldn't leave until he was certain Alku was safe.

There was an uneasy relief in deciding not to run.

There might even be some positives to his time back in his old stomping grounds. He was making a plan to introduce Evangeline to his favorite local restaurant—a little two-table deli in the DeWitt-Seitz Marketplace with the best smoked salmon in the Midwest—when her number appeared on his phone perched on the dashboard holder.

He ordered his cell to accept the call. "Sorry I've kept you waiting," he began. "I—"

"There's something new."

Her tone made him sit up straight. "What is it?"

"I just got off the phone with Kyle. He confirmed that two hikers *were* found dead near the CCTC. Right outside the school, in fact. And they didn't die in the '80s. They were found in 1998."

Needles pricked Harry's spine.

"On November 2, 1998, specifically," Evangeline said. "Five days before the Korhonen murder."

"Holy hell."

"Yeah," Evangeline said. "But that's not everything. Kyle also discovered a missing person from Alku. Someone who disappeared that same week that the hikers and then the Korhonen family died. It was a regular trauma bonanza in the town."

The road hummed beneath the tires, the muddy steel of Duluth flashing by Harry's windows. He didn't know whether he was holding his breath or had forgotten how to breathe. "Who disappeared?"

"Ansa Tervo. Pekka and Rannie's mother."

CHAPTER 29

Rannie
November 1, 1998

"Children who don't follow the rules disappear. The blood witch gets them."

Rannie whirled from the window, hiding the slick-paged catalog behind his back. His heart beat ferociously. Ansa stood in his bedroom doorway. He didn't want her to know that a woman had knocked on the Tervo door, selling makeup. The woman had lips the color of berries and had asked Rannie if his wife was home, but then her face flushed, and she asked if instead his mother was home.

He'd shaken his head. She'd offered him the glossy catalog, still blushing. Asked him to pass it on.

He'd smelled it first, after she left. It was powdery and sweet. The pages themselves felt soft as rabbit fur. And the pictures inside? He couldn't stop staring at them. All the women had pretty colors painted on their eyelids, butterfly colors, and they wore bright clothes. It made his heart dance to see them, but his mother would be angry—no, she'd be *furious*—if she knew he'd accepted the catalog.

"I'm not a child," he told Ansa, clutching the magazine away from her view. "I'm a man."

A man with a plan to hide a catalog, if he can.

His mother scowled. The rank smell of alcohol poured off her, floating across his bedroom like skunk stink. She drank all the time now. It made her eyes blurry and swelled her belly. "I didn't mean *you*. But a child is a child, no matter their age. You should know you're never too old for a reaping. Never."

Finish your vegetables or the veri noita will get you in the next reaping. All the naughty children will disappear. Words she'd said to him as a child, but totally out of place now. His mother was forgetting which timeline she was living in. It hurt Rannie. He wished he knew how to help her, but for the first time in his life, she didn't want him around. It made the house lonely. Pekka had married and moved out. His dad was at work more than he was home. Rannie thought Nils was trying to avoid Ansa. That left her here with Rannie all day.

"Don't look at me like that." Ansa swayed.

Rannie dropped his eyes. "Yes, ma'am."

She coughed, the sound like wet paper ripping. "You're a good boy."

Her voice had softened. Rannie risked a peek. She was staring at him, her head rolling on her neck like a snake hypnotizing its prey. "Such a good son." Her voice trailed off. "One day bleeds into the next, you know. Then you wake up and all of a sudden, you're old. What do you have then but family? What meaning does your life carry if your people aren't safe?"

Her eyes suddenly cleared and she stood ramrod straight. She almost looked like herself again. "You should go out for Kekri," she said firmly.

Rannie bellowed with joy. She'd *never* let him play with the other kids during the remembrance of the dead celebration. She only allowed him to walk to the edge of the yard with his dad the night before to welcome the spirits, as was traditional. But the second day, when the people of Alku donned their masks, which were otherwise only allowed in the Sacred Spot? Ansa had made Rannie stay home for that his whole life. Said it was too dangerous, told him he'd become too agitated going door-to-door in a mask and demanding hospitality, threatening to destroy their ovens if the request wasn't honored.

Your oven will break and I'll make you ache unless you give me cake!

Kekri had always sounded like the best big fun to Rannie, and he'd only ever been able to watch it from the front window.

Was he being allowed because he was twenty-two now? Was that the magic number?

Didn't matter. He'd better hurry before she changed her mind. He ran over to kiss her cheek. He was too excited to hide the catalog, but she didn't seem to notice it.

"That's my little kekripukki," she said, patting his arm. It'd been many years since she could reach the top of his head. "Will you honor me when I'm dead?"

Rannie had been turning away, but that stopped him cold.

She saw his face and laughed darkly. "Don't worry, kekripukki. Your mother is going to live forever."

Her tone scared him. It sounded like a threat rather than a happy thing. But she'd been so sick-looking lately. She was probably teasing because she didn't want him to worry.

"I'm going to wear the goat mask," he said.

"What else would you wear? Be sure to watch yourself, now."

He did. He watched himself real good. When he started to get too excited, his voice too loud, he removed his mask. That cooled him right down. Everyone at the houses they'd visited had been so nice to him and the kids he was with, too. They gave them enough treats that they could eat until their stomachs were ready to pop. All that was left to do was burn the giant straw goat in front of the church. His mom was the one who lit it, traditionally. He was proud of that. He wanted to walk to the church with her, so he hurried home.

His father's face when he entered the house was his first clue that something was terribly wrong.

The second was that Pekka was there. He should have been with his wife.

"I ate salted licorice!" Rannie said. He knew that wasn't the right thing to say, not exactly, but the two men in the living room were making him uneasy.

Pekka had been talking to his dad, his back to Rannie and his voice a stitched whisper, but he turned when Rannie hollered. "That's really great, buddy. Was it good?"

Rannie knew that tone. He was being humored. It usually bothered him, but right now, he wanted more of it. Anything to keep his dad from telling him why he looked like he was trying not to scream.

"It's time to burn the goat man," Rannie said. "Where's Mom?"

Nils strode forward and punched a hole in the nearest wall, creating a boom and cloud of dust.

Rannie felt skin-slapping fear.

Pekka jumped at the noise, then adjusted his round glasses. "Mom's gone, Rannie."

Rannie stared around the room like he could see her. "Gone where?"

"It doesn't matter," his dad said, still facing the wall. Had he gotten his hand stuck? He sounded funny, like when Rannie sang underwater in the bathtub. "She's not coming back."

Rannie tried to smile. He was used to being the slow one, but now his dad and Pekka were being slow. Mom wouldn't leave *forever*. In fact, just a few hours earlier she'd told him that she was always going to be here. "She has to light the goat man."

Nils spun on him. "She's gone. You'll never see her again." But then his anger drained out. He was shrinking right in front of Rannie's eyes. "Gone forever," he mumbled, shuffling toward the stairs.

Rannie turned to Pekka. His brother had always been so patient. He was a good explainer. "I want to see Mom," Rannie whined.

Pekka shook his head sadly. "You can't, buddy. I'm so, so sorry."

Rannie stared at the hole his father had made. He could hear his dad weeping from upstairs.

"I don't want to stay here without Mom," he said.

Pekka's face relaxed, like someone had lifted a load off his neck. "You pack a suitcase, Rannie. Pihla and I would be happy to have you."

CHAPTER 30

The next morning, Evangeline drove them northwest from the Pine View Lodge to the CCTC. They were on their way to ask Pekka about his missing mother and for more details about the ill-fated hikers. Those two events happening the same week the Korhonen family was murdered was unlikely to be coincidence.

Harry and Evangeline were also hoping for a tour of the rest of the school. They didn't have a search warrant or a reason to request one, but a case followed the new information that turned up, and those hikers had been murdered near the building. Examining the area simply made sense. If their request to poke around was denied, that would provide its own kind of intelligence.

The a.m. sun had melted the surface of the snowdrifts alongside the road, frosting them in a sugar glaze. Harry thought it would make the most satisfying noise to break the surface. Caroline had loved those kinds of sounds—the delicate crunch of lace ice across puddles, the *click-clack* of river rocks underwater, the glitter-snap of biting into freshly made honeycomb toffee.

"I had another nightmare last night," Evangeline said.

Although his stomach tightened—*it wasn't about me, can't have been about me*—he managed to remain focused on the confection of the landscape. When they'd retired to their adjoining rooms early last night, he assumed they both worked. He'd slept well thanks to the bedtime qigong routine, but this morning it became clear that Evangeline hadn't, yet again. Her hair and eyes lacked their usual gloss, and her face appeared swollen. Now that she was finally sharing why, he didn't want to scare her with too much attention.

He made a burr of encouragement in the back of his throat. "That prison cell again?"

"Yeah." She turned on the radio. Country twang poured out. She jabbed a button, and the music was replaced with a tirade against "illegals." She turned off the radio. "That same man, sitting on a bed in a cell, his back to me. Pure evil pouring off him. It looked like those stink lines in cartoons."

She certainly painted an image. "And the cell looked like the double-locked one at the CCTC?"

She was quiet for so long that he almost turned to her. Finally: "Yeah."

He opened his mouth. Closed it. "Are your nightmares visions?"

There it was. As plain as he could say it. A charge flickered between them, and she grew as still as a painting. Harry realized he was holding himself still, too. He'd wanted to ask her in Costa Rica if her nightmares were visions, but it had felt so foolish. He'd considered it again on the Taken Ones case, when she shared details she had no human right to know, but it still had seemed like a ludicrous question.

Here, on the uncertain terrain of the Northwoods, where people talked of blood witches and mashed skulls, and his own ghosts were so near? He couldn't stop himself from asking, as much as he feared the answer.

Yes, and I see you in them. I see what happened with your sister.

"Shit!" She jerked on the steering wheel, barely avoiding running over a white animal. Rabbit? Weasel? The swerve reached their back tires, and she had to steer deep into a fishtail to stay on the road. She tapped the brakes as she jerked the wheel right and left, right and left, gradually bringing the SUV to a stop on the side of the road. Her chest was rising and falling. Harry's too.

After a few beats, she looked at him, her expression distilled agony. "I don't know if they're visions," she said.

His mouth went dry.

He could see she was lying.

He nodded stiffly and straightened his shirtsleeves at the wrist. He was in no position to judge her for choosing which secrets to keep, if judging were his style. "We'll ask to look inside that cell next time we're at the prison." His voice sounded like someone else's. "Ask somebody with more authority than Silas Smith."

Evangeline glanced down, her head bobbing rapidly, and then eased the vehicle back onto the road.

Harry felt a powerful urge to embrace her, or to run, run as fast and far as he could, not stopping until he reached Saint Paul. Instead, he turned toward the endless prairie frosted with dirty snow. What a desolate, unwelcoming land to immigrate to. He'd never visited Finland. Maybe the two were comparable, and this bleakness had felt familiar to the original seven families. But what had driven them, with their medical training, to leave their homeland in the midst of a pandemic? He recalled Evangeline's comment about Alku reminding her of the belly of her experience growing up in a commune. Was it the insularity of the town? The way the natives held their secrets so tightly against the world? He didn't want to ask her, not now, not when they were both so unsettled.

The streets of Alku were deserted as they drove through. Harry was relieved he didn't need to observe the townspeople, to swim through the eeriness of their uncanny movements. The Alkuans knew far more about the murders than they were divulging, and Harry intended to find out what it was.

He and Evangeline had decided not to call ahead to the CCTC.

They wanted to catch them by surprise.

CHAPTER 31

Pekka appeared harried when he approached them in the lobby, his movements jerky, his hair askew. He looked like he'd slept about as well as Evangeline. He still led with his characteristic politeness.

"I'm so sorry, did I forget a meeting we scheduled?"

Evangeline smiled warmly. "No. We wanted to talk with you, actually. Can we go to your office?"

Harry glanced around. No one was seated at the welcome desk, and the whole building had a stillness to it. "School's not in session?" he asked when Pekka didn't immediately respond to Evangeline's request.

"They're on holiday break."

The same thing Sister Catherine had said, except something rang false about it from Pekka's mouth. What had Max said outside the Korhonen house?

We get a long weekend for Easter.

That had been on Monday. Today was Wednesday. Well past a long weekend.

"How nice for them," Evangeline said. Her expression remained friendly. Harry suspected she was thinking the same thing he was: the kids were being kept at home so they couldn't talk to police.

"The children certainly think so," Pekka agreed. His mouth was tense. "Since we're the only ones in the building, is it all right if we talk here?"

Harry kept his eyes trained on Pekka as Evangeline pulled out her notebook. "We wanted to ask about the first week of November 1998."

Pekka didn't blink. If anything, his face wiped clean. "Yes, yes, the week we lost the Korhonen family." His hands were tightening and releasing, tightening and releasing.

"Also the week the hikers were killed." Evangeline let that hang in the air. He hadn't corrected them when they'd initially referred to the hikers being mauled in the '80s. Had it been an oversight, or a deliberate misdirection?

Pekka flinched and then nodded, not acknowledging the previous date. "It was a difficult week."

Harry was again struck by how sincere he appeared. While he might be obscuring the details, he wasn't lying about the toll the week had taken on him. A man that empathetic must struggle with the reality of operating a prison for violent offenders.

"We've discovered that it was also the week your mother disappeared," Harry said.

The statement had a startling effect on Pekka. It stripped away the years, his sudden trembling chin and wide eyes giving the impression of a boy standing before them wearing a man's clothes. He swallowed several times before he spoke.

"It was an affair," he said. "A scandal. She ran off with another man. It was the worst week of my life, truly. It broke my father's heart."

"I'm sorry," Harry said.

Pekka's jawline jumped. "Rannie came to live with Pihla and me after Mother ran off. He could have stayed with our father, but you have to know they had a traditional marriage. My mother did everything. The cooking, the cleaning, the planning. We thought it best Rannie move in with us. He—"

The click of a door opening on the second level hit Pekka like a blow. He snapped his mouth shut and stared up the curving staircase, where Pihla now stood.

"Hello, dear," he said, his voice growing higher. "I forgot you were here. I was just telling the agents about Mother's disappearance and Rannie coming to live with us."

Pihla's eyebrows shot upward. She wore casual clothing, a green turtleneck sweater and brown cords, her hair in its characteristic Nurse Ratched horns leading to a bun. She didn't speak until she reached the main floor.

"Why do you want to know about Ansa?" She aimed the question at Evangeline.

Evangeline cocked her head. "I think a more relevant question is, Why did you tell us she'd died?"

Pihla's face twisted like a wet towel. "I don't remember that."

"In the church basement," Harry said coolly. "You said you thought it might have been 1997."

"That there had been a major snowstorm," Evangeline offered. She and Harry had speculated why Pihla would have lied about such a thing. Evangeline was certain it was a cover-up. Harry had suggested it might have been something more innocuous.

In either case, they were about to find out.

Pihla's mouth opened and then closed, two red circles blooming on her cheeks like clown paint. Pekka walked over to grab her hand before returning his attention to Harry and Evangeline.

"You'll have to forgive me," he said. "It's *my* request that we not share my shameful family details with people not of Alku. Of course that doesn't apply to law enforcement, but Pihla was simply honoring my wishes."

Pihla stiffened but didn't correct him.

Evangeline's eyes traveled from husband to wife. "Ansa disappeared the same week the Korhonen family was murdered. Don't you think that's an odd coincidence?"

"I think it's a *terrible* coincidence," Pihla said decisively, finding her tongue as she reclaimed her hand from her husband. "And the worst week in Alku's history. You must understand why we'd rather not talk about it. It took weeks for us to get Rannie to sleep on his own, what with his mother disappearing and then spotting the hikers shortly afterward."

Evangeline's shoulders snapped back, and Harry felt his throat tighten. "Rannie found the hikers?" he asked.

"*Saw* them," Pekka corrected. "He was playing in one of the empty rooms upstairs. Mother never let him attend school here for reasons unfathomable to me. It'd been his dream, and so after she ran off, Pihla and I agreed he could visit the school whenever he wanted. He was delighted." His voice softened at the memory. "He'd bring books and snacks and play school."

Pihla's eyes did the opposite, growing as cold as winter glass. "On one of the days he was supposed to be up there, he ran into a classroom to tell a teacher that he'd seen dead people on the edge of the woods. She called the police, who came out with an ambulance. It turned out to be two hikers who'd been mauled by an animal the night before."

"Can we see that room?" Harry asked. "The one he spotted their bodies from?"

Pekka was about to speak, but Pihla silenced him with a look. She was back in charge. "I'm afraid we're understaffed today. It's just Pekka and me."

"We don't need a guide," Evangeline said, keeping her voice pleasant. "You can just point us in the right direction."

Pihla's lips disappeared. "Not today," she said. "Maybe tomorrow."

"We both think Pekka was lying about being the reason Pihla told us his mother was dead, right?" Harry asked as they drove away from the school.

Evangeline touched her finger to her nose. "We absolutely do."

"What do you think they're hiding?" He cranked the heat as high as it would go to ward off the chill.

"I think they're hiding *everything*," Evangeline said, shaking her head. "They're like if a cover-up screwed a mystery and gave birth to a secret. What *exactly* they're covering, your guess is as good as mine." Her phone dinged. "Holy shit, I have signal."

She veered to the side of the narrow forest road between the Gothic school and the fork that led to the prison, both buildings out of sight. It was just thick woods crowding toward them. She put the car in park but kept it running.

"Not a text. It's an email from the Helsinki folklore studies professor," she said, flicking her screen. "Hold on."

Harry nodded. The black, skeletal tree trunks against the white snow reminded him of an Ansel Adams photograph. He studied the stark forest, letting his mind wander. In the Korhonen murders, Matty the Mallet had been the only suspect. When that theory had to be thrown out, law enforcement decided the killer had been a drifter and dead-ended there.

Weiss dying in the same grisly way shot that all to hell. The most logical way to identify who'd murdered the Korhonens would be to apprehend Weiss's murderer. That put Harry and Evangeline dangerously close to stepping on the Duluth PD's toes. They'd have to tread carefully. Harry would check in with Deepty and Johnna to see if they'd uncovered anything new in the evidence they'd been sent, but he'd also like to visit the scene of the Weiss murder, if Detective Emery didn't object.

"He says he's spent a significant amount of time studying the Alku immigrants," Evangeline said, skimming the email. "Turns out they left Finland at the height of the tuberculosis epidemic because they'd been persecuted, like you found in your Wikipedia search."

Harry thought he spotted some movement in the woods. A deer? "But persecuted for what?"

Evangeline snorted. "Apparently, people in their village thought they were vampires."

That got Harry's attention. "Please."

She aimed her phone screen at him, then pulled it back. "Yep. Vampires. Seems that folks didn't know what tuberculosis was, they just knew their families were sick. They brought the afflicted to the Tervos, as they'd always done. When most of their relatives died while in medical care, they became suspicious. So suspicious, the professor writes, that they dug up their graves. Inside, they found their recently deceased relatives looking fresh and bonny, with blood still in their bodies."

"They wouldn't have known about the decomposition process," Harry said.

Autolysis, the first stage, lasted two or three days. The tissues broke down and carbon dioxide built as the bacteria the immune system had kept in check took over. It was a gruesomely exquisite reclamation of organic matter. But barring a significant injury, all the blood would remain in the body, and the green and black of necrosis would not yet appear. Pre-bloat, to an untrained eye, would look as though the victim were merely sleeping, cold and plump.

"Sounds like," Evangeline said. "They figured their relatives had been turned into vampires by the *original* vampires—the Tervos specifically, but by extension, all seven of the founding families, since they all worked closely together. The whole group was accused of being blood witches." Her voice grew serious. "But there's more: the villagers murdered the children of the original seven in front of them as punishment." She rubbed her face as if to clear away the image. "They called it 'the reaping.' The adults were supposed to be killed after their children were slaughtered, but they managed to escape due to 'great personal fortitude.'"

Harry drew a sharp breath.

"Exactly," Evangeline said. "According to the professor, they barely got out alive."

The movement in the woods caught Harry's eye again. He was about to ask Evangeline if the email had any more information when he spotted a flash of red.

It wasn't a deer out there.

It was a person.

CHAPTER 32

Two children and one man, to be exact.

Harry and Evangeline jumped out of the car. On Evangeline's barked order, Rannie, Max, and Honeybee stayed put until she and Harry reached them fifty yards into the woods.

"Where are you going?" Evangeline demanded.

They were all three bundled up against the cold, Rannie as wide as a linebacker in his quilted black parka, Honeybee hiding behind her brother but sneaking peeks at Harry.

"Not going to my fort, that's what we're not doing," Rannie said, too loudly.

Harry smiled despite himself.

Even Evangeline cracked a grin. "I don't think you'd be very good at poker," she said.

"P-p-p-poker face!" Rannie sang delightedly. Max nudged him hard, and his face closed up.

Harry didn't know what had just passed between them, but Evangeline's suddenly serious expression suggested that she did.

"Why were you going to your fort, Rannie?" she asked.

"Kids aren't safe." Rannie spoke with the loud whisper of someone sharing a secret. Then he raised his voice to nearly a yell, sending it in the direction of the school. "But I wouldn't ever take any kids to my secret fort."

Rannie's unease was contagious, but the silence of the woods was complete except for the occasional lonely chirp of a chickadee or crone leaves rustling as a light breeze blew through. A red fox darted across the path, pausing briefly to glance back at the group before disappearing into the underbrush. Harry was the only one who caught it. Other than that, they were alone in the woods.

"What makes you think kids aren't safe?" Harry asked.

"Children who don't follow the rules disappear," Rannie said. "They get got in the reaping."

Harry's neck tightened. "Who told you that, Rannie?"

Rannie glanced at Max, who gave him a quick headshake.

"No one," Rannie said. He was the biggest thing in the forest, thicker even than the ancient trees surrounding them. "No one told us that. They didn't tell us not to hike into the woods, either. Didn't even tell us not to go in the swampboggins." His voice changed, going low. "If you go to the boggins, you deserve what you get, so you better bet I don't forget the threat!"

"Rannie." Evangeline placed her hand on his wrist, her voice gentle. "Who told you all that?"

He yanked his hand back. "No one told me all that! No one told me never to go into the swampboggins! Just like no one got hurt at Sandwich Rock. Just like that!" His voice was growing louder, and he began to visibly shake.

Harry was worried that they were going to have to restrain the huge man when Max jumped in front of him.

"Rannie!" he said, waving his arms up high. "Cool it, man. Cool it."

Rannie focused on the boy, who was a quarter his size, and he went still, blinking like he'd just woken up. His arms relaxed and his eyes cleared. "Can I go to art class with you if I cool it?"

Max giggled, his relief evident. "Aw shucks, Rannie. You're too old for school. But we can go sledding before all the snow's gone. Just show us what you were gonna show us."

Rannie's expression turned canny, his smallish eyes growing tighter. Something about it chilled Harry, but before he or Evangeline could ask a follow-up question, a tornado siren screamed through the forest. It was coming from the direction of Alku.

"No way," Evangeline said, looking at Harry. "A tornado?"

Max had turned as white as the forest snow. "No tornado," he said. "We have to hurry back to town. Someone's hurt."

CHAPTER 33

When they reached Alku, Rannie and the kids riding in the back seat, Evangeline still at the wheel, the flashing lights drew them to Willow Street. A woman stood on the sidewalk across from the Korhonen place, her face streaked with tears. She wore only a short-sleeved blouse and slacks, her pageboy haircut wild around her swollen face. Detective Emery was trying to lead her inside, but she kept shoving him away.

"That's Arlie's mom," Max said. His voice was pinched.

Arlie, the freckle-dusted girl wearing the red cap with the rainbow pom-pom. Harry wanted to tell Max not to worry, but he recognized the stricken expression on Arlie's mom's face. He unbuckled and hurried out of the car, Evangeline on his heels.

"She said she was sick." The woman's voice was almost a wail. "She went into her bedroom, but she's gone now. Gone!"

"I understand, Mrs. Wenner," Emery said, his voice soothing. "But she might be close. Heck, she could be visiting a friend."

"You don't understand!" she shrieked, wrenching free. "I'm one of the original seven. I have the blood. This isn't right! It's not right!"

The sidewalks had been empty, but people were appearing. Harry had a moment to wonder why they hadn't left their houses earlier, the moment they heard the alarm. And who had activated the siren? It almost seemed like they were only leaving their houses now that Evangeline and Harry were here, putting on a show whose purpose he could not comprehend.

Hannele was the first to reach Mrs. Wenner. She threw her arms around her. "There there, now, dear," she said. "We'll all start searching for Arlie. You say she's not home?"

Mrs. Wenner tried to wriggle out of the woman's grasp, but Hannele gripped her tighter. "Hurry, Torben!" Hannele called out to a middle-aged man who'd appeared on the front porch of the home next door, tugging on a parka. He was unremarkable except for his oversize nose, which set him apart from the other Alkuans. "We're needed!"

Harry felt like he was in the middle of an insect swarm as nearly a dozen people crowded around Mrs. Wenner, jostling Evangeline and him. He had to actively push back against fight-or-flight mode as he heard chittering noises and caught flashes of too-high foreheads and bright eyes and, for a moment, what looked like sharp teeth behind red lips. He rubbed his cheeks, told himself it was the conversation from earlier bleeding into his head, that and the hideous synchronicity of a girl gone missing.

Caroline.

But not Caroline. Arlie Wenner. Harry thought back to meeting her outside the Korhonen house. *I'm ten,* she'd said, her pom-pom bobbing.

Same age as Caroline when she went missing.

He recognized the corroded edges of panic. Were the faces of the townspeople slipping? Growing blurry, then sharp? Was he falling?

"Harry."

It was Evangeline. She was up in his face, one hand on her weapon, the other gripping his elbow.

"This is Emery's scene," she said. "Let's step back."

Harry nodded, let her lead him to the SUV. He fell against it, hands on his knees as he drew deep breaths. He didn't want to look at the townspeople, so he watched the other police cars screech onto the street, officers popping out.

"You okay?" Evangeline asked. She still had her hand on her weapon.

Harry inhaled through his nose. "Yeah. Sorry. I don't know what happened to me."

Evangeline studied him. With her white hair and light eyes, she looked almost like she could be Finnish herself. But not of Alku. She was too safe, too present. He didn't know what he'd seen back there, but it was sitting in his belly like a cold stone.

"You stay here," Evangeline said. "I'll be right back."

She strode over to one of the arriving officers just as Pihla showed up, shooting Harry a dark look before disappearing into the middle of the mob that had encircled Mrs. Wenner. Harry should be offering to help, he wanted to help, but his legs didn't seem to be working properly.

Evangeline returned to his side in a few minutes. "They're starting a search party."

He was glad he'd packed his boots. "What area are we taking?"

She smiled grimly. "I requested the swampboggins. The place Rannie says we definitely, absolutely aren't allowed to go."

CHAPTER 34

The arctic sunlight poured liquid gold across the enormous rocks. They reminded Harry of huge, round Stonehenge stones, one lying flat and the other leaning against it.

"Something creepy about those." Evangeline shivered.

"We should have dressed warmer," Harry said, unwinding his scarf to give to her.

She waved him off. They'd been tromping through the woods, not stopping until they reached the large boulders. "Not enough time. The swamp is due east from here, according to Emery. Rannie was weird about it, right?"

"Yes," Harry said. "But it might not have anything to do with the missing girl."

Evangeline made a noncommittal sound.

"What did you react to before?" Harry asked. "When Rannie repeated 'poker face'?"

Evangeline stared at him. "You serious?"

Harry didn't think that warranted an answer.

She shook her head in disbelief. "It's a song. A very, very popular one by Lady Gaga. Rannie sang the first part of the chorus."

Harry nodded as her reason for concern immediately clicked into place. "But they have no access to magazines or popular music here."

Evangeline rubbed her mittened hands together, still looking up at the enormous rocks. "At least that's what the adults think. Kids always find a way, even when they're this isolated."

Harry heard something in her voice. "Did you? When you were young?" He didn't want to mention Frank's Farm by name.

A bittersweet expression touched her face. "Yeah, only it was candy for us, not music, though I loved that, too." Her mouth twisted. "Really messes you up when the place that's supposed to be the safest—your home—is the most dangerous."

Before Harry could think of a response, his phone lit up his coat pocket.

"Reception!" Evangeline said.

He tugged out his cell. "Johnna." He hit the "Accept" button but lost the call immediately.

Evangeline pointed at the large flat rock. "Try up there."

"It's a myth," Harry said, "that moving to higher ground gets you better reception."

What he didn't want to say was that the rocks made him uneasy, too. Had his class visited this area on their field trip? Enjoyed a picnic here? When Evangeline had no comeback, he sighed and walked over to the massive stones. What geologic activity had carried them here? He saw where smaller boulders had created a natural stairway onto the bottom rock. A quick climb and he was at the top, where he was peeved to discover that Evangeline's suggestion had worked. He had one bar.

Luck.

"Johnna," he said when she picked up. "I don't know how long I have reception for."

"Got it." Johnna Lewis, the second half of Harry's team in the lab, was a genius at collecting and processing trace evidence. She also had a famously strong constitution. If Harry had a scene that he knew would be particularly violent or decayed, there was no better agent for staying focused and getting the job done. Like Deepty, Johnna was also quick on her feet.

"I was able to enlarge the Weiss photos you sent, plus I magnified the ones we have from the original Korhonen scene," she said, jumping right in. The noise of paper riffling—or static—came down the line. "They're not great. A close-up shotgun blast obviously obliterates much of the detail. I didn't glean anything new on the Korhonen case, but I came up with a weird-ass theory on Weiss."

Harry's pulse quickened.

She hedged her words before saying them. "Deepty looked at it, too, and she agrees."

Harry knew Johnna to be exceptionally forthright. Her reticence unsettled him. "Agrees on what?"

A deep sigh. "It looks like there were two contact points to Weiss's head, separate from the gunshot."

"That makes sense," Harry said. "A hammer or some other blunt tool could have been brought down twice. Were they side by side?"

"No," Johnna said, "and that's the thing. They were opposite. Immediately over his ears, in fact, as if someone grabbed his head and squeezed it like a melon until it popped."

"Shit." Harry wasn't much for swearing, but in this case, he'd been unable to hold it back. He was about to apologize when a shape appeared and then disappeared in the woods across the clearing. His mouth went dry.

"Arlie!" he yelled, pointing.

Evangeline saw it, too. She took off running.

Harry ran to the edge of the rock. "I have to call you back," he told Johnna.

He didn't know if he hung up or lost the connection, and it didn't matter. He shoved the phone in his pocket, leaped down, and raced after Evangeline.

Knuckled tree limbs grabbed at him, but he plunged onward. The child wore a cap, but it hadn't had a rainbow-colored pom-pom. Had it even been a kid? His heartbeat pumped in his veins. He barely ducked in time to miss a branch. He had the disorienting sensation of knowing exactly where he was, even though he'd never been here before. He felt a sucking-down pull, the fear-twist of a lifting plane suddenly plummeting, and then he landed back in his childhood home on the last day he saw Caroline.

He'd been leaving for the party but, on impulse, had hurried to her room. He thought he saw Myrna at the end of the hall, her shadow swishing toward the servant stairs, but that didn't make sense. She hardly ever came to this wing, not since Caroline was born, and certainly wouldn't bother when there was a party to stress over.

He knocked on Caroline's door. When she told him to come in, he found her sitting on her bed, her walls covered with the crayon clouds she'd been drawing on them since she was little. Myrna had tried every punishment she could think of to get Caroline to stop drawing them—spanking, grounding, no dessert—but the clouds were the one thing Caroline stood firm on. She said she couldn't live without them. Myrna must have gotten tired of making her scrub them off the walls.

Caroline had been crying right before Harry came in, but her face lit up at the sight of him.

"Was Mom just in here?" Harry asked.

Caroline nodded miserably. Her ponytails had been replaced by french braids, and the blue mascara Myrna would not in a million years let her leave the house wearing was smudged. She wore raspberry lipstick, too. She looked like a beautiful doll, ten going on twenty. "She said I look like a whore. I don't even know why she came up here. She's been awful since you left, Harry. Worse than you can even imagine. I'm scared living here." She drew in a ragged breath. "I'm gonna run away."

To Harry's eternal shame, his first emotion had been regret that he'd poked his head in. What if Jennyfer left before he even reached the party? He loved Caroline, but a ten-year-old girl saw the whole world as built around her, either holding her up in her rightful position or unfairly dragging her down. And hadn't Myrna vacillated between ignoring Caroline and being mean to her for Caroline's entire life? It could take hours to sort out. He really should say something to Myrna about her behavior—someone should—but not today.

He hoped he managed to keep all that off his face. "I'm sorry, Caro," he said. He had one ear aimed toward the front door. Were guests already arriving? It was later than he'd thought.

"No you're not." Caroline shook her head vigorously, sending her long, pale braids swinging. "You don't even want to be here."

That got his full attention. She was right, and he could do better. His little sister missed him. So what if he was a few minutes late to a party? He dropped into the chair across from her.

"I've always got time for you," he said. "What's scaring you?"

She peeked from beneath her bangs. An impish smile lit up her dimples. "Ghosts."

He groaned, and her smile disappeared.

"Fine," she said. "I'll just go ahead and run away."

Mom had mentioned Caroline had been throwing out this threat a lot since she'd started hanging with Olive. Apparently, the girl ran away from home on the regular. Each time she came back, her mother was so happy that she took her shopping.

"Good luck," Harry said. "Mom would send the National Guard to find you."

"Ooh," Caroline said, her eyes dancing. "Do you think one of them would be cute? Like John Stamos? Olive says John Stamos is lame looking, but I know she's just playing it cool." She laughed, the sound like sparkling wind chimes. "Do you think when I grow up that John Stamos would want to marry me? I know some guys think I'm pretty. You know how I know?" Her eyes grew big. "This guy drove past Olive and me while we were walking by the lake in front of the Malt Shoppe a couple days ago. He was nice to me, but he creeped out Olive. Further evidence of how she has to always be cool, you know? The dude had—"

But Harry was already tuning her out. She was on one of her flights of fancy. So he gave his sister his face, but his mind and heart had traveled to Jennyfer. Just thinking about her made him hot. The things she used to do to him. When his mind started re-creating their last night together, he abruptly crossed his legs.

"—two different lies." She paused, tilting her head. "I guess it *was* a little creepy."

"What was?"

Her mouth curled up into a rosebud. "You weren't listening."

He stood. "I swear I was, Caro. It's just that I gotta go. You and Olive will figure it out, right? And then you can fill me in tomorrow over breakfast."

Her face fell hard. "Please don't leave, Harry. Please stay with me."

She sounded so desperate that for a second—and only a second— he contemplated staying behind. But then he'd miss his chance to see Jennyfer. Myrna always said Caroline was born dramatic, and this was just his baby sister being overdramatic. They'd talk tomorrow. Maybe by then he'd work up the courage to have the long-overdue conversation with his mother, too, tell her she was a bully. The world had always bent to Myrna. It seemed easier—or at least less terrifying—to tiptoe around her than to stand up to her. But if she was visiting Caroline's room to criticize her, it meant things were escalating. Harry had to stand up to his mother, for his sister's sake.

"We'll hang out tomorrow, Caro, okay?" Harry said. "We'll fix everything."

She didn't respond, but Harry felt warm in his chest. She'd see. Everything would be fine. He slipped out the door and to the party.

It was the last time he ever saw her.

She left for Olive's as planned, walking because neither Harry nor their dad was around to give her a ride. A single witness thought they saw her get into a green four-door. Police would later discover that the vehicle matched the description of the car driven by the man who'd talked to Caroline outside the Malt Shoppe.

Olive could only describe the vehicle, not the man.

Olive had thought he was creepy, so only Caroline had approached his window.

Only Caroline saw him up close.

Harry had seen how miserable Caroline was at home. He knew she wanted to run away. And she'd tried to tell Harry all about it, and about the man who would abduct her, had begged him to stay home with her.

If he'd been listening, he'd have a description. Better yet, if he'd been listening, he would have known she'd been telling the truth when she said she was scared. But he'd blown off Caroline because he had a hard-on for a girl, plain and simple.

He was the reason his sister had never been found.

In his darkest moments, he wondered what his mother had been doing to her, if her constant verbal abuse had escalated, and what cowardice had driven him to delude himself about how unbearable Caroline's homelife had always been. And he fought to reclaim those lost seconds, to replay the tape of that final conversation with her so he could *hear* the words he'd tuned out, remember what came between "the dude had" and "two different lies," certain there was some clue in there, some bit of information that would lead him to his baby sister, the person he loved most in the world, the one he had let down.

But those words were gone forever.

Ahead of him, Evangeline moved with an uncommon grace. Harry picked up speed, his nerves crackling. He'd failed his sister. Finding Arlie wouldn't bring her back, but it could save another family from the misery he lived with every day. Except . . . they were following the same route he thought he'd seen Arlie run, and there were no footprints in the crusted snow.

His pace put him on Evangeline's heels as they broke into a clearing. The smell hit him first, the scent of slaughter. Then his eyes caught up. The clearing was beaten-down grass with a staked woman at its center.

A moan escaped his lips.

CHAPTER 35

Rannie
November 2, 1998
Early Morning

When Pekka told Rannie he could live with him and Pihla, Rannie had one impulse: run.

When Mom is gone everything's wrong.

He burst out the door and raced away as fast as his legs would carry him.

He made it a couple miles before he had a thought: maybe Mom was in the woods. Maybe she found out about the fort he'd built in the swampboggins! That notion made him dead stop at Sandwich Rock. That was it! She'd discovered his hidey-hole in the place he shouldn't be, and she was waiting there to thrash him!

He grinned in the dark. He didn't want a beating, but he sure did want his mom. He put on an extra burst of speed, never doubting he was gonna find her. *Hoo-eee*, was she gonna be mad!

Except she wasn't in his fort.

She wasn't anywhere.

She was gone.

Once that plunked into his heart and then crashed down to his belly, he began to shiver. He'd run away without a jacket, but that wasn't even it. What sort of kid doesn't have a mom? He might be full grown, but he was still a boy. Everyone in Alku knew Randolph Tervo was good at directions and that he was going to be a kid forever.

He hugged himself. He kept walking. He backtracked to Sandwich Rock and then kept going to the clearing where they held the ceremonies and the celebrations. He stopped in the center. Maybe his haltija would show up and tell him what to do. It'd never happened before, but neither had his mom ever left him. He waited for the goat man, fighting the gloomy sleep that pulled him under when he was scared, but the stress was too much. He lay at the base of a tree and closed his eyes.

By the time he opened them again, he was an ice cube. He had to run in place to get feeling back. It started with an agony like a thousand needles pricking him all along his side, so now he was in pain *and* sad. He couldn't go home, because he wasn't even sure where that was anymore. He couldn't sneak into the old dormitories, either, now that they were a prison, but he *could* go to the school. The more he thought about that, the better the idea seemed. His mom was the one who'd forbidden him from going, and now his mom was gone.

He started running again, this time with purpose.

It's my turn to learn without a mother's concern.

He smiled. That was a good one. Rhymes had always soothed him, but the best ones were like a hug from a friend. His mouth opened when he smiled, and the smell of bloody meat rushed in so hard it punched the back of his throat. He quickly snapped his mouth closed. He better be careful because something was hunting, that's what that smell told him. The school building was just ahead, through the tall ferns that looked like black paintbrushes stroking the sky. He'd be safe there.

He walked another ten feet before he tripped over the first body, falling to his knees. He turned back, certain it was someone sleeping (*silly willy, don't sleep where it's chilly*), but the ground around them was a shadowy red, their head as flat as pie. He reeled back and felt something warm beneath his hand.

It was an arm.

He turned hopefully toward it—someone to help him!—but the limb was attached to another dead body, its head smashed as good as the first. He moaned and leaped to his feet, running toward the school. He was sure the monster was right behind him, chasing him, just one lick away from his heels. He thought he saw its reflection in one of the big school windows, but it couldn't be the monster.

It looked just like his dad.

When he reached the school, the door was locked, so he huddled in the alcove.

Pihla found him there the next morning, half-frozen.

He couldn't know that twenty-five years later, she'd lie to two BCA agents about the details.

CHAPTER 36

"It's that damn blood witch effigy from the front of the church," Evangeline said, staring up at it. "I don't know where the smell is coming from, though."

The snow around the veri noita was heavily trampled but white.

"Over there," Harry said, struggling to contain himself. His throat felt raw, the world off-kilter. He grasped for his three principles but he couldn't remember them. All he could do was stumble away from the staked figure and toward a ravaged form on the edge of the clearing. The closer he got, the stronger the smell of slaughter, until he saw it was a deer, its head gone but the corpse otherwise intact. It rested in a pool of blood ice that glittered in the moonlight like terrible rubies.

Harry crouched by the carcass, tugging on a glove and running his hand over the stiff body. "No visible wounds other than the missing head. Decapitation may have been done with an ax. The edges are rough." The first principle came back to him, and with it, a wash of relief: *insight adheres to structure.*

Evangeline squatted next to him. "What kind of hunter would do that?"

Harry stood, removing the glove with a snap. "None that I know of." He glanced back at the witch. "It looks more like a ritual killing. An offering." The second principle: *structure provides safety.* "Did you see a girl running through here? Is that who you followed?"

Evangeline's eyes were shadowed. "I saw a shape. It definitely did not look like a girl. You saw *a girl*?"

His jaw tightened as he played back the last several minutes. "I don't know. I honestly don't. I was sure of it when I stood on that rock, but now?" He shook his head, then cupped his hands around his mouth and yelled, "Arlie! It's Agents Reed and Steinbeck. If you can hear us, please let us know."

His voice echoed across the icy terrain, bouncing off black tree trunks and rebounding back to them.

There was no response.

Evangeline made a hissing noise. "This cacked town." She tugged her phone out of her pocket. "No reception," she said. "You?"

Harry pulled out his. "None. We should go back and check on the search status. They could have found Arlie."

Evangeline looked him in the eye. "You really think so?"

He knew they hadn't. They would have heard the commotion, even a couple miles from town. The discovery of a lost child was an event. The search dogs would be barking, people yelling. He turned a full circle, his feet crunching in the crystalline snow. The woods were as cold and lonely as a heartache. He couldn't fathom leaving a child out here, even though he knew they wouldn't find her. "Let's do a grid pattern in this immediate area, just to be sure it wasn't her I saw. If we don't find her, we check in with Emery and decide next steps."

She gave him an appraising look. He thought she was going to argue, but instead she started searching her end of the clearing.

A lone figure stood in front of the Wenner home when they pulled up, Davidson, repeatedly cracking his knuckles as he glanced back at the house. It was a challenge for Harry to walk rather than run to him. The lack of a police command post could mean only one thing.

"They found her?" Harry's voice was surprisingly clear.

Officer Davidson nodded, his forehead folded like he was still processing disbelief. "Turns out the kid was never missing. Mom said she was in her bed the whole time. Can you believe it?"

Harry fought the urge to punch him in the mouth.

"No," Evangeline said, stepping alongside Harry. "I can't. Can we speak to Mrs. Wenner?"

"That's a big nope," Davidson said with regret. "She's pretty drained, as you can imagine. I was told to wait for you two; otherwise everyone else has gone home. When we couldn't reach you by phone, we figured your reception must be bad." He tapped the cell clipped to his belt. "Happens a lot out here."

"Have you *seen* her?" Harry asked, pulse throbbing.

Davidson appeared genuinely confused. "Who?"

"Arlie," Harry bit out. "The missing girl."

"No."

"Did any officer?" Harry pressed. "Did anyone confirm that she's inside?"

Davidson tried to keep a pleasant expression, but confusion was winning out. "I'm sure they did."

Harry felt something growing inside him, unfurling, like heat, or stomach acid. No way was little Arlie Wenner with her rainbow pom-pom cap and freckle-dusted nose in that house. Someone or something in this town had taken her, and the rest of Alku was covering.

"Thank you for waiting to tell us the good news," Harry told Davidson through gritted teeth. "We'll be returning to our motel now."

Evangeline did Harry the professional courtesy of waiting until they were inside the vehicle to swear at him. "There's no way that kid's in there."

"I suspect you're right." Harry clipped his seat belt into place. "And we both know that if she's been abducted, we have seventy-two hours, tops, to locate her if we want to find her alive. So let's get to work."

Evangeline gripped the steering wheel. "You know I'm in, but where do we begin? You heard the deputy. They've decided she's not missing, and we have no jurisdiction to behave otherwise."

Harry's brain began to organize all the threads, weaving them into a semblance of order. "We begin where we started. We find out who killed the Korhonens and then Weiss. And to find out who, we have to find out why." He tugged his sleeves down over his wrists. Habit. "I'd like to interview Silas Smith outside of the CCTC. Without Pihla around to intimidate him."

Evangeline raised an eyebrow. "You don't think Emery will assume we're stepping on his toes if he hears we interviewed Smith?"

Harry frowned. If they overstepped, they could get kicked off the cold case, but he found he didn't want to give Emery a heads-up. Yet he'd never broken protocol on the job, hadn't even bent it.

Suddenly, a solution landed. He picked up his phone, texted Emery to let him know that he and Evangeline would be talking to Smith off-site. He hit send.

His phone dinged almost immediately.

"It went through?" Evangeline asked, incredulous.

"No," Harry said. "That was my 'failed to send' notification." He tapped his phone. "I tried. That counts as due diligence."

Evangeline hooted as she started the car. "You better slow down or you'll wake up one morning and have accidentally removed the *entire* stick up your ass."

He grimaced at the window. "Not a chance."

CHAPTER 37

They stopped at a gas station between Alku and Duluth. Harry offered to fill up while Evangeline tracked down Smith's address and reached out to the Finnish professor to ask if there was more to the story of Alku's founding.

The sharp apple crispness of the air took Harry's breath away, reminding him that though today might have felt like spring, this far north, they were still in the last whip of winter. The sound of gas pumping into the car was rhythmic, almost hypnotizing. He recognized that he was detaching from obsessing that Arlie might be out in this frigid night. The only way he could help her was to do his job, and quickly.

The loud *thump* when the gas reached the pump's sensor made Harry flinch, revealing a scar a few inches above his wrist. He tugged his coat down.

Put it all in the compartment. Focus on what you can do right now.

It was an old-fashioned pump, one that required him to pay inside. He jogged toward the station, which was little more than a lit-up glass room. Back in the day, he and his friends had called these "farmer stops." The store would stock a cooler or two with pop, there'd be a rack of chips near the counter, lottery tickets, and if you were lucky, a bathroom key taped to a block of wood. No espresso machine or deli or sparkling water at a farmer stop.

The white-bearded man at the counter barely tossed him a glance.

Harry walked to the nearest cooler. Evangeline preferred the neon-colored sodas, but he couldn't bring himself to buy her one. He'd instead purchase two waters and set hers between them. It'd probably anger her, but then again, she might drink it. Stranger things had happened.

He made his way to the counter. "Just the waters and the gas."

The man flipped the page of his newspaper, still not looking up. "You're those two agents, aren't you?"

Harry's radar clicked on. "I suppose we are. You're from Alku?"

"Ha," the man said, finally glancing up. "Do I *look* like I'm from Alku?"

The hair beneath his feed cap matched the white beard. His eyes were brown, his nose a bulbous red. He lacked the Alku features and way of moving. "Do you get a lot of Alku residents through here?"

The man's face cramped. "Yeah. They keep to themselves. Pay in cash. I got no problem with them." He finished ringing Harry up, glancing pointedly at Harry's credit card when he ran it through the machine. "Need a bag?"

"No, thanks." Harry grabbed the waters and made toward the door.

"They're strong folk in Alku, I'll give them that."

Harry stopped. Turned. "Because of what they've survived?"

"Naw. Because they can lift heavy things." His voice was free of sarcasm. He flipped his newspaper page again.

Harry took a step back toward the counter. "Excuse me?"

The man was nodding. "Saw one of them push a car off another's foot right out front here." He pointed toward the opposite side of the parking lot, the halogen lights bathing the ground in an eerie, pulsing glow. "People can do that when they're scared or in a lot of pain, yeah?"

The door jingled, letting in a new customer, a nondescript middle-aged woman. She waved a hand at the man behind the counter, and his face tightened again. His eyes dropped to his newspaper.

Harry stood near the counter, thoughts swirling. "When was this?"

The man lifted up his paper, snapped it, and set it back down. "I was pulling your leg," he said, not looking at Harry. "A little storytelling, is all."

The woman stood in front of the rack of chips, her long-nailed finger dragging across the front of each. The sound was unnerving. Harry wanted to choose one for her, rip it off the clip, anything to stop the high, feathery noise.

Instead, he addressed her. "Nice night."

She smiled, turning from the chips too slowly, her neck too long, her forehead too high. "It is."

When Harry's phone buzzed in his pocket, he was just able to stay inside his skin. He pulled out his cell. The message was one word, and it was from his mother.

Urgent.

CHAPTER 38

Though it was evening, Myrna answered the door wearing an immaculate taupe pantsuit with a single strand of pearls around her neck. Her expensive silver hair was tightly curled to her scalp, her makeup subtle and elegant. She looked ready to steer a board meeting.

Except for the way her eyes kept sliding off to the side, unable to hold Harry's gaze.

"What is it?" Harry demanded. He'd tried calling once they were back within range of a cell tower. She either hadn't heard her phone or had chosen not to pick up.

"Please," she told him and Evangeline, "let's take this in the parlor."

"Mother." Harry paused, hearing the sharpness in his tone, and breathed deep, calling up his qigong practice. Myrna was not in visible danger. He could let her control the narrative, at least for a few minutes. "Fine," he said. And then to Evangeline: "After you."

They followed her down the hallway, the thick cream-colored carpeting swallowing their footsteps. Harry thought of foster children in here, any children at all. He couldn't picture it. He'd barely visited since Caroline disappeared. How could he? Every time he looked at Myrna, he thought of how she'd treated Caroline, and how he'd let her.

When the three of them settled into the stiff furniture, Myrna crossed her legs at the ankles and brushed a nonexistent hair away from her face, ensuring she had Harry's and Evangeline's full attention before speaking.

"I was just going about my business when it occurred to me: What if the Alku murderer was the one who took Caroline?"

Evangeline audibly inhaled.

At Harry's father's funeral, one of Harry's few return trips, his mother had careened between criticizing his father's memory and crying about her loss. If Caroline had been there, she would have said their mother was going Full Myrna. It was a tornado with Myrna at the center, trying to suck everyone in. But Caroline hadn't been there, would never be there, so he'd needed a new coping mechanism to navigate the funeral. He'd envisioned himself in a glass container, one only he could inhabit. It was thick, so thick and heavy that Myrna's tornado couldn't pick it up. It muffled her words and her manipulations.

He pictured that container around him now. "Caroline's disappearance has nothing to do with the Alku crimes."

"How do you know?" Myrna was twisting her hands, her coral-colored fingernails churning. "That family was murdered the same year that Caroline went missing."

Harry thought of the work they should be doing this very moment, of poor little Arlie Wenner, of the cluster of crimes focused on Alku, of Caroline having absolutely zero connection to Alku, not even a field trip visit there. His mother was simply trying to assuage her guilt. "A lot of crimes happened in 1998 all over Minnesota, Mother. The murder of the Korhonen family in Alku was twenty miles and six months away from Caroline's disappearance."

Myrna leaned forward, argument in her eyes.

Evangeline spoke first. "Most criminals have a specific way they operate, Mrs. Steinbeck. A modus operandi. A mass murderer is seldom an abductor of children as well."

The air grew sharp and still, shattering Harry's container. Evangeline didn't know what she'd just stepped in, contradicting Myrna. He should have warned her, but now it was too late. Myrna's mouth puckered.

"Do you color your hair?" she asked. "It's so very white. I can't imagine that's natural."

Evangeline's face went momentarily rigid, then relaxed. "It's free to be mean, but it pays to be kind," she said. Then she smiled.

Myrna's eyes widened. Her attack had been the pettiest of petty. She'd always been larger than life in Harry's mind, holding ultimate authority over him. Had he *ever* stood up to her? No. Seeing his mother through Evangeline's eyes, though, he suddenly realized how fragile she really was, how tender her grasp on her tiny kingdom. It made him sad.

It also freed his tongue, finally.

"That was rude, Mother. You owe Evangeline an apology."

Myrna reeled back as if he'd slapped her, and he supposed that made sense. He was breaking the rules of their relationship. "And I owe you an apology, too," he said. "I've not spoken honestly with you in the past. I'll do better."

His chest flared at the words, a combination of fear and hope. Maybe, if he put the boundaries where they belonged, he'd no longer have to wear them like a cage.

Myrna's lips disappeared until they were just a razor cut across her face.

Harry was steeling himself for her to slide into the hard, glassy innocence she liked to wear as a shield. But that wasn't right, either. Caroline's loss had damaged all of them. Myrna had chosen the safety of a high perch. His dad disappeared into himself. Harry had taken a different route, living by his three rules, denying himself real intimacy and connection.

Who was he to judge which path had been the better choice?

He stood. Kissed his mother on the cheek. "Evangeline and I are going now. We're in Duluth on a serious case. Please don't text me like that again unless it's a true emergency."

Harry indicated Evangeline should lead the way out, and he followed. He knew his mother loved him, in her own way. She was apparently trying to love other children, too, or at least give them a safe haven. Could he make room for her in his life? Mature their relationship beyond the past it was locked into? It seemed like a wide ravine to cross, one that would require him to finally talk with her about how profoundly they'd failed Caroline, to address Myrna's past emotional abuse and Harry's cowardice in standing up to her, to speak plainly about how he'd covered for the family—minimized or ignored the bad outright, and shined up the good—at Caroline's ultimate expense.

Would he also finally tell someone that Caroline had described her abductor and begged him to stay, and he'd tuned her out?

For the second time since they'd arrived in Duluth, he wondered what it would feel like to confess to Evangeline. To get off his chest what he'd done.

But neither spoke as they got in the SUV and pulled away from the mansion.

Some words, if you waited too long, could no longer be spoken.

CHAPTER 39

Silas Smith's roommate sent them to a bar up the street called Kowalski's. He said Smith could be found there most nights he wasn't working. From the outside, Kowalski's looked like a shabby neighborhood dive glittered with neon Coors and Budweiser signs, but the inside was surprisingly warm with high ceilings and a beautiful antique mahogany bar. The lights were dim, and the bartender was the only woman in the room other than Evangeline.

Smith sat at the barstool farthest from the door.

"Hey, Silas," Evangeline said, perching on the seat next to him. Harry remained standing.

Smith glared at them both before returning his attention to his red, white, and blue Pabst. "You two again. I got nothing more to say."

"Why don't we move to a table?" Harry asked. "We can buy you a drink."

"Won't pass up a free beer," Smith said, chewing on the inside of his mouth. "Still not gonna talk, though."

He made for the nearest table. Evangeline lifted her hand and ordered a bourbon on the rocks for herself, a second Pabst for Smith, and without asking, a water for Harry. He hid his smile. She'd noticed but not taken the extra bottle he'd picked up for her at the gas station.

Harry took the chair across from Smith. "Did you know a girl went missing today?"

Smith's eyebrows shot up. He appeared genuinely surprised. "No shit? From Duluth?"

Harry shook his head. "No, from Alku."

Smith snapped his mouth closed so fast that he caught his lip on a tooth. "Yeah, like I said, I'm not talking. Not even about that witch, Pihla."

Evangeline joined them at the table, setting Silas's fresh beer in front of him. "Witch, huh?" she said. "Funny choice of words."

"Witch, whore, bitch. All the same to me."

Harry frowned. "That language is unnecessary."

Smith barked laughter. "Which one of you is the man at this table?"

Evangeline took a seat without comment. Harry also felt no need to respond.

"I have just one important question for you," Evangeline said.

Rather than speak, she sipped her honey-colored liquor, a look of serenity crossing her face. She closed her long-lashed eyes, her pale skin and hair glowing in the dim bar. Harry thought she must know how beautiful she looked in that moment. Smith visibly relaxed watching her.

A good agent uses every tool in their tool kit.

"Yeah, one question for a beer isn't too much," Smith said, dragging his eyes away from Evangeline with visible difficulty. "Let's hear it."

"You mentioned when we were in the tunnels that Weiss was puffed up about something new the last time you saw him. What was it?"

"Shoot, I should have just told you right out of the gate. Then you would have left me alone." He held up his second beer. "But then I guess I wouldn't have this coming." He grinned. He had unusually smooth teeth, no sharpness to his canines. Dentures? But he was young for that. "It was no big thing. Weiss said he heard some people talking, and their conversation was going to make him big money. Like maybe an inside track on some bet he was gonna place. I don't know."

"Did you believe him?" Evangeline asked.

Smith rolled his eyes. "Before that, he said he was dating a super-model. Look around." He waved his arm, indicating the middle-aged men at the bar. "What do you think? The two of you are about as close as we have to models in these parts, and I don't see either of you dating Weiss."

"Do you like working at the CCTC?" Harry asked.

Smith took a pull on his beer. "I like the paycheck, I like the bene-fits, and I'm not going to do anything to mess up either of 'em."

His meaning was clear. They'd asked for one important question answered, and they got one important question answered. There would be no more forthcoming.

Suddenly Harry was incredibly tired. "Thanks for your time," he said.

Evangeline downed her bourbon and led the way out.

CHAPTER 40

Harry found himself lying awake at 2:30 a.m. running with ghosts. He'd dismissed his mother's concern that there was a connection between Caroline's disappearance and the Korhonen killings, but that didn't mean that his sister wasn't everywhere he looked.

The day she disappeared, a car had raced up to the party Harry had been at, pulling him out of Jennyfer's arms. The officer told him Caroline was missing, drove him back to his parents' home. He saw the police defer to his mother, accepting Myrna's story that Caroline had a wonderful life and was a happy girl, that there was no way she could have run away. When they asked him the same questions, he'd repeated the same lies. It wasn't just cowardice; nineteen-year-old him also figured they wouldn't look as hard for Caroline if they thought she was a regular runaway. But now, as an adult in law enforcement, he knew that he should have given the police all the details, that it was just one more way he'd let Caroline down.

His mind was spiraling, taking him to the depths of the many ways he'd contributed to his sister never being found. He'd told himself he could skate on the surface of the past while he was in Duluth, just as he did in the Cities, but he'd known he was lying to himself. He'd packed the lighter, after all.

He'd first used it the week after Caroline was abducted.

He'd mostly burned himself on his chest, where it was easily hidden, but there were also scars on his arms. He knew the mechanics of nonsuicidal self-injury. Inflicting the pain offered a feeling of control, and the relief following the pain offered a temporary sense of calm as endorphins rushed in.

They were doing everything they could to find Caroline, he was told. There was no reason to derail his future. But he couldn't make sense of a life without his little sister. He felt untethered, literally like he was floating away from his body.

The burning brought him back.

He'd stopped on the first anniversary of Caroline's disappearance, trading the burning for his three rules and a rigid, orderly life. He'd also added a second major: criminal justice. He dressed sharp, went home alone, and did his penance on this earth. But here, in Duluth, dealing with a missing—or not—child, he was too close to it. He was craving the burning like a lover. The agony of it would wake every nerve, yank him out of his shame-colored brain, return him to his flesh.

For an exquisite moment, each cell of his body would sing.

Relief.

He lay on his bed in the lonely, ugly space of his motel room, studying the red plastic lighter. He'd known, hadn't he, when he saw "Duluth" on the file. He'd taken the lighter out of his desk drawer, tossed it in his go bag. He hadn't burned himself in more than two decades, but he also hadn't stayed overnight in Duluth since Caroline's abduction.

He rubbed his thumb across the flick lighter's rough wheel and was surprised by a thought: What would it be like to have a best friend, a true soul who walked alongside him, who *knew* him? He had work buddies, gym buddies, but he didn't let anyone closer than that. He could accept any darkness from Evangeline. Why didn't he trust her to do the same for him? His chest started to crack at the thought of it, but then came the familiar wall of pain.

His heart glued right back up.

Insight adheres to structure. Structure provides safety. Safety requires you let no one in.

He didn't realize he'd fallen asleep until he was jerked awake. He smelled the decay of cigarette smoke baked into the wallpaper, heard the hum of the heater, read the clock on the bedside table. It wasn't yet 3:00 a.m. He'd only been asleep for moments.

What had woken him?

His pulse suddenly tore through his veins as he remembered. *Danger* had woken him, and it was coming from Evangeline's room. The sounds of a scuffle, and then a grunt.

She was in trouble.

He leaped out of bed, unlocked his adjoining door.

Hers was wide open.

He rushed into her room.

CHAPTER 41

Rannie
November 6, 1998

Rannie's mom disappeared on Sunday.

Those two hikers were killed by a wild animal on Monday.

His dad keeled over on Thursday.

Alku folks thought Rannie should be sad about Nils dying. He saw it on their faces. An invitation to *cry or confess or wear the very best dress.* But the truth was, Rannie felt only relief. Everyone else was afraid of his mom, but she'd loved Rannie hard and fierce. Like a momma bear, she'd say. Rannie's *dad* was the one who hit him, hit him into next week sometimes. Nils wouldn't play games with him, didn't read to him. He was just a crabby old man who sat at their dinner table.

Plus with Nils dead, maybe Ansa would come back.

I can attest that putting him to rest is the best.

The only downside, and it was a big one, was that the men of Alku had to take turns sitting with the body for three days, as was tradition. Tonight was Rannie's shift. He glanced at the pyre for the hundredth time. Who wanted to spend a night alone in the woods with their dad's stinky corpse?

But it was the way of Uusialku. All the direct descendants of the original seven must be returned to the woods to feed the haltija. Even so, Pekka had offered to take Rannie's shift. Pekka was so kind. A perfect big brother. But with Dad gone, it was more important than ever that Rannie prove he was a man.

He glanced nervously again at the body. It was wrapped in burlap with the branch-made goat mask resting on its face. But the shape of it sure didn't look like Rannie's dad. Rannie's dad had a big ol' stomach, and this body was flatter, head to toe. Everyone said it was Nils Tervo in there, though, so it must be Nils Tervo. Alku was family, family was everything. You trusted your family, no matter what. He knew that like he knew directions.

People told Rannie that it was a broken heart that killed his dad. To Rannie, it looked like his mom and dad mostly yelled at each other. Was that love? Rannie didn't know, but everyone said Nils's heart had been so big that when Ansa left, it collapsed in on itself.

Fine by Rannie.

A breeze kicked up around the clearing. It made the corner of the burlap wave at him. Did he smell the sweetgas of death? His blood grew refrigerator chilly. What if his dad sat up right now, turned to Rannie, pulled off that mask that looked real scary in the moonlight, and said in a scratchy, leathery voice, *Rannie, I know you didn't love me. You never loved me. I will hug you with my rotting arms until you do.*

Rannie could see it like it was happening right in front of his eyes. Made it feel like his skin flew away while his skeleton stayed put. He wanted to run so bad, but he'd promised Pekka he'd stay, and Pekka did so much for him. He was the closest thing Rannie had to a mom right now.

And Pekka'd promised Rannie that things would feel normal again soon. That it would just take some time until his life was even better than before. Rannie clung to that, holding on like it was a tree trunk in a tornado.

If "better" meant finally going to school, though, Rannie was no longer interested. Finding those bug-smushed bodies right next to the building had cured him of wanting that. He didn't ever need to see something so horrible again. Except, that wasn't all that happened at school, was it? There were also games. And food. Everybody got to eat the same lunch. How fun would that be? You could talk about what you liked and what you didn't like. *You bet I'll take your pickle!* Rannie usually ate lunch alone. No one knew how he felt about his sandwich.

He was imagining a corned beef on rye when a *scratch thump* knocked him out of his thoughts. He whirled around. The trees were so crooked and gnarled that the sound could be bouncing from anywhere, but it sure seemed like it'd come from the center of the Sacred Spot.

From his father's corpse.

Rannie's mind let go of its flimsy grip on his reflexes, and he took off. He was sure he heard the cackle of the blood witch at his heels, exactly as he had the night she pushed the rock on top of Hector. But Pekka had told him that that had been a terrible accident, that there was no blood witch, not really.

And Pekka never lied.

Rannie was a good distance away from his dad's body before his sense found him. Pekka wouldn't let him stay out in these woods if they weren't safe. Right? All their haltija protected him right now. They'd been eating the bodies of his ancestors, and they were strong and united in his favor.

Rannie stopped running. Caught his breath. Felt himself growing taller.

I'm connected so I'm protected and won't ever be neglected.

That was a good one, so good it grew a smile on his face. He didn't want to head back to the body, though. Surely he'd done his time there. Yup. Shift over.

He started toward town.

He didn't get far before he heard voices. Rannie knew what it was like to feel sneaky. It wasn't a good feeling. It was like he'd eaten too much candy and barf was knocking at the back of his throat. But right then, his body was commanding he be sneaky, and he couldn't tell it any different. He crouched low in the forest and crawled quiet as a mouse toward the noises.

It was Pihla, Jarmo, Mr. Wenner, and Mr. Esko. They were all bundled up. Like they were ready to do their own watch with Nils, but they'd already pulled their shifts. Maybe they knew Rannie wouldn't last long. His cheeks grew warm in the cold dark.

Mr. Wenner was talking to Pihla.

"The monster is destroying us," he said.

Rannie's ears perked up.

"What would you have me do?" Pihla responded. "Those are the ways. Those are the rules. The blood witch protects Alku. Alku is family. Family is everything."

Rannie was struck by how much Pihla reminded him of his mother. It wasn't just the words. It was how she held herself. Like a storybook queen.

Jarmo spoke. "Ansa came around to it. You know she did."

Rannie's insides grew soggy at the mention of his mom. He sure missed her. Pihla couldn't ever take her place, no matter how she walked and talked.

Jarmo glanced to Mr. Wenner and Mr. Esko for support. They were silent, so Jarmo was forced to say the rest, his flashlight aimed toward the ground like it was embarrassed to be part of this. "*We need to get rid of the prison.* It's poison. The monster feeds on the hate inside. Look at what's happened so far this week."

Rannie glanced behind him. He *had* heard the monster out there. Pekka had been lying to him about the veri noita being real! Well, if getting rid of the prison would make the witch stop being so angry, then Rannie voted yes to that. But he didn't get a vote. Randolph Tervo was good at direction, he sure liked nice smells, and he remembered that you didn't do anything to somebody that you didn't want done to yourself. But he was no leader. Pihla had said that. She said that when she took his vote for herself.

Someone else was crunching down the path toward the secrety group. In a few moments, Pekka emerged, holding his own flashlight. He was hardly recognizable. It was like the weight his mother and father had carried now pressed down on his shoulders like God's thumb. Made him small and bowed.

"Pihla, you know they're right," he told his wife.

She glared at him. "We can't close the prison. We need it."

"You've got stone balls," Mr. Wenner said to her. "I'll give you that."

Rannie wondered what good stone balls would be. They would just lie on the ground. Give him balls that bounced any day.

"If the prison goes, we *all* have to go," Mr. Esko said, seconding Pihla's declaration. "No money without it."

"If the prison *doesn't* go, my family and I are moving," Jarmo said.

Pihla gasped. No one left Alku. Ever.

Pekka put his arm around her to calm her. "At least let us vote, Pihla," he said.

Rannie couldn't see Pihla's eyes in the shadows, but her voice was pulled tight as barbed wire. "You know what'll happen."

"Please," Pekka said. "Just one vote. I promise I'll abide by it."

There was so much tension among them that Rannie started to feel tired. As quiet as he could he made a little nest at the base of a tree and fell asleep.

CHAPTER 42

Harry slapped on the light in Evangeline's room. She was sitting up in bed, still moaning loudly. She appeared dazed. Harry's head was on a swivel, trying to see everywhere at once, desperate to locate the intruder.

But he saw no one. Only Evangeline.

He reached out toward her from across the room, wondering if he was dreaming.

"Are you all right?" he asked.

She shook her sleep-ragged head. "It was a nightmare." She scrubbed her face. Turned on the bedside lamp and looked at him.

When her eyes widened, he realized his mistake.

He'd fallen asleep wearing silk pajamas, but he hadn't buttoned the top. His chest scars were visible.

Her gaze crawled to his face, searching. "Is that something we need to talk about?"

He quickly buttoned his pajama shirt. "An accident."

She kept her gaze on him. He held it.

And then her face crumpled. "It was that prison cell again. Pure evil rolling out of it, thick, like black oil." She held herself. "Then Frank Roth showed up."

The man who demanded all the children of the commune call him Father. Harry took a step closer to her bed, rustling an empty chip bag underfoot.

"He said he needed me to help him teach the girls a lesson," Evangeline said. Beautiful, crystal tears appeared on her bottom lashes. Harry wanted to brush them away.

"I'm sorry," he said, keeping his distance. The words were true. Unyielding. He hoped she could fit into them, find protection there.

But instead, she began shivering. He shouldn't hold her, but she was his friend, wasn't she? *Wasn't she?* So he sat next to her on the bed, gently, and took her hand.

She started crying. It surprised him. It shouldn't have. Everyone cried. But Evangeline Reed was forged of stone and steel.

He was relieved, almost, to see her like this.

"When I finally got out of the commune, I saw a therapist for a while," she said, swiping her nose with the back of her free hand. "He told me that the shittiest people in our lives actually help us. They scrape away our whole outer layer, like a power wash. Good and bad, scoured off. What's left beneath is new pink skin that can grow into any shape we want it to." The look she gave Harry was so vulnerable that it hollowed him out. "Do you believe that?"

He thought of Myrna. Of the cold metal coiled inside her. How the only way she knew to cope was by controlling everyone around her. Yet she was now opening her home to children in need. Was she growing into a new shape?

"I don't know," he said honestly.

"Are you okay, Harry?"

He knew what she was asking. Until tonight, he'd managed to hide his scars—the ones inside and out—from everybody. Even her, the best detective he knew. Coming up north had made him careless. His pins were coming loose.

"I'm just tired," he said. It was a coward's lie.

She yanked her hand away. The bedside lamp behind her hid her expression, but she was seeing the truth of him, he had no doubt. He rose from the bed. He needed to get back to his room.

"Will you leave both doors open between our rooms?" she asked, her voice small.

He paused at the doorway, his hand on the jamb.

"Of course," he said. "Let me get you some tissues and water first."

CHAPTER 43

"I'll try your waffles this time," Evangeline told Lydia.

"All right, honey," the waitress said, scratching the order on her notepad. "And for you? Oatmeal and tea again?"

Harry nodded brusquely. There'd been no talk of last night on the walk across the highway. They were back to being colleagues working a case.

They'd agreed that Harry was going to reexamine the Korhonen and Weiss files, looking for anything they'd missed, and Evangeline was going to continue researching Alku. Harry was so deep in his reading that he tensed when Lydia set their food in front of them. The stress had irritated his stomach, but he'd eat so as not to draw attention to himself.

Evangeline grabbed the syrup and drowned her waffles. Bile rose in the back of Harry's throat. Her eyes flicked up and recorded his reaction, leading her to jut out her chin and tip the syrup jar so it poured even more vigorously.

Harry felt a glimmer of a smile.

"We don't want any trouble with the good folks of Alku," Lydia said.

Both Evangeline and Harry glanced over at the waitress, who'd returned to top off Evangeline's coffee. She'd spoken in a near whisper.

"Excuse me?" Evangeline said, the syrup forgotten.

The waitress's voice was brittle. "I'm nobody," she said. "I'm just a woman who married a nice guy who forgot how to be nice. I wait my tables, and I go home to my shows. But we don't want any trouble here. Understand? Nobody else might fight for what I have, but I'm happy with it. So forget what I told you before. All of it. Just my imagination, that's all."

The front door opened, and Lydia's neck jerked. The man who entered had dark eyes, dark skin. Lydia relaxed.

"Do you know anything about the girl who was reported missing yesterday?" Harry asked.

Her face squeezed up on itself just like the gas station attendant's had yesterday. "Heard that was a false alarm," she said, grinning too wide. "Hope you enjoy your breakfast." She hurried back to the kitchen even though a middle-aged man in a trucker's cap was holding his cup out for a refill.

Evangeline shoved a huge bite of waffle into her mouth. She chewed, swallowed. "Looks like somebody got to them."

Harry frowned. "The question is, why?"

Evangeline's cell started dancing on the table. "I swear the tower out here has legs." She glanced at the phone's face. "It's the professor calling me back. Don't eat my waffles."

Harry watched her walk outside, taking small bites of his oatmeal as he flipped through the records, his stomach gradually unclenching. His focus started returning. That's why when he spotted the name Antero Wenner in Weiss's file, it lit up like a sparkler. When he'd first read the documents, he had no idea who Wenner was. Now that Arlie Wenner had gone missing—or not—the name was impossible to ignore. According to the file, Wenner had been a guard on duty during Weiss's last shift before he was murdered. Wenner hadn't been interviewed, just his name listed with all the employees who'd worked that same shift.

It was potentially a coincidence, the man's connection to Weiss and then his daughter reported missing. A coincidence that deserved a closer look.

By the time Evangeline returned, Harry's oatmeal was gone and her waffles were cold. She slid into the seat across from him and pushed her plate away.

"Didn't find out much," she said. "Other than that Finnish folklore professors sound an awful lot like the Swedish Chef from *The Muppets*. Remember that show?"

Harry tipped his head. "I didn't think you were allowed television at the commune."

"Wasn't. Watched it as a grown-up." She poured cream into her coffee and stirred, blending the white clouds into the black. "The professor reiterated how bad he felt for the Alku folks. Said it was a real 'witch hunt' that pushed them out of town. His words. That they were true innocents and that it was a miracle the adults managed to survive the entire village coming for them."

"Not much help there."

Evangeline made an amenable noise, and then an impish grin brightened her face. "Good thing Kyle had some dirt. I called him after I hung up with the professor. Remember that big rock you climbed like a dork yesterday to search for reception?"

Harry raised an eyebrow. "I believe I *strode* on top of it."

She waved a hand. "The important thing is that in September of 1984, a person was crushed beneath the rock leaning against it."

Harry thought back to the structure of the stones. "You mean the perpendicular one used to be balanced on the bottom one?"

She nodded. "Exactly. There's more. The person who was killed? A friend of Pekka's. Not an Alku guy."

Harry rubbed his temples. "That's a bad break."

"Yeah. The two of them were camping below, but Pekka got out in time. Freak accident. But there's even more." She leaned forward, her eyes sparking. "Fast-forward to May 1, 1990. A CCTC inmate was offed in his cell."

Harry's blood was humming now. He didn't even glance at Lydia when she cleared the plates. "Manner of death?"

"Head crushed."

Harry whistled and opened the timeline doc he'd created on his laptop. "I want to add this new info." He began typing. "The rock falls in 1984, killing a man. In 1990, an inmate of the CCTC is killed, a cranial injury the reported cause of death." He paused. "How close was his cell to Mr. Millard's?"

Evangeline drummed her fingernails on the Formica table, her nose wrinkling like it did when she was excited. "Would you believe they were cellmates?"

He nodded. "I would." He reviewed what they'd already gathered. "There're no more reported killings until the first week of November 1998, eight years after the prison death."

"November 1, Ansa Tervo goes missing. November 2, two hikers are mauled. Kyle confirmed that it was written off as an animal attack, by the way. Nobody loves the timing, same week as the Korhonen family is wiped off the face of the earth." Her voice grew quiet. "No one but Emery, maybe."

"Do we have a complete description of their wounds?"

She chewed her top lip. "You're thinking they might bear more than a passing resemblance to the injuries of the other victims?"

Harry nodded.

"Too bad." Evangeline turned her hands palms up. "Kyle says that information is lost to the ages."

"All right," Harry said, disappointed but not discouraged. "November 2, two hikers killed. November 7, the Korhonen family is murdered. As far as we know, there's not another suspicious death until Peter Weiss's killing five nights ago. Is that everything?"

"Yup," Evangeline said. "As long as we believe Ansa Tervo's disappearance that same week doesn't belong under the category of 'suspicious death.'"

"Do we know when Nils Tervo died?"

Evangeline tugged her ear. "We do not. Honestly, he might be alive for all we know. We have only Pekka's word that he's passed."

"Worth confirming." Harry's fingers paused over the keyboard. He knew what he was about to say was a long shot, bordering on conspiracy theory. It was uncomfortable territory for him. "Did the professor happen to say anything about the original Alku folks having remarkable strength?"

Evangeline's head jerked back. "What, like as part of their vampire superpowers?"

Harry cleared his throat. "Last night, when I went into the gas station, the attendant made a comment about the people of Alku being strong. He said he'd witnessed a resident push a car off someone else's foot."

Evangeline looked like she was trying to decide whether to punch him or laugh at him. "You're serious?"

"It might be nothing," Harry said.

She nodded and wrote herself a note. "Or it might be something. I'll ask Kyle."

"Thanks," Harry said, skimming his timeline. "Looking at all these murders lined up, I'd say we're overdue for a visit with Detective Emery."

Evangeline slapped her notebook shut. "Now you're speaking my language."

CHAPTER 44

When they entered Emery's office, the detective flashed a tense smile. He looked like he'd spent the night lying on a bed of glass. Even his sideburns were drooping. "Busy day, folks," he said, indicating they should both take a seat. He took a slug of coffee from a chipped mug and grimaced. "We're not the BCA. We don't have the luxury of working one case at a time."

Harry saw no reason to correct his perception. "Thanks for seeing us. I wanted to tell you we interviewed Silas Smith yesterday."

Emery's cheek twitched. "I said to keep me in the loop."

"I texted you." Harry held his stare. "It must not have gone through." Though he wasn't one to hide behind half-truths, he was happy to do it now. Something about Emery was no longer sitting right with him. "Is there any update on Arlie Wenner?"

Emery's territorial posture disappeared, and he leaned back in his chair, the gesture bordering on arrogant. "Never was missing. Didn't Davidson tell you? We should sue the mother for resources." He scrubbed his face with both hands, making a scratchy sound. "But we won't. I need to get to work. We all good here?"

Evangeline opened her notebook to a blank page, which Emery couldn't see. "Can I just run through a quick timeline with you?"

"Sure," Emery said.

"Thanks." She flashed him a stunning smile, but it had no effect. The man was done flirting. Without skipping a beat, she began reciting the order of deaths that Harry had typed up at the diner. "First suspicious death in Alku happened in 1984. A man crushed beneath a rock."

"If you say so," Emery said, his eyes narrowing. "Before my time."

"In 1990, an inmate was killed at the CCTC."

Emery glanced off to the side. "Also before my time, but I remember that one. Open and shut. Matty the Mallet's arms were working, even if his legs weren't. He obliterated his cellmate. The prison was retrofitted after that. Everybody got their own room no matter how incapacitated they seemed." He shrugged. "Nobody missed the guy he offed."

"Did the state want to try anyone?" Harry asked.

"Like I said, open and shut, with the killer serving consecutive life sentences."

Evangeline paused, studying Emery evenly. "November 2, 1998, two hikers murdered outside the school."

Emery held up his hand. "Not murdered," he said. "Killed by a bear. At least that's what the records say, so unless you can prove the animal had intent . . ."

"You found the records?" Harry asked.

"Excuse me?" Emery sounded irritated.

"You said previously that if there were any records of the 'accident,' they'd have been purged."

His mouth twisted. "I guess my assistant found them," he said dryly. "And 'records' is generous. What we have is as short as a leprechaun: two people killed by a wild animal, assumed to be a black bear."

"A lot of deaths for such a small town," Evangeline murmured. "Those, plus the Korhonens. And Weiss, if we're including him."

Emery nodded, his posture relaxed but his face carved of pure stone. "Yep."

"Yep?" Evangeline asked incredulously.

Emery struck Harry as one of those men who smiled when they were angry. The wider it was, the more furious they were. Emery's grin grew enormous.

"*Yep,*" he confirmed. "Sometimes bad luck hits a town, and it hit Alku with a big, meaty fist. I believe I mentioned that to you when you first arrived."

Hearing the timeline had clearly upset him. What was at the root of it? Did he think the BCA was stepping on his toes? If so, it wouldn't be the first or the last time a local detective felt squeezed. Or was he simply overworked and tired? Very possible. But it might be a third option: someone on his crew had messed up somewhere along the line, and he was protecting them.

"Do you know where the Alkuans bury their dead?" Harry asked. "Do they have a cemetery near town?"

"You'd have to ask them." Emery's smile was staying put with terrifying brightness. He got to his feet and leaned forward, fists on the table, like a silverback giving warning. "If that's it, I've got things to do."

"One more question," Evangeline said, still sitting, appearing thoughtful. "The pizza delivery person who called in the murder. Can we get a copy of the interview with her? I didn't see it in the file."

Harry felt a flare of pride. He'd personally failed to notice the interview wasn't in the records they'd been given access to.

"Nothing much there," Emery said, stiff-jawed. "She approached the door with a large supreme. The door was open. She called out. When no one answered, she peeked in and saw Weiss. The responding officer folded those details into the report."

"Could we talk to her?" Evangeline asked.

"If you can find her." Emery ground his knuckles deeper into the paper on his desk. "She quit her job the next day, and who can blame her? Minimum wage doesn't cover therapy."

"What about Peter Weiss's family?" she asked. "They've been interviewed?"

Emery drew air in through his nose and relaxed his hands, spidering his fingers. "Hey now, I thought you were working the cold case."

"We are," Evangeline said, her tone neutral. "There's a shit-ton of crossover between the two. We might be talking to Weiss's family today, and we'll let you know if we're able to track down the delivery person. So *heads up*."

Evangeline was playing a dangerous game. If she pushed Emery, he might shut down their access. But if he did, he'd need to offer a reason.

"That'll work," Emery said through clenched teeth.

Evangeline jumped to her feet and offered her hand. "Great," she said. "It's nice when we can work together, isn't it?"

She waited until they were outside of the police station to speak. "I think my relationship with Detective Emery has died on the vine. And the bastard is terrible at his job."

Harry felt a very ungentlemanly burst of pleasure.

CHAPTER 45

Peter Weiss's only family in the area was a brother, one Richard Weiss, who lived in a row house on the west side of Duluth. Two steady days of sun had forced winter to retract its claws, exposing a sidewalk and street gutter decorated with cigarette butts, rotting leaves, and weather-bleached wrappers.

Richard Weiss's front porch was clean, though, and his windows had curtains, which set it apart from the houses surrounding it. The door opened as Harry raised his hand to knock.

"Ope, you caught me on my way out." The man in the doorway was in his sixties, clean-shaven. He wore a kelly-green jacket with Premier Plumbing and Heating printed into the chest, the name Richard stitched below. His eyes flicked from Harry to Evangeline. "Aren't you two a pretty pair." He turned immediately red. "Sorry. That just spilled out. Can I help you?"

"We're with the Bureau of Criminal Apprehension." Harry offered his hand. He was met with a firm, dry grip. "We were hoping to ask you a few quick questions about your brother."

Weiss didn't act surprised, though it took him a few seconds to respond, as if he were weighing the request. "Sure, I can be a few minutes late for work. Come on in out of the cold."

The interior reminded Harry of his own house. Austere, uncluttered, furniture with clean lines. Except for the Ducks Unlimited art on the wall, he'd feel completely at home.

"I'm afraid I don't have time to offer you tea and cookies, though." Weiss crossed his arms, the move appearing more habitual than defensive. "What do you want to know?"

"We're actually investigating a cold case," Evangeline said. "The Korhonen family murder of 1998. Are you familiar with it?"

Weiss frowned. "I'm familiar with it, yeah. Everyone in the area is, at least if they're as old as me. And I think it's a damn good idea you're connecting it to Pete's murder."

"Why is that?" Harry asked.

Weiss snorted. "Not a lot of shotgunning and head crushing going around, is there? Just my brother and that family." His shoulders drooped. "When I got the call about Pete, I asked if I could identify the body. You know what they said? They told me there wasn't enough of his face left."

"I'm sorry," Harry said.

"Yeah," Weiss replied, "me too. Pete was a bastard, but he was the only family I had. One of those guys who knew everything about nothing, right?"

"I've met the type," Evangeline said. "Did your brother like his job at the CCTC?"

Weiss rubbed the back of his neck. "Well, I don't want to speak out of school, but now that he's dead, I don't suppose it matters. Pete was a drinker. The last few years, it started interfering with his ability to work. Thought he was gonna lose his job at one point, but then the woman who runs the place made him an offer."

Harry's pulse skipped. "Do you remember her name?"

"No, I don't. I just remember that she wanted my brother for a special shift. He'd be guarding one cell."

"Guarding?" Evangeline asked. "We have down that he was a nurse."

"True, true. I got the impression this was more of a babysitting job."

Evangeline and Harry exchanged a look. "Do you know who he was assigned to guard?"

"Naw." Weiss seemed disappointed in himself. "You think it has something to do with who killed him?"

"At this stage, we're just collecting all the information we can," Harry said.

"All I know is he told me he had lifetime job security. Hell, I was proud of him. Then all of a sudden, he's murdered. How's that for irony?" Weiss hooked his thumbs into his jeans pockets. "If there's nothing more, I need to get to work. Cool?"

"We appreciate your time," Harry said. "Here's my card if you think of anything else."

His blood started itching on the walk to the SUV.

"We think that 'job security' is related to whatever he told Silas Smith he overheard, yeah?" Evangeline asked once they were inside the vehicle.

"It's possible." Harry fastened his seat belt. "But what did Weiss overhear?"

"Something the Alku folks didn't want him to."

Harry considered this. "There's still the possibility that the murderer is one of the CCTC's ninety-seven inmates, pretending to be incapacitated and escaping."

"But not Matty the Mallet?"

Harry's phone buzzed. "Not judging by how he looked when we first visited, but I wouldn't mind going back." He tugged his cell out of his pocket. It was Deepty. He accepted the call.

"Harry, we have an update," she said.

"Can I put you on speakerphone?" Harry asked. "I'm here with Agent Reed."

"Sure."

He clicked the button.

"Hey, Deepty," Evangeline said quickly. "Before the update, can I ask you to pass on a message to Kyle? Can you ask him to track down the phone number and any existing addresses for the pizza delivery driver at Northern Lights Pizza in Duluth, the one who found Peter Weiss's body?"

"You got it." Clicking noises in the background indicated Deepty was typing herself a note. "Anything else?"

"Nope," Evangeline said. "Thanks."

"All right, because I've got something big." She launched right in. "We have a ballistics match. The shell found at the Korhonen scene was fired out of the same shotgun as the shell discovered at the Weiss scene."

Evangeline nodded in grim satisfaction.

"Not sure it'd stand up in court because it's a shotgun shell," Deepty continued, "but the firing pin had an imperfection that showed up on both casings, and the breech face markings were identical in both shells. I'm comfortable saying that the same gun was used twenty-five years apart."

Harry's brain was working the angles. "Good work. Were you able to get any DNA from either of the shells?"

"Still working on that, but there *is* something else." The sound of plastic sliding along a surface. "We ran forensics on Weiss's phone. I've got a message I want you both to listen to. And before you ask, the message came from a burner phone. We're gonna try tracking down who bought it where, but that's a long shot. Ready?"

"Ready," Harry said.

There was no click, just a guttural voice. "You better not tell anyone what you saw."

Harry waited for more. Nothing came. "That was it?"

"Yep," Deepty said. "He received it the day before he was killed. Could have been a prank, could have been his murderer. All we know for sure is that he was dead less than twenty-four hours later."

Harry's skin buzzed as he wondered if two dots could be connected. "Deepty, you mind also asking Kyle to research whether Mr. Weiss was working at the CCTC back in 1990, on the day an inmate was murdered in his cell?"

CHAPTER 46

Rannie
November 7, 1998

It happened too quick for Rannie, but most things did.

He woke up in the woods. He was alone. He hurried back to Pekka's. It was still dark. A terrified-looking Pekka grabbed him as soon as he walked through the door.

"You've got to hide, Rannie. Quick! And don't come out no matter what you hear. Promise me." Pekka was so scared his eyes were rolling around like marbles.

It made Rannie scared, too. "Sure, I promise," he said.

He was halfway up the stairs to his bedroom when he heard a terrifying hum, like the ancient *buzz whirr* of an army of cicadas. When he came down to see what it was, Pekka was gone. He figured it couldn't hurt to tiptoe to the front window and peek out as long as he tucked himself behind the drapes.

What he saw made his hands and feet grow cold.

The rest of the town was approaching the house. They wore their masks. He knew they were his family (*Alku is family*), he'd seen those masks a hundred times before, but not like this, not a wild pack in the streets. The cored-out eyeholes were the deepest black, and everyone was holding guns. They looked like monsters, but that couldn't be right. Rannie knew them, knew the people behind the masks.

Still, staring at them, his bladder relaxed, warm liquid pouring down his legs.

Pihla walked right past Rannie like he was invisible (*you hid yourself good, Rannie my dude*), stepped out the door to join the mob wearing her Tervo goat mask. While the door was open, Rannie clearly heard their soft chant, more a razor's edge than a noise. It sneaked up inside Rannie, coiling and cutting.

"Kill the monster before it destroys the town."

"Kill the monster before it destroys the town."

They were telling him a terrible secret, the words crawling in his ears like a spider laying its eggs. But they didn't even know he was there. He stayed tucked behind the curtains, just one eye peeking out, the tang of his own urine making his cheeks burn.

It was the middle of the night. When his mom was around, no one wore their masks at night, not outside the Sacred Spot. This was so bad. But if they were going to kill the monster, that was all right, wasn't it? Rannie's head hurt. He wished he were stronger and braver. He was a grown man, yet here he was, hiding and peeing his pants like a baby. He should grab his own goat mask and run after them, slip right into the crowd. Nobody would be looking close.

I crave to be brave and leave the cave.

But he'd promised Pekka he'd stay hidden, and the idea of breaking a promise to his brother was so awful that he started to grow tired. Stress and pain, they both put him to sleep. Pekka had once told him that he was better than a regular Tervo goat—he was a *fainting* Tervo goat, which was a special breed.

Rannie tried to fight it when the floor called to him, twisted the tender skin of his underarm to keep himself alert, but it was no use. The gloomy sleep won, like it always did.

When he woke up, a rolling red light washed over him. It was so pretty and soothing that he watched it for several seconds. But he was cold. *The pee.* His pants were still soaked. He hadn't slept for long. When he sat up, he spotted the police car outside the Korhonen house across the street, and his stomach kicked his heart.

They'd been too late, the townspeople.

They hadn't gotten the monster before the monster got one of them.

He stood and walked toward the door. He noticed his shirt was red and sticky. He sometimes picked his scabs when he slept. It got so bad that his mom would put socks on his hands.

Only a dud lets blood come out in a flood, bud.

But there was too much blood for that. He licked his lips and tasted it, like licking a salty penny. When he curled his nose, it hurt. He must have hit his face when he got so tired that he fell to the floor. That was it. He had a bloody nose. He hoped it wasn't broken, but there wasn't time to check. He had to hurry outside right now and see what was going on. He'd already missed so much. He opened the front door. Stepped outdoors. Ambled toward the police car. Didn't like that he felt so stiff.

The officer turned around. Rannie recognized him. He was of Alku, once or twice removed. Sometimes he'd come to church. His eyes grew concerned when he spotted Rannie.

"Go back inside, Randolph. Go back inside and put those clothes in the woodstove. Burn them till they're all gone and take your shower. I don't want to see you up again tonight."

Rannie nodded.

He felt like he was sleepwalking.

CHAPTER 47

Harry woke the next morning in the prickly motel bed to a phone call from Deepty confirming that she'd found DNA on the Weiss shell but that it hadn't matched anyone in the system. She and Johnna must have been working late nights, early mornings, or both.

When Harry told Evangeline the latest, she'd agreed on the next step: gather Alku's sitting board of directors, the descendants of the original seven.

A phone call to Lou had gotten them their names: Pekka Tervo, Antero Wenner, Helmi Esko, Torben Virtanen, Edvin Laine, and Joona Harju. Once they had the list of directors, Kyle had managed to arrange for Harry and Evangeline to meet with them at the school.

He'd told the board it was urgent.

The winding forest road brought Evangeline and Harry into the achingly cold shadow of the medieval-looking CCTC building, more cars parked in front of it than they'd yet to see. Harry wondered whether Evangeline felt the same sense of foreboding as he did. A brutal story was emerging through the mist, but it felt both sharp and slippery, dodging and weaving when they got close. Were the people of Alku victims? Killers? Both?

"You ready?" Evangeline asked as she parked the SUV behind a row of cars.

"I am." Harry grabbed his leather case.

The weather had dipped back below freezing. The sky was clear, the morning sun shining, but he could see his breath. Silas Smith waited for them inside the entrance, Pihla at his side. Harry tried to read their body language, but the two were holding themselves apart, their gazes forward.

"Good morning," Evangeline said.

Smith's eyes slid to Pihla.

"They're all waiting in the boardroom," Pihla said by way of greeting. Her gray sweater looked hand-crocheted, a soft counterpoint to the severity of her face. "I understand you won't tell us why we needed to gather."

When neither Harry nor Evangeline responded, she sniffed. "Follow me," she said. She led the way up the stairs, her crepe-soled footsteps echoing. Smith stayed on the ground level, watching them ascend.

"Can I get the Wi-Fi password?" Evangeline asked on the way up.

Pihla's shoulder jerked. Harry thought for a moment she might tell them there was no internet. But Evangeline tipped her phone so he could see. CCTC Admin was the only available network.

"It's alku123," Pihla said after a few beats. "All one word, all lowercase."

"Thanks." Evangeline typed it into her phone.

They passed a window on the west side offering a view they hadn't yet seen. Below was an ice-crusted, unwelcoming forest that appeared untouched, as if nature itself held its breath. It was both captivating and intimidating. "Is that where the hikers were found?" Harry asked.

This time, Pihla didn't hesitate. "It is. That was a terrible tragedy."

"Were you here?" Evangeline asked.

"Working, you mean?" She shook her head. "No, it happened after hours."

"And Pekka found the bodies?" Harry asked.

"Rannie," she said, before she had a chance to censor herself. Her knuckles going white on the banister told Harry that she regretted the slip. "This way."

The boardroom they entered had once been a grand space, likely a library judging by all the empty shelves, but the paint was now peeling off the moldy ceiling in great sheets, and the flowered wallpaper had faded to the color of dried blood. Even so, the view of the front lawn was spectacular, the sprawling pine green of the forest almost black against the snow.

The twelve-person table appeared laughably small in the room's center. Six men sat around it, all of them bearing the characteristic craniofacial features of native Alkuans. It made Harry's skin prickle when they turned in unison at their entrance.

"Much thanks for meeting with us," Harry said.

"It really is no trouble," Pekka said from the head of the table. The way his fellow board members held themselves suggested that wasn't true, but he forged on. "We were due for a meeting anyhow. Can we ask what this is about? Agent Kaminski didn't have much detail to offer."

"As you know," Harry said, following Evangeline toward the two open seats opposite Pekka, "we're investigating the Korhonen tragedy."

"And we thought it would save time to interview you all at once," Evangeline continued. She pulled out her notebook. "Could each of you please share what you remember of the night of November 7, 1998? You too, Pihla," she said, swiveling to invite the woman to the table.

"Antero Wenner," said one of the men, introducing himself. "We were all asleep." *Arlie's dad or grandfather?* Harry thought. The man looked to be in his sixties, wearing bifocals and a sour expression.

"When Jarmo didn't show up for work or answer his phone the next day, I went to check on him," Torben Virtanen said, rubbing his generous nose. Harry'd bet good money the man never introduced himself as "the husband of Hannele." Torben continued, "No one answered the door, so I stepped inside, called out. Still no answer, so I went upstairs. I saw the blood and called the police."

"What time was that?" Evangeline asked.

Torben looked to Pihla.

"About eight in the morning, wasn't it?" she said. "Jarmo had an early shift."

Torben nodded. "That sounds right."

"No one witnessed anything strange in town that day?" Evangeline pressed, glancing around the table. "No new people visiting, no odd behavior from the Korhonens?"

"Nothing out of the ordinary," Pekka said. The rest nodded in agreement.

It was exactly what Harry and Evangeline had expected, exactly what was in the file.

But they hadn't come for an interview.

"While we have you here," Harry said, setting his evidence collection kit on the table, his tone mild, unthreatening, "we were hoping for a DNA swab from each of you."

Pihla was the first to find her words. "What on earth for?" she asked.

"We've obtained what may be a breakthrough piece of evidence," Evangeline said, remaining deliberately vague. "And we'd like to rule out everyone in this room."

Both pieces of information were true, taken alone. They didn't belong together. Harry could live with that. "Is that all right?" he asked. They couldn't force them to comply. The collection had to be voluntary.

"We were in and out of the Korhonen house," Wenner said, his eyes flicking around the table. His face was relaxed but his fingers were drumming. "Every one of us."

"Understood," Harry said, removing his swab kit. "Once we rule out the people who had a reason to be there, we know which DNA to focus on." Again, true, and not entirely the truth.

"If it'll help," Pekka said, his tone admonishing as he glanced at his fellow board members, "of course we'll do it."

The rest of the Alkuans appeared unhappy, but no one protested.

Harry started with Pekka. Evangeline asked questions while Harry worked his way around the table, swabbing as the Alkuans opened their mouths like reluctant baby birds. Did they have a list of all the people Jarmo had worked with the day of the murder? Who watched the children when Jarmo and Janice were out? Were there any new employees at the CCTC the month before the crime? When she reached her question about Pekka and Rannie's father, the answer rolled right out of Pekka.

"He died on the fifth of November."

That was new information. Harry managed to keep his eyes trained on his work, though he was dying to glance at Evangeline. He knew she was thinking the same thing as him: that week had been a death spree in Alku. He popped his last swab into a bag and labeled it.

"Two days before we lost the Korhonens," the man who'd identified himself as Joona Harju said. He was the youngest board member, by appearance. Hair more black than gray, face relatively unlined, his red plaid shirt reflecting a rosy glow onto his face. "A broken heart killed him."

A blend of humor and regret played across Pekka's face. "That's what we told Rannie, and it may have been true. More likely, though, it was his diet and a lack of exercise. My father was not a healthy man."

"I'm sorry," Harry said.

Pekka nodded. "We had a complicated relationship, Nils and me. But I do miss him."

Harry inserted the swabs into their assigned pocket and began closing up the kit.

"We appreciate your time," Evangeline said. "Before we leave, we'd like another interview with Mathias Millard as well as Amon Dooley, if you don't mind, plus to do one more walk-through of the prison's exercise yard."

"But—" Pihla started, stopped by Pekka's hand.

"Do you prefer to take the tunnel or drive?" he said.

"Drive," Evangeline said so quickly they might have assumed she was scared of the tunnel. They didn't need to know that a BCA officer had driven up from Saint Paul and was waiting on the county road for the samples.

Or that Harry had requested Deepty check for myostatin-neutralizing antibodies while running the other tests, hoping to disprove a theory so ludicrous that he had yet to say it aloud to Evangeline.

CHAPTER 48

Harry and Evangeline followed the guard down the echoing hallway. They found Millard's cell as bare as it had been last time, outfitted with only a stainless-steel sink and toilet with heavy-duty rails around both. His bunk was attached to the wall, a Hoyer lift in the corner. No art, no color, just a frail-looking man seated in a wheelchair in the middle amid the faint odor of human waste and sanitizers.

"Good morning," Harry said. "My name is Agent Steinbeck, and this is Agent Reed. We visited a few days ago. We were hoping to ask you questions."

The serial killer stared forward, his gaze vacant, his mouth half-open. His hands remained twisted in his lap, their brown-spotted flesh waxen against the bright orange of his jumpsuit. His left foot was rested at an angle, the toes nearly touching the inside of his right ankle. The bottom of his sock was clean.

Exactly as he'd appeared the last time they'd visited.

"Five people were murdered in 1998 in the same style as your seven victims," Evangeline said, not bothering to keep the venom out of her voice. "Last week, the killer struck again. All the dead had connections to the Carlton County Treatment Center."

Millard's head twitched, his breath growing heavy. Harry initially thought he was in distress, but the breathing came in rapid huffs.

The man was laughing, his eyes remaining as blank as pits.

Evangeline glided forward in a flash, gripped Millard's chin, and turned it to the right so he faced the wall. It wobbled there like a ball on a stick. With his gaze facing away, she pinched the skin of his outer left thigh through his jumpsuit's thin fabric, twisting so sharply that even Harry winced. It was over before he could intercede, and Millard hadn't so much as flinched. He kept up his dry laughing, the terrible husking noise of a trapped gremlin finding joy.

He hadn't felt the pain.

Evangeline released him. "I'm done here," she told Harry, pushing past him.

Harry followed her out of the cell. "That was unethical," he said when he caught up to her.

Evangeline's face was flushed. "Not by his rules. The man tortured every one of his victims before he smashed their heads in. He skinned one woman alive. She died of shock when he was only a quarter of the way done. *She was nineteen.*"

Harry knew this. He'd read the same files as Evangeline. "He still has rights."

"Tell that to his victims." Then she stopped, hands on hips. "What did you think we were going to do in there? Ask him again whether his legs worked, but this time do it so *politely* that he had no choice but to answer?" A guard passed them. She lowered her voice and uncocked her shoulders. "Fine. I'm not sorry I did it, but I won't do it again. Okay?"

Harry's brows furrowed. "Please don't."

She tossed her head, looked like she wanted to say more, and then swallowed. "We're still talking to Amon Dooley before we leave?"

Thanks to orders from Pekka, they could visit any prisoner they liked, unsupervised, with just a guard to let them in and out of any locked cells. It had so far been fruitful. Evangeline had almost drawn blood she'd pinched Millard so hard. Harry believed the man truly had no feeling in his legs.

He wasn't their killer.

That didn't mean he wasn't communicating with someone. His mind was still working—Evangeline had proven that, too. He wouldn't have approved her methods if she'd run them by him first. That's why he was glad she hadn't asked. He wondered how much more efficient his job would be if he skirted the rules like Evangeline. But that would never be him. He simply wasn't wired that way.

"Yes," Harry confirmed. "Dooley next."

They located the prisoner in the same large recreation room where they'd first encountered him. Four other inmates sat on the weathered couch kitty-corner to him, watching a *M*A*S*H* rerun. Two of them glanced at Evangeline and Harry as they entered, then at each other, then back to the television. With more time to study the game room, Harry saw it was neat—the white walls free of scuffs, the floor freshly mopped, games stacked on the TV—but that it was strangely frozen in time. It wasn't just the sound of Hawkeye and Hunnicutt exchanging their 1970s banter. There was the pool table, its green felt covered by paperback novels out of publication for decades. Patient jumpsuits that would have suited any time in the last century. A damaged lightbulb flickering in a far corner that combined with the sunlight-slicing window bars to give everything a herky-jerky sepia tone.

"Mr. Dooley?" Harry asked, approaching. "We were here a few days ago. We're BCA agents."

Dooley's chair faced the window looking over the front lawn of the CCTC. Harry could see their SUV below parked at the edge of the employee lot.

"I remember you," the man said.

"I'm glad," Evangeline responded. "You were pretty worked up that day."

He pivoted his wheelchair to face them. Pekka had told them that Dooley suffered from hallucinations, that he'd been transferred to

CCTC because of a degenerative neurological disorder. He appeared surprisingly clear-eyed.

"It was only a nightmare," he told Evangeline. "You know about those."

She tensed from head to toe, a small movement but more powerful for it. "What do you mean?"

His shoulder lifted. "In your line of work."

"You mentioned a witch sucking Matty's blood," Harry said, taking lead from Evangeline so she could collect herself. "You were referring to Mathias Millard?"

"Sure, but I was wrong." Dooley glanced behind Harry. When Harry turned, he saw a guard watching them. Alkuan? "I had a nightmare that I was rolling past Matty's room, and I peeked in, saw somebody leaning over, sucking his blood. Ha ha ha," he said, tapping each syllable like a drumbeat. "A nightmare, right?"

Evangeline leaned toward Dooley. Harry worried she was going to assault a second inmate, but her voice was conspiratorial. "What do you know about Matty? Think he walks at night?"

Dooley's nose wrinkled. "Naw, his legs are worthless, man. Arms too. He can't even feed himself. Can't talk." His expression grew crafty. "His mind's there, though. He's a sharp little devil inside that body cage."

"No way," Evangeline said, widening her eyes. "You know that for a fact?"

"It's no secret," Dooley said. "He can blink yes or no, but it's not even that. When he thinks no one is looking, his eyes glow." He shuddered.

"Glow?" Harry asked.

"Not for real, but there's just so much hate in 'em."

"But you didn't see anyone in his room?" Evangeline asked. "Not really?"

"Can you do anything for me?" Dooley asked, licking his lips. "Get me a shorter sentence, or even a room with a bigger window, or food that doesn't taste like shit soup?"

Evangeline stood up. Shook her head.

"That's what I thought," he said. "Naw, I didn't see anything, anywhere. Now, if you'll excuse me, I'd like to watch some TV."

CHAPTER 49

"The CCTC is connected to the whole town, and the town is a mystery." Evangeline spoke quietly as they left the rec room.

Harry felt uneasy as they walked the empty corridor, a different route than they'd come in. The stark white walls stretched endlessly, devoid of life or warmth. Fluorescent lights buzzed overhead, casting a cold, clinical glow. Unsettling sounds echoed—the distant clank of metal against metal, the creak of a cell opening, a hushed whisper that vanished before it could fully register. This was a place designed to suppress and control.

Harry wouldn't talk about the case here, and Evangeline wasn't asking him to. She was processing something out loud.

"Or is the whole town connected to the CCTC, and the CCTC is the mystery?" She began to hum. Harry recognized the tune as "Dem Bones." He was thinking of the lyrics (*hip bone connected to the backbone, backbone connected to the shoulder bone, shoulder bone connected to the neck bone*) when Evangeline stopped abruptly in front of a cell door.

The one she'd tried to get in the other day, the one from her nightmare, the one with the double lock. Harry noticed the cell number this time: 36.

Two guards appeared at the far end, laughing at something. Harry called to them. "Excuse me," he said, speaking before he could talk himself out of it. "Can you come here?"

One of the guards broke away to approach them. He didn't have Alkuan features. "Yes?"

Harry showed him the day pass they'd been given as well as his BCA identification. "Who's in cell 36?"

The man pushed out his bottom lip and shook his head. "It's empty."

"Can we see inside?" Harry asked, his heart hammering.

"I don't see why not." He pulled back the dead bolt, then took the key card from his waist and held it in front of the lock. It buzzed and clicked, and the door popped open.

Evangeline stayed outside while Harry stepped in. It was a standard prison cell with empty walls, a made bunk attached to the wall, a shelf, a stainless-steel sink and toilet, and a detention-glazed window overlooking the rear courtyard. The rich smell of black dirt was strong near the bed, but the blanket was clean.

"Who was the last inmate to stay in here?" Harry asked.

The guard hollered down the hall, "Jones. You know anyone ever housed in 36?"

Harry heard the negative confirmation.

"Same," the guard told Harry. "This one's always empty. At least as long as I've worked here, and that's been over a year."

Harry thanked him. Step by step, they were being led to a dark truth, but it was frustrating how slick it was. What were they up against? In a prison of serial killers staffed by a town built on secrets, who was telling the truth?

Your neck bone connected to your head bone,
I hear the word of the Lord.

CHAPTER 50

The prison yard's silence was as profound as before, the deep green of the pine trees hugging the razor-wire-topped fencing still creating a sound barrier. The effect was one of isolation and emptiness, as if the entire world were frozen.

Pure white snow. Silver fencing. Emerald trees.

There was a strange, alien beauty to the bleakness.

Harry wondered for the second time how much use the exercise yard got. There were no new tracks since they'd last been here. Most if not all the prisoners had mobility issues, but they still deserved fresh air. Were they confined to the building all winter long?

"What do we know for sure?" Evangeline asked as they crunched along the interior perimeter.

"Mathias Millard is incapacitated. Amon Dooley believes he saw someone harming Millard, but he played it off as a nightmare."

"You caught that, too," Evangeline said gratefully. "He could've witnessed another prisoner messing with Millard. Someone who bribed a guard to let him in. Happens at prisons all the time."

"If the person being messed with has caused trouble or was a pedophile, yes. Neither of those describes Millard, not that we know of."

Evangeline inhaled deeply. "I'm going to miss this smell. Cold air and pine trees. There's nothing cleaner."

She was right about the fresh air. He welcomed the invitation to appreciate the frozen beauty. "We also have reason to suspect that the two crimes are connected. What motivation is there to kill a family and a nurse, twenty-five years apart?"

They'd walked the first length of fencing. Evangeline took a sharp left to start the second. "Best guess is that back in '98, Jarmo or Janice saw something they weren't supposed to. Sounds like the same thing happened to Weiss."

They both glanced over at the ugly prison. It was the architectural opposite of the original building, broad and aggressive where the school was graceful and sweeping. Harry thought he saw a flash of a face in a lower-level cell, but the prison otherwise appeared to be asleep.

"Did they see the *same* thing, twenty-five years apart?" he asked.

"That would be quite a long-lived scandal, if so," Evangeline said. "Maybe they both witnessed the Tervo family turning into vampires?"

Harry assumed—hoped—she was joking. "But then why kill the children?"

"I don't know." She sounded exasperated. "Maybe the Korhonens were the vampires, and the town killed them to prevent them from hurting others." Her mittens punctuated the air. "Or maybe it was a drifter the first time, like the police thought, and he came back around again with the same shotgun."

Neither of them believed that. A scrabbling sound in the forest drew their attention. Harry saw it first, nose quivering, nearly the same color white as the snow. "A rabbit," he said, pointing. Then he saw the lumps. "But what's right behind it?"

They walked toward the end of the second length of the fencing until they reached the farthest point from the prison while still being inside the exercise yard. The rabbit was twenty feet beyond, crouched in a clearing they could just see between the tree trunks.

"Stones?" Evangeline asked. There were at least fifty lumps, some covered in snow, others protected by the trees.

Harry pulled out his phone and snapped a photo between the fence wires, focusing on the nearest, largest of the objects. Then he made the image in the photograph even bigger.

Evangeline hissed. "*Grave*stones."

He enlarged the photo further. It was blurry, but the etched writing was legible: NILS TERVO, PATRIARCH, 1926–1998.

Evangeline whistled. "A founders' graveyard, is my guess," she said. "Take a photo of the two stones to its left. Is either his wife?"

Harry did, squinting. "No," he said. "Both Tervos, but they're his parents, by the dates."

"And no headstone to the right," Evangeline said. "Not for at least ten feet. They really think she's still alive."

Harry slid his cell back into his pocket. "You don't?"

Her mouth grew tight. "I don't think anyone leaves this town, dead or alive."

They started walking again, lost in their thoughts. They'd nearly reached the prison when Evangeline's phone dinged. "The Wi-Fi!" she said.

Harry waited while she read her text.

"Kyle tracked down the pizza delivery person who discovered Weiss's body. Her name's Aimee Fleck. He's got a Highway 61 address for her." She turned to Harry. "Where's Highway 61 from here?"

"North of Duluth," he said.

Evangeline nodded. "Says he left her a message telling her to expect us. I want to canvass Alku again on our way through. You in?"

"Of course," Harry said.

"Good," Evangeline said. "Let's drop by the Korhonen place, too. Something's telling me we need another walk-through."

CHAPTER 51

Alku's placement on the open prairie meant much of its snow had melted. Small, dense glaciers still hung on in alleys and beneath the shade of trees, but most of the town had the soggy, beat-up look of a bear emerging from hibernation.

The streets remained as empty as a movie set at midnight, same as every time Harry and Evangeline had been here. Harry knew the kids weren't at school. Neither were they outside playing. Harry and Evangeline walked from house to house, knocking, but no one answered their door. There wasn't even movement inside indicating someone was hiding or watching. Many residents would be working at the prison, but not every single person in Alku, not the children.

"I feel like I'm selling car-wash coupons," Evangeline said as they approached the Wenner house.

"That's a very specific reference." Harry tucked the loose end of his cashmere scarf into his coat. It might be a few degrees warmer in Alku than in the woods, but the wind had teeth.

"It's a job I held for a minute in college," she said, flashing him a wry smile. "Answered an ad in the college newspaper for 'unlimited money, you pick the hours.' Turned out to be one click off a scam. The company owners drove a bunch of us idiots out to the suburbs and had us sell ten-dollar car-wash coupon booklets for twenty bucks. When I sassed back on the first day, they stranded me in Fridley. This was before cell phones, mind you." She stamped her feet against the cold. "I had to hitchhike home."

"'Sassed back'?" Harry asked. "On day one?"

She shrugged, stepping onto the Wenner porch. "You'd understand if you were there. I got a job as a maid right after." She kept talking as she knocked. "That gig lasted a little longer, only because I loved snooping through people's things. Good prep for this job."

Harry was horrified. "You riffled through strangers' personal effects?"

"Didn't take anything." Evangeline stared at the quiet door. "They operate in sync here, don't they?"

"They do," Harry agreed, wondering if she'd riffled through *his* things. But when would she have had a chance? "They either have something to hide, or they're hiding from something."

"Harry Steinbeck," Evangeline said in mock wonder, "is that you speculating—out loud and in public—without evidence?"

"I am *inferring* based on behavior."

She chuckled. "'Guessing' is what us laypeople call it."

"*We* laypeople," he said before he could stop himself.

"What?" she asked, stepping off the porch.

"Nothing." They'd visited fourteen houses so far. "Want to keep going?"

She glanced up and down the street. "No one is going to talk to us, not without a direct order from Pekka or Pihla. Might as well hit the Korhonen house and then go talk to the pizza delivery gal."

Though no one had answered their door, Harry felt certain many folks were home, possibly hiding in their basements—where else would they all be?—but the Korhonen house wore its emptiness on its sleeve, its clean, wide glass staring vacantly at the street.

The front door was unlocked, as before. The interior looked the same, like a museum left open for tourists to walk through, commenting on the china and silverware of people from the past.

"Let's open drawers and look under furniture this time," Evangeline said.

They started at the radio and worked their way around the room, away from each other, until they met on the other side. First the living room, then the dining room, then the kitchen, then the bathroom, looking in, on, and under everything. It was meditative. They discovered only the uncomplicated materials of a past life, nothing electric. Silverware. Linens. Basic tools: hammer, screwdriver, tape measure. Kitchen utensils: silver serving spoons, a potato masher, spatulas.

Remove the refrigerator and this house could have been abandoned anytime in the last hundred years.

In the soothing movement of opening and closing drawers, mentally cataloging the detritus of life, Harry was brought back to a memory of playing house with his sister. She was around five, so he must have been fourteen or fifteen. She loved playacting a happy home at that age, clattering through the kitchen, pretending to bake cakes and to order him—she insisted he play her husband—around. It's what she thought wives did.

That particular day, she'd taken out the large Red Wing cake bowl their mother cherished. Caroline had been forbidden to play with it. Myrna had inherited the bowl from her own mother. Myrna neither baked nor spoke kindly of her mom, but for some reason, she loved that piece of pottery. Harry pretended to read the newspaper in a husbandly fashion, smoking an imaginary pipe, while Caroline stirred air and complained about fictional friends, criticized her invisible daughter, and talked about the new diet she was going to start, some of Myrna's favorite topics of conversation.

Harry didn't know how long their mother had been watching them.

He only knew that her jaw was rigid, her face fresh with tears when he finally noticed her.

"We're pretending!" he said, but Myrna strode away without comment.

Harry wanted to run after her, but it was Caroline who stopped him, saying in her sweet, tinny five-year-old voice, "If she doesn't like it, she should behave differently."

Then she went back to fake stirring.

For the first time, Harry wondered what his mother had given up to raise two children. He knew about her degree, her potential career, but what other dreams had been thwarted? What connections severed as her life was shrunk to the size of her home, first with Harry, and then when she was almost free, with the birth of Caroline? What healthy impulses toward creation and travel were stunted, redirected to resentment and control, and—in the case of Caroline—to cruelty? The thought made Harry uncomfortable, but he didn't know whether it was the fact that he'd never considered Myrna's side of it before or that he was potentially letting her off the hook for how she'd treated Caroline.

"Let's move it upstairs," Evangeline said, glancing sideways at the basement door. "I'm in no hurry to go down there."

"Fine by me." Harry followed her up. They started in Jarmo and Janice's bedroom, slipping back into their rhythm. Harry got the closet, still full of clothes. He checked all the pockets and inside the shoes while Evangeline dug deep in the chest of drawers. After forty-five minutes, they came up empty and moved to the children's room.

"You take the beds," Evangeline said. "I'll start at the dresser."

Harry nodded, striding to the nearest twin mattress. He ran his gloved hands across the blankets, the pillow, examined the space between the bed and the wall. It wasn't until he lifted up the mattress that he discovered something.

"Look at this," he said, still holding the mattress aloft.

Evangeline came to stand beside him, both of them staring down at the *Rolling Stone* magazine.

"Guess we know where the kids in this town hang out when no one's looking," she said.

"Is that woman wearing an AR-15 bra?" Harry asked.

"That's Lady Gaga, and yep, sure looks like it," Evangeline agreed. "This is an old one. Published July 2010."

"I wonder where they got it?"

"Kids find a way, their tenacity in direct proportion to how much effort their parents put into hiding the world from them." She paged through it. "Nothing hidden inside."

Harry was about to ask her if she wanted to put it back when the closet sneezed.

CHAPTER 52

Harry dropped the mattress as Evangeline drew her weapon.

"Come out with your hands up," she commanded.

When there was no response, she strode to the door and whipped it open. The closet was wide but not deep. Max, Rannie, Fred, and Honeybee stood inside. The man and boys appeared shamefaced, while Honeybee beamed with delight at Harry.

"Don't shoot!" Fred exclaimed, fear accentuating the whistle between his tooth gap.

Evangeline holstered her weapon.

"Sorry!" Rannie said, his bulk too large and his voice too loud for the cramped space. "We were hiding! You took forever!"

"How long have you been here?" Harry asked.

Max still had his hands up. "We came about half an hour before you showed up. We sometimes hang out upstairs." His eyes strayed to the bed that hid the *Rolling Stone* magazine.

"Like a clubhouse," Harry said. *That also happens to be the scene of a mass murder.* But that would have been well before their time, at least for everyone but Rannie. "Where you read magazines and . . . ?"

Max's cheeks blazed.

"You can drop your hands," Evangeline said.

"I stole that magazine from the motel office," Max said. "Last summer. We were just biking around and exploring. If we sat exactly right in the woods, we could see what the guy at the desk was watching on the TV. He left for something, and I sneaked in and stole the *Rolling Stone*." He dropped his head. "I'm sorry."

"Don't lie," Rannie said. "If you lie, you make people cry, and you might as well say goodbye. I was the one who took it. I'm very bad, so bad that sometimes I forget."

Honeybee slipped out of the closet, her hands held behind her. She must have been wearing a hat earlier because her wispy blonde hair was tight to her scalp for a few inches and then became a magnificent frizz bomb at the end. She walked to Harry and offered him the daffodil she'd been hiding.

"She's been carrying that around all day," Max said. "And Rannie's telling the truth about forgetting. Passes out cold when he's stressed or hurt. No reason for him to get in trouble about the magazine. We all looked at it." He blinked rapidly. "You won't tell on us, though, right?"

Harry clutched the daffodil. The stem was warm and wilted, but the flower was a vibrant, buttery yellow. "Thank you," he said. "And we won't tell about the magazine."

Honeybee smiled and ran to hide behind Rannie.

Max watched her, his expression pained. "Rannie says we're not safe."

"Super unsafe," Fred whistle-said.

"They're coming for us, aren't they?" Max asked.

Harry and Evangeline exchanged a look. "Who's coming for you?"

"You don't know?" Rannie asked. He seemed disappointed.

"We'll know if you tell us." Harry fought to keep his voice level. If the kids told them what was happening, they could protect them.

Max shook his head and glanced up at Rannie. "They don't know."

Rannie nodded. Max's and Fred's faces fell.

"Do you know where Arlie is?" Harry asked.

"At home," Max said unhappily, staring at his feet. "We should get back to our families."

He grabbed Honeybee's hand and guided her out of the closet. Harry was desperate to make them stay, to reveal their secret, but he wouldn't force children to talk even if he could, and he knew their parents would never give permission. He held the flower and watched them walk out of the bedroom.

Evangeline jumped, which made Harry jump.

"What?"

"My phone buzzed." She tugged it out. "You were right. This town is a hive. This place has access to the same Wi-Fi as at the CCTC."

Her voice dropped. "Ho-lee cats. Emery just texted: 'Come to the station. We have a confession.'"

CHAPTER 53

Rannie
April 8, 2023

Rannie formally met Peter Weiss while exploring the school basement one day while everyone was in class. It'd taken him years after he stumbled over those bear-chewed bodies to work up the courage to return to the building. Pihla promising he could use the new crayons and play hide-and-seek in the empty rooms was what finally got him. He was scoping out good places to hide when he discovered Peter smoking near the tunnel door.

"You shouldn't smoke." He'd seen smokers outside the restaurant when he and Max biked out there. He knew it was bad. But then he recognized the guy's horseshoe-shaped mustache, even though it'd been years and years and years since he'd seen it, that night of the Hela celebration when he'd followed his mom and Jarmo into the prison. "Hey, are you the skeleton crew?"

Peter had seemed worried when Rannie appeared around the corner, but he suddenly relaxed. "You're that Tervo boy, aren't you? The special one."

Rannie smiled proudly. "Pekka's my brother. He's married to Pihla, so she's my sister. Ansa is my mother, and Nils was my father."

Peter's eyes narrowed. He dropped his cigarette, squashed it with his boot, then picked up the butt and dropped it into a cellophane wrapper. "Your mother alive?"

"Yeah." Rannie didn't like how his gut burned saying that. "But my dad isn't. His bones, the ones that were left, are buried in the graveyard. My fort is past that."

He knew he shouldn't tell anyone about his fort, but he was proud of it.

"Fort? I'd like to see it sometime," the man said. "And yeah, I work late some nights, but I'm no skeleton." He held out his hand. "I'm Peter. I'm a good friend of your brother's."

Rannie deliberately sought out Peter after that. Rannie loved Max and Honeybee, and he liked the other kids, but there was something nice about talking to a grown-up. Peter treated him like an adult. He'd talk to him about the prison inmates and tell him stories about the terrible things they did. Hearing those gory tales made Rannie's stomach twist and bubble, but he listened politely because Peter would sprinkle in bits about a movie he'd seen, or a gooey cheese pizza he'd eaten, or something else good from the outside world. He must have noticed Rannie's face when he talked about food, because he started bringing him crinkly little bags of candy or chips, most of which Rannie socked away to share with Max and Honeybee.

It got to be where Rannie knew he and Peter were friends. He trusted the man, and he wanted to finally bring him to his fort.

It was a simple one-room structure, safe and snug. It even had a woodstove that Nils had put into storage after buying a new one for their house. Rannie was sure Peter would think it was cool. Only problem? Max didn't like the bony, big-bellied nurse with the horseshoe mustache, and the fort was part Max's. Though Rannie had built it, it was Max who turned it cozy. It was his idea to color it sky blue inside using paint taken from the school basement, to put up bright lemon-colored curtains, to bring in blankets so they could snuggle warm while they hid away from everyone. They'd even painted a sign that said RANNIE'S RANCH and hung it over the door. Rannie didn't understand what a ranch was, even after Max tried to explain it to him, but it made Max giggle to call it that.

"His laugh is mean," Max had said after meeting Peter, "and any-how, no guy that old should be hanging out with kids."

"But I'm not a kid," Rannie said. "I'm a grown man, yes I am, so I can. Besides, you don't know him like I do. I want to bring him to the fort."

Max made a grumpy face, but he hadn't argued. Rannie liked that about Max. He said his piece, but he let you make up your own mind. He was the best friend Rannie had ever had. But that didn't mean he was Rannie's *only* friend. Rannie decided he was going to bring Peter out no matter what Max thought.

It wasn't a lie. It wasn't sneaky.

Rannie had told Max, and Max didn't have to like it for Rannie to do it.

Still, his heart was beating slam-bam as he led Peter through the woods. He'd promised him last week he'd take him to his fort, but today was the first day it would work. He told Peter to bundle up good—the smell of the air and the angry steel of the sky told Rannie there was a monster of a blizzard on the way—and meet him thirty paces west of the school door. He didn't tell Peter that's where the bear had killed the hikers, but it would have been easier if he'd known. Then Rannie could just say to meet him at Bearkill, which was what he called it.

The snow in the open was as deep as their knees, but Bearkill was in the protected woods. It was only ankle-deep there and had a hard crust. They stayed on top of it.

"You're going to love my fort," Rannie said.

Peter had grunted. "Their graves are back here, aren't they?"

It took Rannie a moment to understand that he meant where the founders slept, not the hikers. "Sure, we walk right through them to get to the fort."

"Tell me when we get to them."

Peter sounded bossy, which he sometimes did. Rannie didn't like it, but Pekka had once told him that friends needed to accept each other, good and bad, so Rannie didn't say anything until they reached the gravestones. Evening was coming, and the shadows were getting long, but he could have found them in his sleep.

"Here we go," Rannie said. "The first cemetery."

"First?" Peter asked, crouching in front of Rannie's father's grave. He pulled a phone from his pocket and turned on the flashlight.

"Sure." Rannie was mesmerized by the phone. He'd spotted them through the windows of the motel and the diner when he and Max were spying, but not up close. The phone was flat, not much bigger than a deck of cards. "The second is where the others are buried."

Peter flashed the light right into Rannie's eyes, blinding him. "The *others?*"

Rannie held his arm in front of his face. "From the hospital times. There are thousands in the field right beyond the forest. Their gravestones lie flat in the ground. Not raised, like these."

"Jesus," Peter muttered. "You people."

Rannie didn't like the way Peter said that. He started to think maybe he didn't want him at his fort after all. Should he have listened to Max? *Of course* he should have. "Dangit," he said out loud.

"What?" Peter's flashlight scanned the nearby headstones.

"I don't want to go to my fort anymore. I'm hungry."

Peter shoved his free hand into his pocket. "I brought you chips."

"I like chips." Rannie hadn't given himself time to think before speaking. He bit his lip until he could arrange his thoughts. "But I don't want them." That was a lie. "I want them, but I don't want to take you to my fort, not anymore. Let's go back to Bearkill."

The light in his face again. "Bearkill?"

"I want to go home." Rannie started walking back the way they'd come, his steps high and jerky.

"Tell me about your mom," Peter said, catching up to him.

Rannie didn't slow. "She was smart and beautiful and she loved me."

"No." Peter grabbed Rannie's arm. Other than his protruding gut, he was a tall, lean man, but Rannie had fifty muscled pounds on him. Pekka had hammered into his head that the bigger you were, the gentler you must be. Rannie breathed through his nose like he'd been taught and allowed Peter to stop him.

"I want to know what your ma was like right before she disappeared."

Calm like balm think of Mom.

"She wasn't herself," Rannie said. "She drank so much it swole her tummy, just like yours." He pointed at Peter's belly and kept talking. "She would cry. She was forgetful. That's why I think she wandered off. She forgot who we were."

Peter snorted. "Sounds like she was pregnant to me. Probably ran off to have that baby and start a new life."

All the training in the world couldn't have touched Rannie then. He was filled with a blind rage, his strength overpowering and terrifying, just like his father's had been. He drove his fist into a tree and then the world went black.

CHAPTER 54

Pekka Tervo sat at a metal table in a Duluth Police Department interview room. He wore corduroy pants and a dark-yellow sweater that matched the rims on his round glasses, and his thinning hair was combed and neat. His hands were clasped resolutely in front of him, resting on the table. He made eye contact with Evangeline and then Harry the moment they walked in.

"I'm responsible for all the deaths," he said, speaking clearly. "The poor Korhonen family. Peter Weiss. It's all my fault."

Harry's eyes flicked to Emery, who'd met them at the PD's front door, his eyes on fire.

Pekka Tervo strolled in and claimed responsibility for the murders. All of 'em.

He'd led Harry and Evangeline straight to the room and then positioned himself behind Pekka. Harry was struck by the disconnect between the ease of Emery's pose—arms and ankles crossed as he leaned—and the rigidity of his body, every muscle humming, ready to leap.

"You murdered them?" Evangeline asked.

"It's my fault they're dead," Pekka said emphatically.

Harry took one of two chairs across from Pekka. The scrape of the metal legs on the floor was sharp in the close room. He didn't know what was actually going on here, but he suspected Pekka was in a dissociative state. The man was hardly blinking, and when he spoke, only his mouth moved.

"Did you kill them?" Harry asked, repeating Evangeline's question.

"I allowed serial killers into Alku. *Serial killers.* Murderous men who had to be tended by the husbands and wives and—eventually—children of Alku. And when there were too many for us to care for, I invited in outsiders, people who do not understand our ways or . . ." He closed his eyes tightly. "Share our moral code."

Evangeline was wound as tightly as Emery. "Who killed the Korhonen family?"

"Don't you see?" Pekka's face collapsed in misery. "We *all* did. The board members are responsible, and I'm the chairman of the board. Please. I claim full responsibility."

"Did you pull a trigger?" Evangeline asked.

Pekka groaned. "I might as well have." His hands twisted, his eyes beseeching. "I need to do this. For the town. For our peace. For our solitude. We can get it back, have a fresh start, but first someone must take responsibility." He held out his wrists. "I confess."

The tension in the room was so taut that they all twitched when someone rapped at the door.

"This better be important," Emery barked as he opened it.

Pihla and the long-nosed Torben Virtanen stood on the other side. Emery paused for a moment before stepping aside.

"Pekka, you shouldn't be here," Pihla said from the doorway. Her features were composed, but her face was red and swollen. She'd been crying.

"Can he come with us?" Torben asked Emery, his tone desperate.

Emery paused, then: "He came of his own free will, he can leave of his own free will."

"There are no charges?" Torben asked.

"Not at this time," Emery said.

It was a legitimate answer. Pekka Tervo wasn't confessing; he was having a psychological break. He needed help, not a jail cell. "I believe you're under a great deal of stress," Harry told Pekka. "Do you have resources available to you?"

Pihla strode over and put her hand on her husband's shoulder, her fingers disappearing nearly to the first knuckle. "We have the best mental health staff in the region at our disposal," she said. "What Pekka needs is *rest*."

She leaned down, her mouth touching his ear. "Come, Veli-Pekka. It's time to go home."

He nodded, his expression vacant. Torben stepped aside so Pihla could lead her husband out.

She paused at the door and turned to Emery. "You should have called us sooner."

Emery scratched his left sideburn. "He came to me, Pihla. No one picked him up."

She nodded, her mouth set in a grim line. "We will expect you in church on Sunday. It's been too long."

Then she, Pekka, and Torben disappeared.

CHAPTER 55

Harry's flesh crawled. "You're of Alku?"

Emery had his hand on the doorknob, head down. "Told you my grandpa was Finnish." He kept his back to them. "He grew up in Alku, died years ago."

"You're shitting me," Evangeline said. "You're related to the *original founders*?"

Emery showed them his profile. "Blood's pretty thin by now, but I imagine there's a link. I've never lived there. My parents, either. I've attended a few services. Holidays. That sort of thing."

"You didn't think to mention that?" Harry was incredulous. The lead investigator on an active murder investigation had failed to reveal a connection to the potential suspects and was now acting like it wasn't of note.

Emery turned around all the way, slowly. He looked *prickly*. His expression, his mood. "Here's how it is. When there's a game on, sometimes I drop by Burgers at the Beacon in Hermantown to watch. The Super One grocery store on the hill has some great specials on Saturdays. There's a gas station in Proctor that'll change your oil for nineteen dollars and not even ask for a coupon. It's like that with the Christmas service in Alku. I drop by on occasion, make sure I look happy being there." His voice sounded like rocks grinding. "You work LE up here, you make sure to connect with the community for twenty miles in each direction."

"Did you know Arlie Wenner?" Harry asked, wondering why he'd never noticed before how punchable Emery's face was.

"I've encountered the Wenner family prior to the scene in Alku, sure, if that's what you mean." He held Harry's gaze. "I've likely seen the child as well."

"Did you see her after the parents told you she'd never been missing?" Harry pressed.

Emery's mouth curved. "I think I can guess where you're going with this, but you saw for yourself how out of her mind the mother was. You think if her daughter had really been missing, she would have just *forgotten* about it?" He shook his head. "Everyone loves their kids, but no one loves them like Alku folks."

"Did you *see* Arlie Wenner after her parents told you she'd never been missing?" Harry repeated, his voice a growl.

"No." Emery fired the word. "And I didn't need to because Mrs. Wenner confirmed that her daughter had been in her bedroom the whole time."

Evangeline shook her head in disbelief. "What if she was told to say that, to pretend Arlie wasn't missing?"

"And why would anyone tell her that?"

"Because they took the girl," Evangeline said.

"They?" Something dangerous coated Emery's words.

"They," Evangeline said, stepping toward him. "The town of Alku. Something stinks there." She aimed her chin at him. "And now you stink, too."

Harry spoke slowly so as not to be misunderstood. "Do you have any other ties to Alku or the case we should know about?"

A muscle in Emery's cheek was jumping. He and Evangeline were still in a stare-off. "I didn't think you needed to know about *this*."

"Thanks," Harry said. "We'll be in touch."

He waited for Emery to open the door, and then he followed Evangeline out.

He knew in his bones that they were running out of time to keep the Alku children safe.

CHAPTER 56

"That was some steaming horseshit." Evangeline tossed Harry the keys. "You're driving. I need to call that professor in Finland."

"What about this time?" Harry slid behind the wheel.

"What Emery said. About how everyone loves their kids, but not like the Alku folks. I want to know if Professor Herdingher agrees."

Harry's forehead creased. "That's his name?"

"Close enough."

Harry started the car. "We're going to interview the pizza driver who found Weiss?"

Evangeline was punching numbers into her phone. "Who else?"

Harry's phone lit up with Aimee Fleck's address. Even angry, Evangeline was efficient. He opened the directions in Google Maps and began driving north, toward Two Harbors. He and Evangeline had to hurry. The children of Alku were in danger, it was connected to the murders, and if they didn't act fast, they would lose.

Poor Arlie, rotting Alku, slippery Emery.

It had a powerful emotional resonance with the loss of Caroline.

She'd described her likely abductor. She'd told Harry exactly what he'd looked like, Harry was sure of it. The only piece he'd caught was "two different lies." What had that meant? Was it like this case, with half-truths and cratered secrets? Or had the man who'd taken his sister lied about two different things? His name, where he worked, his age, when he would meet her next?

Evangeline was rattling off background details to the person on the other end of the phone, presumably the professor. She told him about a girl disappearing, about Emery saying no one valued their kids like Alku folks. She even threw in Harry's question about super strength, pausing for a response after each question. When she hung up, she was silent for a few moments.

Harry let her process.

"He confirmed what Emery said, that the Alku folks worship their children—at least they did when they lived in Finland. He asked if it was only one child who'd likely gone missing."

"'Only'?" Harry asked.

She stared out the window. "He said if it was more than one that it might be a 'reaping.' That's what the village townsfolk called it when they murdered the Alku children back in Finland in the 1800s. 'A necessary reaping.' It was part of their belief system."

Harry gripped the steering wheel. "But who would be hurting their children here in the United States, in this century?"

"A hate group? One reenacting the violence of the past?"

Harry shook his head. "That seems a stretch. Crossing an ocean to reenact an ignorant genocide from five generations earlier?"

"Yeah, but we've both seen weirder," Evangeline said, sighing. "The professor fleshed out the vampire stories a bit, too, though he didn't offer anything new. A person suffering from tuberculosis is so pale they look like they're being bled to death, and a freshly dead corpse will still bleed. The ignorant townsfolk misread both those facts to decide that their doctors—the Tervos et al—were vampires preying on them."

"I heard you ask about super strength."

"Interesting, that." She turned to him, eyebrows raised. He could almost feel her trying to crawl inside his head. "There *were* stories about the people in the village being particularly strong. Able to pull carts, carry multiple buckets of water, that sort of thing. You intuited that from an offhand comment from a gas station attendant?"

Harry made a noncommittal noise. He still wasn't ready to reveal his outlandish theory. There weren't enough facts. He could wait to share it, one way or another, until he got the DNA results from Deepty.

Evangeline needed more. "So what does it mean that there were rumors of super strength?"

"Maybe nothing," Harry said honestly. "Scared people see things, and false stories spread faster than true ones. It's another piece of information to add to what we know."

"And what exactly do we know?" Evangeline threw up her hands. "Either there's a serial killer in the prison who's escaping, or someone in that town is a serial killer. In either case, everyone is covering for them."

"That makes the latter more likely, doesn't it?" Harry asked. "I can't see Alku running interference for a stranger. I *can* see them going to the mat for one of their own." He flicked on his turn signal and pulled into a short asphalt driveway. "See the earlier behavior of one Pekka Tervo."

"This the pizza delivery person's place?" Evangeline glanced at her phone and then at the two-story apartment building seemingly dropped onto the Lake Superior shore five miles north of Duluth.

"It's the address you sent."

"After we talk to her, I want to circle back to Silas Smith. I need one more crack at him," Evangeline said, sliding out of the car.

Aimee Fleck answered the door wearing flannel pajama bottoms and an oversize Calvin and Hobbes T-shirt. She was in her late twenties. She had blonde hair with black roots, black eyebrows, and wide brown eyes.

"Can I help you?" she asked.

"I'm Agent Van Reed, and this is my partner, Harry Steinbeck." They both held up their IDs. "I believe my colleague, Agent Kaminski, told you to expect us."

"Sure," she said, without stepping aside. Her voice was high, trembly. She looked like she hadn't been sleeping well. "But I don't have anything new to say. I kinda want to forget that night, you know?"

"We don't blame you," Harry said. "May we come in?"

She glanced at the ground. "I'd really rather you didn't. The detective told me I should only talk to him, you know?"

"Which detective?" Harry asked.

"I don't remember his name, but he had face hair like Wolverine. From the X-Men?"

Emery. "You don't need to tell us anything new," Harry said. "If you could just review what you saw that night, exactly as you told him, we can be on our way."

She appeared unsure, but then Evangeline said one simple word. "Please."

Harry continued to be surprised at how completely Evangeline's demeanor changed around victims. The bearing that made her always look braced for a fight relaxed. Her voice and gaze softened. She leaned forward, nodding often. Harry had known agents for whom this behavior was a performance, one they shed like an itchy coat the minute they left a victim's side. With Evangeline, it seemed like the opposite was true, like she became her true self around people who'd survived trauma.

Aimee Fleck's hand dropped from the doorjamb. "I tell you what I told him, and you go?"

"Yep," Evangeline said. Her voice was sunny.

"Fine." The woman sighed. "It was a snowstorm. Lots of people ordering pizza that night. They don't wanna risk their lives to eat but don't mind if someone making minimum wage does, you know? Pizza was delivered to his place at least two hours late and as cold as stone, but he's lucky I got it there at all." Her cheeks grew red. "I mean, he wasn't *lucky*. It's just that . . ."

"We get it," Evangeline said. "Given the weather, it was hard to get around."

"Exactly." She pushed her hair behind an ear with seven brassy piercings up its ridge. "The snow was so thick, I couldn't see a foot in front of my face, not really. That's why I saw the mirage, or whatever. The hallucination. That's what Detective Wolverine told me. Said it was the snow playing tricks on my eyes, refracting light or something like that."

Harry's pulse danced. "What did you see?"

"I parked at the end of the driveway, you know? So I wouldn't get stuck. I had my good boots on, so it was no big. Grabbed the pizza, hoofed it to the house, and that's when I saw it. Some creature shrinking as it walked. Like a stop-action person, you know? They started out big, then shortened right in front of my eyes. Big, medium, little, *gone*. It was a human body with a scarecrow face in all three versions."

"One person, three sizes?" Evangeline asked.

"At *least* three sizes." She rubbed her arms. "The snow was thick, and I was tired. Not high, like the detective kept saying." She shook her head. "I almost dropped the pizza and beat cheeks after I saw that, and maybe I should have, but even through the blizzard I could see that the front door was open. What if someone in there was hurt, I thought. I wouldn't want someone to be that close to helping me and then drive away." She shook her head in horror. "Can you imagine? Hearing someone just outside when you needed saving?"

Evangeline nodded encouragingly.

Aimee bit her lip. "But that guy couldn't hear anything at all, not anymore, could he? I peeked into his house and there he was, his head mashed in. I ran back to my car, locked my doors, and called 911."

CHAPTER 57

When no one answered at Silas Smith's apartment, Evangeline wanted to pick the lock. Harry talked her into waiting in the SUV, though it hadn't been easy. The man was their only non-Alku CCTC connection, and Evangeline wanted at him. Smith showed up forty-five minutes later, a bag of groceries in one arm.

They strode up while he fumbled with his key.

"We know Pihla is paying you on the down-low," Evangeline said coolly.

They, in fact, knew no such thing. Evangeline was stabbing in the dark, hoping to rattle Smith.

He whirled, his garter snake eyes glittering like dark water. "No down-low."

He switched his bag to the other arm and almost dropped it. Inside were generic pretzels, high-sodium boxed meal kits, and bacon. No fruit. No vegetables. "It was a raise," Smith continued. "I been there long enough."

Bingo.

Evangeline adjusted her height and somehow seemed more threatening and smaller at the same time, her elfin features sharp. "That's not what the IRS will say, not when no one else has gotten an equivalent raise. They'll say it's a bribe."

Legally, they could lie to a suspect to get the information required, a practice that had never sat well with Harry. But Smith wasn't a suspect. Still, Harry kept his mouth shut.

Smith sneered. "Don't matter to me. She gave me a raise to mind my business. Nothing the IRS can do about that."

"What business, exactly, does she want you to mind?" Evangeline extended her arms to take his groceries. He glared at her, then handed them off, turning back to his door.

"I don't know what she thinks I know, but I don't know a thing, except that Matty the Mallet gets tears in his eyes when Pihla walks into the room. Good, I say." He slid the key into the lock, opened the door, and reached for his groceries.

Evangeline held them tight. "You ever see Pihla hurt Matty?"

Smith traced an X over his chest. "Cross my heart and hope to die, I haven't. But I'd offer to help if I ever did. Man's a stone-cold bastard. You read his record. You know. Plus he laughs at everyone, all dry and cocky, like he knows something we don't."

"Who do you think killed Weiss?" Harry asked.

Smith threw back his head and bellowed. "Tell me you're bad at your job without telling me you're bad at your job." His eyes slitted. "Now give me my groceries and leave me the hell alone."

Evangeline handed the bag back. "What's in cell 36, Silas?" Her voice had changed, gone husky. Harry suspected they were getting to the real reason she'd wanted to talk to Smith. Her nightmares must be worse than she'd let on.

He tipped his head, studying her with interest. "You know about it, don't you."

She nodded.

His head bobbed, and his mouth tipped up at the edges. "Then you know it's empty. No inmate." He turned and stepped into his apartment. Turned back again. Grinned wider when he saw Evangeline's pleading expression. He seemed ready to leave it at that, taking pleasure in her unmet need, but then he paused.

"I've seen Pihla coming out of there some mornings looking ashamed, that's all I got," he said. Something in the slant of his voice suggested he was telling the truth. He shrugged. "I think she's got problems at home and sometimes sleeps in there." He widened his eyes and covered his mouth in a mockery of concern. "Think that's the thing she wanted me to keep to myself?"

Then he closed the door in their faces.

CHAPTER 58

"Lou just texted. She wants us to stop by her office."

"Your lawyer friend?" Evangeline had taken the keys back from Harry and driven them away from Smith's. "The one who got us the names of the Alku board members?"

"That's her." Harry told her where to turn.

Evangeline drove for a ways. "I've been thinking about something," she finally said. The side of her head rested in her hand, her elbow on the window ledge. She steered with her free hand. "What if they're experimenting on prisoners up at the CCTC? Not creating zombies. Medical studies. Psychological tests."

Harry felt a buzz of concern. He admired Evangeline's vivid intelligence, but this was veering off into conspiracy territory. "To what end?"

She exhaled through her nose. "That's what trips me up. There isn't money in it. Maybe they do it out of a sense of responsibility to a larger community? To get to the root of deviance so they can cure it in the next generation?"

"Every society throughout history has had deviants. It's sewn into our DNA."

"Deviance from cultural norms, sure, and it can be a good thing. It spurs evolution." She rubbed her nose. "But I'm talking violence, brutality. Impulses that serve no purpose in any society. What if the Alkuans are working to isolate those darker drives at the CCTC?"

Harry felt like she was stepping toward a ledge. "What evidence do you have?"

"Evidence?" She lifted her head and started drumming the steering wheel. "None. But it tracks with how they present themselves as caregivers. Remember how they donated to the families of those hikers? They believe they have a responsibility to others. And it would explain everything: their secrecy, the prisoner killed back in 1990, what Dooley thinks he saw recently, Pihla coming out of that cell. Maybe the Korhonens were going to tell, and then Weiss was going to tell, and so they had to be killed."

Harry scrubbed his voice of judgment. "In such a horrific manner?"

"That's where my bonkers theory falls apart," she agreed.

Harry's shoulders relaxed. "Take a left here," he said. "And park in front of the tan three-story. That's Lou's offices."

She pulled in. "What if one of their experiments escaped, though?" she asked, her voice suddenly rushed. "What if it had been in cell 36, and it got out? A murder monster?"

"Evangeline," Harry began.

Her chuckling stopped him. "Got you. Even I wouldn't put that on the table. My nightmares are telling me something terrible is in 36, though. I dreamt about that exact cell before I saw it."

"We looked inside. The cell is empty."

"A moment in time is not forever, Harry Steinbeck." She released her seat belt. "Shall we?"

"Dale Emery is related to Alku?" Lou asked, her voice loaded with disbelief.

Her office was pulled out of the lawyers page of an interior design catalog. Dark paneling, rich leather furniture, bookcases lining two walls. She sat behind an elegant wood desk. "I had no idea." She tapped her chin with a pen. "I don't know that it means anything that he is, though. Especially if he's two generations removed from living there."

Evangeline crossed her legs and leaned back in her chair. She obviously disagreed with Lou on that front but had the tact to keep silent.

"It was a surprise to us," Harry said. "Your text mentioned information?"

"Yessir." She opened a file on her desk. The thin afternoon light from the sole window hit her head, making her hair cartoon glossy. "I tracked down the Alku corporation bylaws, and it wasn't easy."

Evangeline sat back up. "Thank you," she said.

"It was no big deal." Lou smiled and leaned forward conspiratorially. "Actually, it was a *huge* deal. The bylaws were buried several layers deep. I had to pull nearly every string to access them, but what good are favors if you don't call them in?"

"Anything stand out?" Harry asked.

"They're fairly standard, considering they govern the board and a town. There's only one unusual item."

Both Harry and Evangeline were on the edge of their seats.

She pulled out a sheet of paper and turned it to face them. "Clause 41b. Any change made to the bylaws, and by extension any change made to the financial or governing status of the town or its businesses, must be unanimously agreed upon." Her eyes left the paper and locked onto Harry's. "And no board member may ever move out of Alku."

Evangeline made a scoffing noise. "But how can you force someone to stay in a town?" She realized the answer nearly before she finished the question.

"You kill them," she and Harry said in unison.

CHAPTER 59

Rannie
April 14, 2023
Predawn

When Rannie learned that Peter, the nurse with the mustache like a horseshoe, died after their visit to the graveyard, he didn't know how to feel. The man was gone by the time Rannie woke up near the founders' cemetery. Rannie was cold, his fingers stiff from lying on the frozen ground.

So Rannie didn't like that the man had left him there.

He also didn't like that the man had said his mom had been pregnant.

But he didn't want anyone to die. Especially not *how* that man died. From what Rannie overheard Pekka and Pihla whispering, Peter had been turned into head soup just like the prisoner in the cell back in 1990. The blood witch was hunting again, protecting Alku.

That's why those two agents were in town.

To investigate the murder of Peter Weiss, Rannie's sorta friend, the horseshoe-mustache nurse.

And they were getting close. That's why Rannie had to take care of Arlie. She was a Wenner, but she liked to talk. He was hoping dealing with her would be enough, but the agents were still here.

That meant he had to take Fred Laine, too.

He had no choice anymore.

Didn't mean he liked doing it, though. Tears burned a track down his cheeks as he tromped through the forest, Fred over his shoulder, dangling like a sack of potatoes. Rannie wiped at his face. He glanced down and saw a cluster of tender purple flowers on the edge of the path, their orange tongues dusty. They'd found a sweet spot in the deep woods where the sun could hit them. He appreciated the message they sent, because he was getting so sleepy. He wanted to set Fred's body down and have a good rest, but he had to stay awake.

Focus like a crocus.

He couldn't go to sleep. Not this time. Not with those agents so close. He liked them, too, especially the lady. She was so pretty with her light hair in that genie ponytail. And her side of the car had been messy, like Rannie's room. He picked up his speed, grateful for the first time in his life that he got the monster curse.

You'll cower from the power of a Tervo, for sure, though.

CHAPTER 60

Harry and Evangeline agreed that Pekka Tervo was their best chance at breaking the Alku gridlock. His attempt at a confession established he was the weak link. They raced toward Alku, planning to make a quick pit stop at the motel for Harry's laptop. Deepty had texted that she had new lab results for them, sent encrypted.

"What're we thinking?" Evangeline said as she drove. "That the Jarmo family wanted to get out of Dodge, and the town hired a killer to take care of them? Or released someone from the prison for the sole purpose of murdering them?" She made a frustrated noise. "Or maybe the whole town lined up and did away with them?"

The road was speeding by. Harry fought to keep his hand off the dashboard. It would annoy Evangeline now and serve no purpose in a crash. "Say that last part again."

"That the whole town lined up and did away with them?"

He closed his eyes, feeling a quick slip of vertigo as the world went from speeding to still. He pictured their first visit to the Korhonen house, studying the pockmarks around the bed, feeling them like braille beneath his hands. He nearly heard the satisfying *clink* as a piece finally fell into place. "That disruption around the Korhonen beds? I think it was rock salt."

She considered this for a moment, then punched his arm. "One gun had the real shells, and the rest were loaded with filler so no one had to bear the weight of murder! Like an old-school firing squad." She paused. "But then why the cranial trauma?"

Harry shook his head. "No idea. And I'm not comfortable running it past Emery at this point, either."

"You and me both." Evangeline squealed into the motel parking lot. "You grab your laptop and download Deepty's encrypted data. I'm going to take a trucker's shower and meet you in your room. Good?"

Harry wouldn't go so far as to call that *good*, but Evangeline was already headed to her door. He exited the SUV and stepped into his room.

The first thing he noticed was the open window on the forest side of the room, cold spring air pouring in.

The second was the two children peeking out of his bathroom.

"Max?" Harry asked, his mouth dry. "Honeybee?"

They stepped into the bedroom, Honeybee hiding behind Max.

"Fred's gone," Max said, his eyes red. "They're not going to tell you, but he's disappeared. They got him. The reaping has started."

CHAPTER 61

Max wouldn't reveal anything more about Fred, no matter how Harry and Evangeline asked. The most he would agree to was remaining in the motel room with Honeybee while they went to Alku to check on Fred. Harry settled the kids on his bed with the TV on and salty snacks courtesy of Evangeline's stash while she reached out to Kyle for the Laine family address.

They got it and took off.

It was the same street that all the Originals—the Wenners, Virtanens, Tervos, Eskos, Harjus, and Korhonens—lived on, and it was a commotion of frenzied bodies when Evangeline and Harry pulled up. The mob was arguing beneath a single streetlight, their voices raised, all of them with the Alku features, the loping movements. Their gray and black clothes looked almost militaristic against the shadowed red of their houses and the fading white of winter.

"Mr. Laine?" Evangeline called out.

The crowd separated. Harry counted thirteen people, many of whom he recognized from the board meeting at the school, though Pekka was nowhere in sight. Some of the mob wore surprised expressions; others looked like they were itching to get back into whatever they'd been fighting about.

Edvin Laine stepped forward, a tall man, built like a farmer, with broad shoulders and meaty hands. He'd been sitting to Pekka's immediate right at the DNA swabbing. Today, his cheeks were flushed.

"Are you Fred Laine's father?" Harry asked.

Torben Virtanen stepped forward, Pihla by his side. "What is this concerning?"

"We believe Fred's gone missing," Evangeline said, "and that Arlie Wenner has disappeared as well."

Edvin's face was gnarled in the truest expression of pain Harry had ever seen. "Fred's not missing. He's in the house."

"Can we talk to him?" Evangeline asked evenly.

"We don't need you," Pihla spat. "We take care of our own." She wrapped her arm around Laine's waist in an intimate gesture and began leading him back toward his house. The rest of the folks followed, forming a line as they filed into the steep-roofed home. Arlie's mother was with them, appearing twenty years older than she had last time Harry had seen her.

Whatever the town's involvement with the Korhonen family and Weiss murders, they appeared shocked by their kids disappearing. Shocked, but still presenting a united front against outsiders.

Harry had a realization as he watched the Alkuans file into the house. "I didn't have time to look at the results Deepty sent before we came over here," he said. "And I have no reception to ask her for a summary."

Evangeline glanced at her phone. "No Wi-Fi for me here, either. I bet they shut it off." She looked over at Harry, her face worried. "Are you okay stopping by the prison before we head back to the motel? We need to talk to Pekka."

CHAPTER 62

No one had thought to retract Pekka's earlier permission to let them come and go as they pleased, so Harry and Evangeline were admitted at the gate and rolled up to the prison well after visiting hours. At the door, Evangeline's weapon was taken but they were otherwise given free rein.

When they found Pekka's office empty, Evangeline insisted they go to cell 36.

"There isn't time," Harry said, glancing down the hallway, toward the tunnel. "We should look for him at the school."

Evangeline put her hand on his arm. "Do you trust me?" she asked.

Harry looked into her eyes. He saw desperation there. Her nightmares meant something to her, something that made Harry deeply uncomfortable. He'd risked his career to trust her nightmare-informed "hunch" on the Taken Ones case. Could he do it again now, when two children were missing and the clock was ticking?

When he'd researched her before they'd first worked together, he'd discovered that she'd had one partner for her entire ten years on the force. His name was Bart Lively. He'd died eighteen months before she came to the BCA. Immediately upon his death, Evangeline's MPD colleagues began actively harassing her.

He was her first true partner since her time at the Minneapolis PD.

His decision at this critical juncture would affect not only their working relationship. It would affect *her*. The choice was easy.

"Let's go to cell 36."

She'd drawn herself straighter as if gearing up for battle, but at his words, her eyes filled with tears. "All right, then. Time's a-wasting."

They walked casually but quickly past a dozen guards and more nurses, all of them doing their jobs, paying Harry and Evangeline little mind. When they reached cell 36, though, the halls magically cleared, the corridor's ominous, bleak nature magnified by the silence.

"Look through the window in the door," Evangeline said. Her tone was fragile and resigned, and it made Harry's blood cold. "There's a scratch in the corner that should let you see in."

Harry did, his mouth dry. What he saw inside made him pull back. "How'd you know?" he asked, his voice hollow.

She nodded, biting her lip. "If it's the town doing the killing, then the man who confesses is the greatest danger to them." A security card hung from the knob. She held it to the card reader, and the door clicked open.

"I think they're giving him a time-out," she said. "I think they do that a lot."

"Pekka?" Harry asked, stepping into the cell ahead of Evangeline.

Pekka Tervo, psychiatrist, head of the Alku board, lay on his back, eyes closed, hands crossed over his waist. There was a crocus on the shelf across from him, already wilting from being plucked. Next to it sat a gallon-size Ziploc bag full of what looked like black dirt, open and scenting the cell. It was otherwise barren, exactly as it had appeared when they were there earlier.

Evangeline stepped alongside Harry, her posture making clear she'd rather be anywhere else. She was scanning every corner of the cell. "This isn't right," she said. "Not like my dreams."

"According to Carl Jung, dealing with darkness in others requires knowing our own darkness," Pekka said, his eyes still closed, his voice soothing. "We can't just hope for the light to replace what's dark in us—we must pull the dark into the light. It's terrifying to accept the whole of ourselves, but it's the only way to awaken." He opened his eyes. Blinked. "I wish I could remember Jung's words exactly, but that's close enough. The lesson is that we can't be fully conscious until we see ourselves truly."

"Why are you locked in here?" Harry asked.

"It's for my own good." Pekka sat up, swung his legs over the side of the bed, and leaned his elbows on his knees. He wore the same golden sweater and cords he'd had on at his earlier "confession."

"We have reason to believe that Arlie Wenner is still missing and that Fred Laine has disappeared as well," Harry said. "Can you confirm that?"

Pekka ran his fingers through his thinning hair and then dropped his face in his hands, the image of a man in agony. "I cannot."

"Who killed the Korhonen family, Pekka?" Evangeline squatted in front of him. "There's relief in confession. We can protect you."

"Not me," Pekka groaned. "It's Rannie you need to protect. It's always been Rannie."

"Come with us," Harry said. "We can help you."

"No." He shook his head vigorously, like an upset child. "Pihla wouldn't allow it. I'd only hurt the town."

Evangeline stood. "What's with the bag of dirt?"

Pekka looked toward it, his eyes bleary. "It's from the homeland. The head of Alku must always have it near to remind him of where we came from, what we survived."

Evangeline tossed Harry a *what the actual hell?* look and placed the cell key and her card on the shelf between the crocus and the dirt. "If you want to get out of here, Pekka, you have the key. If you want help, call. But we've got things to do." She left the cramped room.

Harry wanted to yell. The case was an M. C. Escher horror of staircases that led to nowhere, all of them tantalizingly promising, tragically pointless. He gave one last look at Pekka, whose shoulders were trembling, his face again buried in his hands, and joined Evangeline in the corridor.

"Back to the motel?" she asked.

Arlie missing. Fred missing. Who was next?

"Yeah," Harry said, feeling the walls closing in.

CHAPTER 63

Harry knew he should inform Mr. and Mrs. Esko that their children were in his motel room. Law enforcement officers had lost their jobs for less, and justifiably. In a field where you held sway over the life and freedom of others, appearance was as important as behavior.

But he couldn't bring himself to make the call.

Instead, he and Evangeline picked up four tin packages of meat loaf and mashed potatoes from the diner and brought them to Harry's room. Honeybee was asleep on the bed, her blonde hair tossed on the pillow, Max's parka laid across her. She was so tiny. Max was watching television with the sound on low. He glanced up, startled, when they walked in.

"Did you find him?" Max asked. But he read Harry's expression and dropped his eyes before Harry had a chance to respond. "I didn't think you would."

"We still can," Harry said. "Is there anything you can tell us to help him?"

Max shook his head, then dragged his eyes back to the bright screen.

Evangeline watched him for a moment before grabbing one of the meat loafs and going to her room.

"We brought you food," Harry said, setting it on the nightstand.

"Thank you," Max said dutifully, but he didn't stop watching. "I'll eat when Honeybee wakes up."

Harry studied the child in profile. He looked so tender from the side, his brown hair tousled, his nose a soft slope, skin smooth and unmarked. There was something so endearing, so responsible about the boy that it was hard to remember he wasn't even a teenager.

"Max?"

"Yessir," Max said, eyes trained on the screen.

"How'd you and Honeybee get here?"

"Hitched," he said, holding up a thumb.

Harry was barely able to stop himself from scolding the child for such a dangerous choice. There were bigger dangers to worry about, more important questions to ask. "Has Honeybee ever spoken?"

Max closed his mouth, and his Adam's apple bobbed. He turned to Harry, his eyes in shadow. "Yeah. Used to all the time. Couldn't shut her up."

Harry nodded. "When did she stop?"

Max turned his hands palms up. "When she got her words scared out of her." The angle of the light made his eyes two deep, black holes.

"What scared her?" Harry asked, realizing he was afraid to move.

Max kept his shadowed gaze trained on Harry for a few more beats, then turned back to the screen.

Harry let out a deep breath. Max thought that by holding his secrets close, he was protecting someone, most likely his little sister. And hadn't Harry done the same for his own mother? His mind traveled back to Honeybee. Selective mutism was not unheard of in someone who'd experienced trauma. It served as a shield, allowing the child to create a temporary barrier between themselves and the overwhelming emotions tied to the traumatic event.

What had Honeybee seen?

Harry glided to his desk and fired up his laptop, the doors still open between his room and Evangeline's. He could hear her quick movements. They both understood the urgency. Harry had no illusion they'd suddenly break a case that'd gone unsolved for twenty-five years. He just hoped to uncover enough to protect the children. Evidence of ritualized abuse or medical neglect, some complaint filed against a parent of Alku in the last two-plus decades that he could use to buy them some time.

He logged on and began reading the email Deepty had sent him.

And rereading it, horror trailing its dead fingers over his skin.

Exactly what he'd been looking for had just been handed to him, but it was so incomprehensible that he could only sit in the dingy motel chair, stunned, his mouth hanging open. When he was able to collect himself enough to open and read the data file she'd attached, he reeled all over again.

The data file definitively confirmed what her email had said.

Harry glanced at Max, his innocent face washed in the blues, greens, and reds of the television he was leaning toward like it was a warm fire on a cold night. Honeybee was the picture of a cherub as she slept, mouth partly open, long lashes lying across plump cheeks.

He stood. Walked stiffly through the doorway separating his room from Evangeline's.

It was difficult to speak.

She was staring at her own computer. "This dial-up is as slow as a snail in peanut butter. Do you—" She glanced over. Stood immediately. "What is it?"

His voice sounded far away. "Deepty sent over the results of the trace DNA collected from the shell casing found at Weiss's." His mouth was so dry. He licked his lips. "It's a 50 percent match with the DNA we collected from Helmi Esko."

Evangeline cocked her head, about to ask a follow-up question, but then realization dawned. She reached for the desk. "Dear God."

Harry heard a noise behind him. He turned. Max stood there, his thin shoulders resolute.

"That means you know, right?" he asked, his face brutal. "You know it's us kids who do the killing."

CHAPTER 64

Harry felt like he'd been punched in the gut. Evangeline's mouth dropped open.

Max immediately broke down weeping. Harry led him all the way into Evangeline's room so Honeybee could sleep. Harry let the boy curl into his chest, thinking how like a puppy he was. Bony. Energetic. Vulnerable.

And also a cold-blooded killer?

"It's called laki," Max said when he caught his breath.

Evangeline handed him tissues, her eyes brimming with compassion now that she'd recovered from the initial horror.

Max took one and wiped his nose, speaking haltingly. "It means, like, justice. We wear these masks assigned to our families. The Eskos are owls." He swiped his nose again. "We mostly wear them to celebrate, but sometimes for other things, like funerals." His voice dropped. "Or when someone hurts the town and they have to pay. They want us to learn Alku's ways young, us kids of the patriarchs. So we can carry on the traditions."

He began trembling violently, and Harry motioned for Evangeline to hand him a blanket. Max didn't seem to notice it being draped across him. "I don't know anything about what happened to the Korhonen family," he said, "but I went along to Mr. Weiss's house. Me, Arlie, Fred, Honeybee. It was our first laki."

Max's breathing became quick and shallow, his shoulders tensing up and his face turning ghostly white. He must be reliving the trauma. Evangeline grabbed the paper bag the meat loaf dinners had come in and handed it to Harry. He rubbed Max's back while the boy breathed into the bag. Harry felt sick. Children, taught to kill. He wanted to bundle Honeybee and Max into the SUV and drive as fast and as far away as he could.

When Max caught his breath, Harry gently asked him if he knew who had left a shotgun shell behind at Weiss's apartment.

Max blinked. "Only a couple guns carry the killing shells. The rest are full of rock salt. No one's supposed to know who has what, but I shot my gun at the wall, not at Mr. Weiss. When the shell came out, I shoved it in between the mattresses so those assigned to clean wouldn't see it." Max's voice dropped to a whisper. "Mr. Weiss was so scared, all of us in our masks."

"How many?" Evangeline asked.

Max shook his head and stared at his hands, one still holding the grease-spotted bag. "That's telling."

Harry and Evangeline exchanged a worried look over his head.

"Max," Harry asked, "do you know what the Korhonen family did that would have required laki?"

The child was chewing the inside of his cheek. "They were going to tattle. That's what we were told, that Mr. Korhonen was going to leave Alku and tell everyone our secrets, and it would destroy everything. We wouldn't be able to all live together anymore, the school and prison would be closed. It would be the end of Alku." His lips quivered. "So when we were told that Mr. Weiss was going to do the same thing, that he was going to destroy Alku, I was kind of excited. I wanted a chance to fight for my family." He glanced up at Harry, his eyes pleading. "I didn't know. I didn't know how scared he would be." Max looked down. "He peed his pants when we came in," he whispered.

Harry kept his hand on Max's back because it seemed to comfort him. The boy's shoulders were so narrow, barely an outline of the man he'd grow up to be.

"I stayed close to Honeybee," Max said, his voice low. "She's so little they didn't even give her a gun, so she didn't shoot anybody. But she didn't talk again after that night, either. The adults told us to treat her like she'd always been that way and that her voice would eventually come back." He was quiet for a few moments. "Me, Arlie, and Fred told Rannie all about it. We said that we couldn't do it again, no matter what kind of trouble it got us into, no matter if we had to run away and start a new life." He brought his wide brown eyes up to Harry. "I think that talk gave Arlie or Fred enough guts to tell their parents they were done with those traditions. That's why they disappeared. I bet they had laki done to them, too."

Harry swallowed. "We don't know that they're dead," he said. "Is it possible they're hiding somewhere?"

"I don't know where that could be," Max said. "The whole town—" He stopped himself, his mouth forming a perfect O.

"The whole town what?" Evangeline asked.

His mouth snapped shut. "Nothing."

Harry wished he could enter Max's head and scoop out the information. "Max, please," he said. "If you know where they might be, tell us so we can help."

Max shook his head vigorously. On this point, he would not budge.

"Max," Evangeline said, "I'm sorry I have to ask this, but Mr. Weiss wasn't just shot. Somebody crushed his head."

Max nodded slowly, like a puppet with loose strings. "The monster comes after we leave. It needs to be fed."

CHAPTER 65

"The monster?" Evangeline asked, shooting Harry a worried glance.

"Our protector," Max said. "The veri noita. She watches over the people of Alku."

He'd stopped shaking. The idea of a blood witch brutalizing the body of a supposed enemy was so ingrained in his understanding of the world that it didn't even upset him. Harry marveled at the courage it had taken the boy to tell them as much as he had.

"What do the masks look like?" Harry asked. He wanted to keep Max talking about less traumatic parts of the story so he could reset his nervous system.

Max ran the back of his hand across his nose. "Branch faces with eyeholes. We learn to make them in art class at school. There's rules about who gets to wear them and when."

Harry remembered the willow twigs he'd seen on the interior church steps when Pihla and Hannele had shown them the records room. Leftovers from a recent celebration or the murder of Peter Weiss? It was surreal to hear this tale in a dingy roadside motel with wallpaper the color of cigarette smoke, the gassy smell of meat loaf polluting the air.

"Tattling is the worst thing we can do in Alku," Max said, looking scared again. "You never tell on your family, no matter what they do, and Alku is my family." He squeaked out the next words. "But I have to protect Honeybee. I can't let her take part in another laki. That's no big brother who'd let his sister get hurt like that twice."

You never tell on your family, no matter what they do. Harry's brain felt hot. "Max, you've done the right thing by talking to us. I need you to know that. Evangeline and I'll do our best to protect you both. We need to make some phone calls now, but we'll have to go outside to get reception. I'd like you to go back to my room and eat something, then rest if you can. We'll be right outside the door. Is that okay?"

Max nodded. He stood, swayed a bit, then gathered himself, disappearing into Harry's room.

Evangeline looked as shocked as Harry felt, but she was already in action, tugging out her phone as she strode to the door. "I'm going to call Chandler to get approval to go over Emery's head."

"Good idea," Harry said, on her heels. "I need to talk to Deepty. Then one of us is calling Child Protective Services."

The night was frigid, its chill matching the temperature of his heart. The trauma the children of Alku had already endured was inconceivable. But there was no percentage in remorse, not right now. They needed to act fast to prevent more damage.

"Deepty," he said, relieved the call went through and that she picked up on the second ring. "There's a lot riding on this. Tell me the procedures you followed for that DNA run on the shell casing."

He hoped she knew him well enough to understand he wasn't questioning her science. She quickly confirmed what he already knew: the data was clean. A child or parent of Helmi Esko had held that casing, and since Helmi was the patriarch of the Esko clan, that left only Max or Honeybee.

Still. "Can you please ask Kyle to confirm there are no living Esko grandparents?" Given Max's confession, it was unlikely, but Harry would do this right.

"You got it," she said. "And I wanted to ask. How'd you know to look for the myostatin-blocking mutation in their blood?"

Somehow, the fact that one male member of the Alku board had a genetic mutation offering super strength had been the least interesting reveal in the data Deepty had sent over.

Myostatin was a protein that kept muscle growth in check. Blocking its production resulted in a condition known as myostatin-related muscle hypertrophy, which showed up as increased muscle mass, low fat, and incredible power. A handful of children had so far been diagnosed with the condition, most famously a boy in Michigan and another in Germany. The gas station attendant's comment had made Harry consider the death at Sandwich Rock, if possibly one enormous boulder had been pushed off another.

"A couple comments here," he said. "Rumors of excessive strength in the founders of Alku and their descendants. Their lean, muscular build."

"Ah," Deepty said, her tone mock serious. "You used a *hunch* to lead you to science."

"Something like that." He gave her a quick rundown on the situation.

She whistled. "I'll coordinate with Chandler and Kyle on this end. We'll get CPS right over so you and Van can locate those other two kids. I'll let Chandler advise on what sort of backup to send to Alku. Given what you've described, I'm thinking the National Guard might be *under*kill, but don't worry—I'm on it."

"Thanks, Deepty."

When he walked into his motel room, he felt the closest thing he could to relief. Max and Honeybee were going to be safe. He and Evangeline could plan next steps while they waited for CPS to show up. He was feeling focused until the coolness in his room hit his face, disorienting him.

The forest-side window was open.

Max was nowhere to be seen.

Honeybee still slept.

And suddenly, Caroline was in the room with him, her white-blonde hair in braids, her blue eyes wide, rattling off her internal monologue as his mind ran to Jennyfer.

I know some guys think I'm pretty. You know how I know? This guy drove past Olive and me while we were walking by the lake in front of the Malt Shoppe a couple days ago. He was nice to me, but he creeped out Olive. Further evidence of how she has to always be cool, you know? The dude had . . . two different lies.

He was the reason his sister had never been found. A good man would have confronted Myrna earlier, would have listened to his sister's fears, would have stayed with her when she begged.

Even a child of Max's age knew that much.

But I have to protect Honeybee. That's no big brother who'd let his sister get hurt like that twice.

And now, Harry had lost Max as well.

"Where is he?" Evangeline demanded, appearing in Harry's line of sight. He hadn't heard her come in. "Harry, what's wrong?"

He was frozen in place, staring at Honeybee, who looked just like Caroline as she slept. It was happening all over again. "I'm the worst person to be doing this."

Evangeline's brow creased. She followed his gaze, and understanding settled across her face, twisting and then smoothing it. She gripped his arms. "Harry, it's not your fault your sister was abducted. There're monsters in the world," she said. "You can't protect everyone all the time."

"I shouldn't have let Max out of my sight," Harry said.

"*We* shouldn't have." She gave him a shake. "We did what was right in the moment. Now let's go find him."

The tissue paper separating his past from his present was gone. He was nineteen, the reason his sister had never been found, the shame so strong that he was sure it would choke him, almost prayed for it to. "I'm a terrible man," he whispered.

Evangeline's hand flew upward. He thought it was willpower alone that kept her from slapping him. "Harry, that's BS, and you know it."

Harry looked in her eye and laid it bare. It was time. Past time.

"Caroline and I were close. She trusted me implicitly. The day she was abducted, she told me she wanted to run away. Myrna was abusive, don't you see? It was bad when I lived there, but I think it got much worse when I went to college. And I looked the other way, wrapped myself in the quiet lies people tell so as not to upset the family apple-cart. And Caroline didn't just confess that she was going to run away." He swallowed. "She also told me about a man who'd been following her. He drove the same color and model car as the one she was last seen getting into. She was so worried—I don't know if it was about Myrna or the man—that she begged me to stay with her. I left her. She was never seen again."

Evangeline's jaw locked. "What else did she tell you about the man?"

Harry's voice was raw. "That's just it. I had a date later that afternoon, and I tuned her out. *She described her abductor to me and I didn't listen.*" He rapped on his head, hard enough to make a hollow noise. "Somewhere in there is the key to where she is, and I was too focused on meeting up with an old girlfriend to hear it. How's that for pure selfishness?"

There it was, the truth of who he was at his core. He was surprised to discover that he didn't regret saying it, though his heart was racing and it felt like his skin had been replaced with glass. Evangeline deserved to know what caliber of man he was so he wouldn't impede the investigation any longer. "I'm dangerous to children. How many have disappeared on my watch now?"

She was studying him, a kaleidoscope of expressions flashing across her face. The attention was excruciating, but he'd earned it. He was waiting for words of reproach, or for her to storm out with Honeybee in her arms—either would be appropriate—but instead, she placed her left hand over her heart and her right over his.

Her touch cracked the glass he was encased in, and then her words shattered it.

"What happened to Caroline was terrible." She pushed gently on his chest, her voice aching with compassion. "It's going to hurt here forever. Now that you've told me, I can take some of it, but most of that is yours to carry." She closed her eyes, long lashes resting on her cheeks. "I am so sorry that's how it is, but I don't make the rules. But Myrna's abuse is hers to bear, not yours."

Harry opened his mouth to argue, but Evangeline shook her head sharply, her eyes flying open. "Yes, you could have said something, and you should have. And of course you would have stayed with her if you'd known what was at stake. But making any mistake one time, no matter how consequential, doesn't mean you're a bad man, and it certainly doesn't mean you can't be a spectacular agent. Harry, you're the best there is. I need you." She pushed on his chest again, even more softly than the first time. "Max needs you."

The last of the glass fell to the ground, leaving him raw, naked, the very air hurting his skin. The exposure was excruciating, but he didn't retreat from it, didn't hide. Evangeline was here. She was *seeing* him. And rather than running away, she was calling the best part of him to step forward. A salt tear rolled down his cheek. It was agony, pleasure pain, to meet someone in such an honest place.

"We don't know that the other children are dead," she continued, her tears matching his. "We don't know that your sister is dead." She still had her hand on his heart, warming him. "Tell me what we *do* know about the Korhonens, about Alku, about the CCTC that can help us to find Max and the monster."

He put his hand over hers, feeling Evangeline's truth, her strength. Something strange was bubbling in his veins, responding to her courage and her friendship, an emotion he hadn't experienced in so long, not since Caroline disappeared.

It was hope.

CHAPTER 66

Harry began reciting facts from memory, growing more grounded as he spoke. "We know that in the late '80s, the Minnesota legislature stopped funding centralized institutions in favor of a more community-based support system, striking down Alku's main source of income. Two years later, what had once been sanitorium dormitories were converted to the Carlton County Treatment Center, where violent but nonambulatory men were incarcerated." It felt good to combine all the pieces they'd gathered into a cogent story. "We know that all the board members of the corporation that controls Alku had to vote to approve this, including Jarmo Korhonen."

Evangeline had out her notebook and was flipping pages furiously back and forth as Harry spoke.

"The Korhonen family—Jarmo and Janice, and their three children, Jutta, Johanna, and Jaakko—were murdered on November 7, 1998," he continued. "That same week, Ansa Tervo, mother to Pekka and Randolph, supposedly disappeared, and her husband, Nils, supposedly died of a heart attack. Two hikers also died within sight of the original CCTC building," Harry said. "Twenty-five years later, in April of 2023, Peter Weiss, a CCTC nurse, was murdered in the same violent and unique way as the Korhonen family."

Evangeline nodded in agreement.

Harry steeled himself. "We have a witness to the Weiss murder, an eleven-year-old by the name of Max Esko, who claims that the homicide was part of a tradition called laki, where the board members and their offspring ritually kill anyone who they perceive threatens Alku. We have a reasonable belief that the Korhonen family was considering leaving Alku, which their bylaws forbid. We have a second reasonable belief that if Max's story is true, the same tradition of laki was responsible for the Korhonen family deaths."

"Two reasonable beliefs are as good as one fact," Evangeline said.

"They are not," Harry said, massaging a sudden chest pain. Something occurred to him. "The laki Max described, with both adults and children in masks leaving Weiss's house, would account for Aimee Fleck's belief that she saw a single killer shrinking. They might have looked like one confusing person in a blinding blizzard."

Evangeline nibbled the end of her pen. "Good call. We also know that the people of Alku worship a blood witch alongside their Christian beliefs and that at least Max believes the blood witch is responsible for the mutilation of the Korhonens and Weiss."

"We don't believe in blood witches or monsters," Harry said, ignoring Evangeline's contrary expression, "but we do know that Pekka—and possibly all the Tervo males—have a genetic mutation that leads to enhanced strength, which is likely one of the reasons they were so vilified in their homeland."

Evangeline squinted. "When were you going to tell me *that*?"

Harry sighed. "I just received confirmation. Deepty sent it over in the encrypted file."

"And you didn't want to share your 'hunch' with me until it was confirmed because it was absolutely banana pants," she said, smiling. "I see you, Harry Steinbeck. I'll coax you over to the dark side yet." She shoved her notebook back into her pocket. "It would make sense that the same 'creature' that mutilated the Korhonens and Weiss also killed the hikers, and possibly the CCTC inmate who was murdered in 1990. It also makes sense that what they call the monster is actually a Tervo with a rare genetic mutation that enables him to pop skulls with his bare hands, yes?"

Harry couldn't believe what he was about to say. "Those are two reasonable beliefs."

"So a fact," she said.

Harry felt a flicker of a smile. "Those two *beliefs* are supported by the Korhonen and Weiss crime scene photos. All the victims' ears were intact, which would have been statistically unlikely if the heads had been crushed from above. It appears as though great force was instead simultaneously applied to both ears. Two hands, pushing together."

"Christ, that's horrifying." Evangeline shook her head, and then her eyes grew large. "It's Rannie, isn't it?"

Harry sighed. "It's likely one of the two Tervos, and Rannie's got the size. And according to Max, he's the only adult who knew that Max, Fred, and Arlie were going to refuse to participate in future killings and that they were potentially going to expose the town's secrets."

"He struck me as such a kind soul," Evangeline said. "You think he took Arlie and Fred?"

"Yes," Harry said. "And I think Max knew that, and either Rannie sneaked in and nabbed him while we were out front on our phones just now, or Max left on his own to rescue them. We're going to operate as if all three kids are alive."

Evangeline's smile bloomed like a flower in the forest. "I knew you were in there, Harry. Now that you've returned, how do we find them?"

Harry felt an unexpected rush of emotion at her faith in him, still, after hearing his darkest secret. Before he could respond, he felt a softness in his hand. He glanced down at a tender green shoot of a flower, its white petals wilting.

Honeybee had woken and slipped it into his hand. Her hair was fuzzy from sleep, her cheeks rosy. Her expression was expectant, hopeful.

"That's goldthread," Evangeline said wonderingly, crouching down for a closer look. "We had it around the farm growing up."

The green was vibrant and vulnerable in the harsh light of the motel room. Harry realized Honeybee had handed him a treasure. "Where did it grow?" he asked Evangeline.

She examined it more closely. "At the swamp on the edge of the property."

Her head shot up as she realized what Harry was thinking. "The swampboggins," she said.

"Honeybee." Harry knelt so he was on her level. "We need to find Max, and we think he's at Rannie's fort. Can you take us there?"

She put her finger over her mouth in the universal symbol for *be quiet*.

"Are you saying it's a secret?" Evangeline asked.

Honeybee nodded, but she kept her eyes on Harry. They were so wide, so trusting.

"When you decide whether or not to keep a secret," he said, keeping his voice gentle, "you have to ask yourself one very important question: Is the secret protecting something that's good, or something that's bad?"

She blinked, her turquoise eyes clear. She wiped her nose with her knuckle. And then she took Harry's hand and led him toward the door.

CHAPTER 67

Harry bundled Honeybee into her winter gear while Evangeline called Kyle.

"I'm not dying dumb," she said as she stepped out the door. "I'm going to let him know where we're going and also tell him to issue an APB for a boy who might have been hitchhiking back to Alku from here."

Once Honeybee was outfitted, Harry let her lead him to the SUV, amazed by the beauty of the April night. Overhead, a slender crescent moon hung against the indigo backdrop. The clarity of the northern sky allowed even the faintest stars to sparkle, the air crisp with the electric smell of winter's last stand.

Evangeline finished updating Kyle as she followed Harry and Honeybee, her final request that he prepare CPS to be ready for a whole town's worth of children, pickup location to be determined. She ended the call and tossed her phone in the passenger seat. Harry had already buckled Honeybee in the back, himself alongside.

Honeybee glanced out her window until they reached Alku, where she dropped low in her seat, her expression faraway and miserable. It was a ghost town, not a light on in any window. She waved her little hand forward, indicating they should keep driving.

"She said to keep going," Harry told Evangeline.

They momentarily locked gazes in the rearview mirror. They didn't want to bring Honeybee, but there was no one safe to leave her with and no time to wait.

Honeybee sat back up once Alku was in the rearview mirror. When they reached the road to the CCTC, Harry wasn't surprised when Honeybee pointed at it.

"Turn here," he told Evangeline.

Honeybee tapped the window vigorously when they reached the spot in the forest where they'd seen her walking with Max and Rannie.

"I'm guessing this is it," Evangeline said, parking the SUV along the winding road. Harry made sure Honeybee's coat was zipped as high as it would go, her mittens tucked into the cuffs, her cap low over her ears. He was glad Max had brought her winter gear. Both Harry and Evangeline had talked brave about the kids being alive, but Harry knew that if they were, they wouldn't be for long. Time was everything.

With everyone bundled, they took off into the achingly still woods. Harry's and Evangeline's shoes tore up the crusty snow, but Honeybee glided as quietly as a rabbit. When they reached the towering school, she put her finger over her mouth and pointed at their feet. They both looked down but didn't move.

Her face screwed up in frustration, she wrapped a mittened hand around Evangeline's ankle and lifted. Evangeline let the girl guide her foot from the ankle-deep snow into an established footprint. Then she pointed at Evangeline's other foot.

"She wants us to stick to the trail instead of breaking our own," Evangeline whispered. "It'll be quieter."

Harry nodded. They should have been doing that from the outset. Were the remaining Alku Originals inside the school? Or were they outside searching for their children so they could kill them themselves? The horror of tradition. But was it really that? Or was it a younger generation afraid to call out the terrible behavior of their parents, just as Harry had been? He was humbled by the courage of Max, Arlie, Fred, and Honeybee deciding to break the cycle.

Honeybee led them through the founders' graveyard and around the sacrificial ground where they'd discovered the bloody deer. The veri noita effigy was no longer staked in the center of the clearing. They walked for so long that after a while, Harry began to imagine the silence had a sound, a vast seashell hum. But then it began to grow shape, and texture, and he realized someone was speaking ahead, their tone agitated. He tucked Honeybee in the safety of a large tree and signaled that she should stay hidden. She nodded, blending into the base of the trunk. Harry moved forward low and quiet, Evangeline at his side, her weapon drawn. It was another ten feet before the flickering glow of a flashlight became visible.

They crouched behind a bush.

A rough hut had been built in the woods twenty feet in front of them. It had a single window. A tree too large for Harry to hug lay on its side in front of the door.

Pekka stood facing the hut, a headlamp perched on his forehead, the beam bouncing off every point surrounding the fort. Harry's heartbeat pounded. Had he followed the same clues as Evangeline and Harry? Did he know what his brother had done?

But then Pekka stepped forward.

He held a shotgun in one hand, Max Esko in the other.

Max was so terrified that his eyes were rolling in the back of his head.

CHAPTER 68

Harry registered only a flash of movement to his left. Thankfully, Evangeline had the reflexes of a cat. She grabbed Honeybee with one hand before the child launched herself into the clearing to save her brother.

"Rannie, you know this must happen," Pekka called out, his voice gravelly. "The monsters will destroy the town if we don't cull them."

"They're not monsters!" Rannie yelled from inside the fort. "They're my friends."

"The law decrees that anyone who harms Alku is a monster who must be eliminated. I'm sorry." Pekka shook his head, the light bobbing and weaving across the black forest. "I know how hard it is, but you must do it for family. Without it, we have nothing."

Pekka set his shotgun on the ground and reached for the tree partially blocking the fort's door. Still hanging on to Max, he used his free hand to pull the log away, dragging it as easily as if it were a bag of dog food.

Harry was watching the spectacle, but he was having difficulty processing it. *Pekka* was the monster who must be fed. He'd been locked in a room not to keep him from revealing the truth but to keep him from crushing skulls.

Evangeline's nightmare of the evil inside that cell *had* been a vision.

It wasn't Rannie the town had been protecting.

It was Pekka.

"I had a moment of weakness when I went to the police, Rannie," Pekka said, his voice seemingly everywhere. "You know how much I value Alku, but I had a crisis. The killing is hard, I won't deny it, but the board showed me the error of my ways. Who are we if we let go of our traditions?"

Rannie moaned from inside the fort. "But what does family mean if we have to hurt each other so bad to save it?"

"*Alku* is family, Rannie. It's bigger than any one of us. We must do what needs to be done for the town. The children can't be allowed to tell. It'll ruin us."

"Family is love!" Rannie yelled, his voice carrying. "Family is safety! When it's not that, it's not family." He groaned again. "Can't you please just let me and Max and Arlie and Fred and Honeybee move away? We'll all leave. You won't see me, let us be free!" His words were running together. "I didn't tell anyone you're the blood witch, Veli-Pekka. I didn't tell anyone we lock you up at night."

An icicle dropped from a branch over Harry's head and landed on the snow next to him. Pekka turned, the movement slow, languorous, the light perched on his too-tall forehead casting skull shadows across his profile.

Harry saw Evangeline's jaw drop open.

In that moment, Pekka looked exactly as she'd described the celled man of her nightmares.

Pekka turned back toward the fort, dismissing the noise. "I'm sorry, buddy, but we can't let anyone leave. You know we can't. That's the most important thing Mom ever taught us." He paused, lowered his voice. "I know Weiss told you that I killed her, Rannie. That's why we had to eliminate him. Don't you see? You're part of this. You're one of us."

The drum of silence beat in Harry's blood.

"He never told me that," Rannie finally called through the window, his voice quivering. "*Did* you kill her?"

Pekka stepped back and picked up the shotgun. "I had to," he said, speaking matter-of-factly. "She was pregnant. She'd already produced an idiot and a sociopath. I couldn't let her make another mistake. I did it for the town." He raised his voice. "But I can save *you*. If you give me those two children, I can offer them to the town along with Max, and that'll be enough. I'll make sure of it." Pekka's voice broke. "Please let me save you, Rannie."

"No," Rannie said. It sounded like he was shifting something inside the fort. "You protect secrets, not people. *You* were the one who taught me to treat people like you wanted to be treated."

"You're telling me you don't want to be protected?" Pekka said, his voice ramping up. "You don't want to be cared for, and fed, and loved? Once we get rid of the prison, it'll be better, I promise. It's poison, having that evil so close." Spittle was flying from Pekka's mouth. "Jarmo understood, but his mistake was that rather than stay to help, he tried to leave. To desert us."

Harry recognized the signs of an extreme manic state. Had the genetic mutation that had given Pekka strength also given him sociopathy? The ability to hide his true self from the world, to manipulate others? It didn't particularly matter in the moment. Pekka needed to be incapacitated so the children could escape.

But as long as he held Max and the shotgun, their options were limited.

Harry signaled to Evangeline. He would sneak around the perimeter until he was as close to Pekka as he could be while still remaining hidden. He would grab Max. She would disable Pekka.

She shook her head violently. *Too risky*, she mouthed, still holding Honeybee in one hand, her weapon in the other.

But he was already in motion. Memories of Caroline were pushing to the surface, agonizing vignettes of her telling him he was the best big brother, how he was smart and strong and wouldn't ever let anything happen to her. He tried to lock into the present, but Caroline was in his ear. The distraction meant he was parallel to Pekka before he could see the truth. Pekka had the hood of Max's jacket twisted in his grip, the child's face slack with terror. Unless the hood gave way, Harry had no chance of snatching him back, not against Pekka's strength.

You're a good man, Caroline's voice urged. *You know what to do.*

And suddenly, he did.

He stood, revealing himself, hands over his head. "Pekka, it's over. The police are on their way."

Pekka swung to face Harry, his headlamp temporarily blinding. The glare moved when Pekka shook his head sadly, his voice back to the calm doctor's tone he'd used when they'd first met. "I didn't want to do any of this, you know, but Alku must keep her secrets."

He shoved Max away so he could bring the shotgun to his shoulder. He swung the barrel toward Max, who shivered like a rabbit at his feet.

Harry launched himself forward, shielding Max's body. The pellets drilled into his back, the pain so intense his brain went white. He heard the crack of another shot. Pekka dropped to the ground in Harry's sight-line, blood blooming across his chest. Both men stared at each other for a moment, and then Harry's vision faded.

The last sounds he heard were a great scraping, and then Rannie screaming, "Don't kill my brother!"

There was one more gunshot before the world tilted black.

CHAPTER 69

Rannie
April 15, 2023

Rannie stared up at the pretty crescent moon, at the stars having a glitter party all around it. His body hurt so bad, but the moon was smiling down at him. Rannie loved Alku. The land. The people. That ol' moon sliver that watched over them.

But Pekka was the blood witch, had been the whole time.

He'd killed Hector, must have pushed that rock right on top of him. Pekka had refused a sip of alcohol ever since that night. Rannie now knew why. But it hadn't made any difference because even sober, Pekka had killed that prisoner. Then the hikers. Fed his hunger on the poor Korhonen family, then Peter Weiss, the nurse with the horseshoe mustache.

Pekka had been begging for so long that they get rid of the serial killers, that they were poisoning people.

He meant himself. They were poisoning *him*.

Killing Hector might have been a onetime mistake, but listening to murderers unburden themselves day in and day out had driven Pekka to be his worst self and smush heads. That wasn't nice. But he couldn't have gotten away with it for so long if the town hadn't let him. Why'd they let him? And why had they been willing to sacrifice their own children in a reaping rather than upset the old ways?

Rannie wanted to stay awake so bad so he'd remember all this, but he couldn't.

He was too tired.

Don't blunder and let the sleep pull you under, you dunder.

But he'd never been able to fight the sleep, not when he was sad or hurt, and right now, the pain was so bad he felt like snakes were clawing their way out of him. He was hot, too. His view of the moon was shrinking.

He thought he heard singing. No, it was sirens. Sirens and then Max crying.

"I knew Mr. Steinbeck would keep you safe, Honeybee," Max was saying. "I knew it."

Rannie felt his face crease into a smile even though he couldn't see anymore. Honeybee was okay. And Rannie had managed to hide Arlie and Fred, kept them safe even though it meant betraying Alku.

Maybe that's what family was. Not the people you'd been born to but the people you'd do the right thing for no matter what it cost you. The people you'd risk everything to protect.

Ditch the witch, we've got each other, brother . . .

And then he said goodbye.

CHAPTER 70

"Two different eyes," Harry murmured. "Brown and blue."

Evangeline jumped to her feet. "You're awake!"

He craned his neck to study his heavily bandaged left shoulder.

"Buckshot," Evangeline said. Her eyes were creased with worry, her clothes rumpled from sleeping in a hospital recliner. "Your falling saved your life. Three pellets tore straight through, another three were embedded, the rest missed. Your shoulder looks like Salisbury steak, but the doctor thinks you'll regain full use of it."

The hospital room was bathed in a warm, golden glow. Sunlight streamed through a large window, refracting off melting icicles, sending rainbows across the walls. The machines next to Harry worked silently. A curtain through the middle of his room separated him from the hall-way but didn't stop the occasional muffled conversation of medical professionals passing by, creating a reassuring hum of activity.

"I remember what Caroline said to me," Harry croaked. As the memory flooded back, his heart constricted with a mix of shock and sorrow. He tried to sit up, but the movement was excruciating. Evangeline gently eased a pillow behind him. He coughed, cleared his throat. "Her description of the man who abducted her. She said he had two different-colored eyes."

"You lost a lot of blood," Evangeline said.

"I remember," Harry insisted. It felt like warm water coursing over his skin, finally reclaiming that memory, like receiving the greatest gift in the world. "The trauma of the gunshot brought it back." He repeated Caroline's speech word for word, seeing it as clearly as if he were reading her words off a script. "'The dude had black hair, for-real black, not dark brown. He had a nice smile, like Tom Cruise, where the front tooth is a little off. But his eyes were weird. One brown, one blue. Can you believe it? Two different eyes. I guess it was a little creepy.'"

Evangeline crossed her arms. Glanced toward the window. Harry read worry in her expression.

"It isn't much to go on," he said. The weight of the revelation had settled in his stomach, grounding him. "I know that. But it's a start."

"Yeah," Evangeline said, making up her mind about something, "it is."

Harry shot up involuntarily this time, despite the pain. "My God, how are the children?"

Evangeline smiled, her worry taking a back seat. "Arlie, Fred, Max, and Honeybee are safe and healthy."

He dropped back, his shoulder screaming. He was so relieved he could weep. "And the rest? What happened after I blacked out?"

"Strap in," she said, rolling over a chair, "because I had to put a bullet in two Tervos the other night. Pekka as he was about to fire on you a second time, Rannie as he charged out of the fort at me, trying to stop me from killing his brother. Pekka took a gutshot, but Rannie I was able to down with a bullet to the leg." She shook her head. "He looked like a bull charging me. The good news is they're both alive and in this hospital."

"I'm sorry you had to shoot," Harry said. It was a last resort for a good officer. "But grateful."

"You definitely owe me," she said, nodding. "But there's more. Guess which Alku citizen is turning, despite initially insisting that 'you never tell on family'?"

"Arlie's mom?" Harry asked. "Or Fred's?"

"Nope," Evangeline said. "But those are good guesses. It's Pihla. She said she believes her husband is a serial killer and that she and him are solely responsible for all the deaths dating back to the prisoner in 1990."

Harry frowned. "Protecting the town to the end. What reason did she give for supposedly killing the Korhonens and then Weiss?"

"The Korhonens wanted to leave, just as we suspected. Jarmo and Janice had initially been opposed to turning the CCTC into a prison, but they didn't demand it be shut down until it started to affect Pekka. Unfortunately, the board couldn't be convinced to eliminate their only source of income. When Pekka went off the rails and murdered his mother and then the two hikers, the Korhonens had had enough. They were planning to sneak out, and the town got wind of it."

Harry put a hand over his eyes. Those poor Korhonen children, slaughtered because their parents tried to do the right thing too late. "And Weiss?"

"Pihla says she tried three methods to help Pekka control his violent urges. One was locking him in cell 36 at night. The second was allowing him to mutilate the already dead. The third was a good old-fashioned confession." She shook her head like she still couldn't believe what she was about to say. "Apparently, Pekka used Matty the Mallet like his priest. Told him about his crimes in brutal detail, on repeat, whispering them right into his ear. He knew Matty couldn't speak so would never be able to tell anyone. Except Weiss overheard him one time and started blackmailing him. He'd already had suspicions about the Alku folks. When Pihla discovered that not only was Weiss extorting money from Pekka but also had started grooming Rannie and filling his head with ideas about the town and his parents, she said she had no choice but to shoot Weiss, with Pekka there to destroy his head."

It would make a gruesome sense, if not for Max's confession. "Dooley must have seen Pekka leaning over to confess to Millard, and that's why he was screaming about a vampire sucking Matty's blood."

"Seems likely," Evangeline agreed. "Max ran away from us because something you said to him made him realize that Rannie must be the one hiding Fred and Arlie. He wanted to make sure they were okay."

"What courage," Harry marveled. "How is the state possibly going to try this case?"

"Their problem, not ours." Evangeline made a dusting motion with her hands. "For now, they've got the National Guard stepping in at the CCTC. In a darkly ironic twist, Pekka might not be able to walk again. He may end up incarcerated at his very own nursing home for serial killers."

The thought chilled Harry. "What will happen to the children of Alku?"

"They're all going into temporary foster care while this whole mess is sorted out." She tossed him the oddest expression. "You're not going to believe who's requested two of them."

Harry searched his brain, still fuzzy from pain medication. Then he sighed. "Myrna."

"Yup. She's getting Max and Honeybee."

He raised an eyebrow, and Evangeline shrugged. "Your mom said that you and she have a long-overdue conversation coming, that she wants you to know about all the work she's done on herself since Caroline disappeared." Evangeline held up her hands at his doubtful expression. "I say you give her a chance. She obviously still has control issues, but that doesn't mean she doesn't have her own regrets about how she treated Caroline or new skills when it comes to caring for children. She's activated her network to foster the rest of the Alku kids, so there's a good chance they'll all get to live in the same neighborhood and go to the same school until next steps are decided. She wanted to make the transition as easy as possible for them, under the circumstances."

"Myrna Steinbeck, using her power for good," Harry said. He was working his penance, and she was working hers. Had he sold her short all these years? "It means we'll get updates on how they're doing."

"I hope so," Evangeline said, her eyes dancing, "because between you and me, Max and Honeybee have grown on me. Don't tell them, though."

"Too bad we're here." Max peeked around the hospital curtain. His smile was toothy, though his eyes were too sad and wise for his age. He had his arm around Honeybee, who smiled behind her hand. A woman followed, likely a social worker.

"We wanted to say thank you," Max said, nudging Honeybee forward.

She held out a daffodil. Caroline's flower. It was as bright and hopeful as the sun.

"Thank you," Harry said, accepting the gift. "But it's the two of you we need to thank. I don't know that we would've been able to solve this without your help. A lot more people could have been hurt."

Max approached Harry's bedside. He pointed at the bandage. "That's where you were shot?"

Harry nodded.

"Did it hurt bad?"

"Still does," Harry said honestly. "But I'm going to be fine."

Max grew serious. "Rannie didn't kill anyone, you need to know that. He was never allowed to go out for the laki on account of his being special."

Evangeline and Harry exchanged a glance. "Thank you for that," Harry said. "We'll make sure that information goes in the file."

Max played with the edge of Harry's blanket. He clearly wanted to say something, so Harry gave him the space. After a few moments, the words poured out in a hot rush. "It's my fault the nurse was killed and that you and Rannie got shot. If I'd said something sooner, like when I knew there was going to be a laki, none of this would have ever happened." Two tear globes raced down his cheeks.

Harry took his hand. "Max," he said, "you're not responsible for what other people do. I know it feels like you should have done more, and it always might, but the truth is you did what you could when you were able. You showed great bravery."

The tears kept flowing. Max wasn't hearing him.

"Can I tell you something?" Harry asked, sitting up and leaning forward despite the pain. "About my own sister?"

Max's shoulder lifted, a half shrug that said *suit yourself*.

So Harry told him the story, leaving out the disturbing parts.

"She's still gone?" Max said when Harry finished. He glanced worriedly over at Honeybee, who was listening, rapt.

"She's still gone," Harry said, "but I'll never stop looking. The reason I told you that, though, is because, for the first time in my life, I realize how pointless it's been for me to take so much responsibility for actions that weren't mine all these years. I don't want that for you."

"But you're not the one who took your sister!"

It was in the innocence of Max's words that Harry was finally—dear God, *finally*—able to hear them for himself, the truth penetrating the walls of guilt that had confined him for more than two decades, releasing knots of anguish. It was the most powerfully bittersweet emotion he'd ever felt.

"And you're not the one who shot anyone," Harry said gently.

"That's true." Max spoke slowly, tasting the words. "I made sure to fire away from Weiss, and I didn't shoot anyone outside the fort." He glanced at Evangeline apologetically.

She raised her hands. "Don't feel bad for me. It's my least favorite part of the gig, but it's the job I signed up for."

Max nodded more vigorously. "I think I get it. Not in my head, but I feel a little different here." He patted his chest. "And I know you'll save your sister, Harry, because you saved me. You saved all of us."

In that moment, Harry couldn't have stopped his tears to save his soul.

EPILOGUE

Van

I sit in the Steinbeck mansion staring out across Lake Superior, thinking I might like living here. The power of the waves pushing up great ice heaves, the way the vast silver lake meets the horizon so you can't tell where the water ends and the sky begins.

It's humbling and comforting at the same time.

But this mansion is ridiculous. It'd be like living inside that CCTC school, except locked in the '90s (*19*90s, not 1890s). And for a medium-size city, everyone in Duluth seems to know each other. No, give me the anonymity of the Cities any day.

Harry's in the other room talking to his mother. It makes my bones buzz to think about what he's been through, what he's survived. How he seemed to leave his old skin behind at the hospital and walk out shiny and new. Max and Honeybee have been set up in his childhood bedroom. Myrna'd been willing to give up her Caroline shrine so they could have separate rooms, but Max didn't want Honeybee out of his sight, and who could blame the kid? He survived a horror town, nearly everyone around him a killer or training to be one. And that brave little bucktoothed dude had managed to bring it all down *and* get his sister out of there.

As I stare at the eternal lake, I can't help but think of coincidences.

Max protecting Honeybee brought Harry full circle in confronting the loss of his sister. That buzz again. Harry is the purest man I've ever met. Smart and strong. Loyal and true. It hurts to think of all the time he's spent carrying a load that should never have been his.

How if he'd confided in me earlier, I could have helped him.

But of course, I have my own dark secrets. My visions. The three locks of hair hidden in my bathroom back in Minneapolis.

My mind wanders from coincidences to the invisible weights every one of us carries, whether we acknowledge them or not, how similar burdens tend to draw people together across space and time. Then my brain moves to how the people of Alku chose the easiest path and called it love—feeding Pekka's addiction rather than addressing it. And to how all this brought Harry back to his own mother, and to a possible reconciliation.

Myrna has apologized for how she treated Caroline, said it wasn't until she was diagnosed with manic depression a decade ago and started treatment that she was able to see what she'd done. Her confession allowed Harry to talk about the guilt he's borne all these years. I can hear him in the other room right now making plans to come back and visit Myrna, Max, and Honeybee next weekend, to return to this wild and ancient place to begin rebuilding a family.

He'll need help driving for a while because of his arm. I might offer to chauffeur. *Might.*

I think all this as I study the lake and it studies me, taking my measure.

Coincidences, the weight we carry, what draws us to people.

The way we lie to ourselves that shared secrets are the same thing as love.

And those thoughts lead me directly to Frank Roth, my tormentor, the man I called Father. Frank, who governed his farm with a cruel fist, who presented a smiling face to the world as he went out and made business connections across the state of Minnesota, driving his green four-door from town to town, including Duluth.

Who would sometimes return with children for the commune, bright and terrified.

Who, in the year Caroline disappeared, had black hair and a Tom Cruise smile.

Who'd always had two different eyes.

One blue. One brown.

ACKNOWLEDGMENTS

A big sloppy thank-you to my dream team at Thomas & Mercer, led by the incomparable, brainstorming, research-and-weird-story-loving Jessica Tribble Wells and including Charlotte, Jon, and Kellie. You all sift through the dirt of my stories to find the gold, and I am forever grateful.

Thanks also to my incredible agent, Jill Marsal. I don't know what luck brought us together, but I am so happy it did. Jessica Morrell, you've edited an early version of every (!) book I've written since 2002, and I am so thankful for all you've taught me.

I owe a debt of gratitude to Ann Marie Gross, BCA forensic scientist extraordinaire, for helping me get the science in this book right. All errors are my own, made either in service of the story or because I was too clueless to know better. While it's true that the BCA has a cold case division, and while the history of the BCA as presented here is accurate, the day-to-day operations of Cold Case and general workings of the BCA in this book are a product of my imagination.

Carolyn, our weekly writing sessions are a highlight of my writing career, and your friendship is a gift. To my Squad: How did I ever do this without you? And finally, to my babies, my superstars, Zoë and Xander: thanks for making life fun.

If you have information on a Minnesota cold case, or any case, you are encouraged to call the BCA tip line at 1-877-996-6222 or email bca.coldcase@state.mn.us. You may also submit an anonymous tip via their online web form.

AUTHOR'S NOTE

The idea for *The Reaping* came to me as I was touring the grounds of the gorgeous, sprawling, abandoned, and surely haunted Regional Treatment Center in Fergus Falls, Minnesota. The treatment center was constructed as a state hospital in 1890. It followed the Kirkbride plan of mental health treatment: vast, isolated complexes built to allow patients access to fresh air, sunlight, and hard work. Kirkbride believed that mental health issues were the great levelers—they didn't see race, class, or gender—and that they were curable.

Those were radical ideas in his time.

Digging into the RTC background led me to a deep history dive into sanitoriums all over Minnesota, which was how I learned about the Faribault State School and Hospital. It's gone through many iterations since it was opened as the Minnesota Institute for the Deaf, Dumb, and Blind in 1863. In 1919, a study purported to be written by two of the institute's employees was published. It was called *Dwellers in the Vale of Siddem*, and it claimed to be an investigation into the genetic nature of mental disabilities and deviance. The authors asserted that they'd researched the heavily intermarried families in a pocket of the Minnesota River Valley that they renamed the Vale of Siddem to protect the inhabitants' privacy. This poem introduces the book's first chapter:

All the wicked people
In the Vale of Siddem

Thought of things they shouldn't do
And then they went and did 'em.

I read the whole eighty-page book, and you can, too. It's free online. You may find, as I did, some interesting facts buried among deeply offensive and flawed language and concepts. What you won't find is verification that it was ever an actual study, though it's written like one. I was able to track down an interview with a famous neurologist who refers to the book, but other than that, the truth of whether there's ever been a town in Minnesota with an unusually high deviance rate has been lost to the ages.

But the idea that there *could* have been hooked me.

And when I learned from another mystery writer that the Faribault hospital where the *Vale of Siddem* authors worked had been converted to a medium-security prison in 1989, and that this prison was not only built on top of tunnels but also had a dedicated unit for inmates who were immobile but still dangerous—essentially, a nursing home for killers?

Forget about it.

I immediately contacted my editor, Jessica Tribble Wells, and we bounced creepy ideas off each other until we developed the skeleton of *The Reaping*'s plot.

The nursing home for serial killers as written in my book is entirely fictional, however.

Another truth I took liberties with was the New England vampire panic that tore through Connecticut, Massachusetts, Maine, New Hampshire, Vermont, and Rhode Island in the late 1700s through the late 1800s. It was the result of the tuberculosis epidemic affecting much of the world. At the time, tuberculosis was known as consumption because its victims appeared to be *consumed* from the inside out, withering away and coughing blood. Those who succumbed to the hysteria of the time believed that the dead subsequently rose to eat others. When they dug up the graves of the newly deceased and found that some still had blood in their bodies, they took this as confirmation.

To deal with this "evil," they'd turn corpses over, behead them, or burn their organs and then breathe in the smoke or swallow the ashes to protect themselves.

While tuberculosis did hit all of Europe, including Finland, and while many Finns left their home country because of tuberculosis, there is no evidence that they were chased out for being vampires; that fear was largely contained to New England.

And finally, I know of no Finnish cult in northern Minnesota. I needed a group of immigrants for this story, and my editor said I couldn't pick on the Germans—my people—again, not after *Bloodline*.

So I chose the closest thing we have in Minnesota: Finns.

My research found that Finland consistently ranks as one of the happiest countries in the world. It has an amazing education system, provides top-tier postnatal care to children and mothers, has one of the freest presses in the world, and is a beautifully forested country with tens of thousands of lakes.

I'd like to apologize to Finland, as none of that made it into *The Reaping*.

Thank you for reading.

ABOUT THE AUTHOR

Photo © 2023 Kelly Weaver Photography

Jess Lourey is the Amazon Charts bestselling author of *The Quarry Girls*, *Litani*, *Bloodline*, *Unspeakable Things*, *The Catalain Book of Secrets*, the Reed and Steinbeck thrillers, the Salem's Cipher thrillers, and the Murder by Month mysteries, among many other works, including short stories, young adult fiction, and nonfiction. Winner of the Anthony, Minnesota Book, and Thriller Awards, Jess is also an Edgar, Agatha, and Lefty Award–nominated author; TEDx presenter; and recipient of The Loft's Excellence in Teaching fellowship. Check out her TEDx Talk for the true story behind her debut novel, *May Day*. She lives in Minneapolis with a rotating batch of foster kittens (and occasional foster puppies, but those goobers are a lot of work). For more information, visit www.jessicalourey.com.